LINDA LAEL MILLER

AN OUTLAW'S
Christmas

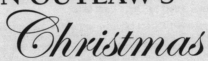

ISBN-13: 978-0-373-77856-0

AN OUTLAW'S CHRISTMAS
Copyright © 2013 by Harlequin Books S.A.

The publisher acknowledges the copyright holder of the individual works as follows:

AN OUTLAW'S CHRISTMAS
Copyright © 2012 by Linda Lael Miller

ESCAPE FROM CABRIZ
Copyright © 1990 by Linda Lael Miller

Recycling programs for this product may not exist in your area.

This edition published by arrangement with Harlequin Books S.A.

For questions and comments about the quality of this book, please contact us at CustomerService@Harlequin.com.

® and TM are trademarks of Harlequin Enterprises Limited or its corporate affiliates. Trademarks indicated with ® are registered in the United States Patent and Trademark Office, the Canadian Trade Marks Office and in other countries.

Printed in U.S.A.

www.Harlequin.com

CONTENTS

AN OUTLAW'S CHRISTMAS

In loving memory of Dale Macomber.
Knowing you was a gift I'll always be grateful for.

CHAPTER ONE

December, 1915

ALL BUT HIDDEN behind a rapidly thickening veil of snow that cold afternoon, Blue River, Texas, looked more like a faint pencil sketch against a gray-and-white background than a real town, constructed of beams and mortar and weathered wood and occupied by flesh-and-blood folks. Squinting against the dense flurries, Sawyer McKettrick could just make out the pitch of a roof or two, the mounded lines of hitching rails and horse troughs, the crooked jut of the occasional chimney. Here and there, the light of a lamp or lantern glowed through the gloom, but as far as Sawyer could tell, nobody was stirring along the sidewalks or traveling the single wide street curving away from the tiny railroad depot.

Beside him, his buckskin gelding, Cherokee, nickered and tossed his big head, no doubt relieved to finally plant four sturdy hooves on solid ground after long hours spent rattling over the rails in a livestock car. Sawyer's own journey, sitting bolt upright on a hard and sooty seat in the near-empty passenger section, had been so dull and so uncomfortable that he probably would have been happier riding with the horse.

Naturally, Cherokee didn't hold up his end of a conversation, but he was a fine listener and a trustworthy companion.

Now, the engineer's whistle sounded a long, plaintive hoot of fare-thee-well behind them, and the train clanked slowly out of the station, iron screeching against iron, steam hissing into the freezing air.

They waited, man and horse, until the sounds grew muffled and distant, though for what, Sawyer couldn't have said. He hadn't expected to be met at the depot— Clay McKettrick, his cousin and closest friend, lived on a ranch several miles outside of Blue River and, given the weather, the trail winding between there and town must be nigh on impassable—but just the same, a momentary sense of loneliness howled through him like a wind scouring the walls of a canyon.

With a glance back at the station, where he'd left his trunk of belongings behind, meaning to fetch it later, Sawyer swung up into the saddle and spoke a gruff, soothing word of encouragement to the horse.

There was a hotel in Blue River—he'd stayed there on his last visit—but he wanted to let Cherokee walk off some stiffness before settling him in over at the livery stable with plenty of hay and a ration of grain, and then making his way back to rent a room. Once he'd secured a bed for the night, he'd send somebody for his trunk, consume a steak dinner in the hotel dining room, and, later on, take a bath and shave.

In the meantime, though, he wanted to attend to his horse. Sawyer gave the animal his head, let him forge his own way, at his own pace, through the deep snow and the unnerving silence.

The buildings on either side of the street were visible as they passed, though only partially, dark at the windows, with their doors shut tight. Most folks were where they ought to be, Sawyer supposed, gathered around stoves and fireplaces in their various homes, with coffee brewed and supper smells all around them.

Again, that bleak feeling of aloneness rose up inside him, but he quelled it quickly. He did not subscribe to melancholy moods—it wasn't the McKettrick way. In his family, a man—or a woman, for that matter—played the cards they were dealt, kept on going no matter what, and tended, to the best of their ability, to whatever task was presently at hand.

Still, there was a prickle at his nape, and Cherokee, rarely skittish, pranced sideways in agitation, tossing his head and neighing.

Sawyer had barely pushed back his long coat to uncover his Colt .45, just in case, when he heard the gunshot, swaddled in the snowy silence to a muted pop, saw the flash of orange fire and felt the bullet sear its way into his left shoulder. All of this transpired in the course of a second or so, but even as he slumped forward over Cherokee's neck, dazed by the hot-poker thrust of the pain, spaces wedged themselves between moments, stretching time, distorting it. Sawyer was at once a wounded man, alone on a snow-blind street except for his panicked horse, and a dispassionate observer, nearby but oddly detached from the scene.

He didn't see the shooter or his horse, but the calm, watching part of him sized up the situation, sensed there had been a rider. If anybody had seen anything, or heard the muffled gunshot, they weren't fixing to rush to his rescue, and he didn't have the strength to draw his .45, even if he could have seen beyond Cherokee's laid-back ears.

Fortunately, the horse knew that—in cases like this anyway—discretion was the better part of valor. Cherokee bolted for safer territory, leapfrogging through the powdery snow, and Sawyer, hurting bad and only half-conscious, simply lay over the pommel, with the saddle horn jabbing into his middle like a fist, and held on to reins and mane for all he was worth.

Maybe the gunman lost sight of them in the storm, or maybe he just slipped back through the edges of Sawyer's awareness, into the pulsing darkness that surrounded him, but the second shot, the one that would have finished him off for sure, never came.

His mind slowed, and then slowed some more. He was aware of the *thud-thud-thud* of his heart, the raspy scratch of his breath, clawing its way into his lungs and then out again, and the familiar smell of wet horsehide, but his vision dimmed to a gray haze.

Cherokee kept moving. Sawyer's consciousness seemed to retreat into the far corners of his mind, but growing up on the Triple M Ranch in Arizona, he'd practically been raised on the back of a horse, and the muscles in his arms and legs must have drawn on some capacity for recollection beyond the grasp of the waking mind, because he managed to stay in the saddle.

It was only when the horse came to a sudden stop in a spill of buttery light on glistening snow that Sawyer pitched sideways with a sickening lurch, jarred his wounded shoulder when he struck the snow-padded ground, and passed out from the pain.

PIPER ST. JAMES, seated at the desk in her empty schoolroom and glumly surveying the scrawny, undecorated pine tree leaning against the far wall, wished heartily, and not for the first time, that she'd never left Maine to strike out for a life of adventure in the still-wild West.

Her cousin Dara Rose, in love with her handsome rancher husband, had painted a fine picture of Blue River in her letters, telling Piper what a wonderful place it was, full of good people and wide-open to newcomers.

Piper sighed. Of course Dara Rose would see things that way—she was so happy in her new marriage and, being a generous soul, she wanted Piper to be happy, too. Life had been hard for her cousin and her two little girls, but Clay McKettrick had changed all that.

Piper's pupils—all thirteen of them—were safe at home, where they belonged, and that was a considerable comfort to her. She'd spent the entire day alone, though, shut up in the schoolhouse, feeding the potbellied stove from an ever-dwindling store of firewood, keeping herself occupied as best she could. Tomorrow was likely to bring more of the same, since the storm showed no signs of letting up—it might even get worse.

Piper shuddered at the thought. She had plenty of food, thanks to the good people of Blue River, but her supply of well water was running out fast, like the wood. Soon, she'd have no choice but to pull on a pair of oversize boots, bundle up in both her everyday shawls *and* her heavy woolen cloak, raise the hood to protect her ears from the stinging chill, and slog her way across the school yard, once to the woodshed, and once to the well. To make matters worse, she was getting low on kerosene for the one lamp she'd allowed herself to light.

She told herself that Clay, Dara Rose's husband, would come by to check on her soon, but there was no telling when or if he'd be able to get there, given the distance and the state of the roads. For now, Piper had to do for herself.

The wind howled around the clapboard walls of that small, unpainted schoolhouse, sorrowful as a whole band of banshees searching for a way in, making her want to burrow under the quilts on her bed, which took up most of the tiny room in back set aside for teacher's quarters, and hide there until the weather turned.

She might freeze if she did that, of course, and that was if she didn't die of thirst beforehand.

So she put on the ungainly boots, left behind by Miss Krenshaw, the last teacher, wrapped herself in wool, drew a deep breath and opened the schoolhouse door to step out onto the little porch.

The cold buffeted her, hard as a slap, trapping the breath in her lungs and nearly knocking her backward, over the threshold.

Resolute, she drew the shawls and the cloak more tightly around her and tried again. The sooner she went out, the sooner she could come back *in,* she reasoned.

She stopped on the schoolhouse porch, peering through the goose-feather flakes coming down solid as a wall in front of her. Was that a horse, there in the thin light her one lamp cast through the front window?

Piper caught her breath, her heart thudding with sudden hope. There *was* a horse, and a horse meant a rider, and a rider meant company, if not practical help. Perhaps Clay *had* braved the tempest to pay her a visit—

She trudged down the steps and across the yard, every step an effort, and got a clearer look at the horse. A sturdy buckskin, the animal was real, all right. The creature was saddled, reins dangling, and she saw its eyes roll upward, glaring white.

But there was no rider on its back.

Although Piper had little experience with horses, she felt an instant affinity for the poor thing, evidently lost in the storm. It must have wandered off from somewhere nearby.

She moved toward it slowly, carefully, partly because of the bitter wind and partly because of her own rising trepidation. She didn't recognize the horse, which meant that Clay *hadn't* come to look in on her, nor had any of the other men—fathers, brothers or uncles of her students—who might have been concerned about the schoolmarm's welfare.

The buckskin whinnied wildly as she approached, backing up awkwardly, nearly falling onto its great, heaving haunches, lathered despite the chill.

"There, now," Piper said, reaching for the critter's bridle strap. There was a shed behind the schoolhouse— some of the students rode in from the country when class was in session and tethered their mounts there for the day, so there was some hay, and the plank walls offered a modicum of shelter—but just then, that shack seemed as far away as darkest Africa.

Before she could take hold of the horse's bridle, Piper tripped over something solid, half buried in the snow, fell to her hands and knees, and felt the sticky warmth of blood seeping through her mittens.

She saw him then, the rider, sprawled on his back, hat lying a few feet away, staining the snow to crimson.

Sitting on her haunches, Piper stared down at the unfortunate wayfarer for a few long moments, snowflakes slicing at her face like razors, confounded and afraid.

Bile surged into the back of her throat, scalding there, and she willed herself not to turn aside and retch. Something had to be done—and quickly.

"Mister?" she called, gripping the lapels of his long gunslinger's coat and bending close to his face. "Mister, are you alive?"

He groaned, and she saw one of his eyelids twitch.

The horse, close enough to step on one or both of them, whinnied again, a desperate sound.

"You'll be all right," Piper told both the horse and the

man, on her knees in the snow, her mittens and cloak damp with blood, but she wasn't at all sure that was the truth.

The man was around six feet tall—there was no way she could lift him, and it was clear that he couldn't stand, let alone walk.

Piper deliberated briefly, then stumbled and struggled back into the schoolhouse, through to her room, and wrenched the patchwork quilt—she'd done the piecework herself and the task had been arduous—off the bed.

Warmer now, from the exertions of the past few minutes, Piper rushed outside again and somehow managed to get the quilt underneath the bleeding stranger. He opened his eyes once—even in the dim light she could see that they were a startling shade of greenish azure— and a little smile crooked the corner of his mouth before he passed into unconsciousness again.

In a frenzy of strength, she dragged man and quilt as far as the steps, but there was no getting him up them. She had no way of knowing how long he'd been lying in the school yard, injured, and frostbite was a serious possibility, as was hypothermia.

She gripped him by his shoulders—they were broad under her hands, and hard with muscle—and shook him firmly. "Mister!" she yelled, through the raging wind. "You've got to rally yourself enough to get up these steps—I can't do this without some assistance, and there's no one else around!"

Miraculously, the stranger came to and gathered enough strength to half crawl up the steps, with a lot of help from Piper. From there, she was able to pull him over the threshold onto the rough-plank floor, where he lay facedown, bleeding copiously and only semiconscious.

"My horse," he rasped.

"Bother your horse," Piper replied, but she didn't mean it. The stranger, being a human being, was her first concern, but she was almost as worried about that frightened animal standing outside in the weather, and she knew she wouldn't be able to ignore it.

"Horse," the man repeated.

"I'll see to him," Piper promised, having no real choice in the matter. She collected another blanket from her quarters, covered the man, and steeled herself to hurry back outside.

Ever after, she'd wonder how she'd managed such an impossible feat, but at the time, Piper worked from a sense of expediency. She got ahold the horse's reins and somehow led him around back, through what seemed like miles of snow, and into the dark shed. There, she removed his saddle, the blanket beneath it, and the bridle. She spread out some hay for him and found a bucket, which she filled with snow—that being the best she could do for now. When the snow melted, the creature would have drinking water.

The horse was jumpy at first, and Piper took a few precious moments to speak softly to him, rubbing him down as best she could with an old burlap sack and making the same promise as before—he *would* be all right, and so would his master, because she wouldn't have it any other way.

On the way back to the schoolhouse, she fought her way into the woodshed and filled her arms with sticks of pitch-scented pine.

The stranger was still on the floor, upon her return, lying just over the threshold, either dead or sleeping.

Hastily, murmuring a prayer under her breath, Piper dumped the firewood into the box beside the stove, went back to the man, pulled off one ruined mitten and felt for a pulse at the base of his throat. His skin was cold, a shade of grayish-blue, but there was a heartbeat, thank heaven, faint but steady.

There was still water to fetch—why hadn't she done this chore earlier, in the daylight, as she'd intended, instead of starting a pot of pinto beans and reading one of Sir Walter Scott's novels?—and Piper didn't allow herself to think beyond getting to the well, filling a couple of buckets, and bringing them inside.

She marched outside again, moving like a woman floundering in a bad dream, taking the water buckets with her. Just getting to the well took most of her strength and, once there, she had to lower the vessels, one by one, by a length of rope.

She'd discarded her mittens by then, and the rough hemp burned like fire against her palms and the undersides of her fingers, but she lowered and filled one bucket, and then the other. Her hands ached ferociously as she carried those heavy pails toward the schoolhouse, up the steps, and once inside, she set them both down an instant before she would surely have spilled them all over the man lying in a swoon on her floor.

There was no time to spare—if there had been, Piper might have had the luxury of succumbing to helplessness and giving herself up to a fit of useless weeping—so she filled a kettle and put it on the stove to heat, right next to the simmering beans.

With one eye on the inert visitor the whole time, she peeled off her bloody cloak and shawls and stepped out of the boots. Her hands were numb, and she shook them hard, hoping to restore the circulation, which only made them hurt again. When the water was warm enough, she poured some into a basin and scrubbed sticky streaks of crimson from her skin.

The stranger didn't stir, even once, and he might very well be dead, but Piper talked to him anyway, in the same brisk, take-charge tone she used when her students balked at staying behind their desks, where they belonged. "You can stop fretting over your horse," she said. "He's safe in the shed, with hay and water aplenty."

There was no response, and Piper made herself walk over to the man, stoop, and, once again, feel for a pulse.

It was there, and it seemed the bleeding had slowed, if not stopped altogether.

She was thankful for small favors.

Noticing the ominous-looking gun jutting from a holster on his right hip, she shivered, extracted the thing gingerly, by two fingers. It was heavy, and the handle was intricately carved, as well as blood-speckled. She made out the initials *S.M.* as she held the dreadful weapon in shaking hands, carried it into the cloakroom and set it carefully on a high shelf.

Heat surged audibly into the water kettle, causing it to rattle cheerfully on the stove top. Piper moved, with quiet diligence, from one effort to another, emptying the basin in which she'd washed her hands through a wide crack in the floorboards, wiping it out with a rag, settling it aside. She had cloth strips to use as bandages, since one or the other of her pupils were always getting hurt during recess, and there was a bottle of iodine, too, so she fetched these from their customary places in the cabinet behind her desk.

Her mind kept going back to that dreadful pistol. No one carried guns these days—it was the twentieth century, after all—except for lawmen, like Clay, who was the marshal of Blue River, and, well, *outlaws*.

Had the stranger used that long-barreled weapon to hold up banks, rob trains, accost law-abiding citizens on the road? She'd seen no sign of a badge, so he probably wasn't a constable of any sort, but he might have identification of some kind, in his pockets, perhaps, or the saddlebags, left behind in the shed with the horse and its attendant gear.

Put it out of your mind, she ordered herself. There was no sense in pandering to her imagination.

Since she couldn't quite face searching the fellow's pockets—it seemed too intimate an undertaking—she turned her thoughts to other things. After collecting a pair of scissors from the drawer of her battered oak desk, Piper undertook the task she would rather have avoided, kneeling beside the man's prone form and gently rolling him onto his back.

The singular odors of gunpowder and blood rose like smoke, one acrid, one metallic, to fill her nostrils, then her lungs, then her fretful stomach. She gagged again, swallowed hard, and forced her trembling hands to pick up the scissors and begin snipping away at the front of the man's once-fine coat.

The bullet had torn its way through the dark, costly fabric, through the shirt—probably white once—and the flesh beneath.

When Piper finally uncovered the wound, she was horrified all over again. She slapped one hand over her mouth, though whether to hold back a scream or a spate of sickness she couldn't have said.

The deep, jagged hole in the flesh of the stranger's shoulder began to seep again.

Piper shifted her gaze to the supplies she'd gathered, now resting beside her on the floor—a basin full of steaming water, strands of clean cloth, iodine—and was struck by their inadequacy, and her own.

This man needed a surgeon, not the bumbling first aid of a schoolmarm.

She raised her eyes to the night-darkened window and the huge flakes of falling snow beyond, and mentally calculated the distance to Dr. Howard's house, on the far side of Blue River.

At most a ten-minute walk away, in daylight and decent weather, Doc's place might as well have been on another continent, for all the chance she had of reaching it safely. Furthermore, the man wasn't a physician, but a dentist, albeit a very competent one who would definitely know what do to in such an emergency.

Since she had no means of summoning him, she would have to do what she could, and hope the Good Lord would lend a hand.

Piper spent the next half hour or so cleaning that wound, treating it with iodine, binding it closed with the strips of cloth. Stitches were needed, she knew, but threading a needle and sewing flesh together, the way she might stitch up a patchwork quilt, was entirely beyond her. If she made the attempt, she'd get sick, faint dead away, or both, thereby making bad matters considerably worse.

Mercifully, the stranger did not wake during the long, careful process of applying the bandages. When she'd finished, Piper covered him again, brought a pillow and eased it under his head, and, rising to her feet, looked down at the front of her dress.

Like the cloak and the mittens, it was badly stained.

Piper rinsed the basin, filled it with clean water, and retreated into the little room at the back of the schoolhouse. She stripped to her petticoat and camisole, shivering all the while, and gave herself a quick sponge bath. After that, she donned a calico dress—a little scant for the season, but she'd need her gray woolen one for some time yet and wanted to keep it clean. Once properly clad again, she took her dark hair down from its pins and combs, brushed it vigorously, and secured it into a loose chignon at her nape.

Needing to keep herself occupied, Piper burned her knitted mittens in the stove—there was no use trying to get them clean—and then assessed the damage to her cloak. It was dire.

Resigned, and keeping one eye on the unmoving victim, Piper took up her scissors again and cut away the stained parts of her only cloak, consigned the pieces to the stove, and folded what remained to be used for other purposes.

Waste not, want not. She and Dara Rose, growing up together in a household of genteel poverty, had learned that lesson early and well.

She ate supper at her desk—a bowl of the beans she'd been simmering on the stove all afternoon—and wondered what to do next.

She was exhausted, and every muscle ached from the strain of dragging a full-grown man halfway across the school yard and inside, tending to the horse as well as its master, fetching the wood and the water. She didn't dare close her eyes to sleep, though—the stranger might be incapacitated, but he was *still* a stranger, and he was accustomed to carrying a gun. Suppose he came to and did—well—*something?*

From a safe distance, Piper assessed him again, cataloging his features in her mind. Caramel-colored hair, a lean, muscular frame, expensive clothes and boots. And then there was the horse, obviously a sturdy creature, well-bred. This man was probably a person of means, she concluded, but that certainly didn't mean he wasn't a rascal and a rounder, too.

He might actually be dangerous, a drifter or an unscrupulous opportunist.

Again, she considered braving the weather once more, making her way to the nearest house to ask for help, since Doc's place was too distant, but she knew she'd never make it even that far. She had no cloak, and in that blizzard, she didn't dare trust her sense of direction. She might head the wrong way, wander off into the countryside somewhere and perish from exposure.

She shuddered again, rose from her chair, and carried her empty bowl and soup spoon back to the washstand in her quarters, where she left them to be dealt with later.

Still giving the stranger a fairly wide berth, she perched on one of the students' benches and watched him, thinking hard. She supposed she could peel that overcoat off him, put it on, and tramp to the neighbors' house, nearly a quarter of a mile away, but the effort might do him further injury and, besides, the mere thought of wearing that bloody garment made her ill.

Even if she'd been able to bear *that,* the problem of the weather remained.

She was stuck.

She retrieved her knitting—a scarf she'd intended to give to Dara Rose as a Christmas gift—and sat working stitches and waiting for the man to move, or speak.

Or die.

"Water," he said, after a long time. "I need—water."

New energy rushed through Piper's small body; she filled a ladle from one of the buckets she'd hauled in earlier, carried it carefully to his side, and knelt to slip one hand under his head and raise him up high enough to drink.

He took a few sips and his eyes searched her face as she lowered him back to the floor.

"Where—? Who—?" he muttered, the words as rough as sandpaper.

"You're in the Blue River schoolhouse," she answered. "I'm Miss St. James, the teacher. Who are you?"

"Is…my horse—?"

Piper managed a thin smile. She didn't know whether to be glad because he'd regained consciousness or worried by the problems that might present. "Your horse is fine. In out of the storm, fed and watered."

A corner of his mouth quirked upward, ever so slightly, and his eyes seemed clearer than when he'd opened them before, as though he were more present somehow, and centered squarely within the confines of his own skin and bones. "That's…good," he said, with effort.

"Who are you?" Piper asked. She still hadn't searched his pockets, since just binding up his wound had taken all the courage and fortitude she could muster.

He didn't answer, but gestured for more water, lifting his head without her help this time, and when he'd swallowed most of the ladle's contents, he lapsed into another faint. His skin was ghastly pale, and his lips had a bluish tinge.

He belonged in a bed, not on the floor, but moving him any farther was out of the question, given their difference in size. All she could do was cover him, keep the fire going—and pray for a miraculous recovery.

The night passed slowly, with the man groaning hoarsely in his sleep now and then, and muttering a woman's name—Josie—often. At times, he seemed almost desperate for a response.

Oddly stricken by these murmured cries, Piper left her chair several times to kneel beside him, holding his hand.

"I'm here," she'd say, hoping he'd think she was this Josie person.

Whoever she was.

He'd smile in his sleep then, and rest peacefully for a while, and Piper would go back to her chair and her knitting. At some point, she unraveled the scarf and cast on new stitches; she'd make mittens instead, she decided, to replace the ones she'd had to burn. With so much of the winter still to come, she'd need them, and heaven only knew what she'd do for a cloak; since her salary was barely enough to keep body and soul together. Such a purchase was close to impossible.

She wasn't normally the fretful sort—like Dara Rose, she was hardworking and practical and used to squeezing pennies—but, then, this was hardly a normal situation.

Was this man an outlaw? Perhaps even a murderer?

He was well dressed and he owned a horse of obvious quality, even to her untrained eyes, but, then, maybe he was highly skilled at thievery, and his belongings were ill-gotten gains.

Piper nodded off in her chair, awakened with a start, saw that it was morning and the snow had relented a little, still heavy but no longer an impenetrable curtain of white.

The stranger was either asleep or unconscious, and the thin sunlight struck his toast-colored hair with glints of gold.

He was handsome, Piper decided. All the more reason to keep her distance.

She set aside her knitting and proceeded to build up the fire and then put a pot of coffee on to brew, hoping the stuff would restore her waning strength, and finally wrapped herself in her two remaining shawls, drew a deep breath, and left the schoolhouse to trudge around back, to the shed.

The trees were starkly beautiful, every branch defined, as if etched in glimmering frost.

To her relief, the buckskin was fine, though the water bucket she'd filled with snow was empty.

Piper patted the horse, picked up the bucket, and made her way back to the well to fill it. When she got back, the big gelding greeted her with a friendly nicker and drank thirstily from the pail.

As she was returning to the shelter of the schoolhouse, holding her skirts up so she wouldn't trip over the hem, she spotted a rider just approaching the gate at the top of the road and recognized him immediately, even through the falling snow.

Clay McKettrick.

Piper's whole being swelled with relief.

She waited, saw Clay's grin flash from beneath the round brim of his hat. His horse high-stepped toward her, across the field of snow, steam puffing from its flared nostrils, its mane and tail spangled with tiny icicles.

"I told Dara Rose you'd be fine here on your own," Clay remarked cordially, dismounting a few feet from where Piper stood, all but overwhelmed with gratitude, "but she insisted on finding out for sure." A pause, a troubled frown as he took in her rumpled calico dress. "Where's your coat? You'll catch your death traipsing around without it."

She ignored the question, wide-eyed and winded from the hard march through the snow.

Clay was a tall, lean man, muscular in all the right places, and it wasn't hard to see why her cousin loved him so much. He was pleasing to look at, certainly, but his best feature, in Piper's opinion, was his rock-solid character. He exuded quiet strength and confidence in all situations.

He would know what to do in this crisis, and he would *do* it.

"There's a man inside," Piper blurted, finding her voice at last and gesturing toward the schoolhouse. By then, the cold was indeed penetrating her thin dress. "He's been shot. His horse is in the shed and—"

Clay's expression turned serious, and he brushed past her, leaving his own mount to stand patiently in the yard.

Piper hurried into the schoolhouse behind Clay.

He crouched, laying one hand to the man's unhurt shoulder. "Sawyer?" he rasped. "Damn it, Sawyer—*what happened to you?*"

CHAPTER TWO

SAWYER, PIPER THOUGHT distractedly—Sawyer *Mc-Kettrick*, Clay's cousin, the man he'd been expecting for weeks now. That explained the initials on the man's holster, if not much else.

Down on one knee beside the other man now, Clay took off his snowy hat and tossed it aside. Piper caught the glint of his nickel-plated badge, a star pinned to the front of his heavy coat. Clay was still Blue River's town marshal, but it was a job he was ready to hand over to someone else, so he could concentrate on ranching and his growing family.

"Sawyer!" Clay repeated, his tone brusque with concern.

Sawyer's eyes rolled open, and a grin played briefly on his mouth. "I must have died and gone to hell," he said in a slow, raspy drawl, "because I'd swear I've come face-to-face with the devil himself."

Clay gave a raucous chuckle at that. "You must be better off than you look," he commented. "Can you get to your feet?"

Solemnly amused, Sawyer considered the question for a few moments, moistened his lips, which were dry and cracked despite Piper's repeated efforts to give him water during the night, and struggled to reply, "I don't think so."

"That's all right," Clay said, gruffly gentle, while Piper's weary mind raced. She'd heard a few things about Sawyer, and some of it was worrisome—for instance, no one, including Clay, seemed to know which side of the law he was on—though Dara Rose had liked him. "I'll help you." With that, Clay raised Sawyer to a sitting position, causing him to moan again and his bandages to seep with patches of bright red, draped his cousin's good arm over his shoulders, and stood, bringing the other man up with him.

"I'll put Sawyer on your bed, if that's all right," Clay said to Piper, already headed toward her quarters in the back. The schoolhouse was small, and everybody knew how it was laid out, since the building of it had been a community effort.

When word got around that she'd harbored a man under this roof, bleeding and insensible with pain or not, her reputation would be tarnished, at best.

At worst? Completely ruined.

The injustice of that was galling to Piper, but nonetheless binding. Lady teachers in particular were scrutinized for the slightest inclination toward wanton behavior, though their male counterparts sometimes courted and then married one of their students, with impunity. A practice Piper considered reprehensible.

"Certainly," she said now, well aware that Clay hadn't been asking her permission but feeling compelled to offer some kind of response.

She hovered in the doorway of her room—little more than a lean-to, really—with one tiny window, high up, while Clay wrestled Sawyer out of his coat then eased him down carefully onto the bed, pulled off his boots.

The effort of going even that far must have been too much for Sawyer, strong as he looked, because he shut his eyes again, and didn't respond when Clay spoke to him.

"I'll get the doc," Clay said to Piper, as she stepped out of the doorway to let him pass. "Do you have any more blankets? It's important to keep him warm."

Piper thought with a heavy heart of the fine, colorful quilts lying neatly folded in her hope chest. She'd always envisioned them gracing the beds of some lovely house, once she was married, like Dara Rose, with a proper home.

"Yes," she said bravely, and though she didn't begrudge Sawyer McKettrick those quilts, she couldn't help lamenting their fate. She'd worked hard to assemble them from tiny scraps of fabric, carefully saved, and many of the pieces were all she had to remember friends she'd left behind in Maine.

She swept over to her bulky cedar chest, raised the lid, and rummaged through the treasured contents—doilies and pot holders, tablecloths and dish towels and the like—until she'd found what she was looking for.

As she spread the first of those exquisitely stitched coverlets over Mr. McKettrick, he stirred again, opened his eyes briefly, and smiled. "Thanks, Josie," he said, and there was a caress in the way he said the name.

Briskly, because she was a little hurt, though she couldn't have pinpointed the reason why such an emotion should afflict her, Piper put another quilt on top of her patient, and then another.

Then, because it was nearly eight o'clock, she went to the other end of the building, where the bell rope dangled, and gave it a tug. Surely none of her pupils would make it to school on such a day, but Piper believed in maintaining routine, especially during trying times. There was something reassuring about it.

The silvery bell, high overhead in its little belfry,

chimed once, twice, three times, summoning students who would not come.

Piper's hands, rope-burned from hauling up well water the night before, stung fiercely, and she was almost glad, because the pain gave her something to think about besides the man sprawled on her spinster's bed, probably bleeding all over her quilts.

She retrieved a tin of Wildflower Salve from her bureau, careful not to make too much noise and disturb Mr. McKettrick. Carrying the salve back to her schoolroom, she sat down at her desk and smiled a little as she twisted off the pretty little lid to treat her sore palms.

There was an abundance of the stuff, since Dara Rose, impoverished after the scandalous death of her first husband, upstairs at the Bitter Gulch Saloon, had once planned to sell the product door-to-door in hopes of making enough money to support herself and her two small daughters, Edrina and Harriet. Instead, Dara Rose had fallen in love with Clay McKettrick, married him, and thus retained what amounted to a lifetime supply of medicinal salve, which she generously shared.

A half hour passed before Clay returned, with Dr. Jim Howard, the local dentist, riding stalwartly along beside him on the mule that usually pulled his buggy.

Everybody in Blue River liked Dr. Howard, whose young daughter, Madeline, was one of Piper's best students. At eight, the little girl could read and cipher with the acuity of an adult. *Mrs.* Howard, however, was not so easy to like as her husband and daughter. Eloise wore nothing but velvet or silk, dismissed the town as a "bump in the road" and told anyone who would listen that she'd "married down."

"Miss St. James," Dr. Howard greeted her, with a friendly smile and a tug at the brim of his Eastern-style hat, as he stomped the snow off his boots on the school-house porch, the way Clay had done a moment before. Doc was a large man, good-natured, older than his wife by some twenty years, and his eyes were a kindly shade of blue. He carried a battered leather bag in one gloved hand.

Piper barely stopped herself from rushing over and embracing the man, she was so glad to see him. The responsibility of keeping Mr. McKettrick alive had, she realized, weighed more heavily upon her than she'd thought it did.

She merely nodded in acknowledgment, though, as he closed the door against the cold daylight wind, and she hung back when Clay led the way through the school-room and into the chamber behind it.

Of course she couldn't help overhearing most of the conversation between Clay and Dr. Howard, given that the whole place was hardly larger than Dara Rose's chicken coop out on the ranch, classroom, teacher's quarters and all.

Clay was asking how bad the injury was, and Dr. How-ard replied that it was serious enough, but with luck and a lot of rest, the patient would probably recover.

Probably recover? Piper thought, sipping from the mug of coffee she'd poured for herself. When Clay and the doctor—more commonly referred to as "Doc"—came out of the back room, she'd offer them some, too. She owned three cups, not including the bone china tea service for six nestled in her hope chest, which would remain precisely where it was, unlike her once pristine quilts.

"I'd like to take Sawyer out to my place," she heard Clay say.

"Better wait a few days," came Doc's response. "He's lost a lot of blood. The bullet went clear through him,

though, which saves me having to dig it out, and Miss
St. James did a creditable job of binding him up. He'll
have scars, but the wound looks clean, thanks to her." A
pause followed. "There's a bottle of carbolic acid in my
bag there—hand it to me, will you?"

There was another short silence, during which Clay
must have done as Doc asked, soon followed by a hoarse
shout of angry protest from the patient. He swore col-
orfully, and Piper winced. She believed that cursing
revealed a poor vocabulary, among other personal shortcomings.

"Can't take a chance on infection setting in," the dentist said peaceably, evidently unruffled by the outburst.
"The burning will stop after a while."

Sawyer muttered something unintelligible.

Piper's hands trembled as she set her coffee mug down
on her desk. Doc's reply to Clay's statement about taking his cousin out to the ranch echoed in her mind. *Better wait a few days.*

All well and good, she thought fretfully, but what was
she supposed to do in the meantime? There was only one
bed, after all, and she couldn't sleep in a chair until the
man was well enough to be moved, could she?

Mr. McKettrick was indeed badly injured, but this
was a *schoolhouse,* frequented by children five days a
week—children who would go home after dismissal and
tell their parents there was a strange man recuperating
in Miss St. James's room. She wouldn't be able to hide
him from them any more than she could hide that enormous gelding of his, quartered in the shed out back. Even
unconscious, Sawyer filled the place with his presence,
breathed up all the air.

Clay emerged from her room just then, took a second mug from the shelf near the stove and poured him-

self some coffee. He was probably cold, Piper realized with some chagrin, having ridden in from the ranch, proceeded to Doc Howard's, and then made his way back to the schoolhouse again.

"I guess we've got a problem," he said now. Was there a twinkle in those very blue eyes of his as he studied her expression?

"Yes," Piper agreed, somewhat stiffly. Maybe Clay found the situation amusing, but *she* certainly didn't.

Clay took another sip, thoughtful and slow, from his mug. He'd shed his long coat soon after he and Doc arrived, and his collarless shirt was open at the throat, showing the ridged fabric of his undergarment. Like Sawyer, he wore a gun belt, but he'd set the pistol aside earlier, an indication of his good manners. "You probably heard what Doc Howard said," he told her, after a few moments of pensive consideration. "I could stay here with Sawyer and send you on out to the ranch to stay with Dara Rose and the girls, but it's hard going, with the snow still so deep."

Jim Howard came out of Piper's room, wiping his hands clean on a cloth that smelled of carbolic acid. "I gave him some laudanum," he told Clay. "He'll sleep for a while."

Piper propped her own hands on her hips. She'd spent a mostly sleepless night hoping and praying that someone would come to help, and she'd gotten her wish, but for all that, the problem was only partially solved.

Perhaps she should have been more specific, she reflected, rueful.

"Must I point out to you gentlemen," she began, with dignity, "that this arrangement is highly improper?"

Clay's grin was slight, but it was, nonetheless, a grin, and it infuriated her. She was an unmarried woman, a schoolmarm, and there was *a man in her bed,* likely to remain there for the foreseeable future. All her dreams for the future—a good husband, a home, and children of her own—could be compromised, and through no fault of her own.

"I understand your dilemma, Piper," he said, sounding like an indulgent older brother, "but you heard the doc. Sawyer can't be moved until that wound of his mends a little."

"Surely you could take him as far as the hotel without doing harm," Piper reasoned, quietly frantic. She kept her hands at her sides, but the urge to wring them was strong.

Dr. Howard shook his head. Helped himself to the last mug and some coffee. "That could kill him," he said bluntly, but his expression was sympathetic. "I'm sure Eloise wouldn't mind coming over and helping with his care, though. She's had some nursing experience, and it would temper any gossip that might arise."

As far as Piper was concerned, being shut up with Eloise Howard for any length of time would be worse than attending to the needs of a helpless stranger by herself. *Much* worse.

"I couldn't ask her to do that," Piper said quickly. "Mrs. Howard has you and little Madeline to look after." She turned a mild glare on Clay. "Your cousin needs *male* assistance," she added. She'd dragged Sawyer McKettrick in out of the cold, cleaned his wound, even taken care of his horse, but she wasn't *about* to help him use the chamber pot, and that was final.

"I'll do what I can," Clay said, "but Dara Rose is due to have our baby any day now. I can't leave her out there alone, with just the girls and a few ranch hands. Once the weather lets up, though…"

His words fell away as Piper's cheeks flared with the

heat of frustration. She could demand to be put up in the hotel herself, of course, until Sawyer McKettrick was well enough to leave the schoolhouse, but that would mean he'd be alone here. And he was in serious condition, despite Doc's cheerful prognosis.

What if something went wrong?

Besides, staying in hotels cost money, and even there in the untamed West, many of them had policies against admitting single women—unless, of course, they were ladies of the evening, and thus permitted to slip in through an alley door, under cover of darkness, and climb the back stairs to ply their wretched trade.

"You do realize," Piper persisted, "that I have nowhere to sleep?" *And no good man will* ever *marry me because my morals will forever be in question, even though I've done nothing wrong.*

Dr. Howard walked over and laid a fatherly hand on her shoulder. "I'll bring over anything you need," he assured her. "And stop in as often as I can. I'm sure Clay will do the same."

Clay nodded, but he was looking out the window, at the ceaseless snow, and his expression was troubled. "I've got to get back to Dara Rose," he said.

Piper's heart went out to him. As untenable as *her* situation was, Dara Rose needed Clay right now, and so did the children. Edrina and Harriet, though uncommonly precocious, were still quite small, and they couldn't be expected to know what to do if their mother went into labor.

"Go home, Clay," she said gently. "Give Dara Rose my best regards. Edrina and Harriet, too."

Clay's expression was even more serious now, and he looked at her for a long time before giving a reluctant nod and promising, "I'll come back for Sawyer as soon as Doc decides he can travel. I appreciate this, Piper. I wouldn't ask it of you, but—"

"I understand," she said, when words failed him again. And she *did* understand. Clay and Sawyer, like Piper and Dara Rose, were first cousins, the next best thing to siblings, and the bond was strong between them.

The snow came down harder and then harder still, and Doc Howard finished his coffee, collected his bag and took one more look at Sawyer, then headed out, after assuring Piper that he'd return before day's end and asking what he ought to bring back.

Blankets, she'd said, flustered, and kerosene, and whatever medicine the patient might need.

Clay attended to Sawyer's horse, said goodbye, and left for the ranch.

Watching him disappear into a spinning vortex of white, Piper felt a lump rise in her throat.

Once again, she was alone, except for Sawyer McKettrick and he, of course, was a hindrance, not a help.

True to his word, Doc was back within the hour, despite the increasingly bad weather, bringing a fresh supply of laudanum, a jug of kerosene, more carbolic acid and several warm blankets, wrapped in oilcloth so they'd stay dry.

He examined Sawyer again—reporting that he was still sleeping but that his heartbeat was stronger than before and he seemed to be breathing more easily—gave Piper a few instructions, and quickly left again, because nightfall would be coming on soon, making the ordinarily short journey home even more difficult than it already was.

Piper thanked him, asked him to give Eloise and Madeline her best, and watched through the front window until he and his mule were gone from sight.

Then, feeling more alone than she ever had, she got busy. She washed down the already clean blackboard.

She dusted every surface in the schoolroom and re-filled the kerosene lamp.

She drank more coffee and fed more wood into the stove.

Before he'd gone, Clay had assured her that Sawyer's horse would be fine until morning, which meant she could stay inside, where it was comparatively warm, so that was *one* less worry, anyhow. Gaps between the floorboards let in some of the cold, but that couldn't be helped. Using the spare blankets Doc had brought, she made a bed on the floor, close to the stove and hoped all the mice were hibernating.

She lit the kerosene lamp as the room darkened, and tried to cheer herself up by imagining the Christmas tree, still in its pail of water and leaning against the far wall, glowing with bright decorations. She took comfort in its green branches and faintly piney scent and thought, with a smile, of the recitations her students were memorizing for the school program.

Christmas Eve, just ten days away, fell on a Friday that year, so school would be in session until noon—weather permitting—and the recital would be presented soon after. After the poems and skits, everyone would sing carols. The owner of the mercantile had promised to donate oranges and peppermint sticks for the children, and the parents would bring pies and cookies and cakes.

This gathering represented all the Christmas some of the children would have, and all thirteen of them were looking forward to the celebration.

She moved, quiet as a wraith, to the window, and glumness settled over her spirit as she looked out.

And still the snow fell in abundance, unrelenting.

IT WAS THE pain that finally roused him.

Sawyer came to the surface of consciousness with a fierce jolt, feeling as though he'd been speared through his left shoulder.

His stomach lurched, and for a moment he was out there on that snowy street again, unable to see his assailant, reaching in vain for his .45.

He went deliberately still—not only was there no Colt at his hip, but he'd been stripped to his birthday suit—and tried to orient himself to reality.

The room was dark and a little chilly, and it smelled faintly of some flowery cologne, which probably meant there was a woman around somewhere.

The thought made him smile, despite the lingering pain, which had transmuted itself from a stabbing sensation to a burning ache in the few minutes since he'd opened his eyes. There weren't many situations that couldn't be improved by the presence of a lady.

He squinted, managed to raise himself a little, with the pillows behind him providing support. Snow-speckled moonlight entered through the one window, set high in the wall, and spilled onto the intricate patterns of the several quilts that covered him to the waist.

"Hullo?" he called into the darkness.

She appeared in the doorway then, carrying a flickering kerosene lamp, a small but well-made woman with dark hair and a wary way of carrying herself.

She looked familiar, but Sawyer couldn't quite place her.

"You're awake, then," she said rhetorically, staying well away from the bed, as if she thought he might grab hold of her. The impression left him vaguely indignant. "Are you hungry?"

"No," he said, because his stomach, though empty,

was still reacting to the rush of pain that had awakened him. "How's my horse?"

In the light of the lantern, he saw her smile slightly. Decided she was pretty, if a mite on the scrawny side. Her waist looked no bigger around than a fence post, and she wasn't very tall, either.

"Your horse is quite comfortable," she said. "Are you in pain? The doctor left laudanum in case you needed it."

Sawyer guessed, from the bitter taste in his mouth, that he'd already had at least one dose, and he was reluctant to take another. Basically distilled opium, the stuff caused horrendous nightmares and fogged up his brain.

"I'm all right," he said.

She didn't move.

He had fuzzy memories of being shot and falling off his horse, but he wasn't sure if he'd actually seen his cousin Clay or just dreamed he was there. He did recollect the doctor, though—that sawbones had poured liquid fire into the gaping hole in his shoulder, made him yell because it hurt so bad.

"Do you have a name?" he asked.

She bristled, and he guessed at the color of her eyes— dark blue, maybe, or brown. It was hard to tell, in the glare of that lantern she was holding. "Of course I do," she replied primly. "Do you?"

Sawyer gave a raw chuckle at that. She was an impertinent little dickens, he thought, probably able to hold her own in an argument. "Sawyer McKettrick," he conceded, with a slight nod of his head. "I'm Clay's cousin, here to take over as town marshal."

"Well," she said, remaining in the doorway, "you're off to a wonderful start, aren't you?"

He chuckled again, though it took more energy than

he felt he could spare. "Yes, ma'am," he said. "I reckon I am."

"Piper St. James," she said then, without laying any groundwork beforehand.

"What?"

"You asked for my name." A pause, during which she raised the lantern a little higher, saw that he was bare-chested, and quickly lowered it again. "You can call me 'Miss James.'"

"Thanks for that, anyhow," he said, enjoying the exchange, however feeble it was on his end. "Thanks for looking after my horse, too, and, unless I miss my guess, saving my life."

Miss St. James's spine lengthened; she must have been all of five foot two, and probably weighed less than his saddlebags. "I couldn't just leave you lying out there in the snow," she said, with a sort of puckish modesty.

From her tone, Sawyer concluded that she'd considered doing just that, though, fortunately for him, her conscience must have overruled the idea.

"You'd have had to step over me every time you went out," he teased, "and that would have been awkward."

He thought she smiled then, though he couldn't be sure because the light fell forward from the lantern and left her mostly in shadow.

"What is this place?" he asked presently, when she didn't speak.

"You're in the Blue River schoolhouse," Miss St. James informed him. "I teach here."

"I see," Sawyer said, wearying, though he was almost as much in the dark, literally and figuratively, as before he'd asked the question. "Was Clay here?" he threw out. "Or did I imagine that part?"

"He was here," Miss St. James confirmed. "He's gone

home now—his wife is expecting a baby soon, and he didn't like leaving her alone—but he'll be back as soon as the weather allows."

Sawyer was quiet for a while, gathering scraps of strength, trying to breathe his way past a sudden swell of pain. "You don't have to be scared of me," he told her, after a long time.

"I'm not," she lied, still cautious. Still keeping her distance.

"I reckon I can't blame you," Sawyer said, closing his eyes to regain his equilibrium. The pain rose to a new crescendo, and the room had begun to pitch and sway.

"The laudanum is there on the nightstand," she informed him helpfully, evidently seeing more than he'd wanted her to. "And the chamber pot is under the bed."

He felt his lips twitch. "I'll keep that in mind," he said.

"You're certain you don't want something to eat?"

"Maybe later," he managed to reply.

He thought she'd go away then, but she hesitated. "You were asking for someone named Josie," she said. "Perhaps when the weather is better, we could send word to her, that you've been hurt, I mean."

Sawyer opened his eyes again, swiftly enough to set the little room to spinning again. "That won't be necessary," he bit out, but he felt a certain bitter amusement imagining what would happen if word of his misfortune were to reach her. Josie was his last employer's very fetching wife, and she'd made it clear that she wanted more from Sawyer than protection and cordial conversation. He'd had the same problem before, with other wives of men he worked for, along with their sisters and daughters in some instances, and he'd always managed to sidestep any romantic entanglements, be they physical or emotional—until Josie.

He'd *wanted* Josie, and that was why he'd agreed to come to Blue River and fill in for Clay, as temporary marshal—to put some distance between himself and the sweet temptation to bed his boss's wife, to burn in her fire, let lust consume him.

He'd left in the nick of time.

Or had he?

Had the shooter been one of Henry Vandenburg's hirelings, one of his own former colleagues, sent to make sure Sawyer stayed away from the old man's wife—forever?

It was possible, of course. Vandenburg was rich, and he was powerful, and he probably wasn't above having a rival dispensed with, but even for him, ordering the murder of one of Angus McKettrick's grandsons would have been pretty risky. His and Clay's granddad, even at his advanced age, was a force of nature in his own right, owning half of Arizona as he did, and so were his four sons. Holt, Rafe, Kade—Sawyer's father—and Jeb, who'd sired Clay, were all law-abiding citizens, happily married men with children and even a few grandchildren, money in the bank and a prosperous ranch to run. Still, the untimely death of any member of the clan would rouse them to Earp-like fury, and Vandenburg surely knew that. In fact, it was that dogged quality that had caused the old reprobate to hire Sawyer as a bodyguard in the first place.

"Mr. McKettrick?" Miss Piper St. James was standing right beside the bed now, holding the lantern high. There was concern in her voice—enough to draw her to his bedside, thereby risking some nefarious assault on her virtue. "Are you all right? For a moment, you looked— I thought…"

She lapsed awkwardly into silence.

He might have reminded her, if he'd had the strength, that, *no,* actually, he *wasn't* "all right," because he'd been *shot*. Instead, he asked slowly, measuring out each word like a storekeeper dispensing sugar or flour, "Do you happen to have any whiskey on hand?"

CHAPTER THREE

"OF COURSE I don't have any whiskey," Piper replied, with a little more sharpness in her tone than she'd intended to exercise. "This is a *school,* not a roadhouse."

"Well, damn," Sawyer said, affably gruff and clearly still in pain. "I could sure use a shot of good old-fashioned rotgut right about now. Might take the edge off."

Having set the kerosene lantern on the nightstand so she wouldn't drop it and set the whole place on fire, Piper took a step back. Rotgut, indeed. "Then I guess it's too bad you fell off your horse here instead of in front of the Bitter Gulch Saloon."

He favored her with a squinty frown at this, and she wondered distractedly what he'd look like in the daylight, cleaned up and wearing something besides bandages, her quilts and the dish-towel sling Dr. Howard had put on his left arm. "Are you one of those hatchet-swinging types?" he asked, with a note of benign disapproval. "The kind who go around hacking perfectly good bars to splinters, shattering mirrors and breaking every bottle on the shelves?"

Piper stiffened slightly, offended, though she couldn't think why she ought to give a pin about this man's—this *stranger's*—opinion of her. "No," she said tersely. "If some people choose to pollute their systems with poison, to the detriment of their wives and children and society in general, it's none of my concern."

He laughed then, a hoarse bark of a sound, brittle with pain. "If you say so," he said, leaving his meaning ambiguous.

Annoyed, Piper was anxious to be gone from that too-small room. She wished she hadn't approached the bed, if only because she could see so much of his bare chest. It was disturbing—though it did remind her of the gods and heroes she'd read about in Greek mythology.

She gathered her dignity, an effort of unsettling significance, reached out to reclaim the lantern. "If you don't need anything, I'll leave you to get some rest," she said, speaking as charitably as she could.

"I do need something," he told her quietly.

Piper took another step back. The lantern light wavered slightly, and she renewed her grip on the handle. "What?" she asked cautiously.

"Company," Sawyer replied. "Somebody to talk to while I wait for this bullet hole in my shoulder to settle down a little—it feels like somebody dropped a hot coal into it. Why don't you take a chair—if there is one—and tell me what brings a proper lady like you to a rough town like Blue River."

Was he making fun of her, using the term "a proper lady" ironically?

Or was she being not only harsh, but priggish, too?

She set the lantern back on the night table and drew her rocking chair into the faint circle of light, sat down and folded her hands in her lap. For the moment, that was all the concession she could bring herself to make. And it seemed like plenty.

"Well?" Sawyer McKettrick prompted. "I can tell by the way you talk and carry yourself that you're an Easterner. What are you doing way out here in the wilds of Texas?"

"I told you," Piper said distantly, primly. "I teach school."

"They don't have schools back where you came from, in Massachusetts or New Hampshire or wherever you belong?"

"I'm from Maine, if you must know," she allowed, suppressing an urge to argue that she "belonged" wherever she wanted to be. "Dara Rose—Clay's wife—is my cousin. She persuaded me to come out here and take over for the last teacher, Miss Krenshaw."

"Dara Rose," he said, with a fond little smile. "Clay's a lucky man, finding a woman like her."

"I quite agree," Piper said, softening toward him, albeit unwillingly and only to a minimal degree.

He studied her thoughtfully in the flickering light of the lantern. "Does it suit you—life in the Wild West, I mean?" he inquired politely. She saw that a muscle had bunched in his jaw after he spoke, knew he was hurting, and determined to ride it out without complaint. Like Clay, he was tough, though Clay wore the quality with greater grace, being a more reticent sort.

Piper paused, considering her reply. "It's lonely sometimes," she admitted, at last.

"Everyplace is lonely sometimes," he answered.

This was a statement Piper couldn't refute, so she made one of her own. "It sounds as if you speak from experience," she said carefully.

He grinned a wan shadow of a grin, lifted his right hand in a gesture of acquiescence. "Sure," he replied. "Happens to everybody."

Even in his weakened state, Sawyer McKettrick did not strike Piper as the kind of person who ever lacked for anything. There was something about him, some quality of quiet sufficiency, of untroubled wholeness, that shone even through his obvious physical discomfort.

"I do enjoy spending my days with the children," she said, strangely flustered, sensing that there was far more to this man than what showed on the surface.

"I reckon that's a good thing, since you're a teacher," he observed dryly.

A silence fell, and Piper found herself wanting to prattle, just to fill it. And she was most definitely *not* a prattler, so this was a matter for concern.

"I might be able to handle some food, after all," Sawyer ventured presently, unhurriedly. "If the offer is still good, that is."

Relieved to have an errand to perform, however mundane, Piper fairly leaped to her feet, took the lamp by its handle. "There's bean soup," she said. "I'll get you some."

When she returned with a bowl and spoon in one hand and the lantern in the other, she saw that her visitor had bunched up the pillows behind him so he could sit up straighter.

She placed the lantern on the night table again and extended the bowl and spoon.

He looked at the food with an expression of amused wistfulness. "I've only got one good arm," he reminded her. "I can feed myself, but you'll have to hold the bowl."

Piper should have anticipated this development, but she hadn't. Gingerly, knowing she wouldn't be able to reach far enough from the rocking chair, she sat down on the edge of the mattress, the bowl cupped in both hands.

The sure impropriety of the act sent a little thrill through her.

Deep down, she was something of a rebel, though she managed to hide that truth from most people.

Sawyer smiled and took hold of the spoon, tasted the

soup. Since the fire in the stove had burned low while they were talking earlier, the stuff was only lukewarm, but he didn't seem to mind. He ate slowly, and not very much, and finally sank back against the pillows, looking exhausted by the effort of feeding himself.

"Would you like more?" Piper ventured, drawing back the bowl. "I could—"

Sawyer grimaced, shook his head no. His skin was a waxy shade of gray, even in the thin light, and he seemed to be bleeding from his wound again, though not so heavily as before. "That'll do for now," he said. "I might take some laudanum, after all, though."

Piper nodded, put the spoon and the bowl down, and reached for the brown bottle Dr. Howard had left, pulled out the cork. "I'll just wipe off the spoon and—"

Before she could finish her sentence, though, he grabbed the bottle from her hand and took a great draught from it. The muscles in his neck corded visibly as he swallowed.

Piper blinked and snatched the vessel from him. "Mr. *McKettrick,*" she scolded, in her most teacherly voice. "That is *medicine,* not water, and it's very potent."

"I hope so," he said with a sigh, closing his eyes and gritting his teeth. Waiting for the opium to reach his bloodstream. "I'd have preferred whiskey," he added, moments later.

Soon, he was fast asleep.

Piper made sure the bottle of laudanum was out of his reach and rose to carry the lantern and the bowl and spoon out of the room, walking softly so she wouldn't wake him—not that there seemed to be much danger of that, from the steady rasp of his breathing.

Once she'd set the bowl and spoon aside, along with the lantern, she wrapped one of the extra blankets Dr.

Howard had brought around her shoulders, in lieu of a cloak, and marched herself outside, into the snowy cold, carrying the lantern again now, lighting her way to the outhouse. Normally, she would have used the enamel chamber pot tucked beneath her bed, but not this time.

The going was hard, though not quite as arduous as when she'd gone out for wood and water before, and to take care of Mr. McKettrick's horse. She heard a reassuring dripping sound—snow melting off the eaves of the schoolhouse roof, probably—and the sky was clear and moonlit and speckled with stars.

For the time being at least, the storm was over, and that heartened Piper so much that, after using the outhouse, she went on to the shed, where the big buckskin gelding stood, quietly munching hay.

She spoke to him companionably, stroked his sturdy neck a few times, and made sure he had enough water. Clay had filled the trough earlier, instead of just setting a pail on the dirt floor of the shed, so there was plenty.

Returning to the schoolhouse, Piper set the lantern down, put the covered kettle of boiled beans on the front step, so the cold would keep its contents from spoiling. Then she shut the door, lowered the latch, and went over to bank the fire for the night.

The lamp was starting to burn low by then, so she quickly made herself a bed on the floor, using the borrowed blankets, washed her face and hands in a basin of warm water, and brushed her teeth with baking soda. Donning one of her flannel nightgowns was out of the question, of course, with a man under the same roof.

Resigned to sleeping in her clothes, she put out the lamp and stretched out on the floor, as near to the stove as she could safely get, and bundled herself in the blankets. The planks were hard, and Piper thought with yearning of her thin, lumpy mattress, the one she'd so often complained about, though only to herself and Dara Rose.

She closed her eyes, depending on exhaustion to carry her into the unknowing solace of sleep, but instead she found herself listening, not just with her ears, but with all she was. A few times, she thought she heard small feet skittering and scurrying around her, which didn't help her state of mind.

At some point, however, she finally succumbed to a leaden, dreamless slumber.

When she awakened on that frosty floor, sore and unrested and quite disgruntled, it took her a few moments to remember why she was there, and not in her bed.

The bed was *occupied,* she recalled, with a flare of heat rising to her cheeks. By one Sawyer McKettrick.

But the sun was shining, and that lifted her spirits considerably.

She shambled stiffly to her feet, hurried to build up the fire in the potbellied stove, glanced with mild alarm at the big Regulator Clock ticking on the schoolhouse wall. It was past eight, she saw, and she hadn't rung the schoolhouse bell.

A silly concern, admittedly, since her students weren't likely to show up, even though the snow had stopped falling and cheery daylight filled the frigid little room, absorbing the blue shadows of a wintry yesterday and the night that had followed. At the front window, Piper used the palm of one hand, no longer sore, to wipe a circle in the curlicues of frost to clear the glass. She peered out, encouraged to see that the sky was indeed blue and virtually cloudless.

Moisture dripped steadily from the roof overhead, and the road was taking shape again, a slight but visible dip in the deep, blindingly white field of snow that seemed to stretch on and on.

The voice, coming from behind her, wry and somewhat testy, nearly caused Piper to jump out of her skin. For a few moments, glorying in the change in the weather, she'd forgotten all about her uninvited guest, her night on the floor, and most of her other concerns, as well.

"Is there any coffee in this place, or would that be sinful, like keeping a stock of whiskey?" Sawyer McKettrick asked grumpily.

Piper whirled, saw him standing—*standing,* under his own power—in the doorway to her private quarters. He was still bare-chested, his bandages bulky and his bad arm in the sling Doc had improvised for him the day before, but, thankfully, he'd somehow managed to get into his trousers and even put on his boots.

He looked pale, gaunt, but ready for whatever challenges the day—or the next few minutes—might bring.

She smiled, relieved. If Sawyer was up and around, he'd be leaving soon. Maybe *very* soon. "I'll make some coffee," she said. "Sit down."

He was leaning against the framework of the doorway now, probably conserving his strength, and he looked around, taking in the small desks, the benches. "Where?" he asked, practically snarling the word.

Piper was determined to be pleasant, no matter how rude Mr. McKettrick chose to be. "There's a chair behind my desk," she pointed out. "Take that."

He groped his way along the wall, proof that he wasn't as recovered as she'd first thought, pulled back the wooden chair and sank into it. "Where's my shirt?" he asked. "And my .45?"

Piper ladled water into the small enamel coffeepot that, like the three drinking mugs, her narrow bed and the rocking chair, came with the schoolhouse. "I burned your shirt," she said cheerfully. "It was quite ruined, between the bullet hole and all the blood. And I put away the pistol, since you won't have use for it here."

Sawyer thrust his free hand through his hair in exasperation. Clearly, the laudanum had worn off, and he hadn't rested well. "I need that shirt," he said. "*And* the .45."

"I'm sorry," Piper answered. "Perhaps Clay will bring you fresh clothes, when he comes to take you out to the ranch." She refused to discuss the gun any further.

Sawyer frowned. His chin was bristly with beard stubble, and he narrowed his blue-green eyes practically to slits. "When will that be?" he growled. "My trunk is over at the train depot. Plenty of clothes in there."

Piper didn't reply right away, since she didn't know precisely when Clay would return, and fetching Sawyer's baggage from the depot was not presently an option. Instead, she put some coffee beans into the grinder and turned the handle, enjoying the rich scent as it rose to entice her. Coffee was normally a treat for Piper, though she'd been drinking more of it lately, being snowed in and everything. Since the stuff wasn't considered a staple, like canned goods and meat, potatoes and butter, the town didn't provide it as a part of her wages. Since she saved practically every penny toward a train ticket home to Maine, Dara Rose bought it for her, along with writing paper, postage stamps and bathing soap.

God bless Dara Rose's generous soul.

Sawyer cleared his throat, a reminder, apparently, that she'd neglected to answer his cranky question. "Clay will be coming back—when?"

"I don't know," Piper said honestly. "Soon, I hope."

His frown deepened as he looked around again. "Where did you sleep last night?"

She measured coffee into the pot and set it on the stove to boil. "You needn't concern yourself with that," she said sunnily.

He gave a gruff chortle at her response, completely void of amusement. Then he pushed back the chair and stood, with an effort he clearly wanted very much to hide. "I suppose the privy is out back?" he asked.

Piper kept her face averted, so he wouldn't see her blush. "Yes," she said. "But the snow is deep and the path hasn't been cleared yet." She paused, mortified. "There's a chamber pot under the bed."

"I'm not using a chamber pot," he informed her, each word separated from the next by a tick of the Regulator clock. Slowly, he crossed the room, snatched up the same blanket she'd used earlier, in lieu of a coat, wrapped it around his mostly naked upper body like an enormous shawl, and left the schoolhouse.

The door slammed behind him.

Piper hoped he wouldn't collapse in the snow again, because she wasn't sure she'd be able to get him back inside the schoolhouse if that happened. She waited tensely, added water to the coffeepot when it bubbled, and resisted the urge to stand at the window and watch for his return.

He did reappear, after a few minutes, and he kept the blanket around him as he made his way back to the desk chair and sat down.

Piper poured coffee for him—the grounds hadn't settled completely, but that couldn't be helped—and set the mug on the surface of the desk.

"Breakfast?" she asked.

He finally smiled, though grudgingly. "More beans?" he countered.

"I have some salt pork and a few eggs," Piper responded. "Would that do, or should I risk life and limb to fetch something more to your liking from the hotel dining room? I could just hitch up the dogsled and be off."

He laughed, and it seemed that his color was a little better, though that could probably be ascribed to the cold weather outside. "You don't lack for sass, do you?" he said.

"And *you* don't lack for rudeness," Piper retorted, but, like before, she was softening toward him a little. There was something about that smile, those intelligent, blue-green eyes, that supple mouth...

Whoa, ordered a voice in her mind, bringing her up short. *Forget his smile, and his mouth, too.* Silently, Piper reminded herself that, to her knowledge, Sawyer Mc-Kettrick had just one thing to recommend him—that he was Clay's cousin—which most definitely did *not* mean he was the same kind of man. Families, even ones as illustrious as Clay's, *did* have black sheep.

"Sorry," he said wearily, with no hint of actual remorse.

She fetched the salt pork and the eggs, which were kept in a metal storage box in the cloakroom, that being the coldest part of the building, and proceeded to prepare breakfast for both of them.

"There's a little house for the marshal to live in," she said busily, after a few stiff minutes had passed. "The town provides it."

"I know," Sawyer said. "I was here in Blue River once before." Now that he had coffee to drink, his temperament seemed to be improving. A hot meal might render him tolerable. "Dara Rose lived there at the time, with her daughters."

"Oh," Piper said, apropos of nothing, turning slices

of salt pork in the skillet, then cracking three eggs into the same pan, causing them to sizzle in the melted lard.

"These accommodations of yours are pretty rustic," he said, evidently to make conversation, which Piper could have done without just then. "The bed feels like a rock pile, and there's no place to take a bath."

Piper, who yearned for an indoor bathroom like the one Dara Rose had now, in her lovely new ranch house, and a feather bed, and many other things in the bargain, took umbrage. *These accommodations of hers,* humble as they were, had very probably saved his life. "I manage just fine," she said coolly.

Sawyer sighed wearily. "I didn't mean it as an insult," he said.

Piper plopped the salt pork and two of the eggs onto a tin plate—also provided by the good people of Blue River—and carried it over to him, along with a knife and fork.

She set the works down with an eloquent clatter and rested her hands on her hips.

"Would you like more coffee?" she demanded inhospitably.

He grinned up at her, enjoying her pique. "Yes, ma'am, I would," he said. "If you please."

She stormed back to the stove, took up a pot holder, and brought the coffee to the desk that doubled as a table. There was a heavy clunking sound as the base of it met the splintery oak surface.

"Thank you," the new marshal said sweetly.

"You're welcome," she crabbed.

A knock sounded at the schoolhouse door just then, and hope filled Piper, displacing her irritation and her strangely injured pride. Perhaps Clay had returned, or Doc Howard—

But when she answered the firm rap, she found Bess Turner standing on the step, looking poised to flee if the need arose. Bess ran the brothel above the Bitter Gulch Saloon, and if she'd ever tried to look respectable, she'd given up on it long ago.

Her hair was a brassy shade of yellow, her thin cheeks were heavily rouged, and her mouth was hard, not with anger, Piper had often thought, but with the strain of bearing up under one tribulation and sorrow after another.

"I'm sorry to bother you," Bess said, almost meekly. She wore a pink satin cloak, completely inadequate for a December day, and her dancing shoes were soaked through.

"Come in," Piper said quickly, stepping back. "There's coffee made—I'll pour you some."

Bess's tired gaze strayed past Piper, dusted over Sawyer, and came back to Piper again. "Thank you," she said, very quietly.

"Stand over here by the stove," Piper urged, with a shiver, hastening to rinse out a coffee cup. "You must be freezing!"

Bess sidled close to the fire, and Piper noticed that the woman's hands were gloveless, and blue with cold. "I can't stay long," she said, stealing another glance at Sawyer. Naturally, she'd be curious about his presence, but she wasn't likely to carry tales, like some of the other townswomen would have done. "My Ginny-Sue is hectoring me something fierce about the Christmas program," she added fretfully. "She's learned the whole second chapter of Luke by heart, that being her piece for the recital, and she's afraid school won't take up again before then, because of the snow."

Piper was touched. Ginny-Sue, a shy ten-year-old, was

one of her brightest pupils. Except for Madeline Howard, she was the best-dressed, too, always neatly clad in ready-made dresses, with her face scrubbed and her brown hair plaited. Her shoes were the envy of the other girls, sturdy, but with buttons instead of laces, and always polished to a high shine.

"Christmas is still more than a week away," Piper said gently, handing Bess the coffee. "I'm sure we won't have to cancel the program."

Bess nodded, looking straight at Sawyer now and making no effort to hide her curiosity. "Now, who would you be?" she asked him, straight out.

He'd risen to his feet, abandoning his breakfast for the moment. "Name's Sawyer McKettrick," he answered cordially. "I'm the new town marshal."

"He's Clay's cousin," Piper added hastily, as though that explained what he was doing in the schoolhouse at this hour of the morning, wearing nothing but boots, trousers and a blanket.

"Howdy," said the local madam. "I'm Bess Turner. Miss St. James here teaches my girl, Ginny-Sue."

Sawyer dropped back into his chair. "Good to meet you," he said, and resumed eating, though he continued to take an undisguised interest in the visitor.

"He was shot," Piper went on anxiously. "Clay and Dr. Howard said he couldn't be moved, so he spent the night here—"

Bess smiled, and a twinkle appeared in her faded eyes, just for the briefest moment. "Shot, was he?" she replied, looking Sawyer over again, this time more thoroughly. "You'd never guess it."

Piper thought of Dara Rose's late husband, who had died in Bess's establishment, and wondered if the two of them had been together at the time of his scandalous demise. Not that she'd ever be so forward as to ask, of course. There were some things a body had to be content to wonder about in perpetuity.

Piper looked back at Sawyer, who moved the blanket aside just enough to show the bandage and part of his sling. He'd guessed that she was embarrassed, evidently, and the fact seemed to amuse him.

"Did you see who shot you?" Bess asked. It was a question Piper hadn't thought to ask, and neither, as far as she knew, had Clay or Doc Howard.

"The snow was too thick," Sawyer answered, with a shake of his head.

"Well, I'll be," marveled Bess, finishing her coffee. "Blue River's always been a peaceful town, for the most part. I hope we're not drawing in all sorts of riffraff, like some other places I could name."

The corner of Sawyer's well-made mouth quirked up in a semblance of a grin, probably at the term "riffraff," coming from someone like Bess, but he didn't say anything.

Bess handed over the empty mug and smiled at Piper. "So I can tell my Ginny-Sue there'll still be a Christmas?" she asked.

"I'm sure of it," Piper said, though that was mostly bravado. Inwardly, she wasn't so sure that the warmer weather would hold—but she *hoped* it would, and fiercely.

Bess nodded a farewell to Sawyer and walked purposely toward the door, Piper following.

On the threshold, Bess paused, lowered her voice and said, "If you need any help, Teacher, just send word over to the Bitter Gulch. My girls and me, we'll do whatever we can to lend a hand."

Piper's throat tightened, and the backs of her eyes burned a little. She wondered how many of the other women of Blue River, besides Dara Rose, of course, would have made such an offer. "Thank you, Mrs. Turner," she said warmly.

"Bess," the other woman corrected, patting Piper's hand before taking her leave. "I never was nobody's missus, and I won't pretend I was."

With that, she started down the slippery steps of the schoolhouse porch, drawing her tawdry cloak more closely around her. The sun glinted in her dandelion-colored hair, and she looked back at Piper, smiled once more, and waved.

Piper waved back, and closed the door slowly.

When she turned around, she saw that Sawyer had finished his breakfast. Still seated at her desk, he watched her over the rim of his coffee mug.

"Christmas," he said, in a musing tone, his gaze skimming over the undecorated tree leaning forlornly against the far wall, slowly but surely dropping its needles. Piper had sent the bigger boys out to find it the previous week, thinking they'd all be able to enjoy it longer that way, though now she wished she'd waited. "I forgot all about it."

"You'll be at Clay and Dara Rose's place by then," Piper said, holding on to blind faith that it would be so, "probably much mended."

"I'll need to round up some presents for those little girls," Sawyer mused.

"I wouldn't worry," Piper counseled, liking him again. Sort of. "They're well provided for, Edrina and Harriet."

He smiled. "Yes," he said. "They would be, with Clay for a father."

The remark stung Piper a little, on Dara Rose's behalf, dampening her kindly inclination toward Mr. McKettrick, even though she sensed no rancor in the remark. Her cousin had had a difficult life, almost from the first, but Dara Rose was and always had been a devoted mother. "If Clay were here," she said moderately, "he'd tell you that he's the fortunate one."

Sawyer sighed. He looked paler than before, though breakfast and the coffee must have braced him up. "I've managed to get on the wrong side of you again," he said. "I *know* Clay loves his wife, and he considers those girls his own, as much as he does the baby he and Dara Rose are expecting."

Piper bit her lower lip for a moment. "I apologize," she said. "I didn't sleep very well last night, and I confess that I'm worried that I might have spoken out of turn to Bess Turner—" She paused, swallowed. "If there's another storm, Christmas will have to be canceled and the children will be so disappointed."

His grin flashed again, brief but bright as the sunlight on the snow outside. "Christmas happens in the heart," he said. "*Especially* the heart of a child."

She regarded him for a long moment. "That's a lovely sentiment," she said, taken by surprise, "and I'm sure it's true, for fortunate children like Edrina and Harriet, and Doc Howard's little girl, Madeline, but there are others, like Ginny-Sue Turner, who need more." She inclined her head toward the forlorn little tree, leaning against the schoolhouse wall. "They need the sparkle and the carols, the excitement and, yes, the oranges and the peppermint sticks, because the other three-hundred-sixty-four days of the year can be bleak for them."

Sawyer, clearly tiring, leaned against the framework of the bedroom doorway again, and smiled sadly. "You really care about these kids," he said.

"Of course I do," Piper replied.

"What do *you* want for Christmas, Miss St. James?" he asked quietly.

She hadn't thought of her own secret wishes for a long time, and the question unsettled her. "You need to rest," she hedged. "Go in and lie down."

"Not until I get an answer," he replied, folding his good arm across the sling that held his injured one in place.

Piper blushed. "Very well, then," she said, throwing out the first thing that came to mind so he would drop the subject and leave her in peace. "I'd like a new cloak, since you bled all over mine and I had to burn all but a few scraps of it."

Sawyer McKettrick smiled again. "Done," he said. And then he turned around and went back to bed.

CHAPTER FOUR

CLAY RETURNED SHORTLY after noon, at the reins of a sledge improvised from lengths of lumber, probably left over from the building of his house and barn, with two enormous plow horses hitched to the front. He grinned and waved when Piper stepped out onto the schoolhouse porch, shielding her eyes from the bright sun with one hand.

"How's that ornery cousin of mine faring?" he called, bringing the team to a halt. The back of the sledge was piled high with an assortment of things—crates and boxes, a supply of hay for Sawyer's horse, a few bulging feed bags and, most notably, the parts of an iron bedstead and a mattress secured with rope.

"He was up and around earlier," Piper replied, staring at the bedstead and wondering whether Clay planned to leave it at the schoolhouse for her or use it to transport Sawyer to the ranch, "but he's resting at the moment."

"Up and around?" Clay echoed, pleased. He climbed off the strange conveyance and approached through the knee-deep but already-melting snow. "I guess I shouldn't be surprised. Sawyer always had more gumption than good sense."

"He's wanting his trunk from the depot," Piper said, as Clay reached her and she stepped back so they could both go inside, where it was warmer.

"I figured as much," Clay told her, taking off his hat

and hanging it from a peg near the door. He'd stomped most of the snow off his boots out on the porch. "Picked it up before I came here."

Sawyer, who must have heard the commotion, appeared in the doorway to Piper's room, looking rumpled and grim. He obviously needed more laudanum, and Piper made up her mind to fetch it and supervise the dosage this time, make sure he didn't guzzle the stuff down again.

"You ready to make the trip out to our place?" Clay asked his cousin, looking doubtful even as he spoke. "I can haul you out there today if you want to go, and in style, too, like Caesar reclining on Cleopatra's barge."

Piper felt a pang of sadness at the thought of Sawyer's leaving the schoolhouse, which was just plain silly, because she ought to be relieved instead. She *really* ought to be relieved.

Sawyer frowned, puzzlement personified. "Caesar? Cleopatra's barge? What the devil are you yammering on about?"

"Either way, I came prepared," was all the answer Clay gave. He was still grinning, proud of his resourcefulness, and he waxed unusually loquacious, for him. "I brought along a kind of sleigh I rigged up last year, out of some old boards—normally use it to haul feed out to the cattle on the range when the wagons can't get through—even brought a bed along, in case you were ready to head out to the ranch sooner than expected. There's hay and some grain for your gelding, too, if you'd rather stay put a while longer. In that case, I'll set the bedstead up for Piper, so she won't have to sleep on the floor until you're out of her hair."

Piper blinked.

"You slept on the floor?" Sawyer asked, practically

glowering at her, as though accusing her of some unconscionable perfidy.

"Where did you *think* she was sleeping?" Clay inquired good-naturedly. "This is a one-room schoolhouse, Sawyer, not a big-city hospital or a grand hotel."

"I cannot have a bed in my schoolroom," Piper put in hastily, though neither man seemed to be listening.

"I'll go back with you," Sawyer said to Clay, though when he took a step, he winced and swayed on his feet so that his cousin immediately stepped forward and took him by the arms, lest he collapse.

Sawyer flinched and his face drained of color.

Chagrined, Clay loosened his grip, though he didn't dare let go completely. "I don't believe you're ready quite yet," he said reasonably.

"My .45," Sawyer said, looking dazed. "She—took it."

"Never mind that," Clay told him. "Right now, we've got to get you back to bed."

Sawyer allowed himself to be turned around and led in the other direction, most likely because he didn't have much choice in the matter. "My *pistol*," he insisted.

Piper glanced toward the cloakroom, where she'd hidden the weapon, climbing onto the food box to push it to the back of a wide, high shelf. She wanted that dreadful thing out of sight *and* out of reach, so none of her students would stumble upon it, once they returned to school, and bring about a tragedy.

For all that, something in Sawyer's tone bothered her. Was he afraid the man who had shot him would return, make another attempt on his life and, this time, succeed in killing him?

Maybe, she concluded, but the fact remained that Sawyer wasn't in his right mind, given all the blood he'd lost and the pain he'd suffered. By now, the shooter was surely putting as many miles as he could between himself and Blue River, no doubt believing that his quarry was dead.

She shuddered, hugged herself against an inner chill.

What if she was wrong? What if, by hiding the gun, she was putting both Sawyer and herself in danger?

In the next room, Clay murmured something, and then the bedsprings creaked as Sawyer lay down again.

Piper paced. She'd ask Clay what to do with the gun when he came back.

He took his time, though, speaking quietly to Sawyer, probably giving him laudanum from Doc's bottle. By the time he returned to the schoolroom, Piper had reheated the coffee left over from breakfast and poured some into a mug for him.

"Thanks," Clay said, accepting the cup and taking a restorative sip before going on. "Has Doc been back? Sawyer's in bad shape."

Piper shook her head no. "He'll be here," she said, with confidence. Weather or no weather, Doc Howard was not the kind to stay away when he was needed. "Clay—?"

He raised one eyebrow. "If you're worried about me setting up that bedstead in the schoolroom—"

Again, she shook her head. "Sawyer's been asking for his gun," she said. "I put it away, but now I'm wondering if I ought to give it back to him. In case—in case—"

Clay's expression was a solemn one. "Where is it?" he asked.

She led the way into the cloakroom and pointed upward.

Clay was so tall that he didn't need anything to stand on to reach the Colt .45 in its hiding place. He extended one hand, felt around a little, and found the pistol. Bringing it down to eye level, he examined it, expertly checking the cylinder to see that there were bullets inside.

"Better give it back to him," he said. "I know Sawyer, and he won't get any real rest as long as this thing is out of his reach."

Piper's heart pounded. "But—" She paused, swallowed, tried again. "He's not himself. What if he doesn't recognize you or me or Doc and shoots someone?"

To Piper's surprise, Clay chuckled, though it was a raspy sound, not really an expression of amusement. "Sawyer's himself, all right," he assured her. "Always is, no matter what. And he won't shoot anybody who isn't fixing to shoot *him,* no matter how delirious he might be."

"How can you be so sure?" Piper persisted. She hated guns. These were modern times, for heaven's sake, and they were not the Old West but the new one.

"I know my cousin," Clay replied matter-of-factly. "We grew up together, he and I. He's been shooting almost as long as he's been riding horses, and he showed a unique talent for it from the first."

Again, Piper shuddered. "You're saying that he's a—a gunslinger?"

"I'm saying he's good with a gun. There's a difference."

"But what if he's a criminal? You've said it yourself— no one is sure, including you, that Sawyer isn't an outlaw."

Clay held the pistol carefully but competently, keeping the barrel pointed toward the floor as he passed her, leaving the cloakroom. "Even if he *is* an outlaw," he replied easily, "he wouldn't shoot anybody down in cold blood. He's also a *McKettrick,* after all."

Piper was exasperated. The McKettrick family had their own distinct code of ethics, hammered out by the patriarch, Angus, and handed down to his sons and their sons after them, but it seemed obvious that Sawyer might not subscribe to that honorable philosophy, given his secrecy about his vocation. On the other hand, Clay trusted his cousin enough to hand over his own badge, and that was no small matter.

Clay carried the pistol to Sawyer's bedside and came back, intent on the next task. "I'll see to my cousin's horse," he said, "and unload the supplies."

Doc Howard showed up while Clay was outside, and the two of them carried the bedstead and mattress, still roped together, into the schoolhouse.

The bed wasn't very wide—it probably belonged to either Edrina or Harriet—but there was no room for it in front, so they took it into the teacher's quarters. Piper fussed and hovered like a hen chased away from its nest, but Clay only said, "You can't sleep on the floor," and proceeded to set the thing up in the little space available—crosswise at the foot of the bed where Sawyer lay, sound asleep.

It made a T-shape, and Piper figured that T stood for *trouble.*

"You'll be quite safe," Doc added, in fatherly tones, after helping Clay assemble the second bed. Sawyer's eyelids fluttered, but he didn't stir otherwise. The pistol rested, a daunting presence in its own right, on the night table. "Mr. McKettrick here is an invalid, remember."

An invalid? Piper thought. Sawyer had gotten out of bed without help just that morning, visited the shed where his horse was kept as well as the privy, and returned to the schoolhouse with enough strength to drink coffee and eat breakfast.

"Safe?" Piper challenged, folding her arms. "By now, my reputation must be in tatters."

"Nobody knows Sawyer's here," Clay reasoned, unwinding the rope that left a deep dent in the middle of the bed. "I haven't said a word to anybody but Dara Rose. She sent some things for you, by the way, staples, mostly, and a book she ordered from back East. Says she'll read it when you're finished."

Piper thought of her cousin with both gratitude and frustration. If only Dara Rose were here, too. As a respectable married woman, she could have defused any gossip by her mere presence.

Doc wouldn't look at Piper, though it took her a moment to notice, and when she did, she saw that his neck had reddened above his tight celluloid collar. He'd told Eloise, of course—his wife would have demanded an explanation for his leaving the house when everyone else was staying home, close to the fire.

"Doc?" Piper prodded suspiciously.

"I've sworn Mrs. Howard to secrecy," he said, but he still wouldn't meet her gaze.

Some things, like a mysterious man occupying the schoolmarm's bed, able-bodied or not, were simply too deliciously improper to keep silent about, especially for people like Eloise Howard. Bess Turner, by ironic contrast, wouldn't say a word to anyone—Piper was sure of that.

She groaned aloud.

"It's too late anyhow," Clay observed lightly, straightening after he'd crouched to tighten a screw in the framework of the bedstead. "If there's damage to your good name, it's already been done."

Piper flung out her hands. "Well," she sputtered, "thank you very much for *that,* Clay McKettrick. But why should *you* worry? *You're* not the one who'll wind up an old maid and maybe even lose her job!"

He chuckled and shoved a hand through his dark hair. "I reckon it's a certainty that I'll never be an old maid," he conceded. "But you probably won't, either. There aren't so many women way out here that men can afford to be choosy."

Doc Howard closed his eyes, shook his head.

Piper would have shrieked at Clay if it hadn't been for Sawyer, placidly sleeping nearby. She didn't want to startle him awake—he might grab for his pistol then and shoot them all.

"Choosy?" she fired back, in a ferocious whisper.

Doc Howard put a hand to each of their backs and steered both Clay and Piper out into the schoolroom. "Now, Clay," the dentist said, in a diplomatic tone meant to pour oil on troubled waters, "any man would be proud to have a lovely woman like Piper here for a wife. Piper, Clay's going to pull his foot out of his mouth any moment now and apologize for the thoughtless remark he just made."

Clay did look sorry. Deflated, too. "I didn't mean that the way it sounded," he said. "I do ask your pardon." When Piper just glared at him, not saying a word in reply, he sighed miserably, turned and headed outside, ostensibly to bring in Sawyer's trunk and the things Dara Rose had sent in from the ranch.

Doc smiled and touched her upper arm. "There, now," he told her. "Matters are rarely as bad as they seem."

Piper opened her mouth, closed it again, remembering childhood counsel. If she didn't have something nice to say, she shouldn't say anything at all.

"I'm going back in there to check the wound and change the bandages," Doc said, leaving Sawyer himself completely out of the equation, it seemed to Piper.

She busied herself building up the fire. Clay carried in a crate filled with supplies, and she spotted not only the promised book, one she'd been yearning to read, but a bag of coffee beans, tea leaves in a tin canister, several jars of preserves, two loaves of bread, and even part of a ham, with the bone intact, so she could make soup later.

Piper said nothing.

Clay, resigned, went out again, lugged a sizable travel trunk over the threshold and on into the little room that now contained two beds instead of one.

As if she'd consider sleeping in such close proximity to a man, an armed *stranger,* no less, of dubious moral convictions.

Spending another night on the floor wasn't a happy prospect either, though, so she put that out of her mind, along with thoughts of Sawyer McKettrick.

Doc and Clay conferred again, and soon came out of the bedroom, single file. Doc's hands were wet from a recent washing—he must have used the basin on Piper's bureau—and he was rolling down his sleeves, shrugging back into his coat to make his departure.

Most likely, he would go straight home and tell Eloise that the problem of sleeping arrangements over at the schoolhouse had been solved. Now the teacher would have a bed of her very own.

Inwardly, Piper sighed. Doc, having only the best of intentions himself, mistakenly believed that everyone else was the same way.

"I'll tie Cherokee behind the sleigh and lead him out to the ranch," Clay told Piper. "That way, you won't have to worry about feeding and watering him if it snows again."

"Thank you," Piper said crisply. This, it seemed, was Clay's version of appeasement, at least in part. "When will you be back?" The question was addressed to both Clay and Doc Howard.

"I'll get here tomorrow if it's at all possible," Doc promised.

"Soon as I can," Clay said, in his turn. "Dara Rose tells me the baby's dropped a little, says it means we'll have another daughter or a son anytime now, so a lot depends on how she's feeling."

"Maybe Dara Rose would be safer in town," Piper said, fretful again as she thought of her cousin way out there on that lonely ranch, heavily pregnant. "Closer to Doc."

"I'm a *dentist*," Doc reminded them both.

"You've delivered babies before," Piper said. It was true; she herself knew of two different occasions when he had served as midwife.

"Only because I didn't have a choice," Doc answered.

"I've brought a few colts and calves into the world," Clay put in, affably confident. "It can't be all that different."

Piper had had enough male wisdom for one day. As much as she dreaded their leaving, a part of her couldn't wait for both Clay *and* Doc to make themselves scarce. Naturally, that meant she'd be alone with Sawyer again, but he slept most of the time anyway.

"Tell Dara Rose I'm grateful for the things she sent to town for me," she said moderately. "Especially the book."

Clay smiled. "She wrote you a letter, too. It's in the box somewhere."

The news heartened Piper, and at the same time made her regret that she hadn't anticipated this and prepared a letter of her own, to send back with Clay. "I hope to see all of you at the Christmas program, if not before then," she said.

Clay looked dubious. "I'll do my best to bring the girls in for the party, if the weather allows, but I can't see Dara Rose making the trip."

"No," Piper agreed sadly. "I suppose not. She's well, though?"

Clay smiled. "She's just fine, Piper. Don't you worry." His eyes lit up. "Tell you what. If Sawyer's better by then, I'll bring both of you out to the ranch Christmas Eve, after the program, and we'll all celebrate the big day together. I'll even see that you get back to Blue River before school takes up again after New Year's."

"I'd like that," Piper said, cheered. The prospect of spending time with her cousin and the children, holding the baby if it had arrived by then, and, yes, taking long, luxurious baths in Dara Rose's claw-footed tub, complete with hot and cold running water, renewed her.

A few minutes later, after bringing in more water and firewood, Clay and the doctor left.

Piper watched them go through the schoolhouse window, Sawyer's buckskin gelding plodding along behind the team and sled. The sky had gone from blue to gray, she saw with trepidation, but she kept her thoughts in the present moment, since worrying wouldn't do any good.

Emptying the crate Dara Rose had filled for her took up a happy half hour—there were notes from Edrina and Harriet, as well as a long, chatty letter from their mother—and Piper, feeling rich, made herself a pot of tea, lit the lantern against the gathering gloom of a winter afternoon, and sat down at her desk to read.

Dara Rose gave a comical account of ranch life, especially in her current condition, assured Piper that she had nothing to fear from Sawyer McKettrick, and related funny things the children had said. Between the approach of Christmas and being virtually snowed in, Edrina and Harriet had an excess of energy and bickered constantly, settling down only when Clay reminded them that St.

Nicholas paid attention to good behavior and dispensed gifts accordingly.

By the time she'd finished reading the letter through for the first time, Piper was both smiling and crying a little. She'd miss Dara Rose and the children terribly if she went back to Maine, she reminded herself silently. They were all the family she had, after all, here *or* there.

Still, in Maine she wouldn't be the schoolmarm who'd housed a half-naked outlaw, as she would be here in Blue River. She could get another teaching position and eventually meet a suitable man and get married. Finally have a home and children of her own.

A hoarse shout from the bedroom startled her so much that she nearly upset her cup of tea. Alarmed, she bolted to her feet and hurried in to investigate.

Sawyer sat up in bed, breathing hard, his eyes wild, his flesh glistening with perspiration even though the room was fairly cold, being far from the stove. He was holding the pistol in his right hand, and the hammer was drawn back.

For one hysterical moment, Piper thought the shooter must have returned, maybe crawled in through the high window, but there was no one else in the room.

She kept her gaze on the Colt .45 in Sawyer's hand. The barrel was long, and it glinted evilly in the thin light.

"Don't shoot," she said weakly.

Sawyer came back to himself with a visible jolt, blinked a couple of times, and, much to Piper's relief, set the gun aside on the night table. "Sorry," he said. "Guess I must have been dreaming."

Piper lingered in the doorway, waiting for her flailing heart to slow down to its normal pace. Doc had done a good job of replacing Sawyer's bandages; they looked clean and white against his skin. "Are you hungry?" she asked. "Dara Rose sent a lovely ham, and some preserves, too."

He blinked again, then gave a raw chuckle. "You keep asking if I'm hungry," he said. "Why is that?"

"You haven't eaten since breakfast," Piper said, a little defensively. "It's almost supper time now."

Sawyer looked surprised, and she could tell he was wondering where the day had gone. "It is?" he asked.

"Yes," she said.

"Did Clay bring me any clothes?"

She nodded. "Your trunk is right over there," she said, pointing it out. "Shall I get you something from it?"

He considered the offer. "I'll do it myself," he said. "The way I figure it, the more I move around, the better off I'll be. Besides, I need to go outside again."

"Your horse is at the ranch," Piper told him. "Clay took it with him when he left."

He grinned. "I know that," he said. "This trip isn't about the horse."

She blushed.

Sawyer swung his legs over the side of the bed. Though the quilt covered his private parts, she couldn't help noticing that he wasn't wearing trousers.

She backed quickly out of the bedroom, followed by the sound of his laughter.

She didn't speak to him or even glance in his direction, minutes later, when he came out of the bedroom, but she knew he was dressed this time, instead of wrapping his upper body in a blanket.

She busied herself heating water—she was desperate for a bath, and planned on locking herself in the cloakroom with her small copper tub later on, when she was sure Sawyer had gone back to sleep—and then sliced Dara Rose's fresh-baked bread and some of the ham, placing the food on plates. She opened a jar of peaches and added those, as well.

Sawyer returned and, forgetting, she looked his way. Saw that he'd strapped on a gun belt when he got dressed. The handle of the Colt .45 jutted beneath his coat, which was shorter than the ruined one, and just as well made.

"Supper," she said, gesturing toward his full plate, which she'd already carried over to the desk, along with a knife, fork and spoon.

Sawyer nodded in acknowledgment of the one-word invitation, closing the door behind him. "I see there's another bed in the back room," he said. "I was going to offer to sleep on the floor so you wouldn't have to, but I guess that won't be necessary."

Piper was at once touched and flustered by this statement, and turned her head so he wouldn't see that in her face. She wasn't about to discuss the second bed, because she didn't expect to sleep in it, but she kept that to herself, too.

"Clay insisted it would be safe to let you have your pistol back," she said, recalling the look in his eyes when he'd awakened from whatever nightmare he'd been lost in and immediately grabbed the gun, prepared to fire. "I don't mind telling you that I'm not convinced it was a wise decision."

Sawyer smiled wanly at this, made his way to her desk, and stood there, looking bewildered. He was wondering where she planned to sit, and she hastened, plate and silverware in hand, to one of the students' places and sat on the bench.

Looking relieved, and singularly worn-out from getting dressed and making the long slog to and from the outhouse, he said he'd like to wash up before he ate.

With a nod of her head, she indicated the basin she'd

already filled with warm water and set on top of a book-shelf, along with a bar of soap and a towel. While Sawyer cleansed his hands and splashed his face, she began to eat. The ham and bread tasted especially good, after a couple of days of boiled pinto beans, and just the sight of those lovely peaches, picked in the autumn from Clay and Dara Rose's own orchard and put up in their kitchen, made her mouth water in anticipation.

Sawyer dried his face and hands with the towel. "I could use a shave," he said, as he returned to the desk and sat down to have his supper.

"Maybe tomorrow," Piper replied. The stubble on his chin made him look like the rascal he probably was, but she didn't find it unattractive. She probably should have, though, she thought. Particularly since they were shut in together, the pair of them, and almost certainly raising more of a scandal with every passing day.

And night.

"I'll buy you a new cloak," Sawyer said, out of the blue.

Piper stopped eating, delicious though the food was. "I couldn't accept," she said hurriedly. "It would be im-proper."

He grinned. "We're way past what's proper already, wouldn't you say?"

It was all too true. Piper colored up again. "You needn't remind me," she said.

The grin held. "I ruined your other cloak, didn't I?" Sawyer asked. "The least I can do is replace it, so you don't freeze to death this winter."

"I'll manage," Piper insisted.

He concentrated on consuming his supper after that, even had a second helping of ham, but his gaze found her every few moments, and each time he looked at her, she saw a twinkle in his eyes.

At last he tired, gathered up his plate and silverware, and looked around for a place to put them.

"I'll take those," Piper said, and did. Since there wasn't a sink in the schoolhouse, she'd wash them later in a basin she reserved for the purpose. By then, she was thinking about the bath she'd take in the cloakroom, once Sawyer had retired to his bed.

Presently, he said good-night and left her alone.

Piper immediately put water on the stove to heat, then hurried outside, to the shed, where she kept the washtub she meant to use.

The snow seemed to be melting, but by the time she returned to the schoolhouse, the hem of her dress was soaked and she was shivering with cold.

It would only be slightly warmer in the cloakroom, she knew, than it was outside, but there was nothing for it. She'd worn these same clothes all of yesterday, then slept in them, and then worn them all day *today*. Now, she felt grimy.

She set the washtub in the cloakroom, filled it bucket by bucket, a process that took a very long time. Sneaking into her bedroom, relieved to see that Sawyer was sleeping peacefully, she collected a flannel nightgown, a washcloth, soap and a towel.

Inside the cloakroom, with a kerosene lantern to light her way, Piper moved the food box in front of the door, just in case, and quickly stripped off her clothes.

Goose bumps sprang up on her bare flesh, and her teeth chattered, but she was resolute. She *would* bathe, even if it was agony, because being dirty was far worse.

The lantern flickered—there was a breeze coming up through the cracks between the planks in the floor—and

the bathwater, having taken so long to prepare, was lukewarm when she stepped into it.

Piper scrubbed diligently, dried off with the towel,
and donned the flannel nightgown.

The prospect of sleeping on the floor again loomed
before her and, as she moved the food box aside, took up
the lantern and fled the cloakroom with her discarded
day garments wadded up under one elbow, she wondered
just how much one small, well-meaning and wholly decent person was meant to endure for the sake of propriety. Especially when that particular horse was already
out of the barn, so to speak.

She stopped suddenly when she realized Sawyer was
seated at her desk again, wearing half a shirt, since he
hadn't been able to put his injured arm through the ap-
propriate sleeve.

He looked up from the book he was reading and
smiled. "I wondered if you were shut up in there," he
said, with a nod toward the gaping door of the cloakroom.
"Even considered coming to your rescue."

"I thought you were asleep," Piper said, still shivering even though—or perhaps *because*—she was wearing her warmest nightgown.

Sawyer's blue-green gaze moved over her like a caress, came back to her face. "Yes," he agreed. "I suppose
you did think that. As it happens, though, I woke up and
that was that. So I came out here, expecting to find you
asleep on the floor, since you're probably too stubborn
to use that bed even after all the trouble Clay went to to
bring it here."

Piper shifted yesterday's clothes, petticoat, bloomers
and camisole included, from her side to her front, like a
rumpled shield. "Don't look at me," she said.

He chuckled, averted his eyes. "That's a tall order,"

he replied, "but whatever else I am, I'm a gentleman, so I'll comply with your request."

"Good," Piper said, not moving.

Sawyer seemed to be reading again, but Piper didn't trust appearances. Nor was she convinced that he was a gentleman.

"Go ahead and take the bedroom," he said. "I'll sleep out here."

CHAPTER FIVE

"Don't be silly," Piper immediately countered, still clutching her clothes against her bosom. Her nightgown was warm enough, but her bare feet felt icy against the planks, where she seemed to be rooted. "You're in no condition to sleep on a hard floor."

Sawyer, remaining at her desk with a book open in front of him, smiled and carefully kept his gaze averted. Or so she hoped—desperately.

"Neither are you, I'll wager," he said dryly. "Anyhow, I saw a mouse run through here a few minutes ago. Bold little critter, too—scampered right through the middle of the room."

Piper shuddered, and not just from the cold. She had a horror of things that crawled, slithered or scurried, though she'd kept that information to herself in case any of the rambunctious boys in her class got ideas about scaring Teacher with a garter snake or any other objectionable creature.

"What kind of name is Piper, anyhow?" Sawyer asked, turning the pages of the book so rapidly that he couldn't possibly be reading from them.

"What kind of name is Sawyer?" she countered, edging toward the stove. If she'd stayed put, she was convinced the soles of her feet would attach themselves to the icy floor. And where, at this precise moment, was that mouse he'd mentioned seeing?

He chuckled. "I'm named after a great-uncle on my mother's side of the family," he confessed. His lashes were long, she noticed, the same shade of toasty gold as his hair. "My folks—Kade and Mandy McKettrick—had three girls before me, so I reckon they were prepared to call me Mary Ellen."

In spite of herself, Piper laughed. She was warmer now, standing so near the stove, but no less embarrassed to be wearing nothing but a nightgown. Oddly, the sensation was not completely unpleasant. "You have three sisters?"

Sawyer nodded. "How about you? Do you have sisters or brothers?"

"I'm an only child," Piper said. *And an orphan,* added a voice in her mind. "Dara Rose and I were raised together, though, so we're as close as sisters."

"That's good," Sawyer responded. He cleared his throat. "Aren't you cold?" he asked.

Piper *was* cold, though the proximity of the stove helped a little. Suddenly, no matter what the shameful implications, she realized she couldn't bear the idea of sleeping on the floor again. "Do you promise to conduct yourself like a gentleman if I agree to spend the night in the spare bed?" she asked, horrified to hear herself uttering such a thing.

Sawyer lifted his good arm, palm out, as if swearing an oath in a court of law. "You have my word," he said.

Piper started for the bedroom doorway, giving him as wide a berth as she could in such a small, cramped space. "Wait until I say it's all right before you come in," she said.

Suppressing a grin, he nodded his agreement.

And Piper dashed past him, into the room that had been hers and hers alone, until night before last. Using

sheets and blankets provided by Dara Rose, along with
the bed itself and the lovely supper she and Sawyer had
shared that evening, Piper quickly made up a cozy nest.
Then, driven by the continuing cold and the shock of her
own brazen boldness, she scrambled under the covers
and lay there shivering until she'd adjusted to the chill
of the sheets.

"I'm—ready," she sang out, after a long time.

She saw the light from the lanterns, the one she'd used
in the cloakroom and the one Sawyer had been reading
by, blink out. He appeared in the doorway, a shadow
etched against the darkness, and Piper's heart began to
pound so that she dared not speak, lest her voice tremble
and betray the nervous excitement she felt.

Sawyer moved through the room, with only a slant
of moonlight to see by, and, with an effort Piper could
hear from beneath her blankets, took off his clothes. She
heard the springs creak as he sat down on the other bed.

"Good night, Miss St. James," he said, with a smile
in his voice. "And sleep well."

Piper didn't answer. She was hoping he'd think she
was already asleep.

Closing her eyes, she pretended as hard as she could.

LYING THERE IN the darkness, Sawyer cupped his right
hand behind his head and smiled up at the ceiling, recalling the delicious look of surprise on Piper St. James's
very pretty face a little while before, when she came
bursting out of the cloakroom in her nightdress and found
him reading at her desk. Her mouth had been blue with
cold at the time, and he'd wanted to wrap her up in a blanket—or better yet, his arms—to warm her.

Given her schoolmarm-skittishness, he reckoned that
would have been about the worst thing he could do, but

knowing that didn't stop him from imagining the way she'd fit against him, curvy and soft against his own hard lines and angles.

The sensual image tightened his groin painfully, a reaction he wasn't going to be able to do a damn thing about and therefore had better ignore as best he could. Sawyer set his back teeth, so great was the effort it took to change the course of his thoughts. Altering the path of a river probably would have been easier, he soon concluded.

He willed himself to relax, one muscle group at a time, starting with the part of his anatomy in the most need of quieting, and when he'd finished, still taut and achy in too many places, he resorted to counting in his head, by odd numbers. After a while, as the imagined digits mounted to astronomical totals, he found he could breathe normally again. Some people prayed, and some people counted sheep, but Sawyer always took refuge in arithmetic.

He closed his eyes, hoping to sleep.

It was no use, though. He was too aware of Piper, lying close by, in her spinsterish nightgown, with her glowing, just-bathed skin, and her dark hair clinging to her cheeks and forehead in moist tendrils. The scent of her was like perfume, faintly flowery, subtle.

"Mr. McKettrick?" Her voice was tentative. Soft. "Are you awake?"

He smiled again, having suspected she was playing possum. She'd called him by his given name once or twice that day, but now that they were both bedded down in the same room, "Mr. McKettrick" probably seemed a more prudent way to address him. "I'm awake," he confirmed.

He heard her draw in a breath. "I was just wondering if—well, if you think the man who shot you might come back?"

Bless her prim little heart, she was scared.

"Not likely," Sawyer said.

"Why not?"

"Because he probably thinks he's already killed me. Anyway, Blue River is small and a stranger would stand out."

"That didn't stop him before," she reasoned. "He just rode right up and shot you, bold as you please."

Sawyer grinned harder. His shoulder hurt, and he was lying a few feet from a woman he wanted and couldn't have, but he was enjoying this exchange. Maybe, he speculated, Miss Piper St. James was scared enough to leave her bed and share his.

"Yep," he said. "That's what happened."

"Suppose he didn't leave Blue River at all? Because of the storm, I mean. He could be holed up around here somewhere, couldn't he? Just waiting for his chance to strike again?"

"Maybe," Sawyer allowed, relishing her concern. If it hadn't meant Piper and her charges could be caught in the cross fire, he might have welcomed such a confrontation, since he'd be able to return the favor and put a bullet in the bastard, thereby evening the score. "It's not likely, though."

"What makes you so sure?"

"I've had some experience with these things," he replied.

"*That* isn't much comfort," Piper said. "Are you saying that you've been shot before?"

He had to chuckle. "No," he said. "I was referring to the nature of my work, that's all."

"What kind of 'work' involves getting shot?"

Sawyer said nothing.

"Are you an outlaw, Mr. McKettrick?" Piper persisted.

"Would you believe me if I said I wasn't?"

She made a muffled sound, like a scream of anger, held captive in her throat. It made him smile again. "I think you owe me an answer," she said, after a few moments.

"You do, do you?" he teased.

"Are you an outlaw?"

He thought it over. He'd killed a man once, though he'd been defending Henry Vandenburg, his former employer, at the time. Vandenburg's attacker, one of those wild-eyed anarchist types, had shoved his way through a crowd, in a busy railway station, and thrust the business end of a gun barrel into the boss's ample belly. Sawyer had stepped in, there was a struggle, and the pistol went off. The would-be killer bled out on the floor before the municipal police arrived in their paddy wagons.

"No," he answered, feigning offense at the question. "Would Clay have asked me to serve as town marshal if I were?"

"Possibly," she replied, after some thought. "You're his cousin, and the two of you grew up together. It might be that he's just giving you the benefit of the doubt by assuming that you are still the person he knew as a boy."

"Could be," Sawyer said, amused. She hadn't been this talkative before, and he wondered if that meant anything. Then he decided she felt safer speaking her mind because they were under cover of darkness, and she couldn't see him, or he her.

In a way, it reminded him of the old days on the Triple M, when he and Clay used to spend the night at their grandparents' house sometimes. The room they'd shared had two beds in it, and the dark of a country night had been like a curtain between them, making it possible to tell each other things they'd have choked on in the daylight.

"That," Piper said, "is a most unsatisfactory answer."

"Clay trusts me because I've never given him any reason not to," Sawyer said, relenting. Now that he wasn't in Vandenburg's employ any longer, he figured he didn't have to be so secretive, but he still wasn't inclined to spill his whole history. "I'm not an outlaw," he added.

"Then what are you? Only outlaws carry guns."

"Clay carries one. Is he an outlaw?"

"Well, *no,*" Piper admitted. "But he's the marshal."

There was a silence.

He waited.

"Are you a lawman?" she asked.

"Not exactly," Sawyer replied. He wondered if she'd warmed up yet, and if she was still scared—in need of a little manly protection. Being nobody's fool, he didn't ask. "How did you become acquainted with a lady of the evening?" he inquired instead, recalling that morning's visit from Bess Turner.

Piper sounded impatient. "You heard what she said— her daughter, Ginny-Sue, is one of my pupils. And if you're 'not exactly' a lawman, what are you?"

"I was paid to protect a man and his family," Sawyer said. "And that's all you need to know." He barely paused before giving her a dose of her own medicine by barging right into her private business. "Generally, respectable women don't befriend people like Ginny-Sue's mother, no matter what the circumstances."

Her tone was huffy. "Maybe I'm not a respectable woman. Did you ever think of that?"

Sawyer laughed. "Oh, you're respectable, all right. You wouldn't be so worried about my seeing you in a nightgown, not to mention our sharing a bedroom, if you weren't."

Piper was quiet for so long that Sawyer began to think she'd fallen asleep. Finally, though, she spoke again, and there was a note of gentle sorrow in her voice. "Bess loves her child, just like anybody else, and besides, however misguided she might be, she's a human being. I see no earthly reason to shun her."

Something thickened in Sawyer's throat, which was odd. He wasn't usually sentimental, especially not over prostitutes like Bess Turner, but something about Piper's offhand compassion touched him in a deep place, and caused a shift in the way he thought of her.

The realization caused him considerable consternation.

"Sawyer?"

He smiled at Piper's use of his first name. That was more like it. "What?"

"I'm—afraid."

"Don't be. I won't hurt you."

"It's not you I'm scared of. It's the man who shot you."

"In that case," he said, only half joking, "maybe you'd better crawl in with me."

"I couldn't do that!"

"Where's the harm in it? Your reputation is probably ruined anyhow."

There was a snap of irritation in her reply. "Be that as it may, I don't want to give you the wrong impression. I am *not* the sort of woman who gets into bed with a man she isn't married to." She swallowed so hard that he heard it. "I'm—unbesmirched."

Unbesmirched.

In other words, a virgin. No real surprise there.

"I won't lay a hand on you, Miss St. James," he assured her. That much was certainly true. He might *want* to do plenty, once Piper was lying beside him in that narrow bed, but he'd never tried to persuade an unwilling woman to share her favors before and he wasn't going to start now.

To his amazement, he heard her get out of the other bed, hurry over, and slip in beside him. The mattress was more suited to one than two; they collided, and Piper almost sprang out of bed again when she realized he wasn't wearing anything but the bandages and the sling on his left arm.

He knew this by the gasp she gave.

"It's *all right,* Piper," he said.

She gave a comical little wail. "You might have told me you were—well—*indisposed!*"

"You didn't ask," he pointed out.

"This is horrible," she lamented. But she was still there, under the covers. With him.

"Hardly," he said. "We're just two people keeping each other warm on a cold winter's night, that's all."

"Maybe that's all it is to *you,*" Piper retorted. "I had hopes of getting married someday, and having a home and a family, before you came along and spoiled everything."

He smiled in the darkness. "If that's so, then I'm sorry," he told her.

"You don't *sound* sorry," Piper accused.

He yawned expansively. "Would you be convinced if I rounded up a preacher and the two of us got hitched?"

She gasped again.

He laughed, but the idea of taking a wife—*this* wife— was already starting to grow on him. He'd have preferred to court Piper St. James properly before he put a ring on her finger and took her home to the Triple M and the rest of the McKettrick family, but she had a point. Whether it was fair or not, she was probably compromised, all right, simply because they'd been alone together for a couple of days and nights. Some folks were just hypocritical enough to assume she'd thrown caution to the winds and succumbed to rampant lust at the first opportunity.

It was downright ridiculous, Sawyer knew, to assume a conscientious schoolmarm would turn into a raving wanton overnight, since she'd given shelter to a wounded stranger of the opposite sex, and never mind the kindness and courage she'd shown by dragging him inside and looking after him as best she knew how. After this, Piper would be no better than Bess Turner, as far as a lot of the locals were concerned.

Piper hadn't answered his question and now, judging by the moisture he felt against the upper part of his right arm, she was in tears.

"Hey," he said hoarsely, "don't cry."

"I can't help it," she sobbed. Since he reckoned she wasn't the kind who cried easily, this was even worse. "Isn't it enough that you *ruined my life?* Do you have to add insult to injury by *mocking* me, too?"

Sawyer was honestly confused. "Mocking you?" he rasped. God, he hated it when women cried, especially when it was his fault. Like now. "When did I do that?"

"When you m-made that r-remark about getting— hitched!"

"Piper," he said, surprising himself as he much as he had her, "I was serious. I'll marry you, if it'll make you feel better."

She struggled to a sitting position, and moonlight turned her tears silvery on her cheeks. Her hair fell loose around her shoulders and down her back, nearly reaching her waist. "But we don't *love* each other!" she cried, in obvious despair.

Gently, he drew Piper back down beside him, holding her with his good arm. She rested her head on his bare shoulder, sniffling. "That's true," he said carefully, "but we certainly wouldn't be the first couple who ever got married for practical reasons. Clay and Dara Rose tied the knot so she and the girls would have a place to live, and that arrangement worked out."

Instead of comforting her, Sawyer's words made her cry harder.

He was confounded, figuring he'd made a good case for holy matrimony.

He patted the back of her head ineffectually, afraid to say anything more in case he got it wrong. Again.

"That's different!" Piper wailed out, after some shuddering and sniffling.

"What's different?" Sawyer asked carefully.

"Clay and Dara Rose are different!"

"Why?"

"Because they were in love with each other from the very first," Piper sobbed. "It just took them a while to notice!"

Against his better judgment, Sawyer laughed. He couldn't help it. "People get married for all sorts of reasons," he reiterated, when he'd caught his breath. "Love isn't always one of them."

"Well, it should be!"

"Lots of things 'should be,' but they aren't." It was the wrong thing to say, but Sawyer didn't realize that until after he'd said it, when she slammed the side of one small fist into his belly. The blow didn't hurt, but it sure startled him, and it knocked the wind out of him for a moment, too.

Piper might be small, but she packed a punch. Raised by and around strong women, Sawyer considered that a good thing.

"I don't even know what kind of man you are," she lamented, though she seemed to be regaining some control of her runaway emotions. "You could be a scoundrel, or worse."

He smiled. "What's worse?" he teased. A strand of her hair tickled his mouth, and he decided he liked the feeling.

"Murder," she said. "Highway robbery. *Bigamy.*"

"Bigamy?"

"Dara Rose thought she was married to Edrina and Harriet's father," Piper blurted out, on one long breath, "and it turned out he already had a wife and children, that stinker!"

Sawyer remembered Clay telling him the story, the year before. He hadn't thought about it since, though. "I'm not married," he said quietly. "Never have been."

She sat up again, looking down at him. "How do I know you're telling the truth?"

Was she considering saying yes?

"You don't," he said solemnly. "You'll just have to trust me."

She ruminated on that for a while, still sitting up. "You didn't—you couldn't have—*meant* what you said? About us getting married?"

"I meant it, all right," Sawyer replied. He actually *liked* the idea, and that was a bit unsettling.

"If we go through with this, it would be a marriage in name only."

Up until now, Sawyer couldn't have imagined himself agreeing to such terms, but he did. "All right," he said. "But I reserve the right to try to change your mind."

Piper mulled that over. He reckoned she was going to come to her senses and pull out of the deal. "Not until *after* we're married," she negotiated.

"Fair enough," Sawyer said, and something inside him soared, as proud and free as a lone eagle against a wide blue sky. "Can I at least kiss you?"

More consideration on her part followed.

He sat up, careful to keep the quilts in place, just above his waist.

They stared at each other for a while, in the light of a waning moon filtering through a weather-grimed window.

Then she closed her eyes, puckered up, and waited.

Sawyer bit the inside of his lower lip, so he wouldn't laugh. Then he placed his hand on the back of her head, very gently, and pressed her face toward his. He kissed her, worked her lips with his own until Piper sighed and opened to him.

He used his tongue. Carefully.

She moaned and slipped her arms around his neck.

He deepened the kiss slowly, because she was so obviously an innocent.

Piper whimpered, but she didn't try to pull away.

It was Sawyer who did that. "Piper," he said, his voice ragged from the strain of giving up what the rest of his body was demanding, "no more. I'm trying to do the right thing here."

"I'd better go back to the other bed," she said shyly.

"That might be a good idea," Sawyer replied. He was hard as tamarack by then, and he didn't want Piper to know it.

She left him, got back into the bed Clay had brought in from the ranch. The small distance between them seemed like miles to Sawyer, who fell back onto his pillows with a heavy sigh.

"Sawyer?" Piper said.

He probably sounded abrupt when he replied. "What?"

"I've never—" She fell silent, embarrassed again.

"I know," he said more gently.

And after that, by some miracle, they both went to sleep.

PIPER'S EYES FLEW open when she realized it was morning, and she'd not only let Sawyer kiss her in the night, but she'd kissed him *back*. She sat up in her borrowed bed, pulling the covers up to her chin, and looked in his direction, but he wasn't there.

She scrambled out from under the blankets, landed both feet on the icy floor, and made a dash for her bureau, where she rummaged for bloomers and a camisole. Clutching them in one hand, she grabbed her woolen dress, the one she'd planned on saving for really cold days, and stuck her head out the bedroom door.

Sawyer wasn't in the schoolroom—he must have gone outside, to the privy.

Piper dressed in seconds, fumbling, hopping about, nearly tripping over her hem in the process, and then did what she could with her hair, winding it into a single plait and twisting it around the back of her head, where she secured it with hairpins.

The schoolroom was warm—Sawyer must have built up the fire—and the delicious aroma of fresh coffee filled the air. She went to the window, looked out. The snow was nearly gone, but she barely took note of that because she spotted Sawyer, dressed and talking amiably with Doc Howard, who didn't get down off his mule. The poor animal was muddy to its knees.

Piper saw Doc smile and nod his head, and she ducked back from the window quickly, hoping he hadn't seen her.

What was Sawyer *saying* out there?

Her cheeks flamed so hot that she pressed her palms to her face, trying to cool them down. *Surely* Sawyer wasn't asking Doc Howard to fetch a preacher, so he and the schoolmarm could "get hitched," she thought frantically. Yes, they'd talked about marriage, and it had seemed like a viable idea at the time, but in the bright light of day it was—well, it was insane, that's what it was. It was *out of the question.*

She remembered the kiss, felt the heat and pressure on her mouth as surely as if Sawyer's mouth was on hers right then.

Her heart pounded, and bolts of fiery lightning shot through her, weakening her knees, melting parts of her that were too personal even to *think about.*

She *was* wanton, she concluded, horrified. She'd not only *gotten into bed* with Sawyer McKettrick the night before, she'd let him kiss her. *Let* him? She'd as good as thrown herself at the man, and then she'd *carried on.* In fact, if Sawyer hadn't sent her back to her own bed, she might have been swept away.

Things, she decided, could not possibly get worse.

Except that they did, and almost immediately.

Sawyer opened the door, came inside, spotted her sitting on one of her students' desks with her hands pressed to her burning face.

He smiled. "There are some kids coming down the road," he informed her. "Your students, I presume."

Piper cried out, bolted to her feet. "No!"

"Yes," Sawyer said. "Doc will be back at three-thirty, with a license and a preacher." With that, he headed for the bedroom, pausing to pour himself a mug full of coffee along the way. From the inside doorway, he looked back at her over his right shoulder. "Better step lively, Teacher," he said. "School's about to be in session."

He was barely out of sight when Ginny-Sue Turner burst in, cheeks pink, eyes eager. "I know the whole second chapter of Luke!" she blurted joyfully. "By heart!"

Piper's smile might have been a little shaky, but Ginny-Sue was too young, and too excited, to notice. "That's wonderful," she said, resting a hand on the child's shoulder.

"And Christmas is going to happen, after all!" Ginny-Sue enthused, glowing as she got out of her coat and mittens and warm woolen hat. "Mama said it would, because you told her so."

Piper's throat tightened, and she managed a little nod. She had no power to keep another snowstorm away, of course, but this child clearly believed she did.

It was a weighty responsibility.

Madeline Howard arrived next, small and blonde and very pretty, like her mother, followed by half a dozen other children.

"May I ring the bell, Miss St. James?" Madeline asked, beaming.

Piper assented, and the other students arrived by twos and threes. Even Edrina and Harriet made it into town for class—Clay had driven them in a wagon drawn by those same two plow horses he'd hitched to the sledge the day before, and he waved and smiled from the seat, reins in hand.

"Has the baby arrived?" Piper asked breathlessly, after picking her way through the mud to stand beside Clay's wagon, looking up at him.

He shook his head. "Not yet," he said, "but Dara Rose

was mighty eager to get the girls out of the house this morning, so I figure she's about ready."

"You'd better get back there, quick," Piper said, worried, but thrilled, too. In her excitement, she forgot about Sawyer McKettrick, hiding out in her bedroom behind the schoolhouse.

He'd be discovered, of course, if only because Edrina and Harriet surely knew he was there, and would want to greet him.

Clay nodded, lifted the reins and released the brake lever with his left hand. "Sawyer doing all right?" he asked, in parting.

Piper colored up, quite against her will, but held Clay's gaze. "Yes," she said.

Clay touched the brim of his hat in farewell, brought down the reins on the horses' backs, setting them in noisy motion, and drove away.

If it hadn't been so cold outside, sunny sky or none, Piper might have lingered in the school yard, putting off the moment when she'd have to face her pupils, but she didn't have a cloak and she'd forgotten to wrap the blanket around her before coming to greet Clay.

So she marched inside, clapping her hands to get the children's attention.

They were gathered around the undecorated Christmas tree, examining it for bird's nests and chatting among themselves. Edrina and Harriet, as she'd expected, were out of sight, and she could hear them talking with Sawyer in the back room.

She closed her eyes for a moment.

"Can we fix up the Christmas tree today, Miss St. James?" one of the boys asked. "Jack and me, we could fix up a stand for it in no time, out in the woodshed."

Piper set her hands on her hips and considered the

suggestion in a teacherly way. "That would be fine," she said, at long last.

The children cheered.

Two of the boys rushed outside, followed by several more.

"Edrina, Harriet!" Piper called pleasantly. "Come out here, please. We're going to decorate the tree."

Dara Rose's children, both beautiful, with heads full of shining curls and cherubic faces, appeared in the bedroom doorway.

Harriet opened her little bow-shaped mouth, most likely on the verge of making some remark about her kinsman's presence, but Piper quickly pressed an index finger to her own lips, shushing her.

Though she was very young, only in the first grade, Harriet read Piper's signal and bit back whatever she'd planned to say.

For the next hour, the children kept busy, cutting strips of colorful paper, saved especially for the purpose, and pasting them together in loops, so they turned into long chains.

The boys returned from the shed, triumphant, with several pieces of wood cobbled together to serve as a stand for the tree.

After much ado, the stem of the tree was wedged into the simple stand. Piper found the box of handmade ornaments on the cloakroom shelf and brought it into the schoolroom, where the lid was ceremoniously raised.

Inside were other chains, made by other students and other teachers, along with a few carefully wrapped glass balls, tiny rag-doll angels, and stars cut from tin. Some of the stars had rusted, which only added to their charm, and the children were as enthralled as if they'd just found a pirate's treasure.

Soon, the tree stood glittering, ready for Christmas.

By midday, the weather was turning gloomy again, the sky dark and heavy with snow, and fathers and uncles arrived in wagons and on horseback, to collect their offspring and see them safely home. Two of the mothers came as well, and peered curiously at Piper, as though they weren't sure they recognized her.

When the first fat snowflakes drifted down, Ginny-Sue took her leave, squeezing Piper's hand before she hurried outside. "Don't worry, Teacher," she said.

"Christmas will still come—you'll see!"

CHAPTER SIX

OF ALL PIPER'S pupils, only Edrina and Harriet remained at the schoolhouse, waiting for Clay to come for them. Heedless of the continuing snow, they laughed with Sawyer, who had hauled Piper's rocking chair out of the bedroom and now sat with one of the little girls on each knee, telling stories about himself and Clay as boys.

The fire in the stove warmed the room and steamed up the windows in a cozy way, and the Christmas tree lent a definite air of festivity, but Piper was nervous, just the same.

From a practical standpoint, she knew that Clay wasn't late—it was not quite three o'clock and he had farther to travel than most of the other parents—and even if he'd gotten off to an early start, the weather would surely slow him down.

No, it was Dara Rose she was concerned about.

Hadn't Clay said, that very morning, that Dara Rose had seemed anxious to get her daughters out of the house? Wasn't that an indication that the baby might be coming?

Piper bit her lower lip and busied herself at her desk, pretending to study her attendance records. Dara Rose was healthy, she reminded herself, and strong. She'd had two other children with no problem at all, hadn't she?

But Edrina and Harriet had been born in a large *city,* with a real doctor present at each of their births, and Dara Rose had been younger then.

Was she giving birth right now, this minute, way out there on that isolated ranch?

Had she run into some kind of trouble with the delivery, the kind Clay didn't have the knowledge or skill to handle?

At three-fifteen Piper heard the squeal of wagon wheels being braked, the snorting and tromping of horses, and rushed to the front window to wipe away some of the mist and look outside.

Clay, wearing a heavy coat, with the brim of his hat pulled low over his eyes to shield his face from the blustery weather, jumped down from the wagon box and left the team standing, their nostrils puffing out white clouds of breath.

Piper looked harder, trying to discern something from Clay's bearing or manner—his face was still hidden from view by the angle of his hat—but he revealed nothing as he made his way toward the schoolhouse with long, even strides.

Edrina and Harriet must have heard the team and wagon, too, because they were beside Piper in a matter of moments, standing on tiptoe, fingers gripping the windowsill, trying to see out. Perhaps they'd been more anxious than they'd let on.

Clay finally reached the porch, paused to stomp the snow and mud from his boots.

Piper wrenched open the door, but stepped aside when Edrina and Harriet scrambled past her.

Clay stepped over the threshold, shut the door, and crouched, putting out an arm for each of the girls. His hat fell backward and the beaming smile on his face was revealed.

"Girls," he told his stepdaughters, his eyes misting over like the windows, "you've got a brand-new baby brother waiting for you out at the ranch. Your mama's just fine, and she's hankering to show the little fellow off to you."

Edrina and Harriet jumped up and down with happiness as Clay straightened, nodded a brief greeting to Sawyer, then shifted his gaze to Piper.

"It was an easy birth," he told her quietly. "Dara Rose is well, if a mite worn-out, and the baby is big enough to fight bear with a switch."

Piper wept tears of joyful relief and gave Clay a quick, sisterly hug.

"Congratulations," she said, stepping back and smiling up at him.

That was when she felt Sawyer standing behind her. He rested his good hand on her shoulder briefly before reaching past her to extend it to Clay.

The two men shook hands.

"Another McKettrick," Sawyer said. "I'm not sure the world is ready for that."

Clay laughed. His face and ears were red with cold, but his eyes gleamed with love and pride. "We're going to call him Jeb," he said, "after my pa."

"Will you stay for coffee?" Piper asked, out of practicality. "It'll help keep you warm on the way back home."

But Clay shook his head in refusal, nodded to the girls to get their things together so the three of them could get going. "If we hurry, we can make it before dark," he said, more to Piper and Sawyer than the children, who were busy bundling up for the long, chilly ride ahead. "Dara Rose will fret if we're not back in time for supper."

Piper felt tearful again, full of longing. Oh, to go with Clay and Edrina and Harriet, to make supper for the family and fuss over Dara Rose and the new baby.

Clay seemed to read her mind. "It'll be Christmas

soon," he said, gruffly gentle. "You'll see Dara Rose and make Jeb's acquaintance then."

She swallowed, nodded, and hastened to help Edrina and Harriet with their coats and hats and mittens and scarves. She kissed each one of them goodbye—when the other pupils were around she tried hard not to show favoritism—and said she'd see them in the morning, if the weather allowed.

"You need anything?" Clay asked as an afterthought, glancing at Piper but mainly addressing Sawyer, after he'd put on his hat and sent the girls racing for the wagon out front.

"No," Sawyer said, with warmth and amusement in his voice. "You go on home and look after your family, cousin. We'll be just fine on our own."

Inwardly, Piper stiffened. In all the excitement over the new baby, she'd forgotten all about Doc's imminent return, with the preacher in tow.

No sense bringing that up in front of Clay, though. It would take too much explaining, and he might feel torn between going home to Dara Rose and the baby and staying for the wedding.

Not that there was going to *be* a wedding.

Piper meant to make that abundantly clear as soon as she and Sawyer were alone. She'd made a rash decision, she'd tell him, but now she'd changed her mind.

Only when Clay and the girls drove away did she turn around to face Sawyer.

He was standing so close that his injured arm, still in its sling, bumped against her breast. A slow, sultry smile lit his eyes and touched his mouth. *That* mouth. Piper could almost feel it against her own, seeking, exploring, and finally, commanding.

She caught her own breath. "About last night—"

Sawyer grinned, easy in his skin and damnably sure of himself, and curled his right index finger under her chin. "A deal's a deal, Miss St. James," he told her huskily. "Besides, the word's surely out by now. There's a man over at the schoolhouse, that's what folks are saying, and something unseemly is going on for sure."

Piper pressed her back teeth together. He was right, of course. She'd seen the way those mothers, those *hens,* had looked at her, when they came to gather their chicks under their figurative wings. They'd known, even before their children got a chance to give an account. Eloise Howard must have spread the word, just as Piper had feared she would.

Besides, the Blue River schoolhouse was too small to contain such a secret; even though Sawyer had been courteous enough to stay out of sight while the students were there, they would have guessed that Edrina and Harriet weren't addressing empty space when they'd hurried into the back room that morning, chattering like happy little magpies. Why, they hadn't even paused to take off their coats.

Piper gave a little groan of frustration. "What if we're making a terrible mistake?" she whispered hoarsely.

Sawyer smiled, placed a brief, feather-soft kiss on her mouth, instantly awakening every wanton tendency she possessed—and the number of those tendencies was alarming.

"Most of your questions start with 'what if' or 'how do I know,'" he observed. "There aren't any guarantees in this life, Piper. The whole proposition is risky from the get-go right up to the end." He paused, wound a finger idly in a tendril of her hair, a gesture almost as intimate as last night's kiss. "I can promise you this much, though—I'll provide for you, I'll protect you, and I'll never lay a hand on you except to give you pleasure."

Pleasure? She blinked at the word. She'd always considered that the province of men and, perhaps, women like Bess Turner.

But, wait, she reflected, avoiding Sawyer's eyes by looking down and to the side. Dara Rose wasn't a loose woman, and she certainly seemed to enjoy married life. She hadn't said so outright, but Piper *had* wondered, a time or two, about the way her cousin and Clay smiled secrets at each other. The way they touched when they thought no one was looking.

Sawyer touched the tip of her nose just then, and her gaze swung straight to his, connected with a jolt, like a metal latch. "You're blushing," he said, in a low, pleased drawl. "Was it the word *pleasure?*"

"Of course not," Piper lied. She'd been raised, like most women of her generation, to believe that "pleasure" and "wickedness" were one and the same thing. Luckily, she was saved from having to make a case for propriety by a knock at the door.

She jumped at the sound, startled because she hadn't heard a wagon or a horse approaching the schoolhouse.

Sawyer merely smiled.

She whirled away from him, in a billow of gray skirts, and opened the door, thinking Clay and the girls must have found the going too hard and turned back. Nothing would have stopped Clay from returning to Dara Rose and the baby, she knew, but that didn't mean he'd put Edrina and Harriet's safety at risk in the doing of it. He'd leave them with her, if he thought they were in any danger.

Instead of Clay and the girls, though, she found herself face-to-face with Doc Howard, his smugly disapproving wife, Eloise, and the Methodist circuit preacher, a towering, bearded man of dour countenance, fearsome as an Old Testament prophet bringing word of impending doom. He looked ready for battle, too, as though he'd come to that little schoolhouse to fight the devil himself, hand to hand, standing there with snow dusting the shoulders of his tattered coat and the brim of his once-fine hat.

"C-come in," Piper said, stepping back to admit them all. She was only too aware of Sawyer standing nearby, looking on with amusement.

Blast him, he was *enjoying* this, she just knew it.

"You've made a wise decision," Mrs. Howard said loftily, pulling off her elbow-length kid gloves and narrowing her eyes at Piper as she spoke. She wore a dark blue woolen cloak over a dress almost the same color, and her hat was huge. With the snow, it looked as though the woman was carrying a miniature landscape on her head.

Dislike welled up in Piper, but she held it in check. She was, regrettably, in no position to make her opinions known, especially since Mrs. Howard was on the school board and could have her dismissed without any difficulty at all.

"Have I?" Piper countered, with false sweetness.

Eloise Howard narrowed her china-blue eyes even further, to little lash-trimmed slits. Doc Howard, the preacher, and even Sawyer seemed to recede into the now-fuzzy surroundings. "I'm sure you'll agree, *Miss* St. James," Eloise said, through her tiny, perfect teeth, "that the moral well-being of our children must be the paramount consideration here."

Piper was mad enough to spit. She was a good teacher and, besides, it wasn't as if she'd been teaching her pupils to dance the hurdy-gurdy. This situation, meaning

Sawyer's presence at the schoolhouse, had *befallen* her—she'd done nothing to bring it about, nothing at all.

Except for trying to do the right thing.

She was to be held accountable, nonetheless, and that, in her opinion, was a travesty.

"Now, Eloise," Doc interceded, after clearing his throat, "leave the preaching to Brother Carson, here."

Nobody laughed at the paltry joke, if it was intended as one, or even smiled.

No one besides Sawyer, that is. Out of the corner of her eye, Piper saw the corner of his mouth twitch.

"Morality is a serious matter," Brother Carson pontificated, in a thundering voice. He held a huge Bible in the crook of one arm, as though poised to use it as a weapon if the need presented itself. His gaze sliced, lethal and dark with condemnation, between Sawyer and Piper. "God is not mocked," he added. "We must root out sin wherever we find it!"

Piper didn't know how to respond to that, except to flinch slightly and take half a step backward, which caused her to collide with Sawyer.

Determinedly jovial, Doc Howard chose that moment to shove a parcel at Sawyer—it was wrapped in brown paper and tied with string. "Here are the things you asked me to fetch from the general store," he said, a little too loudly. Then, spotting the Christmas tree, he went on, "Now isn't that a merry sight!"

"We can thank the Germans for that bit of frippery," the preacher boomed, without appreciation. "A fire hazard at best, idolatry at worst."

"What's this world coming to?" Sawyer mused lightly.

Piper resisted the temptation to elbow him, hard. She couldn't take a chance on doing further injury to his bad shoulder.

Eloise was still watching her, with a sort of curious abhorrence, the way she might watch some poor soul traveling with a freak show, but she directed her words to her husband when she spoke. "What about the marriage license, James?" she asked, in a condescending tone. "Did you 'fetch' one of those, too?"

Doc Howard blushed slightly, and Piper felt sorry for him.

Her own dealings with Eloise Howard were intermittent ones. His were constant.

He patted the front of his suit coat, then reached into the inside pocket and drew out a folded document. "It's right here," he said. "Judge Reynolds agreed that this is an emergency, so he issued the license without the usual waiting period."

Brother Carson opened his Bible, flipped through the pages until he found a sheet of paper tucked away in the Psalms, and cleared his throat. "Dearly beloved," he growled out, squinting down at the words scrawled in black ink, "we are gathered here—in the sight of God—"

"Wait," Piper interrupted, but after that, words deserted her.

Brother Carson looked up, his black eyebrows bushy as caterpillars.

Eloise Howard blinked once.

"I know this must seem hasty," Doc put in bravely, after an anxious glance at his wife, "but there's nothing for it. Marriage is the only solution."

"But—" Piper protested.

Sawyer cupped a hand under her elbow just then, and, somehow, that gave her strength. They were being railroaded into this, both she and Sawyer, but she supposed the situation could have been worse.

He might have been old and ugly, for instance.

And she might have been repulsed, rather than excited, by his kisses.

She sighed. "Go ahead," she said wearily.

And so it happened that Piper St. James was married—*married*—to a man she barely knew. Instead of a wedding gown, she wore her gray woolen schoolmarm's dress. There were no real guests, no family members present; she didn't even have a bridal bouquet.

The whole ceremony was over in under ten minutes, in fact.

Piper was in such a daze that she barely registered Sawyer's perfunctory wedding kiss.

They each signed the marriage license, and Doc snatched it up like it was a Spanish land grant or something, saying he'd file it with Judge Reynolds and bring back a copy when he could.

The preacher slammed his Bible shut on his handwritten wedding vows, nodded abruptly, and turned to leave without so much as a goodbye.

Doc, too, seemed anxious to escape, and he all but dragged Eloise out of the schoolhouse. Mrs. Howard, Piper suspected, with rancor, would have preferred to stay and gloat for a few minutes.

In what seemed like a blink of an eye, the others were gone, leaving Piper alone with her new husband.

She squeezed her eyes shut, willing herself not to cry.

The rustle of paper caught her attention, and she looked sideways to see that Sawyer was opening the parcel Doc had given him earlier. He'd set it aside, without comment, in order to make his marriage vows.

A garment made of rich, russet-colored wool lay folded inside, along with a narrow gold wedding band, perched atop one of the folds.

Smiling, Sawyer slipped the band onto her finger.

Amazingly, it was a perfect fit, like Cinderella's glass slipper in the fairy tale.

Piper couldn't speak. Moments before, she'd been on the verge of tears, and now she wanted to laugh like a madwoman. She was hysterical, that was it.

And, furthermore, she was *Mrs. McKettrick*.

Who *was* that, exactly? How was she to proceed?

Using his right hand, Sawyer caressed her cheek. "I'll keep my word, Piper," he said. "For now, we're only married on paper."

Her eyes widened. "For now?" she echoed. Surely this was all a dream—a terrible, wonderful dream—and she'd awaken at any moment.

Again, that wicked tilt appeared at the corner of his mouth. "I have every intention of seducing you," he said, his voice at once quiet and forthright, "sooner or later. In the meantime, you're a respectable woman again."

Piper might have taken umbrage at that, if he hadn't chosen that moment to unfurl the beautiful russet-colored cape he'd bought for her. It had a deep, elegant hood and was trimmed in black silk piping.

She'd seen the garment on display over at the mercantile, not once but many times, but it cost the earth and she'd never given a single thought to owning it. Neither had most of the other women in town, she'd bet, since it was the sort of thing a grand lady would wear to the opera.

Needless to say, there was no opera in Blue River, Texas.

Spellbound, she accepted the cloak, draping it around her shoulders, marveling at the weight of it, and the supple softness of the fabric, almost like velvet, and the way it seemed to wrap her in grace.

"Do you like it?" Sawyer asked. He sounded almost

shy. "I guess it wouldn't have been a proper gift before, but now that we're married—"

She raised shining eyes to him. "Oh, Sawyer," she said, in a rapt whisper. "I've never seen anything so beautiful."

"Neither have I," he said then, very gravely.

And he was looking at her as he spoke, not at the cloak.

Piper's native practicality reasserted itself a few moments later, and she took the cape to the cloakroom and hung it up there, out of the way, where it wouldn't be stained, or get snagged on something.

"Thank you," she said, with crisp dignity, when she came out again.

Sawyer was feeding wood into the stove by then. "You're welcome," he said.

Shyness overwhelmed Piper in that moment. She didn't know how to be this new person, this Mrs. Mc-Kettrick she'd become with almost no warning at all. "You were forced into this," she murmured. "Just as I was. It isn't fair."

"I guess we're victims of circumstance," Sawyer replied philosophically. "Nothing to do now but make the best of things."

"I'll start supper," Piper said quickly, maintaining a safe distance. It wasn't that she didn't trust Sawyer, exactly; if he were a masher, she'd have known it by now. Even with one arm bound up in a sling, he could have taken advantage of her at almost any point in their brief acquaintance.

No, she realized, it was *herself* she didn't completely trust.

She'd gotten into bed with this man the night before.

She'd allowed him to kiss her—not only allowed it, but *reveled* in it.

It made her blush to think what she might have let Sawyer do after that, if he hadn't had the decency to send her away.

The truth struck her, hard.

Even the forced marriage hadn't been entirely beyond her control—she could have packed a satchel, boarded a train and left Blue River forever, started over somewhere else, maybe even changed her name. Or she could have put her foot down, that very afternoon, when the Howards and Brother Carson showed up, and flatly refused to go through with the ceremony.

There would have been repercussions, of course. But wasn't being married to a man she barely *knew* a repercussion?

There was no getting around it. Some part of her had *wanted* this, had seen the chance and reached out to grab hold.

Piper was baffled by all this, even stricken, and yet—excited, even thrilled. Her life had always been so proper, so predictable, so *ordinary*.

Now, all of a sudden, some other, unknown Piper had come to the fore and quite handily taken matters into her own hands. This was a bold and brazen Piper, a person she'd never imagined she could be.

Leaving her to her confusion, probably blithely unaware of it, being a man, Sawyer went outside for wood and water, managing these chores ably with one arm, and it struck Piper that he was recovering rapidly. He still needed a shave, but his hair was combed and his color was good, and he seemed to have significantly more stamina than one might have expected, after such a severe and recent injury.

Soon, he'd be well enough to leave the schoolhouse.

Maybe he'd even change his mind about accepting the marshal's job, and go back to his former occupation, whatever that was. He'd said he'd been paid to "protect a man and his family." Was that just a polite way of saying he was a common *henchman?* An outlaw, for all practical intents and purposes?

As for the marriage, well, that might have been some sort of ruse on his part. Men walked out on wives and families all the time, didn't they?

Piper gave herself a mental shake as she sliced more of Dara Rose's ham and laid it in the skillet waiting on the stove. She was letting her imagination run away with her. If Sawyer already had a wife tucked away somewhere, *someone* in that sprawling McKettrick clan would know about her, wouldn't they? According to Dara Rose, Clay exchanged letters with half the family. Surely, he'd have heard the news from one of his many relations, if not Sawyer himself. And honor would have demanded that he step in and prevent an illegal marriage.

Except that Clay hadn't *known* she and Sawyer were about to get married. She hadn't had a chance to tell him, wouldn't have known what to say if she had, and it was a good bet that Sawyer hadn't said anything to his cousin, either.

Sawyer came in, bringing the scent of snow and pine pitch along with him, and dropped wood into the box next to the stove.

"I don't think this weather is going to last," he said. "The snow's melting as soon as it hits the ground."

Piper nodded, biting her lower lip and spearing at the slices of ham with a fork as though the task required all her concentration. This was her wedding night, she thought, with glum amazement, catching sight of the golden band shimmering on her finger.

How had this *happened?*

Just a few days ago, she'd been an ordinary school-teacher, a little discontented with her lot in life, perhaps, but certainly not unhappy. Now, she was legally Mrs. Sawyer McKettrick—but what did that mean, exactly? Would she even be able to keep her job?

Married women rarely taught school—it was considered improper and a poor reflection on the husband's ability to provide—even if said husband was a worthless layabout, drinking his way to the grave. The wife and any children unfortunate enough to be born of such a union were expected to politely starve to death, without so much as a whimper of complaint, if only for the sake of appearances.

Appearances!

Piper forgot herself and swore aloud. "Thunderation!" she blurted out.

Sawyer reminded her of his presence with a question. "Did you burn yourself?" he asked, from somewhere behind her. He sounded calmly concerned.

"No," Piper said. "I was just thinking about—things."

"Things?"

"Men. Women. Marriage."

He eased her aside, took over the fork she'd been wielding, repeatedly turning the meat in the skillet, whether it needed turning or not. "I'll do this," he said. "And what about men, women and marriage?"

She flounced to her desk chair and plunked down in it, glad to have something to think about besides what might happen when the lamps went out later in the evening. She had no confidence whatsoever in her own ability to conduct herself like a lady.

"Women get a raw deal," she said. "We can't even *vote,* for pity's sake."

"I agree with you there," Sawyer replied, surprising her. "It isn't right."

Piper was picking up steam, like a locomotive chugging out of the station. "Men can go right ahead and beat women, if they want to, wives *and* children. If they're no-accounts, their wives can't go out and earn a living, even to put food on the table or keep a roof over their heads. They wind up like Bess Turner if they try."

"Whoa," Sawyer said affably, forking the meat onto two plates and bringing one to her, along with a slice of the bread she'd already sliced and buttered and a spoonful from the jar of peaches she'd opened the night before. "If that's what you think marriage is going to be like, it's no wonder you're jumpy."

Piper drew in a deep breath. "I might have gotten a little carried away," she admitted, touched that he'd brought her supper to her. Except for Clay, who doted on Dara Rose even though he was unquestionably the head of their family, she'd never seen a married man do that.

He went back for his own plate and sat on the edge of the desk to eat. "I wouldn't beat you," he said, after a long time. "Or any kids we might be lucky enough to have. For that matter, I wouldn't beat a dog or a horse or any other living creature."

She looked up at him. "Not even a man?" she asked.

"That's different," he said, his gaze level as he studied her.

"Is it?"

"Yes," Sawyer replied, after a few moments of thought. "I don't go around looking for fights, Piper, but if one comes my way, I mean to hold my own. And if I run into the yahoo who shot me, I'll shoot him without missing a breath."

"You are a very complicated man," she observed presently, having mulled over what he'd said.

He cocked a grin at her. "I reckon I am," he said. "Keeps things interesting, wouldn't you say?"

She sighed, let the question go unanswered, since she knew it didn't need a reply, and presented one of her own. "What happens when you're well, Sawyer?" she asked, with a glance at his sling and bandages, bulging under one side of his half-buttoned shirt. "Will you stay here in Blue River, and serve as marshal?" *Or will you retrieve your fancy horse from Clay's barn and ride out, leaving me behind?*

"I'll be here long enough to track down the son-of-a— the man who shot me, and make sure justice is served. Come spring, though, I expect to head north, home to the Triple M. Build a house and settle down."

In all that, there was no mention of bringing a wife along, but Piper didn't point out the omission. For one thing, she was much more concerned by Sawyer's implacability, and his plan to bring in his assailant.

He could get killed doing that.

Or become a killer.

Both possibilities terrified Piper.

They finished their suppers in silence, and Piper did the dishes—Sawyer tried to help, but she elbowed him aside.

Darkness gathered, thick, at the windows, and the little stove labored hard to keep out the evening chill, though the snow had stopped coming down, at least.

Sawyer rummaged around and found the battered checkerboard and chunky wooden game pieces Miss Krenshaw or one of her predecessors had left behind.

Piper sometimes allowed the children to hold tournaments, on days when they'd behaved particularly well and completed their lessons to her satisfaction.

He set the board up on her desk. "Black or red?" he asked.

Piper, drying her hands, turned away from the dish basin, the task complete. "What?" she asked.

Sawyer grinned. "Do you want the red pieces, or the black ones?"

She frowned. "You want to play checkers?"

His grin widened. "There are things I'd rather do," he admitted, "this being our wedding night. But I'm a man of my word, Mrs. McKettrick. A virgin bride you are, and a virgin bride you will remain. For the time being, that is."

She blushed. "Red," she said.

He gestured toward her chair, and she sat down. He rested one hip on the other side of her desk, as he'd done before, when they were having supper.

"Your move," he said.

CHAPTER SEVEN

THIS WASN'T HOW she'd envisioned her wedding night, Piper reflected, as she and Sawyer played game after game of checkers, on the surface of her desk—which wasn't to say she'd ever had a clear idea of what was *supposed* to happen. Oh, she knew the fundamentals, of course, the strictly anatomical part, but the rest belonged to the realm of speculation—mostly. She *had* felt some very interesting sensations when Sawyer kissed her the night before, ones that made her want more of the same, but her fear equaled her curiosity, perhaps even exceeded it.

The congress between a man and a woman, she had been taught, mostly by inference and whispers, was mainly a nasty and painful business, something to be tolerated, endured, with the husband's happiness as a reward and, of course, the possible conception of a baby.

To Piper, the bearing, raising and cherishing of a child of her own—and preferably several—was a sacred calling indeed. Although she loved teaching, she knew the vocation was, at least for her, a prelude to mothering.

As for the husband…well, a good one, like Clay, was a blessing. A *bad* one, on the other hand, would be a curse. Which kind *she'd* gotten remained to be seen.

Keeping her gaze focused on her game pieces—she was losing, badly, *again*—Piper considered Dara Rose, and the way she lit up from the inside whenever Clay was around. She hummed a great deal, Piper had noticed on visits to the ranch, and even sang under her breath while she went about her household tasks. And even though there was never any overt sign of their intentions, Dara Rose didn't seem to dread being alone with her husband at night, behind a closed bedroom door.

The whole thing was downright confusing, and Piper wished she'd been bold enough to ask Dara Rose what marital relations were really like, in their most elemental form.

Sawyer knit his brow, and while his eyes smiled, his mouth played at a frown. "What's going on in your mind right about now, Mrs. McKettrick?" he asked.

She didn't protest the "Mrs. McKettrick" part, even though she thought it contained a trace of benign mockery. "Nothing I want to discuss with *you,* Mr. McKettrick," she replied pertly. He'd blocked her few remaining game pieces into a corner of the board, and any move she made would result in sweeping defeat.

"Who, then?" he asked mildly.

"Dara Rose, if you must know," Piper said, and then wished she hadn't.

"Ah," he said, as though that explained a great deal. Resigned, she moved her checker piece and he picked up one of his own and leapfrogged over her little band of huddled checkers, one by one. "Let me hazard a guess," he went on, at his leisure, watching her with a smile in his eyes. "You're wondering what to expect when a man and a woman go to bed together, not like we did, but in earnest."

Piper's cheeks flamed, and she knew her eyes were flashing, too. She couldn't bring herself to refute the statement, though she would have liked very much to do just that. "I may be a—a virgin," she sputtered, "but

I'm not a complete fool. I *know* what men and women do together."

He began to set up the board for yet another game, concentrating solemnly on the task. "Then why do you want to ask Dara Rose about it?"

"I did not say, at any time, that I wanted to ask my cousin about her very private relationship with her husband," Piper said stiffly. Maybe she *hadn't* said it, but it was very much on her mind, and he'd guessed that, obviously.

"But you do," Sawyer said lightly.

"I do *not,*" Piper lied. This was an unsettling aspect of her new self—skirting the truth—and she didn't approve.

Sawyer's glance strayed toward the front window then, and Piper realized he'd done that a couple of times in the past hour or so. She'd paid it no mind then, figuring he must be thinking about the weather, which was a concern to everybody, but now she sensed that there was another reason. Was he expecting someone? Waiting for something?

He wasn't wearing his gun belt, she noticed now, with relief, but his Colt .45 had somehow found its way to the top of a nearby bookshelf.

"Last game," he said, when the board was ready. He yawned then, but it looked and sounded contrived to Piper.

She studied him suspiciously, decided to call his bluff. "I've had enough of checkers for one night," she told him, rising from her chair and smoothing her skirts, "and this has been a long and trying day." Leaving the nearest lantern for him, she found a second one, struck a match to the wick, wrapped herself in the same old blanket, not wanting to spoil her new cloak, and started for the door.

Sawyer didn't ask where she was going, but he did

reach for his .45, shove it under his belt in a disturbingly practiced way, and follow.

"I'm only going to the privy," she whispered, embarrassed.

"Not alone," Sawyer answered. With that, he squired her outside, down the steps, and around to the back of the schoolhouse. The privy loomed ahead, in a faint wash of moonlight.

Much to Piper's relief, he came to a stop at the corner of the school building and stood still, like a guard who took his duty very seriously.

Piper dashed for the outhouse, used it, and hurried out again, holding her breath.

Sawyer remained where he was, looking around, listening.

"What is it?" she demanded, whispering because that seemed to fit the mood of the moment. There was something clandestine about his bearing, and he was so keenly alert she could feel it.

"Nothing," he said, taking her elbow and hustling her around front at such a pace that she nearly stumbled once or twice.

"I don't believe you," Piper said.

He steered her back inside the schoolhouse, shut the door and lowered the latch. "Go to bed," he told her. "I'll be staying up for a while."

"Why?"

Sawyer turned his gaze to her at last, and she saw a worried smile lurking in his blue eyes. "Would you rather I came with you?" he asked.

She reddened. "Well, no, but—"

"Then go," he broke in, distracted. "I'll put out the lanterns and bank the fire in a little while."

Piper opened her mouth, closed it again. Huffed out a sigh of frustrated curiosity.

"Go," Sawyer repeated.

She went, but only after filling a basin with warm water and carrying it into the bedroom with her.

There, she undressed quickly, gave herself a cursory sponge bath, over in moments, and pulled on her nightgown. She hesitated, debating, then got into the spare bed, where she'd slept the night before.

After a while, the lanterns went out, and she expected Sawyer to join her, but he didn't.

She waited, and then waited some more.

Still no Sawyer. Wasn't he coming to bed? *His* bed, that is? It was getting late, and he'd extinguished the lanterns, though she hadn't heard the stove door open and then clang shut, so he hadn't banked the fire.

She got up, finally, and crept to the doorway, peering into the gloom of the schoolroom, faintly tinged with moonlight. Once her eyes had adjusted, she could make Sawyer out. He was next to the front window, but not in front of it, as unmoving as the eternal hills.

Piper saw the gun then—he was holding it in his upraised hand, at the ready.

She stifled a gasp.

"Go back to bed, Piper," he said quietly. Until then, she'd thought he hadn't known she was there.

"I want to know what's happening," she insisted.

"Go to bed," Sawyer repeated.

Piper bristled—he had no business giving her orders, being her husband in name only—but she did as he said.

Wriggling down between the covers, she fumed, but she was afraid, too. Something was definitely wrong.

She closed her eyes, not expecting to sleep, and was immediately swallowed up by a shallow, uneasy slumber.

IT WAS JUST a feeling, nothing Sawyer could really put a finger on, but over the years, he'd learned to pay attention to the subtler signs. Ever since supper, the fine hairs on his nape had been raised, and there was a familiar sensation, like the touch of an icy fingertip, dead center in the pit of his stomach.

Hell of a wedding night, he thought wryly. First checkers, and now a vigil alongside a darkened window.

He could see part of the school yard from where he stood, being careful not to make a target of himself. The decorated Christmas tree seemed to whisper and sparkle when it captured a stray beam of moonlight, and the desks and stove were nothing but shadows.

Something moved, over by the rope swing dangling from a branch of the oak tree.

A stray dog, probably, or a coyote.

Perspiration tickled his upper lip and his palm felt damp where he gripped the butt of his .45. The wound in his left shoulder throbbed with every heartbeat.

Maybe he was loco—after all, he'd married a woman he'd known for two days, and he'd been delirious part of the time, when he wasn't cotton-headed from the laudanum.

Wasn't that proof that he'd lost his mind?

He swallowed the raspy chuckle that rose to the back of his throat, eased his finger back from the trigger a little. And every instinct urged caution.

There it was again—something moving, more shadow than substance, at least at first. As he watched, holding his breath, silently willing Piper to stay asleep and not come wandering out here to hector him with questions, the shadow took on the shape of a man.

And Sawyer recognized the stance, the way the rifle

rested across one forearm with an ease that bespoke long experience.

He'd worked with Chester Duggins, several jobs back, but he hadn't seen him in years, hadn't thought of him, either. If asked, Sawyer would have said Chester was six feet under by now, in some bare-ground-and-thistle cemetery, long forgotten.

"I know you're in there, McKettrick," Duggins called. His voice was quiet, just barely audible, but it carried far enough. "Come on out here, and let's get this over with, so I can collect my money."

Sawyer glanced in the direction of the bedroom, prayed that Piper would stay put. She wouldn't, of course—when she heard the inevitable gunshots, she'd come running. And if Sawyer didn't happen to be the one still standing, Duggins would shoot her, too.

He drew a deep breath, let it out slowly, and moved to the door.

He raised the latch bar, turned the knob as quietly as he could.

Stepped onto the porch, the .45 in his hand, with the hammer drawn back.

"Duggins," he said companionably. "I thought you were dead."

Duggins chuckled in the darkness. He was just a form, with a hat and a rifle, and Sawyer hoped to God that he himself was no more than that to the other man. "Near to it, once or twice," the gunman replied. He hawked and spat. "I thought I'd finished you the other night," he went on, "but darned if I didn't hear otherwise, over at the Bitter Gulch Saloon. I was laying low over there, waiting out the blizzard, and one of the gals hid me in her room. She told me you were here, living and breathing, getting cozy with the schoolmarm."

Sawyer didn't move. He knew Duggins's friendly chatter was meant to lull him, draw him farther out into the open. Knew there was no way out of this particular confrontation without killing or being killed.

And he was damned if he was going to leave Piper at Duggins's mercy. That, if he recalled correctly, was nonexistent.

"I never figured you for a coward, Chester," Sawyer said easily. They might have been dickering over the price of a horse or a piece of land, from their tone.

Duggins stiffened, raised the rifle slightly. "I was tired of tracking you, McKettrick. Plumb worn to a nubbin. Why, I barely managed to get to this burg before your train came in as it was, and then there was all that snow. Vandenburg had been on me for a good week before that, like stink on a manure pile, wanting you dead." He paused, spat again. "If your death don't turn up in newspapers all over Texas, and right soon, I don't get paid."

Sawyer wasn't surprised to learn that Vandenburg was behind the attack; he'd figured as much. "That," he replied, "would be a real pity."

"Now, don't be thataway!" Duggins whined. "None of this would even be happening if you'd just left the boss man's missus be. Why, if we'd met up in any other circumstances but these, you and me, we'd probably have had a drink together and talked about old times."

"I still think you're a miserable, two-bit coward," Sawyer said cheerfully. He'd heard a sound behind him, in the schoolhouse, and he knew he was almost out of time. Piper was awake, and she'd walk right into this in another few seconds. His tone was easy as he went on. "You bushwhacked me, Chester. In a snowstorm. And you did it that way because you knew you wouldn't have a chance in a fair fight." He stepped down off the porch and moved slowly to one side, so if Duggins fired at him and missed, the bullet wouldn't go right through the schoolhouse door—and Piper's heart.

"I done told you I was fed up with trying to run you to ground," Duggins complained. "Now, you stand still, and we'll have this out."

"I've already drawn," Sawyer told the other man calmly. "Even if you hit me, which you might not, given how dark it is, I'll still get off at least one shot—more likely, two or three. And you know I'll make them count. So why don't you just lay that rifle down on the ground and step away from it with your hands up, before somebody gets hurt?"

Duggins gave a low, rough bark of laughter, like he was fixing to spit again. "Hell," he said. "You're just trying to talk your way out of this. And you're wasting my time and your breath, because I mean to kill you proper this time."

The whole world seemed to slow down then. Sawyer saw Duggins swing the rifle barrel in his direction, and he'd begun to pull the trigger back on the .45, but before either of them managed to fire, the night ripped apart, rent by a crimson flash of gunpowder and a boom so loud that it rattled the schoolhouse windows.

Duggins folded to the ground, with the gruesome grace of a dancer dying in midpirouette. His rifle struck the ground and went off, the bullet making a *whing* sound as it tore away a chunk of the schoolhouse roof.

Sawyer gaped, stunned, his .45 still unfired in his hand, as Bess Turner stepped out of the darkness and into a thin spill of moonlight, lowering a shotgun, both barrels still smoking, and prodding at Duggins's unmoving form with one foot.

"Reckon he's dead?" she asked calmly.

Sawyer approached, crouched to get a better look. She'd blown the back of Duggins's head off. "Reckon so," he replied.

"Good," said Bess Turner, with a sigh of resignation.

Meanwhile, Piper flew toward them on a run, her feet bare, her hair loose. "What—?" she began, but her words fell away when she looked down and saw old Chester lying there.

Sawyer wanted to send her back inside, but she wouldn't go and he knew it, so he saved himself the aggravation and stood, wrapping his good arm around her, holding her against his side.

"Varmint," Bess said, and gave the body another poke with her toe, harder this time. The woman's yellow hair was down, and she seemed to be wearing some kind of silky going-to-bed getup, though Sawyer couldn't be sure because the moon had slipped behind a cloud and the stars weren't shining all that brightly.

"Let's go inside," Sawyer said. "Half the town will be here in the next few minutes."

Bess nodded and favored Piper with a thin smile. "You all right, Teacher? This varmint here, he didn't hurt you none?"

"Er—no—I'm—" Piper choked on whatever it was she'd meant to say after that, and fell silent.

Sawyer steered both women toward the gaping door of the schoolhouse. The puny light of a single lantern spilled through it, a kind of faltering welcome, it seemed to him.

Inside, Piper rallied a little, lit several more lamps, and got busy making a pot of tea.

Bess leaned her shotgun against the wall, near the door, and sat down on top of one of the smaller desks, looking as though the events of the past few minutes might be catching up with her at last.

Sawyer took a blanket from Piper's bed, went outside, and draped it over the dead man. It wasn't much—just a gesture, really—but he couldn't leave the damn fool uncovered, staring blindly up at the night sky.

As he'd expected, folks had heard the shots, and some of them were already gathering at the top of the schoolhouse road, a cluster of moving lantern light and muffled noise.

Sawyer sighed and went back inside, where he found Piper still fussing with tea and Bess Turner still sitting on that desk, her gaze fixed on something far away.

"What brought you here tonight?" he asked Bess, very quietly.

Piper paused in her tea-brewing to turn around. Her hair fell around her shoulders, a waterfall of dark curls, and she wore a flannel nightgown. There was mud on her feet, though she didn't seem to care.

"That feller yonder," Bess said, with a toss of her head toward the front of the schoolhouse. "He got one of my girls to hide him, the night of the big snowstorm. She didn't know it was him that shot you—didn't even know it had happened, there at the first—but then, well, these things get around—and Sally Mae, she finally figured out why that galoot was hiding out. She was scared to tell for a while—guess he must have threatened her—but tonight when he got his rifle and lit out on foot, she came and told me. I got my shotgun and followed him, but I was sure wishing Clay McKettrick didn't live way the heck and gone out in the country." Bess paused to draw a shaky breath. "I was here, when that feller called you out, but I wasn't sure what to do. I reckoned if I yelled at him to put the rifle down, he'd probably turn right around and kill me where I stood, so when I saw that he meant to gun you down for sure, I shot him."

Piper's mouth was open. Out of the corner of his eye, Sawyer saw her close it, very slowly.

"You think they'll put me in jail?" Bess fretted, looking over one shoulder as the voices drew nearer. "My Ginny-Sue can't do without a mama—"

"No," Sawyer said. "Nobody's going to put you in jail."

Piper moved to Bess's side, without a word, and slipped an arm around her shoulders.

A vigorous pounding sounded at the door.

Exclamations were raised when somebody evidently stumbled over the blanket-covered body in the school yard.

"Hold your horses," Sawyer said, crossing to open the door.

Doc Howard spilled into the room, closely followed by several other men.

"Great Scot," Howard nearly shouted, "there's a dead man out there!"

"Yep," Sawyer said.

Attention shifted to Bess, and to Piper, standing stalwartly beside her, chin raised.

Sawyer would forever remember that that was when he realized he was in love with Piper St. James McKettrick, though he supposed it would be a while before he got around to saying so.

"What happened?" Doc demanded.

Sawyer explained, and Piper's eyes seemed to widen with every word he said.

"He's the one that shot you?" Doc said, with a shake of his head. Sawyer had already told them as much, but these were peaceable men, and they had trouble taking it in.

"Well, where the devil are we going to put him?" another man asked. "We don't have an undertaker here in Blue River."

"The jailhouse will have to do, for the time being," Sawyer said.

"Better get him buried first thing tomorrow," Doc put in. "Can't have Christmas spoiled. Do we have to report this to somebody?"

Sawyer nodded. Since he hadn't been sworn in yet, Clay was the logical choice, and he said so. A certificate would have to be drawn up, signed by Judge Reynolds and probably Doc Howard, too.

One of the men agreed to ride out to Clay's place and tell him what had happened.

Sawyer would have preferred to make the visit himself, but he didn't have his horse and, improved though his condition was, he wasn't sure he could make it all that way, anyhow. All this activity had riled up the wound in his shoulder, and it was raising three kinds of hell. Besides, he couldn't leave Piper alone, especially after all that had happened.

When the men went back outside, Sawyer went with them.

Somebody ran to the livery stable, hitched up a buckboard and drove it back to the schoolhouse, and Chester Duggins's mortal remains were hoisted into the back and hauled away.

Doc agreed to make sure Bess Turner got back to the Bitter Gulch Saloon all right, though he seemed nervous about it. Little wonder, Sawyer concluded—that wife of his would kick up some dust if she caught wind of the courtesy.

Inside the schoolhouse, Bess and Piper were sitting there in their nightclothes, calmly sipping tea like two spinsters at a garden club meeting.

The sight touched Sawyer—he thought of how differently this night could have ended. What if Duggins had been startled, and swung that rifle in Piper's direction when she came running out of the schoolhouse door? He might have panicked, pulled the trigger, and killed her.

A headache pounded between Sawyer's temples, and his stomach did a slow, backward roll.

"Let's get you on home now," Doc said to Bess, blinking at the way she was dressed. Evidently, he hadn't noticed until then.

She set aside her cup, smiled graciously, and stood up. "I'll just fetch my shotgun," she said, turning to Piper. "Thank you very kindly for the tea, Miss St. James. I do appreciate your hospitality."

"You're—you're sure you're not hurt?" Piper asked the other woman.

Bess nodded again, looked briefly at Sawyer. "I'm sure," she told Piper.

Doc had averted his gaze to Piper, but it immediately bounced away again, landing square on Sawyer's face. "I'll stop by in the morning," the dentist said. "Have another look at that shoulder. You in any pain right now?"

"No," Sawyer lied. He wanted to be alone with Piper, that was all, and reflect on the glorious fact that they were both still alive.

Doc looked skeptical, but he escorted Bess and her shotgun out into the night, resigned to walking her home.

Sawyer latched the door behind them, turned, leaning against it, and closed his eyes for a moment, willing himself to stay upright.

"Sawyer?" Piper said, very softly. "You look terrible. I'm going to call Doc Howard back."

But Sawyer shook his head. "I'm just—tired."

She slipped an arm around Sawyer, as if to hold him

up, which might have been laughable, given her small stature, if the act itself hadn't eased so many things rioting inside him.

"I'm going to require a lot of answers in the morning," she warned, as they made their slow but steady way across the schoolroom.

Sawyer chuckled at that. "And I'll give them to you," he promised. "In the morning."

SAWYER LANDED HEAVILY on the bed, and barely objected when Piper pulled his boots off his feet and covered him, fully dressed, with the quilts she'd once prized so greatly. She smoothed his hair back from his forehead and bent to kiss his eyelids, first one, and then the other.

He fell asleep so quickly that she worried he'd lost consciousness again, but his breathing was steady and deep, and when she laid her head against his chest, she heard his heart beating with a rhythmic *thud-thud-thud*.

She left him just long enough to put out the lanterns still burning in the schoolroom and bank the fire for the night. He'd set his pistol on one of the desks when he came in earlier, after the shooting, and she picked it up carefully, carried it into the bedroom, and set it on the night table.

For a long time, she sat on the side of the bed, watching him sleep, periodically checking his bandages to make sure he hadn't reopened the wound in his shoulder, but there was no bleeding.

The little room grew colder, and then colder still, and Piper knew she ought to get some sleep herself, but she found she couldn't leave Sawyer, even for the other bed, near as it was.

Finally, shivering, she crawled in beside him, on his right side, snuggling up close for warmth, resting one hand on his strong chest. Again, she felt the thump of his heart against her palm, matched her breathing with his.

And after a while, lulled, she drifted off into sleep, a sound one this time.

The next thing she knew, morning light flooded the room.

Remembering the events of her wedding night, Piper sat bolt upright.

She'd thought Sawyer was still asleep, but she knew by the slow curve of his lips and the way he eased an arm around her that he was very much awake.

"Good morning, Mrs. McKettrick," he said.

"Who was that man and why did he want to kill you?" Piper replied.

Sawyer chuckled and opened his eyes. His chin was stubbly with gold. "I can't say you didn't warn me you'd have questions," he said, "but I *did* expect we'd both be dressed at the time."

Piper clutched at the quilts, drew them up to her chin in a belated effort at modesty, but did not relent. "Tell me," she said.

Sawyer sighed. "His name was Chester Duggins," he said. "He and I worked together once."

"Why did he want to kill you?" Piper reiterated.

"He was sent by a man named Henry Vandenburg— my former employer." He paused, sighed again, but, to his credit, he held her gaze. "Vandenburg believed— mistakenly, as it happens—that I'd enjoyed a dalliance with his wife."

"Josie," Piper breathed, troubled. She couldn't help recalling the way Sawyer had said the other woman's name, like a plea, in the hours after he was hurt.

"Josie," Sawyer confirmed.

"You cared about her," Piper said.

"I was beginning to," Sawyer replied. "That's why I decided to accept Clay's invitation and come to Blue River."

The admission caused Piper a distinct pang, but she found comfort in one thing: Sawyer was telling her the blunt, unembroidered truth. "Do you still care for Josie?" she asked bravely. "Because, if you do, we can have our marriage annulled. Since we haven't—consummated it yet."

He reached up, stroked the line of her cheek very gently with the back of his right hand. "Is that what you want?" he asked quietly. "An annulment?"

Piper considered that. "I don't know," she said, when a few moments had passed. Then, primly, she added, "Answer my original question, please."

Sawyer grinned, like a choirboy caught being wicked. "I do not hold any tender feelings for Josie," he replied.

"But you were *beginning* to—"

He sighed again. As he lowered his hand from her cheek, it brushed briefly over her flannel-covered breast, causing the nipple to turn button-hard and bringing a flush to her cheeks. "There have been other women in my life, Piper," he said. "I don't deny that. But you're the only one I've ever married."

She blinked. Was that supposed to be reassuring? *Was* it reassuring?

"How do I know—?" she began.

He laughed. *"What if'?"* he teased.

"Are there other jealous husbands out there who want to have you killed?" Piper persisted.

"A few rejected suitors, maybe," Sawyer conceded. "But no husbands, at least as far as I know."

"That isn't funny," Piper objected, flustered.

"If they'd wanted to call me out," he said reasonably, "they would have done it by now."

"What happens next?"

Sawyer's mischievous expression turned more serious. "I get well, and then I deal with Vandenburg," he said.

"Let Clay do that," Piper said quickly, though she knew even as she spoke that it was a futile request.

"It's not Clay's responsibility," he answered, regretful but earnest. "It's mine."

"No," Piper argued, in the face of certain defeat. "It isn't. This is why there are laws, Sawyer, and men sworn to enforce them—"

"This is my problem," Sawyer said, "and I'll be the one to set it right."

Piper was almost breathless with panic. She'd thought this waking nightmare was over, now that Duggins was dead, but it clearly wasn't. "By doing what?"

"Never mind that," Sawyer told her, drawing her down beside him, holding her close. She resisted at first, but he felt so warm and strong and solid, and she lost herself in that.

They lay together for a long while, both of them engulfed in a kind of sad silence, thinking their own thoughts.

CHAPTER EIGHT

CLAY SHOWED UP at the schoolhouse soon after the morning fire was built up and the coffee was brewing on the stove, aghast at the news of last night's shooting. Piper and Sawyer were both fully clothed when he finally arrived, she in another inadequate calico, he in trousers and a shirt from his travel trunk.

Having ridden to town on his own gelding, Sawyer's horse, Cherokee, trotting alongside on a lead rope, the erstwhile marshal of Blue River, Texas, left both animals standing in the muddy yard, among ragged patches of dirty snow. A vivid blotch of red remained on the ground where Mr. Duggins had been felled by Bess Turner, making Piper wish for more snow to cover it up.

Sawyer's cousin barely paused to knock, bursting through the front door before Piper could call out a "Come in."

"I'm sorry I couldn't get here before now," Clay announced, passing right on over "good-morning" or even just a "howdy" in his hurry to get Sawyer's report on the events just past. His gaze moved over both of them, probably in search of fresh injury. "It was late when Pete brought word of what happened, and I was tending a sick calf—"

Sawyer, standing near the stove, interrupted with a chuckle. "You might want to hire Bess Turner as marshal, instead of me," he said. "She's mighty good with a shotgun." With that, he poured coffee into a mug and extended it to Clay, who accepted it gratefully.

Piper, wearing an apron to protect her dress, blurted, "Sawyer's got his mind set on going after the man who hired that killer."

"Hold on, now," Clay said, lowering the coffee to look from one of them to the other in plain consternation. "We're getting ahead of ourselves, here. Tell me what happened, and don't leave anything out."

Sawyer, after slicing a mildly reproving glance at Piper, gave a brief but complete account of all that had happened the previous night.

When he'd heard the whole story, Clay gave a long, low whistle of exclamation, and took a thirsty sip from his coffee mug before saying, "*Damn.* And here it is, almost Christmas."

Piper wasn't sure what the approach of the holiday had to do with anything, but she wasn't clearheaded enough to pursue the matter at the moment.

Sawyer stood calmly, his own coffee in hand, the mug raised almost to his mouth but not quite there. "It was an eventful day," he said. "Piper and I got married."

Clay fairly choked on a mouthful of coffee, but he was grinning when he caught his breath. *"What?"* he said.

"I believe you heard me the first time," Sawyer replied. "Given what my staying here has done to the lady's reputation, there didn't seem to be any other course of action."

Clay peered at Piper, who blushed. "You agreed to this?"

Glumly, twisting her wedding band round and round with the fingers of her right hand, Piper nodded. "Yes," she murmured.

Clay gave a burst of delighted laughter but just as

quickly sobered again, his expression turning watchful and wary. "Is this marriage real, or just some kind of ruse to keep the townspeople from gossiping for the rest of the school term?"

There was no need to say that Piper wouldn't be teaching at Blue River again in the fall. For all the good it seemed to be doing her, she *was* married. The school board would probably hire a man to replace her, if they could find one. Failing that, they'd settle for a single woman but, either way, she was as good as out.

"It's real," Sawyer said.

"Sort of," Piper clarified.

"Which is it?" Clay asked, somewhat impatiently, once again looking from one of them to the other. "Real, or 'sort of' real?"

Piper couldn't have answered to save her life. Her throat had closed off and her face felt like it was on fire.

"My wife," Sawyer explained, "is probably referring to the fact that we've yet to consummate the marriage."

Piper's blush deepened. How could the man speak so casually of something so intimately personal? She wanted to throttle him, then and there.

"Oh," said Clay, blushing a little himself. "Well, anyhow, congratulations. Of course Dara Rose will have a thing or two to say about missing out on the wedding, but she'll be pleased, too."

All of them were quiet for a while.

Piper, desperate for something to do, proceeded to walk over and ring the schoolhouse bell, pulling vigorously on the rope, though she knew no one would come to class that day despite the fact that the weather had turned and the trails, if muddy, were passable. There had, after all, been a death, right out there in the front yard, and while the danger was past, folks would probably need a day or two to get used to the idea before they sent their children back.

Clay and Sawyer talked quietly all the while, though the bell drowned them out, which was fine with Piper.

"You brought Cherokee," Sawyer said to Clay, after the last peal died away. He was standing at the front window then, looking out, and there was no mistaking the relief in his voice. This only underscored Piper's fears—Sawyer would be leaving Blue River, and her, soon.

"I was thinking you might be ready to come out to the ranch with me," Clay admitted to Sawyer, looking a little sheepish when Piper caught his eye. "That was before I knew about the wedding, you understand."

Sawyer smiled. "I'll be staying here until after the Christmas program," he said. "Then, if it's feasible, Piper and I will both head out to your place."

Clay nodded, but he still seemed befuddled. "Shall I take the horse back with me, then?" he asked.

But Sawyer shook his head, turning again to admire the magnificent animal through the grubby glass in the window. "I can't ride much, but I ought to be able to handle a few minutes in the saddle, now and then, just so I don't forget how."

Clay smiled at that, but when he looked Piper's way again, she saw concern in his handsome face. "Well, then," he said, just a little too heartily, "I guess it's a good thing I brought that hay and grain in the other day, on the sledge. One question, though, cousin—how are you going to manage that saddle with only one usable arm?"

"I'll find a way," Sawyer said, without a trace of doubt.

Clay finished his coffee, set his cup down alongside the basin, on the small table near the stove. "You say this Duggins yahoo's carcass is laid out over at the jailhouse?"

Sawyer nodded. "Doc Howard wants him buried

right away," he said dryly. "Figures a funeral might put a damper on Christmas."

Clay nodded, rubbing his chin. Unlike Sawyer, he'd shaved recently, and there was no visible stubble. "That wouldn't do," he murmured thoughtfully. "Wouldn't do at all." He crossed to the door, took his hat from the peg where he'd hung it up coming in. "I'll send a wire to the federal marshal in Austin," he said. "Just a formality, really." He paused, cleared his throat. "Of course I'll be mentioning Henry Vandenburg's part in this."

Piper saw a muscle bunch in Sawyer's jaw, even under his thickening beard. "Nobody can be arrested on mere hearsay, Clay. You know that."

"The federal marshal still has to be told," Clay said. Although his manner was cordial, there was steel in his tone. "What he does with the information is his concern, not ours."

"I want to handle this," Sawyer said, glaring at his cousin.

"Fine," Clay retorted, on his way out. "If there's anything left to *handle* by the time you're fit to travel, you just have at it with my blessing. In the meantime, I'm still marshal and I'll do what needs doing."

Sawyer started to argue, Piper saw, but he ended up giving an exasperated sigh and shoving the splayed fingers of his good hand through his hair in frustration. "All right, then," he said, "but I'm going to the jailhouse with you."

Evidently, Clay was willing to concede that much, if nothing more. "You say Bess Turner shot this fella?" he asked, refraining from helping as his cousin struggled halfway into his coat. Sawyer had a harder time buckling on his gun belt but, somehow, he managed it, and slipped the .45 deftly into the holster.

Chilled, and not by the weather, Piper hurried to the window when the men went outside, watched as Sawyer put a foot in the stirrup of Cherokee's saddle, gripped the horn, and hauled himself up onto the horse's back. She saw him clench his jaw again, once he was in place, and close his eyes briefly, but other than that, he seemed steady.

Clay and Sawyer were gone upward of an hour, during which time Piper hoped in vain for a pupil or two to wander in, hungry for learning. Because she believed with her whole heart and mind that idle hands were the devil's workshop, she polished all the desks, swept the floors, made up the two beds and fussed with the straggly Christmas tree, with its burden of unassuming decorations.

When the men returned, Doc Howard was with them, on his mule. All three of them looked grimly introspective, and little wonder.

A man was dead.

In the school yard, Sawyer dismounted on his own, but he leaned against Cherokee's side for an extra second or so before stepping back and surrendering the reins to Clay, who led the animal around back to the shed.

Doc walked up to the patch of bloody ground and scuffed at it with one foot, as though to kick dirt over the place where death had left its distinctive mark. He conferred with Sawyer for a few moments, then followed Clay to the shed, returning with a rusted shovel in one hand.

While Sawyer watched, his feet planted a little wider apart than usual as if in an effort to maintain his balance, Doc used the shovel to turn up enough ground to hide the blood spot.

Piper stepped back from the window just as Sawyer

turned and started for the door. She tried to look surprised when he came inside, closely followed by Doc, but she knew by Sawyer's wry expression that she hadn't fooled him. He'd never glanced in her direction even once, but he'd known she was at the window, watching, just the same.

"I made more coffee," she said, noting the pallor in Sawyer's face.

He merely nodded, and went on into the bedroom. She heard the bedsprings creak as he lay down.

"He might have overdone things a little," Doc remarked quietly, taking off his hat and coat and hanging them both in the cloakroom.

Piper didn't comment on the understatement. "Coffee?" she said instead.

Doc nodded. "Please," he said, looking around for a place to sit down. He was a sturdy man, so none of the students' desks would have held him.

Piper pointed to the chair behind her desk, and he took it gratefully. "I'm a dentist," he said, as though to remind himself and the world at large of his true calling.

She poured his coffee and took it to him, with a slight, sympathetic smile, barely resisting the temptation to pat his shoulder reassuringly and say, "There, there."

Clay came in, having tended to Sawyer's horse, and looked around for his cousin.

"Sawyer's resting," Piper said. "Coffee?"

"Got any whiskey?" Clay asked.

"Sorry," Piper replied, with a little shake of her head.

Clay sighed and said, "I'll take the coffee, then, please."

While Piper poured the brew, he went into the bedroom, stayed a few moments, and came back with the rocking chair. He offered it to Piper and, when she refused with a shake of her head, sank into it with an exhalation of breath.

Piper gave him the mug. "Did you send that wire?" she asked Clay, keeping her voice down even though she was fairly sure Sawyer wouldn't overhear her anyway. "To the federal marshal in Austin, I mean?"

"Yes," Clay said, after taking a sip of his coffee. "And I told him Duggins claimed he'd been hired by a fellow named Vandenburg."

"Well, then," Piper said, unable to hide her relief, "no doubt someone will investigate." And, thus, she deduced, Sawyer would not go riding off, the moment he was physically able, to confront the man who'd wanted him dead.

Clay pondered that for a while, then said ruefully, "Sawyer was right. It's mainly hearsay. The marshal might question Vandenburg, but unless he admits to hiring Duggins, the man's not likely to be arrested."

Piper felt something curl up tight in the bottom of her stomach. How did Dara Rose bear it, being married to a lawman? Was she afraid for Clay every time he pinned on his badge, strapped on a gun belt, and left home to do his job?

"Then *Sawyer* won't be able to get him to admit anything, either," she reasoned, her tone bordering on pettish, though what she really felt was fear.

"Vandenburg hired a killer," Clay reminded her flatly, "and Sawyer was shot. Something has to be done, Piper."

"Maybe Mr. Duggins committed the crime all on his own," Piper argued, more than a little frantic now. "He was a *criminal*. It could be that Mr. Vandenburg knew nothing about the plan."

"Yes," Clay said dryly, "and St. Nicholas might join us for Christmas Eve supper at the ranch. Men like Duggins don't act on their own, Piper. They take orders from somebody else."

Doc Howard cleared his throat just then, reminding both Clay and Piper of his presence. It was strange how such a large personage could take up so little thought-space that he went unnoticed.

Piper glowered at Clay and then at Doc, for good measure, and marched into the bedroom to check on Sawyer.

He lay sprawled atop the covers, with his muddy boots on the bed, further staining the already ruined quilt, but Piper's ire ebbed like an outgoing tide at the sight of him.

She approached Sawyer's bedside, smoothed his hair back from his forehead, and smiled a little. The future was full of uncertainty, but, for this moment at least, he was alive and safe, where she could see him, touch him.

She loved Sawyer McKettrick, she realized. What else could this feeling of sweet desolation mean?

Sawyer didn't open his eyes, but he took her hand in his, gave her fingers a brief squeeze, as if he'd read her mind.

Tears brimmed along her lower lashes as she bent and placed the lightest of kisses on his forehead. *I love you,* she told him silently, and then slipped out of the room because Doc had come in again, his sleeves rolled up and his hands still wet from washing, a basin of clean water in his hands and a roll of bandage cloth under one elbow.

Clay was still in the rocking chair when she returned, looking at the Christmas tree, and he stood up quickly when he realized she was there.

"Sit down, Clay," she said quietly.

But Clay shook his head. "I'd best be heading for home, anyway," he said. "There's not much I can do here, and Dara Rose will be watching the road for me."

Piper nodded, thick-throated again. One of these days,

she reckoned, she might be "watching the road," too—for Sawyer. Only, unlike Clay, he might never come back to her.

She brought herself up short. She wasn't a real wife to Sawyer, after all, and the schoolhouse wasn't their home. When he was well enough, her "husband" would go his way, and she would go hers.

Clay had read her expression before she realized he was looking at her, guessing her thoughts, and he laid a brotherly hand to one side of her face.

"Give Sawyer a little time," he said. "He'll get things straight in his head pretty soon."

"He's leaving," she said, not meaning to but unable to hold back the certainty that it was so.

"I reckon if Sawyer goes anywhere, he means to take you right along with him," Clay replied, very quietly. "I know you have your doubts, Piper, but Sawyer didn't marry you just to save your reputation. He's a fine man, but he's no martyr, and he could have handled this situation a dozen different ways without standing up with you in front of a preacher."

"Name one," Piper challenged, too proud to cry but wanting to, wanting to very, very much.

Clay chuckled. "Well, he could have sent you to Dara Rose and me, for one thing. There would have been a scandal, sure, but once folks had a chance to jaw about the particulars for a while, they'd have gone on to something else, and you'd be right back here in this schoolhouse, like nothing ever happened. For one thing, teachers aren't that easy to come by, way out here. The pay's pitiful, and it's a hard, lonely life."

Piper gave a small, strangled laugh. "How comforting," she said. "What was I worried about, when I have a 'pitiful' stipend and a hard, lonely life to look forward to?"

Clay grinned, shook his head. "I've never been good with words," he allowed. "What I'm trying to say is that everything will be all right in the end."

"I can't imagine what makes you so sure of that," Piper observed.

"Just the same," Clay countered good-naturedly, "I *am* sure. Besides, it's almost Christmas. Have a little faith, will you?"

Have a little faith, will you?

Clay's offhand injunction played in Piper's mind long after Doc and Clay had both left the schoolhouse.

Easy enough for him to say, she concluded, as she built up the fire and rummaged through the food box in the cloakroom for the makings of a simple meal.

Upon awakening, Sawyer still looked like hell-warmed-over, but he insisted on joining her in the school-room for supper. She gave him the desk chair again, and refrained from conversation since he looked a mite grumpy. His fresh bandages were bulky under his sling, and perhaps a little too tight.

"Clay's gone home?" he asked, finally.

Piper refrained from pointing out the obvious. "Yes," she said mildly. "He fed and watered Cherokee before he left, and brushed him down, too."

Sawyer nodded, thanked her when she put a plate in front of him, containing scrambled eggs, some fried ham, and two thick slices of bread toasted on top of the stove. Ate slowly and awkwardly, and with a dignity that pinched Piper's heart.

"In a few days, it will be Christmas," she said, finding the silence unbearable.

"Yes," Sawyer said dully. She knew without asking what was bothering him, or part of it, at least. The aftermath of a death was always sobering, and on top of that, he'd found riding a horse, something he'd probably done almost every day of his life, with unthinking ease, to be suddenly difficult.

"I wonder how Bess is holding up," Piper said. She'd nibbled on some toasted bread earlier, while cooking, but she really wasn't very hungry, so she hadn't filled a plate for herself.

"To hear Doc tell it," Sawyer answered, his eyes bleak, "she's got other concerns. Her little girl's come down with something."

"Ginny-Sue is sick?" Piper asked, immediately concerned.

Sawyer nodded. "Doc wanted to go and see her, but his wife put her foot down. Said she'd leave him, and take their daughter with her, if he showed his face in a brothel, no matter what the reason."

Piper thought of Ginny-Sue's beaming delight over memorizing the second chapter of Luke, her parting assurance that Christmas would happen for certain now, with the big snowstorm over.

And she put one trembling hand to her mouth.

Sawyer, seeing her face, looked regretful. "Doc said it was probably nothing serious," he said. "Sure, Bess is worried, but you know how mothers are."

Piper was already on her feet, hurrying into the cloakroom, taking the lovely russet cape from its hook and swinging it around her shoulders. She was raising the hood to keep the wind from stinging her ears as she emerged into the schoolroom.

Sawyer was standing by then. "Hold on a second," he said, frowning. "Where are you going? It's dark out, Piper, and it's cold."

"Drat that Eloise Howard," Piper muttered, and that

had to suffice for an answer. "I'll be back as soon as I can."

With that, she left the schoolhouse.

It *was* dark, and the wind was brisk, but her cape protected her.

As she crossed the yard, Sawyer called to her from the doorway of the school. "Piper, wait! I'll come with you—"

She turned, still walking, but backward. "You'll be nothing but a hindrance," she called in response. "Stay here, please."

"Piper!" Sawyer yelled, when she turned her back on him again and marched onward.

Thinking only of Ginny-Sue, Piper picked up her pace.

Passing the churchyard, she saw the new grave, where Mr. Duggins had been laid to rest, God forgive him. She wondered if he'd had family somewhere, parents or a wife and children, say, and if anybody would shed tears of sorrow when word of his passing reached them.

On the main street of town, the businesses and shops were all closed up and dark. Except, of course, for the Bitter Gulch Saloon, which seemed to be doing a rousing trade, as usual.

Piper stopped on the plank sidewalk, eyeing the swinging doors with trepidation. Light spilled over and under them, like some smoky liquid, and the tinny clinkity-clink of an out-of-tune piano, badly played, tinkled in the cold air.

Deciding, after much personal deliberation, that she wasn't quite bold enough to walk through those rickety doors into the sawdust heart of a saloon, Piper bustled around back, moving between the buildings, and approached the much less daunting rear entrance.

Standing on a small porch with her chin high and her shoulders squared, she knocked purposefully.

A rotund black woman answered, wide-eyed at the sight of Piper. She laid one hand to her substantial bosom and sucked in a shocked breath. "Lord, have mercy," she said. "It's the schoolmarm!"

Piper drew a deep breath. "Let me in, please," she said. She'd seen the woman once or twice, over at the mercantile, but they'd never exchanged more than a few words. "I've come to look in on Ginny-Sue."

"But, ma'am," the woman argued, "this here's a *bawdy* house!"

As if she hadn't known. Piper looked over one shoulder, half expecting to see Sawyer in pursuit, but he hadn't caught up to her yet. She met the cook's horrified gaze again and whispered, "Hurry. There's no time to lose."

The woman stepped back, admitting Piper to a large and amazingly ordinary kitchen, well-equipped, with a big cast-iron cookstove, bins for sugar and flour, a table surrounded by matching chairs, and a cabinet filled with lovely china. There was even a sink.

"You really shouldn't be here," insisted Bess Turner's cook, in an anxious whisper. "Anybody sees you, there'll be hell to pay!"

Piper put out a hand and introduced herself as Mrs. McKettrick, rather than Miss St. James. It was a small indulgence, she thought. No harm in pretending for a little while.

"Cleopatra Brown," the cook responded. Her eyes looked enormous in her round ebony face. "You wait here, and I'll fetch Miss Bess."

Piper had spotted the rear stairway by then, and she wanted to climb it, open doors until she found Ginny-Sue, see the child for herself. If Ginny-Sue was seriously ill, she meant to get Doc Howard by the collar and *drag* him over here, and to the devil with any objections *Mrs.* Howard might raise.

She paced while Cleopatra was out of the room, went once or twice to peek through the misted-over window in the back door, in case Sawyer had tracked her this far.

Of course, he, being a man, would probably enter by the *front* way.

The rush of annoyance at the idea sustained Piper in the face of her already waning courage.

After a few minutes—very *long* minutes—Bess descended the rear stairway, be-feathered and bejeweled, with her face painted like a garish mask. Cleopatra hovered close behind.

"You shouldn't have come," Bess fretted, pausing halfway down, but there was a spark of something that might have been hope in her jaded eyes.

"Nevertheless, I have," Piper replied briskly. "I must know about Ginny-Sue. How is she?"

"She's poorly," Bess admitted, coming the rest of the way down the stairs. "She's real poorly. It came on sudden-like—she was playing outside without her hat and mittens—said she'd found a cat hiding in the woodpile and she was trying to get it to come inside for some warm milk—"

Piper took both Bess's hands, found them colder than her own, even after the walk from the schoolhouse. "I'll get Doc Howard," she said.

"He won't come," Bess said, with sad certainty.

"He *will,*" Piper replied, "if I have to drag him!"

Bess smiled tentatively. "If you'd just say howdy to Ginny-Sue, I'm sure that would bring her right around," she said. "She thinks you hung the moon right up there in the sky, you know."

Piper's eyes burned. "Take me to her," she said. "Please."

Bess nodded once, turned, and led the way back up the staircase to the second floor, her thin shoulders stooped and mostly bared by the scantiness of her dress. Cleopatra moved aside to let both women pass, but she didn't look at all congenial, no doubt thinking that nothing good could come of the schoolmarm's highly improper visit to the upper reaches of a brothel.

Piper might have conceded the point, if challenged, but she didn't hesitate, let alone turn back.

The upstairs hallway was lined with gilt-framed mirrors, and there was a costly runner, probably Turkish, on the floor. The air smelled of talcum powder, stale sweat, and quiet depravity.

To know that little Ginny-Sue was growing up in this place was almost more than Piper could endure. Given her druthers, she'd have bundled the child up in a blanket and physically carried her out of here, never to return.

Bess stopped in front of a door and rapped lightly at the framework. "Let me in, Emmie," she called out softly.

Piper heard a key turn in the lock, and the door creaked open, revealing a scrawny, bare-faced woman clad in a red silk wrapper. Emmie, presumably.

Relieved to learn that someone had been sitting with Ginny-Sue, and that there was a locked door to protect her from unwanted visitors, Piper smiled at Emmie, though only slightly.

Emmie, stepping back to admit them, widened her eyes. Piper concluded that she probably looked as exotic to the other woman as Emmie did to her.

"She's no better," Emmie said to Bess.

The inside of that room was a revelation to Piper, at complete odds with the structure that surrounded and upheld it, but at the moment she was concerned only with Ginny-Sue.

The little girl lay in a huge and elegant bed, with gilt posts and a painting of sheep and shepherdesses on the headboard. She opened her eyes, smiled a tiny smile when she saw Piper.

"I know the whole second chapter of Luke," Ginny-Sue said.

"Shhh," Piper said, smoothing back the child's hair. Her forehead was hot and dry, though the front of her finely embroidered nightgown clung damply to her small chest. "How do you feel?"

"My throat hurts," Ginny-Sue confided, and her hand fluttered up to rest there, fragile as a hatchling bird.

Piper blinked back tears. Smiled. "Maybe you've been practicing your piece too much—for the Christmas program, I mean."

Ginny-Sue smiled back, but the effort seemed to exhaust her. "Is it Christmas yet?" she asked. "Did I miss the program?"

Piper shook her head quickly. "No, sweetheart. Christmas is still a few days away."

Emmie and Bess slipped out, leaving teacher and pupil alone.

Ginny-Sue closed her eyes, but the smile lingered, faint, on her lips.

Piper looked around then, noticed the fireplace, with a lovely blaze burning on the hearth, the velvet draperies on the windows, the carpets on the floor. Paintings of flowers, delicately wrought in watercolor, graced the walls. There were easy chairs, upholstered in cheery prints, and a door opened onto a bathroom. She could see the side of a long porcelain tub. And there was electricity, at least here, if nowhere else in the Bitter Gulch Saloon.

This, then, was the haven Bess Turner had made for her child, a place apart, a world that belonged only to the two of them.

Piper turned back to Ginny-Sue, gently took her hand, and seated herself on the edge of the fancy bed.

Then she closed her eyes and she prayed.

Ginny-Sue slept on.

Cleopatra came back into the room, bringing a tray laden with tea things. "There's a man downstairs," she said solemnly. "Says you'd better come and talk to him." China rattled as she set the tray down, poured fragrant, steaming orange pekoe into a translucent cup. "What do you want me to tell him?"

"Does he have one arm in a sling?" Piper asked calmly.

"Yes, ma'am, he do," Cleopatra answered.

Sawyer, of course. "Tell him to fetch Doc, or send somebody else if he's not strong enough. Whoever goes is to say that if Mrs. Howard objects, I'll come over there myself and see to the matter personally, and she does not want that to happen."

Cleopatra's eyes widened again, and a smile rested lightly on her full mouth. "Sounds like a bluff to me," she said, but there was respect in her tone.

"Sometimes," Piper answered, "a bluff has to do."

CHAPTER NINE

HALF AN HOUR passed, during which Piper sipped tea, listened to the tick of the elegant clock on the mantelpiece, and watched Ginny-Sue toss and turn in her sleep.

Don't let this be diphtheria, Piper prayed, over and over again. *Please.*

She'd seen that disease too many times, in the few years she'd been teaching school. Among the symptoms were fever and a sore throat, and Ginny-Sue had both. Diphtheria was rampantly contagious, and in most instances it was fatal, as well.

Not Ginny-Sue, she pleaded silently, *or any of the others.*

When a tentative knock sounded at the door of that incongruously grand bedchamber, Piper leaped up, crossed the floor, but then hesitated to turn the shining brass key protruding from the lock, remembering that there was a saloon directly downstairs, and that ladies of the evening and their customers surely frequented the other rooms along the corridor.

"Who's there?" she asked.

"Doc and me," Sawyer answered. "Open up."

Almost breathless with relief, Piper unlocked and opened the door to see a disgruntled Doc Howard standing nervously in the hall, with Sawyer right beside him. Doc looked as though he might bolt at any moment, while *Sawyer* looked as though he'd stop him if he did.

"You came," Piper cried, barely restraining herself from throwing both arms around Doc and hugging him in a fit of gratitude.

"Of course I did," Doc replied, stepping past her and striding over to the bed. He'd brought his bag and hopefully there was something inside that would cure Ginny-Sue. "Why is it that nobody around here seems to remember that I'm a dentist?" he muttered to himself, as he leaned over the child, stethoscope in place.

Did dentists use stethoscopes? she wondered. Evidently so. Perhaps some of their patients suffered palpitations at the prospect of an extraction, or having a cavity filled.

Sawyer smiled at Piper, touched her chin. His fingers were icy-cold, and yet, somehow, he warmed her. Had he walked to Doc's place, in his condition, after following Piper to the saloon earlier? If so, he was probably coming to the end of his strength, considerable as it was.

"I'm all right," he told her quietly. It was unsettling, the way he seemed to be able to read her every expression, as if she'd been thinking aloud. "How's the little girl?"

"I don't know," Piper responded, worried again. "She's feverish, and she told me her throat was hurting."

"Doc will do everything he can," Sawyer promised. He indicated his bandaged shoulder with a motion of his head and then added, "He must be hell on a toothache, if he's this good with a bullet wound."

Piper nodded anxiously but offered no reply, since none seemed called-for.

Bess appeared, letting herself in, since Piper hadn't bothered to relock the door. With Sawyer and Doc both there, she knew Ginny-Sue would be safe.

After nodding a greeting to Sawyer, Bess hurried over

to stand on the opposite side of the bed from Doc. She wrung her hands, and the expression in her eyes was an eloquent plea for good news.

Doc opened his bag, took out a packet, and held it up. "Headache powders," he said. "Stir a teaspoonful into a cup of water, and we'll see if we can't get her to take it."

Bess rounded the bed, took the packet from Doc's hand, and vanished into the bathroom. She was back in a trice with the water, and Piper handed her a spoon from the tea tray Cleopatra had brought up earlier.

The rattle of the spoon against the glass roused Ginny-Sue enough to open her eyes. They glistened, too bright, and seemed to grope and struggle from one face to the next.

"Mama?" Ginny-Sue said.

"I'm right here, baby," Bess said, moving close to the child, sliding an arm around her to help her sit up, forcing cheer into every word and motion, "you've got to drink this whole glass of water right down. Doc brought you some medicine, and it's going to make you feel a lot better, real soon."

Ginny-Sue's confusion was heartrending for Piper, and she was thankful when Sawyer put his good arm around her waist, lending her strength. Almost holding her up, in fact.

The child sipped from the glass, the bitter taste causing her to wince, and it obviously hurt her to swallow. Still, though the process was a long one, she finally emptied the glass.

"What is it?" Piper whispered to Doc, when he walked over to her and Sawyer, looking solemn and thoughtful, though he'd left his bag on the night table and was taking off his coat like a man who meant to stay rather than go. "What's wrong with Ginny-Sue?"

"If we're lucky, she's got a bad cold," Doc answered, keeping his voice low. "If we're not, on the other hand, then this is probably diphtheria, and it works fast. We ought to know by morning."

Piper reached out, took one of Doc's hands in both of hers. Sawyer stood silently beside her.

"Thank you," she said softly, because she knew Doc had made a sacrifice to come here at all.

Doc's smile was genuine, if somewhat feeble. "Don't thank me yet," he replied. "The aspirin powders will bring down the girl's fever if she's just taken a chill, but if that doesn't happen, well, then we're dealing with a much bigger problem."

"Diphtheria," Piper almost whispered.

Doc nodded. "None of us can leave here until we know for sure," he said, with a rueful shake of his head. "If this *is* diphtheria, it'll spread like a fire in dry grass."

Piper looked at Sawyer, whose expression was unreadable, and then Doc. By then, Bess had left Ginny-Sue's side to join them.

"Did you say my girl has diphtheria?" Bess asked tentatively, going pale under all that kohl and rouge and rice powder.

"I said she *might* have it," Doc said, at once stern and compassionate. "How long has Ginny-Sue been sick?" Before Bess could formulate a reply—she seemed to be juggling conflicting thoughts in her mind—he turned to Piper. "Did she come down with this at school?"

"Just since this afternoon," Bess said finally. "Cleopatra said she seemed fine at breakfast."

"And at school, too," Piper added, after reviewing her memory. Even though Ginny-Sue hadn't exhibited symptoms in class, when all the children had been busy decorating the Christmas tree, it was still possible that the illness was already spreading from one end of Blue River to the other. Edrina—Harriet—little Jeb, the new baby—

She wouldn't be able to bear losing a one of them, or any of her pupils, either.

She almost swooned at the enormity of the threat, but Sawyer took a firm grip on her elbow and steadied her, kept her upright.

He guided her to one of the easy chairs near the fireplace and sat her down.

"What about my girls, and the customers?" Bess asked Doc. "Shouldn't they be told?"

"If you say the word *diphtheria*," Doc replied, "there'll be a panic for sure. On the other hand, we can't have those men carrying the sickness home to their own families. I'll put the whole place under quarantine before I let that happen." He paused, grim and brusque. "I just hope it isn't already too late."

From her chair near the fire, Piper watched tears gather in Bess's eyes. "We'll see that the beer and whiskey flow," she said quietly. "And those that don't pass out, well, maybe the girls can keep them here some other way."

Some other way, Piper thought, half-sick. Innocent or not, she knew what that "other way" was, and the ugliness of it nearly overwhelmed her.

But who was she to judge? In Bess's shoes, with Bess's history and lack of choices, she'd probably be no different.

Doc gave a heavy sigh, nodded in agreement with what Bess had said. He had a child to worry about, too, Piper reminded herself, his Madeline. Doc Howard's daughter was probably a large part of the reason he'd finally braved his wife's disapproval, after refusing once, and answered Piper's summons.

Unless, of course, Sawyer had forced the other man to the Bitter Gulch Saloon, at gunpoint. She didn't think he'd be above that.

The possibility made Piper sit up very straight, stiff-spined. "Did you—persuade Doc to come?" she asked, fixing her tired eyes on Sawyer.

"Now, how would I do that, with just one good arm?" he countered.

Piper raised both eyebrows, thinking of the Colt .45 her husband was wearing on his right hip, even then. "One way comes immediately to mind," she said.

Sawyer grinned. "Fortunately," he said, picking up on her meaning right away, "I didn't have to threaten any-body. I guess Doc just figured if I thought it was impor-tant enough to ride bareback to his place with a big hole in my shoulder, he ought to pay attention."

Piper scooted her chair a little closer to Sawyer's, dropped her voice to barely more than a breath while Doc and Bess conferred over by the door. "Didn't *Mrs*. Howard have something to say about it?"

Sawyer's grin broadened. "Oh, she had *plenty* to say. Told Doc she'd get on the train and head East if he set foot outside the house, never mind heading straight for a brothel, where God only knew what he might bring home. Yes, sir, she'd leave him high and dry. He said she oughtn't to make promises she didn't mean to keep, got his bag, and followed me over here. Didn't even take the time to saddle his mule."

Piper was wide-eyed. "You heard all that?"

Sawyer nodded. "I was downright proud of the man," he added.

"If I wasn't so grateful," Piper replied, "I'd have a few things to say *myself,* Mr. McKettrick, about you riding around on a horse in the dark of night in your condition."

"It seemed like a better idea than walking," Sawyer pointed out. "I couldn't saddle Cherokee—it's practically impossible to tighten a cinch with one arm—but he didn't complain. I put a bridle on him, led him out of the shed and over to the porch, and climbed on from there."

"I don't suppose it ever occurred to you to heed me and stay put at the schoolhouse?" Piper retorted, though she wasn't actually angry, just fearful to think of all the things that could have gone wrong. Might *still* go wrong.

"I'll always hear you out," Sawyer said, quietly reasonable. "You're an intelligent woman and most of the time your opinion will probably make sense. That said, if I'm not swayed by your arguments, I'll go right ahead and do whatever strikes me as the best choice."

Piper had no reply for that. She was almost too tired to think.

Doc disappeared into the bathroom then and closed the door, while Bess stretched out on the bed alongside her feverish daughter, holding the little girl close, murmuring a lullaby to her.

Though she was still worried sick about Ginny-Sue and every other child in and around Blue River, Piper went over the things Sawyer had said, oddly exhilarated by them, even in her weariness. Yes, he was letting her know that, as a husband, he wouldn't bend to the kind of pressure women like Eloise Howard exerted, but it was the word *always* that had really caught her attention. He'd sounded as if he expected to share his life with her—as if they'd be working out problems and disagreements *years* from now.

"I thought you were leaving," she said carefully. "Heading out to find Mr. Vandenburg as soon as you could ride that far."

"I might still do that," Sawyer answered, one corner

of his mouth quirking upward ever so slightly. "But I've done some thinking since last night, about how close I came to losing you when it was me Duggins was after. When you bolted from the schoolhouse a little while ago, hell-bent on storming the Bitter Gulch Saloon for the sake of a sick child, and devil take the gossip that was bound to result, I knew you were the one for me."

Piper sat stunned, stricken by hope even in this uncertain and potentially tragic situation. How was it possible for one person to contain so many powerful emotions, especially ones that were at odds with each other?

Doc emerged from the bathroom, drying his hands on a towel and glancing toward Ginny-Sue, and the woman who was holding her.

"That's quite a setup in there," he commented, cocking a thumb over one shoulder to indicate the bathroom. "Running water, hot and cold. Even a flush toilet." Doc paused then to rub his chin and reflect for a moment or two. "If I put in a bathtub over at our place, I reckon Eloise might decide I'm a passable husband, after all."

Sawyer grinned as Doc pulled over an ottoman and sat down close to the fire, rubbing his hands together and staring into the flames.

"And if she doesn't change her mind?" Sawyer asked.

Piper nudged his foot with her own, but he was undaunted and, anyway, it was already too late to stop him from asking such a personal question.

Doc chuckled, the firelight dancing over his face. "Well, then," he answered, "I may be forced to take a pretty fierce stand."

After that, all three of them alternately dozed and talked in quiet voices.

The fire got low, and Doc built it up again.

Once, feeling restless, Piper ventured into the bathroom and inspected the gleaming porcelain bathtub, trying all the while to imagine the sheer luxury of such a convenience. No water to pump or haul up from the well in a bucket, then heat on the stove, then carry and pour, and repeat the whole process all over again. Why, it would be miraculous—even better, at least in her opinion, than a private telephone and electric lights put together.

Around sunrise, pinkish-gold light glowing cold and clear at the windows, Cleopatra returned with another tray, knocking politely at the bedroom door and calling out in a low voice, "Somebody open this door for me. I've got my hands full out here."

This time, she'd brought fresh coffee, along with cups to drink it from, and a heaping plate of cinnamon buns still warm from the oven. The aromas were heavenly.

Concentrating hard, Cleopatra nearly dropped the whole works when a small voice suddenly piped up and said, "Mama? Did I miss Christmas?"

Everyone turned toward the bed to see Ginny-Sue sitting up, pillows at her back, looking a little wan but clear-eyed and alert.

Bess, who had slept beside Ginny-Sue through the night, gathered the child close again and wept for joy. "No, baby," she said, beaming through her tears. "You didn't miss Christmas. You surely didn't!"

Doc went over to touch Ginny-Sue's forehead, and his broad smile told the story. The fever had broken.

"That's one of the finest chest colds I've ever seen," Doc said, in a jocular voice that nonetheless cracked with fatigue. "A few days of bed rest and I'll wager the little lady here is good as new."

Piper turned immediately into Sawyer's embrace, trembling a little, weak with relief. She felt his lips move against her temple. "Go ahead and cry," he told her softly, patting her back. "God knows, you've earned the right."

THERE WOULD BE no school that day, fortunately for Piper, who probably couldn't have kept her eyes open to teach. Doc gave a dime to the local newspaper boy and told him to spread the word, along with the just-printed edition of the weekly *Blue River Gazette*.

He and Sawyer shook hands, and Piper greeted Cherokee, who'd stood patiently at the hitching rail all night long, even though he'd come untied at some point. Stroking the horse's velvety nose, she promised him an extra ration of grain.

Then Doc headed off toward his place, doubtless girding his loins for battle as he went, and Piper and Sawyer made for the schoolhouse, in the other direction, Sawyer leading Cherokee along behind.

Piper couldn't recall when she'd ever been so tuckered out, or so full of happiness. There would be no outbreak of diphtheria, at least for the time being, and Ginny-Sue was going to be all right.

As soon as they'd reached the schoolhouse, Sawyer put Cherokee away in the shed, and Piper went along, partly to help, and partly to keep her word about the grain.

While Sawyer removed Cherokee's bridle and then proceeded to give the animal a quick brushing down, Piper plunged a hand into one of the feed sacks Clay had brought in from the ranch and held out her palm, heaping with grain.

"Watch your fingers," Sawyer warned, but he was smiling as he spoke.

Piper just laughed.

Cherokee ate delicately, for a big-jawed creature with

enormous teeth, and Piper patted his head when he'd finished, and called him a good boy.

"Hey," Sawyer teased. "I'm starting to get jealous."

Piper made a face at him, but then she sobered a little. "Do you think Doc will really stand up to Eloise?" she asked.

Now it was Sawyer who laughed. Having been on the other side of the horse, he ducked under Cherokee's long neck and came up in front of Piper like a swimmer breaking the surface of still waters.

"No," he said. His voice was sleepy and low, and he still needed a shave. "I think he'll bribe her with a fancy bathtub and an indoor toilet, and she'll let him off the hook—until next time, anyway."

She felt incredibly shy, all of a sudden. Maybe it was from lack of sleep. "The poor man *is* a dentist," she said.

Sawyer laughed again. "Come on, Mrs. McKettrick," he said. "Let's get you inside so you can get some shuteye."

They went into the schoolhouse, and Sawyer headed for the stove to build a fire while Piper hung up her beautiful russet-colored cloak. She'd never owned a finer garment in all her life, but she was too worn out just now to properly appreciate it.

She wandered into the bedroom, taking off everything but her bloomers and camisole in the shadowy cold, and practically dove into bed, anxious to get warm.

It was only when she caught a fleeting glimpse of Sawyer standing in the doorway that she realized she'd gotten into the wrong bed, the one she was in the habit of sleeping in.

And she was not about to risk more goose bumps by getting out again.

There was a fire going in the stove, she could smell

the burning wood and hear the popping, but the warmth was still far away.

"A man could misinterpret aspects of this situation," Sawyer remarked, crossing to sit down on the edge of the bed, right next to her.

She realized then that she must have dozed off for a while, because he was clean-shaven, and his skin and hair, which was damp, smelled of soap.

Piper yawned, stretched luxuriously. "Really?" she asked coyly. For some incomprehensible reason, she'd forgotten how to be afraid, how to mistrust another person's motives. If that other person happened to be Sawyer McKettrick, that is.

"Oh, yes," Sawyer replied seriously, kicking off his boots. "That could easily happen."

"What if a *woman* wanted to be held, for example?" Piper's voice was a little shaky now, and her heart was picking up speed with every beat. She'd only had this feeling once before, when she was much younger and speeding down a snowy hillside in Maine on a homemade toboggan.

"That could be arranged," Sawyer said, after pretending to give the prospect due consideration. "But he might be tempted to, well, *persuade* her a little—beyond holding her, that is."

"I guess that would be acceptable," Piper allowed, from beneath the covers.

Sawyer chuckled, and there was some shifting around, and then he was in the bed beside her—her *husband*—resting one hand on the curve of her hip. "It might take days," he said, his voice husky, "but I'm a patient man."

"You are not," Piper argued, as he uncovered her face and quieted her with a kiss.

It was light and soft at first, that kiss, but it soon gathered momentum.

As Sawyer kissed her, he undid the laces at the front of her camisole. "Oh, but I am," he disagreed, when their mouths parted. "Patient, I mean."

Piper slipped her arms around his neck, gasped when he opened the camisole and bared her breasts. Stroking one, chafing the nipple gently with the side of his thumb, he nibbled his way down over her collarbone.

"How could it—take—days?" she asked, a little out of step with the flow of conversation.

"I like to take my time," Sawyer replied, measuring out the words slowly, so slowly, like a man muttering in his sleep. "Especially when I'm doing this." And then his mouth closed, warm and wet and pulling ever so gently, around her already distended nipple.

She cried out with pleasure, instinctively arched her back in a plea for more and then still more.

"Days," Sawyer said idly, moving to her other breast.

The pleasure—yes, it *was* pleasure, and it was glorious, and it was *hers*—unleashed something inside Piper, some vast, elemental state of derring-do she hadn't known existed.

Over the next few minutes—or was it hours?—Sawyer raised Piper to a fever pitch with his fingers, his lips, his words. She wriggled out of her bloomers with a shameful lack of encouragement, making him laugh.

When he slid his hand between her legs and began to work her with a light, circular motion of the heel of his palm, she was lost. And then he took her nipple into his mouth again, and she was electrified, more completely and powerfully *alive* than ever before.

"Oh—*Sawyer*—" she sobbed out.

He lifted his head from her breast, where he'd been

feasting, and said quietly, "Any time you want me to stop, Piper, all you have to do is say the word and I will."

"Ooooooh," she moaned, raising her hips high off the mattress to maintain contact with his hand. *Stop?* Not if she had anything to say about it.

He quickened the pace of his hand, and she went wild with desire, with a need that would not be refused. "There's more," he told her softly, gruffly, tracing the length of her neck with his lips. "There's a lot more. But before any of that happens, I want you to know how it's supposed to feel when I make love to you."

She cried out again, frenzied, flying. Wanting. She was wanton, wide-open to him, and she felt no shame, only freedom and ferocious instincts.

"Sawyer!" she pleaded raggedly.

"Let go," he murmured. "Just let go."

There was a fierce seizing sensation then, deep inside her, a thing of the spirit as well as the body, followed by a release so keen that it seemed to consume all of Piper in sweet blazes of satisfaction. Her body flexed and flexed again, speaking its own language of joy.

Finally, she shattered completely and, after what seemed like a very long time, fell back into herself, in a slow but still dizzying drop, dazed, crooning and purring with every small aftershock.

"That's how it's supposed to feel," Sawyer told her, with a grin, much later, when her breathing had returned to something approaching normality and her heart had ceased struggling to flail its way out of her chest and fly heavenward like a bird.

She snuggled against Sawyer. "But there's more," she repeated sleepily.

"Yes," Sawyer said, with a smile in his voice. His

chin was propped on the top of her head. "We'll have time for that later."

"Mmm," she said, and moved closer still.

Then she felt the hard length of him against her thigh, and she was instantly wide-awake.

"I did say there was more," Sawyer reminded her, his eyes alight with mischief and—just possibly, no it couldn't be, not so soon—love.

"Now I know why everyone says it hurts," Piper announced, feeling her eyes go wide.

"Everyone?" Sawyer asked, teasing. "Is this something you talk about a lot?"

She shook her head, nervous and, at the same time, wanting him. All of him. "Of course not," she whispered, as though imparting a secret in the midst of a listening crowd. "But, well, it does seem—logistically impossible."

At that, Sawyer threw back his head and gave a shout of laughter.

She thumped his chest with the side of one fist, though not very hard. "What's so funny, Sawyer McKettrick?" she demanded, blushing from her hairline to her toes.

He didn't answer right away, but his amusement subsided a little.

Their gazes locked and the mood turned serious again.

"*Will* it hurt?" she asked meekly.

"Probably," Sawyer answered, smoothing her hair away from her cheek. "But only the first time, and for just a little while."

"Oh," Piper said.

"It's up to you," he reiterated.

"Let's try," Piper decided.

"It's not like that," Sawyer told her. "There's no 'try.' You do it, or you don't do it."

"Will it hurt you?"

He kissed her forehead, then the tip of her nose. "No," he answered, in his forthright way.

"And there's only pain the first time?"

He nodded. "Usually. And I'll be real careful, I promise."

She believed him. Her heart widened somehow, and took him in, and that was the moment she truly became his wife. "I love you, Sawyer," she said, and she'd never meant anything more than she meant those words. "I know you probably don't—"

He stopped her from finishing the sentence by pressing an index finger to her lips. "I can speak for myself, woman," he said, with mock sternness. "And it just so happens that I love you, too. I realized it when you took off for the Bitter Gulch Saloon—even before that, really—to see to Ginny-Sue, and there was no talking you out of it."

She blinked. "Really? Why?"

He gave another raspy chuckle and shook his head. "I guess I admire spirit in a woman," he replied, "and you've got plenty of that, all right, with some to spare."

His answer pleased her deeply, settled into her, saturated her with a sense of rightness and perfect safety. "Well, Mr. McKettrick, I think it's about time we consummated our marriage, don't you?"

"You're sure?" He looked troubled, but blue-green fire burned in his eyes.

"I'm absolutely positive," she replied.

Dutifully, she situated herself on the mattress, spread her legs a little, and waited for him to get on top of her.

Instead, he gave another chuckle, and then he drove her to near madness again, caressing her, kissing her, whispering things that made her blood rush hot through her veins.

When Sawyer finally took Piper for his own, in a long, swift thrust, she wanted, *needed* him inside her so much that she barely noticed the twinge of pain as her maidenhead gave way.

Her body responded to his, as if drawing on some ancient knowledge, stroke for stroke, giving and then taking, offering and then demanding, and when he finally stiffened upon her, with a hoarse cry, and she felt him spilling himself into her, ecstasy claimed her once again, even more completely than before, and her cry of triumph rose to meet and mingle with his.

Later, they slept, and it seemed to Piper, as she drifted off, exhausted and utterly spent, a vessel deliciously emptied of all she had to give, that even though their bodies were separate and distinctly individual, their souls had somehow fused into one being, a making-right of many wrongs, large and small, a kind of coming home to all they'd ever really been.

They slept for the rest of that day and all of the night, to Piper's amazement, and awoke to a frost-sparkled morning that had drawn exquisite paisley patterns on the glass in the schoolhouse's few windows.

Sawyer was already up—she could hear him rattling the door of the stove, whistling under his breath.

Smiling, purely happy, she snuggled down in the warmth of the bed, every part of her pulsing with the memory of their lovemaking.

"You'd better get up, Teacher," Sawyer called good-naturedly, from the other room. "School starts in an hour."

Reality jolted through Piper, and she bolted out of bed, immediately beginning to shiver as the cold morning air struck her bare skin. She fumbled for her flannel wrapper and put it on quickly. "An *hour?*" she called back, padding in to squeeze up close to the stove while Sawyer dumped ground coffee beans into the pot.

It was only then that she noticed he'd removed his sling, though not his bandages, and even as he finished putting the coffee on to brew, he was slowly flexing and unflexing his left elbow.

"What are you *doing?*" Piper demanded, instantly alarmed.

"What I can," Sawyer responded. "I still have a lot of use for this arm, Mrs. McKettrick, and I don't want the muscles to atrophy."

"They *won't,*" she said. "Doc Howard would have warned us, if that were the case. He'd have said—"

"Doc Howard, for all his versatility, is a dentist, not a medical practitioner," Sawyer reminded her, still moving his limb. "We've got a couple of doctors in the McKettrick clan, and any one of them would tell me to start using this arm a little every day."

Piper started to protest, and then stopped herself. Reasoning with a man was one thing, and nagging him was another. Besides, she recognized a lost cause when she saw one.

"These McKettricks seem to be an opinionated bunch," she observed, ladling hot water from a kettle on the stove into a basin so she could wash up before she put on her clothes.

Sawyer's grin flashed. "You'll fit right in," he said.

CHAPTER TEN

Afternoon, Christmas Eve

THERE WERE SO many people in the Blue River school-house, Piper thought happily, that even one more wouldn't fit.

And yet, somehow, there was a place for all the late-comers, with their smiles and words of greeting, their homemade fruitcakes and fruit pies.

The evening before, Clay had brought a fresh Christmas tree in from the ranch, deeming the first one a piti-ful sight, past its prime, and Piper and Sawyer had spent a festive hour transferring the ornaments from the old to the new.

Now, Ginny-Sue's eyes widened as Clay lifted her up to touch the feathered wings of the angel that had magi-cally appeared on top of the tree sometime during the night. "Where did she come from?" the child wondered, in an awed whisper. "She wasn't on the *other* tree."

"I guess it's a miracle," Clay told the child, his gaze on Dara Rose, who stood nearby, glowing as she showed off the new baby to one and all. The special angel was their gift to the children of Blue River. "There are a lot of those going around these days, it seems to me."

Ginny-Sue, still weak but mostly recovered, had re-turned to school only the day before, a little subdued but eager to be a part of things. Once Clay set her on her feet, she hurried off with Edrina, Harriet and Madeline to get ready for the program, and Piper, standing next to Dara Rose, smiled and offered a quick, silent prayer of gratitude.

There was so very much to be thankful for.

Indeed, this *was* a season of miracles, just as Clay had said.

Sawyer, neatly dressed in garments from his travel trunk and temporarily without his sling, caught Piper's eye and winked.

She drew a deep breath and went up to the place where her desk normally stood—it had been pushed back against the wall so the raised floor could be used as a sort of stage—clapping her hands smartly to get everyone's attention.

The cheerful talk ceased, but in a scattered, here-and-there way, and every upturned face was friendly—except, of course, for Eloise Howard's.

Piper gave the other woman a warm smile, secretly feeling sorry for her, and addressed the group in general. "The children have worked very hard to prepare for today's program," she said, in a voice trained to carry to every corner of the room without screeching. "We all hope you'll enjoy it."

Bess Turner, standing in a corner with a cluster of her "girls" from the Bitter Gulch Saloon, faded flowers clad in fuss and feathers, beamed with pride as Ginny-Sue took her place and began to recite the second chapter of Luke. Her performance was flawless, delivered in a bell-like voice, and afterward, no one stinted on applause.

Even Eloise clapped, after a fashion, soundlessly touching the gloved fingers of her right hand to the palm of her left, still flushed with the singular pleasure of informing Piper, twenty minutes before, that her teaching services would no longer be required after the school term ended in early June.

Piper hadn't minded, given that she and Sawyer had already made plans to make their home on the Triple M, up in Arizona, starting the journey north as soon as school was out and the new and more permanent town marshal had arrived, but she'd pretended to feel a *little* bit bad, for Eloise's sake. Heaven knew the poor woman was hard up for things to celebrate, which was a sad thing in and of itself, since she had a good husband, a lovely child and a comparatively easy life, far more than many other people could even have hoped for.

Bess Turner, for example, now hugging and congratulating her proud daughter, might have been grateful for the kind of respectability and love Eloise evidently took for granted—as less than her due.

With a sigh, Piper put the whole matter out of her mind. There was no changing other people; one had to accept them as they were and proceed as best one could, making allowances wherever possible.

The boys took the stage next, putting on a little skit of their own composition, in which shepherds and Roman soldiers speculated about the unusually bright star in the sky over Bethlehem. The soldiers had swords fashioned from kindling and the shepherds had staffs and feed-sack headdresses and, though brief, the play met with critical acclaim and much cheering.

Edrina played a lively tune on her ukulele next, with Harriet turning the pages of her sheet music for her, importantly competent throughout.

Recitations followed, mostly poetry, and when the last of those had mercifully ended, all the students assembled to sing "Silent Night," as rehearsed over many, many days. Piper was touched when, one by one, voice by voice, some awkward, some remarkably sweet, the audience joined in.

It was time then for the presents—the owner of the mercantile had, as usual, brought along the promised oranges and peppermint sticks.

The children were delirious with excitement, especially Ginny-Sue, who had confided to Piper earlier, in a brief moment of privacy, that she had a Christmas tree at home, too. There were parcels tucked into the branches, and "the ladies" had lent all sorts of baubles and ribbons and even silk garters for decorations.

Piper had been delighted by the image and kissed Ginny-Sue on top of the head, telling her, "You'll have a happy Christmas for sure."

And Ginny-Sue had nodded vigorously, eyes shining with joy.

Now, with the oranges and peppermint sticks dispersed, the adults chatted and indulged in pie and cake and all manner of country delicacies, each family, even the poorest ones, having contributed something.

Bess made her way to Piper's side and tugged at the sleeve of her new blue dress, a ready-made from the mercantile. She'd splurged on it, now that she wasn't saving her money to go back to Maine, along with small gifts for Sawyer, Dara Rose and Clay, and, of course, the children.

"We'll be going now," Bess said quietly. "I just wanted to say thank you for everything you did, you and your man, and to wish you a happy Christmas."

Piper's eyes burned, and she smiled, her response delayed by a few moments because she was suddenly choked up. "You're welcome," she said, at last. "And a happy Christmas to you, as well."

"It's the best one ever," Bess confirmed, with a fond glance at her daughter.

And then she and her bevy of twittering birds left the schoolhouse, surrounding little Ginny-Sue, in her warm coat, hat, boots and mittens, like a royal guard escorting a princess home to the palace.

Piper watched them go from the front window, knowing she would treasure the recollection forever after, while the party went on behind her. They were a *family,* those fancy women and that sweet child and blustery Cleopatra, as loving and tightly knit as any other. They'd come to the schoolhouse, knowing there would be some who looked askance, resolved to watch Ginny-Sue make her recitation and celebrate with her classmates, and they'd even put up a Christmas tree, festooning the branches with what they had, rather than tinsel and colored glass.

If that wasn't love, what was?

Sawyer stepped up beside her. "What are you thinking right now, Mrs. McKettrick?" he asked quietly.

She loved it when he called her that. "That Christmas comes in many forms," she replied, leaning against him a little, and delighting in the strength of his arm as it encircled her waist. Then she turned her head, looked up into his handsome face. "Do you miss your family? Because it's Christmas, I mean?"

"*You're* my family," he said, smiling into her eyes.

She let her head rest against his shoulder for a long moment. "I love you," she said.

"And I love you," he replied throatily, holding her a little tighter. Then, in a mischievous whisper, he added, "Let's hurry this party along a little. The sooner it's over, the sooner we'll be alone."

Piper smiled. "We're going to the ranch with Dara Rose and Clay and the children, remember? We won't really be alone until after Christmas, when we move into the marshal's house."

Sawyer grinned and gave her a surreptitious pinch on a part of her anatomy he particularly favored. "Clay and Dara Rose have a big house," he reminded her, "and I made sure we got a room well away from everybody else's."

She flushed. "You're a scoundrel," she accused, though she was pleased at the prospect.

"And you wouldn't have me any other way," he answered.

She laughed in agreement.

With that, they rejoined the festivities.

THE RIDE TO the ranch in Clay's largest hay-wagon was long and cold, and Piper, bundled up in quilts and blankets in back, with Dara Rose holding the well-wrapped baby, Edrina and Harriet all sitting with her in a bed of fragrant straw, wouldn't have changed a thing about the experience.

It was already perfect, just as it was.

Clay and Sawyer sat up front, Clay at the reins of a four-horse team, and as they traveled, the stars started popping out in the blue-black sky, to the delighted fascination of the two little girls. Edrina's and Harriet's cheeks glowed, and their eyes danced with happiness and anticipation.

The trail was rough and rutted, the wagon jostled along, and Piper was lulled into a brief revelry by the steady clomp-clomp-clomp of the horses' hooves.

Conversation, it seemed, would be too much effort, at least for the women—the men were discussing something, up there in the wagon-box, and Edrina and Harriet chattered like eager little swallows in springtime—but Piper, for her part, was content just to be with them all.

It was later in the evening, long after they'd arrived at the ranch house, to which Dara Rose and Clay were already adding rooms, when the women finally got a chance to talk. They'd had a big supper, a boisterous affair replete with all sorts of food, and Edrina and Harriet had hung their stockings on the living room mantel and gone to bed with no fuss or delay. Dara Rose had retreated to nurse the baby and tuck him into his cradle near the kitchen table, where they sat, now that she'd returned. Clay liked to build things, when he had the time, and baby Jeb had several cradles, in various parts of the house.

The men had gone to the barn right after supper, and they weren't back yet.

"You seem happy, Piper," Dara Rose ventured gently. She was a pretty woman, with blond hair, like her daughters', and lively eyes, full of joyful intelligence. "Are you? Truly, I mean?"

Piper blushed slightly, and then nodded. "Yes," she said. "I'm *very* happy. I'll miss you, though. When Sawyer and I move to Arizona, I mean."

"We'll write often," Dara Rose promised, reaching out to pat Piper's hand. "And when the baby is older, we'll come for a long visit." The house was warm, being well-insulated, unlike the schoolhouse, with a wood-burning furnace and intermittent electrical services. There were several fireplaces, and the kitchen stove was a magnificent thing, with a hot-water reservoir that could be accessed by a spigot.

"Sawyer says Arizona is a fine place," Piper remarked. It had been a while since she'd seen Dara Rose, due to distance and pregnancy, and there was so much to say that it was hard to choose a place to start.

Dara Rose nodded. "Finally," she confirmed, smiling. "Clay says his granddad thinks it would have been better if Arizona remained a territory, says there'd be less interference from the federal government that way."

Piper had heard stories about Angus McKettrick, the head of the family, who had originally hailed from Texas. Sawyer clearly idolized the man, though he'd come right out and said his grandfather was three years older than dirt and deaf as a fence post, so she shouldn't be alarmed if he shouted at her to "Speak up so I can hear you, little gal!"

"I think I'm a bit intimidated," she confessed. "By the family, I mean. There are so many of them, and they're all strong-minded and utterly fearless, from what Sawyer's told me. Why, his own mother used to be a sharpshooter, traveling with a Wild West show."

Dara Rose laughed. "And Miss Mandy," she said, "is one of the *tamer* ones."

"Good heavens," Piper fretted. She had Annie Oakley for a mother-in-law.

"Don't worry," Dara Rose counseled. "I was only teasing. I've met Clay's folks—they came to visit not too long after we got married, traveled all that way by train—and I was real nervous before then. I took a powerful liking to them both right away, and so did the girls." She paused. "Here's the thing about the McKettricks, Piper. Once you marry into the family, you're one of them, for life. Jeb and Chloe—Clay's mother and father—they don't seem to see Edrina and Harriet as their son's stepchildren, any more than he does. To them, the girls are as much a part of the clan as anybody born with the name. They're extraordinary people, really."

Growing up, Piper reflected, she and Dara Rose had depended mostly on each other, when it came to family. It would be lovely to be part of a large group of kinfolks.

"I just hope they like me," Piper said.

"Believe me," Dara Rose insisted, just as the men came in from outside, accompanied by Clay's dog, "they will."

"Are the girls asleep?" Clay asked, bending to kiss Dara Rose's cheek after hanging up his hat and coat and kicking off his boots to walk about in his stocking feet.

"They're probably pretending they are," Dara Rose said in reply, and all the love she felt for Clay McKettrick showed in her eyes as she watched him lean over the cradle to make sure the baby was warm enough.

Sawyer, dispensing with his own coat and hat—he'd put his sling back on for the ride out from town—crossed to Piper and kissed her ear, sending a fiery shiver through her.

The four of them sat around the table for a while after that, talking quietly while the fire burned low in the furnace downstairs, along with the one in the cookstove. The single bulb illuminating the kitchen blinked on and off periodically, and they used a kerosene lantern in between.

Eventually, Clay went down to the cellar to stoke up the furnace, and Dara Rose lifted their sleeping baby from his cradle, holding him tenderly, his face in the curve of her neck.

"I'll say good-night," Dara Rose told Piper and Sawyer, Sawyer having risen from his chair and drawn back Piper's so she could stand, "and a happy Christmas to both of you."

Piper stepped forward, kissed her cousin's cheek. "Sleep well," she told Dara Rose.

The spare room—Piper had stayed in it before, of course—was on the far side of the house, spacious and comfortably, if simply, furnished. It had its own wood-burning stove, which already crackled with a welcoming fire, but her favorite part of it was the bathroom. Like the one near Clay and Dara Rose's room, which they shared with the girls, this one was well appointed with a pedestal sink, a toilet, and a long, narrow tub made of gleaming porcelain.

Water flowed from a copper tank set into the wall, heated by the small boiler beneath.

Someone, probably Clay, had made sure the boiler was operating properly, and when Piper put the plug in place and turned the spigots, gloriously hot water soon spilled and splashed into the tub.

By the light of the lantern she and Sawyer had brought from the kitchen—there were no electric bulbs in this part of the house—Piper shed her clothes as quickly as she could and climbed in while the water was still running.

She sighed and closed her eyes. "Bliss," she said.

A chuckle from the doorway made her open her eyes again and turn to see Sawyer standing there, watching her. "I'd have to agree," he said huskily.

She didn't think he was referring to the bath, and his words made her blush slightly.

"Join me?" Piper asked. She'd taken regular baths at the schoolhouse, of course, but that had been an awkward proposition to say the least. This was a *real* bath, with plenty of hot water and scented salts in the bargain.

Sawyer remained where he was, giving his head a slight shake. His gaze caressed her as intimately as a touch of his hand. "I'll take a bath later," he replied. "Right now, I'm content to watch you."

She sighed again, a crooning sound of purest contentment, not just with the bath but with the whole of her life, and leaned against the back of the tub, even though the porcelain was chilly where it touched her bare skin, and allowed herself to sink deeper into the rising water. "Nothing," she said, "could be better than this."

Sawyer stepped into the room then, set the lantern on a shelf, and knelt beside the bathtub. "Is that a fact?" he asked, holding out his right arm to her, as he was in the habit of doing when they undressed, and, without replying to his question, she unfastened his cuff link and rolled his sleeve up past his elbow.

He swirled the water around her lightly, splashed some on her belly and her breasts. She quivered as his fingertips brushed those same places, and others, too.

"*One* thing might be better than a bath," Piper admitted, feeling saucy.

Sawyer traced the circumference of her right nipple, again, with a fingertip.

A tremor went through her, with a promise of sweet tumult to follow. She groaned, already surrendering to his caresses, even as the water rose and rose, so warm and soothing. The very marrow of her bones seemed to melt.

Sawyer chuckled at her response; he loved the sounds Piper made when he pleasured her, and he was very good at that.

The tub was full, and he turned off the spigots, reached for a bar of soap.

And he began to lather Piper, gently but thoroughly, washing every part of her, and she gave herself up to the sultry, luxurious sensations of his touch, and of the things he said to her, quiet and strictly their own, almost a private language.

Presently, he leaned over and caught her mouth with his, kissed her deeply, all the while stroking the place between her legs, which had opened for him readily, like always.

His lovemaking always seemed new, and exquisitely daring. He'd taken her standing up in the schoolhouse one moonless night, and even now the memory aroused her almost as much as what he was doing now. She'd taken him into her greedily, crying out in welcome as he took her.

"There's more," he always said to her, after each ecstatic surprise.

"There's more," he said now, getting to his feet and reaching for one of the towels Dara Rose had so thoughtfully provided, along with the fancy soap and the ample supply of hot water.

Wobbly-kneed, Piper stood, let him wrap her in the towel. Stepped over the side of the tub and onto the rug to stand very close to him.

He led her into the warm bedroom, lit only by the light escaping from the edges of the door in the little stove, dried her off, and settled her sideways on the mattress. Easing her onto her back, he kissed her and caressed her for a long time.

She waited, dazed with comfort and anticipation, because when Sawyer said there was more, there always was.

Always.

When he slipped away from her, she tried to pull him back, already wanting him on top of her, inside her, but he eluded her grasp.

And then he knelt again, and parted her knees.

When he took her into his mouth, the most sensitive, intimate part of her, she had to stifle a ragged shout of delight. It was scandalous—it was—

"Sawyer," she whimpered, tangling her fingers into his hair, holding him close to her, pressed hard against her.

His mouth. Dear heaven, *his mouth.* What magic was this? What wild, sweet magic was he working on her?

Without withdrawing from her, he eased both her legs up, setting her heels against the mattress. Her bent knees widened and still he feasted on her, nibbling and tasting, teasing her with just the tip of his tongue until she begged for completion.

One of his hands found her mouth and covered it gently, and that was a good thing, because when satisfaction finally, *finally* overtook her, she was making a primitive sound, part sob and part growl, that would have carried clear to town, never mind to the rest of the house.

Before rising from his knees, Sawyer kissed the insides of Piper's still trembling thighs. Several small, sharp after-releases followed, each one causing her to moan softly and arch her back, as though to find his mouth again.

He arranged her properly in the bed and covered her up. "If Clay hears you yelling like that," he joked quietly, "he'll think I'm killing you and storm the room with a shotgun."

Piper couldn't speak. She was still trying to find her way back to herself, still lost on the outskirts of heaven.

She slept a sweetly shallow sleep, rising to the surface now and then, like some exotic fish. She heard Sawyer running a bath in the next room and, later, felt his weight on the mattress when he climbed into bed beside her. She stirred as, unbelievably, desire reawakened within her, blossoming like some soft-petaled flower.

"Sawyer," she whispered, reaching for him.

He moved on top of her, and she widened her legs for him.

He took her slowly, so slowly, and so deeply that her body instantly responded, even though she was still half-asleep. She began to buckle beneath him, as the first climax seized her, followed by another and then another. They were soft, these releases, and she soared with them as surely as if she'd had wings.

Finally, Sawyer too reached the pinnacle, and gave himself up to her with a long, low groan that seemed to rise from the depths of his soul.

"GET UP!" a little voice crowed. "Get up, get up, get up!"

Sawyer opened one eye, spotted Harriet standing beside the bed, holding up a stocking—one of Clay's, probably—bulging with loot.

"It's *Christmas!*" Edrina piped up, from the other side of the bed.

Piper, buried deep under the covers, murmured something.

"And St. Nicholas was here!" Harriet cried, waving the stocking. "Get up!"

Sawyer laughed. "I thought you didn't believe in St. Nicholas," he said, stalling for time. He wasn't wearing a stitch, and neither was Piper, which meant, of course, that the getting-up part would have to wait until the girls were out of the room.

"Now we've got proof!" Edrina trilled, exhibiting a burgeoning work sock of her own. A doll's head poked out of the top, flanked by what looked like a toy horn of some kind, brightly painted and made of tin.

"And there was a *note!*" Harriet added, her eyes huge with excitement. "St. Nicholas left us presents *in the barn,* and that's why you have to *get up,* so we can all go out there together and see!"

Sawyer thought of the two spotted ponies Clay had been hiding in the barn for three days now, and grinned. The night before, he and Clay had set the small, fancy saddles out in plain sight, on a bale of hay, and draped the bridles over them. "Go wake up your folks, then," he said.

Piper's head popped out from under the covers, and she smiled sleepily at the girls, yawned a good-morning.

Sawyer would have given a great deal for another hour alone with her, right there in the guest room bed, but he knew he was out of luck, given the combination of kids and Christmas.

"They're *already* awake!" Edrina informed him. "Hurry *up*—at this rate, it'll be New Year's before we get to see our presents!"

"Out," Sawyer ordered good-naturedly.

"Go on," Piper urged the girls, with a twinkle in her eyes. "We'll be up and around in a few minutes, I promise."

Possibly because she was their teacher, as well as their mother's cousin and closest friend, Edrina and Harriet scampered out, shutting the bedroom door smartly behind them.

"Hurry!" one of them called back, over the sound of rapidly retreating footsteps.

Sawyer sighed, got out of bed, and gathered up his clothes. He went into the bathroom to dress, and when he came out, Piper was fully clad and pinning up her hair in a loose chignon.

He kissed her nape. "That was quick," he said.

"Christmas waits for no one," she replied, turning in his embrace to kiss the cleft in his strong chin. "Let's go see what St. Nicholas has left in the barn."

One year later
Triple M Ranch, Indian Rock, Arizona

THE WHOLE CLAN HAD GATHERED at the main ranch house, where Angus McKettrick officiated, from his wheeled chair, over a busy and memorable Christmas Eve. Even Clay and Dara Rose were there, with the children, having traveled all the way from Texas on the train.

Since all the McKettricks would have separate celebrations for their own families the next day, gifts were exchanged after supper, and even after months spent with these people, Piper was amazed by the rough-and-tumble love they bore each other. They'd taken her into their lives and hearts back in June, when Sawyer had returned, bringing a new wife with him, and she'd fallen in love with them, too.

She and Sawyer had stayed with his mother and father, Kade and Mandy McKettrick, at first, while they were building their own house and barn on a little rise with a spring and a broad view of the ranch. Mandy was still trim and agile, though she'd long-since given up sharp-shooting to reign over her children and grandchildren, as well as her adoring husband.

Besides aunts and uncles, there were sisters, too, and brothers, and cousins galore.

Piper was still getting to know them all. Sawyer's aunt Katie, Angus and Conception's late-life daughter, a particular favorite of Piper's, was married to a United States senator and divided her time between Arizona and Washington. She was bound and determined to see that women got the vote and constantly pestered her husband and his associates to "catch up with the modern world" and do something about the problem.

On this sacred night, Mandy approached her newest

daughter-in-law and gently touched her protruding stomach. Piper and Sawyer's first baby was due soon—she'd been hoping for a Christmas birth—but that didn't seem likely, since there hadn't been so much as a twinge of a contraction so far.

"You mustn't overdo, now," Mandy counseled. "We're a pretty overwhelming bunch, we McKettricks, especially when we're all in the same place."

Piper smiled, caught Sawyer's eye and received his smile like a blessing. He was standing next to Angus's wheeled chair, listening while the older man went on about the unfortunate changes statehood had brought.

None of them, in Angus's view, were good.

Sawyer winked, and Mandy, seeing the exchange, smiled at Piper again. "At least sit down," she said, steering Piper toward one of the few unoccupied chairs.

Chloe, a lovely red-haired woman and a teacher, like Piper, approached them, having taken a large and gaily wrapped package from beneath the towering Christmas tree. Katie and Lydia and Emmeline, the other aunts, found their way over, too, all beaming proudly.

Chloe handed the parcel to Mandy, who gently laid it in Piper's lap.

Dara Rose joined them, too. From her smile, she was in on the surprise.

"What on earth—?" Piper asked, near tears.

"Open it," Mandy urged eagerly.

Carefully, her hands trembling a little, Piper removed the ribbon, draping it over the arm of her chair for safekeeping, and then smoothed back the tissue paper.

Inside was a quilt, as wildly colorful as the northern Arizona landscape surrounding them all, exquisitely pieced.

"We all worked on it," Katie said.

Lydia and Dara Rose took the quilt by its ends and unfurled it, so Piper could get a good look at the design. The Blue River schoolhouse had been faithfully reproduced in fabric and appliquéd to the center of what, to Piper, was a work of art. There were children embroidered here and there, frolicking in the school yard, and she saw herself standing in the tiny doorway, with Sawyer beside her.

"Sawyer told us he ruined your trousseau quilts by bleeding on them," one of the women said.

Piper's vision was blurred, but she could still make out the words stitched, sampler style, in a rainbow arched above the schoolhouse.

"Piper and Sawyer McKettrick," the thread-letters read. "Blue River, Texas, 1915."

"It's so lovely," Piper whispered. "Thank you."

Mandy leaned down and placed a kiss on her daughter-in-law's forehead. "No, Piper," she said. "Thank *you,* for saving Sawyer's life and for being precisely who you are." Mandy's gaze took in the entire gathering in one swift sweep before returning to Piper's upturned face. "Welcome to the McKettrick family," she finished.

* * * * *

Look for Linda Lael Miller's next original novel,
BIG SKY SECRETS, on sale from
Harlequin HQN Books in January 2014
at your favorite retail outlet.

ESCAPE FROM CABRIZ

For Cheryl, Chris and April,
Dear and special friends.

CHAPTER ONE

THE ROAR OF the ocean followed Zachary Harmon across the weathered deck and inside his beach house. Shivering with cold, he pushed the sliding glass door closed and peeled off his sodden blue sweatshirt, tossing it into the oversize closet where the washer and drier were hidden. Then he hooked his thumbs under the waistband of his orange running shorts.

He was just about to remove them and send them flying after the sweatshirt when the flickering screen of the small color TV affixed to the underside of one of the kitchen cupboards drew his attention. As usual, he'd forgotten to turn it off before going out.

The pit of Zachary's stomach did a carnival-ride pitch-and-spin as he stood there in the middle of the kitchen floor, dripping rainwater and staring.

The voice of the TV anchorman seemed to weave in and out of his consciousness. "The political climate in the small Southeast Asian country of Cabriz is worsening by the hour as warring factions grapple for control of the government. A spokesman for the State Department says Americans in Cabriz may be in serious danger... embassies being closed..."

Zachary shut his eyes momentarily against an onslaught of memories and fears. The Cabrizian man-on-the-street was a pretty laid-back guy, mostly concerned with harvesting a few acres of rice and keeping his ox from being repossessed, but some of the rebels were into imaginative atrocities.

And Kristin was in Cabriz.

The newscaster went on to another subject, after promising regular updates on the situation in Southeast Asia, and Zachary snapped off the TV set. He stood with his hands braced against the counter, mentally sifting through all the memorized data he had on Cabriz—which was considerable, since he'd spent so much time there while he'd been with the agency.

He went to the other counter and poured a cup of coffee. There were several rebel factions in Cabriz—all made up of wild-eyed fanatics bent on overthrowing the existing dictatorship. Just twenty-four hours before, the beleaguered government had broken off diplomatic relations with the United States, Great Britain and Canada because of their refusal to step in militarily.

Kristin, by an act of supreme idiocy, had aligned herself with the royal family. Zachary raised the mug of steaming coffee to his mouth and cursed when he burned his tongue. The fact that Kristin planned to marry Jascha, the crown prince of Cabriz, was still difficult to accept.

It wounded him that their time together had meant so little to her.

Zachary set the mug down with a thump. Kristin's position was precarious, to say the least; she would be roughly as popular in Cabriz as Marie Antoinette had been in Paris after the fall of the Bastille.

The fingers of Zachary's right hand knotted into a fist, and he pounded the counter once, to vent some of his frustration. Kristin couldn't really be in love with that guy; it wasn't possible.

Because he needed something to do, he reached for

the telephone receiver and punched out a number he'd never forgotten.

"Perry King's office," a pleasant female voice chimed.

"This is Zachary Harmon," was the brusque reply. "Put me through."

The secretary hesitated for only a moment, then there was a blipping sound and Perry came on the line.

"Hello, Zachary," he said warmly.

Zachary stated his business, sparing the polite preamble. "What idiot let Kristin Meyers leave for Cabriz when the damn government is collapsing?"

Perry sighed heavily. "She went there to marry the crown prince. Besides, she's the daughter of an ambassador turned cabinet member, in case you've forgotten. It probably took one phone call."

"Any plans to go in after her?"

"God knows, the Secretary wants her out of there yesterday, but we can't forget that Miss Meyers is in the country of her own free will. After all, she's—er—well, like I said, she's supposed to be getting married any day now."

A shaft of pain speared Zachary's middle. "Damn it, P.K., that airhead socialite probably doesn't have the first idea of what she's messing with. Chances are, the prince is planning to use her as leverage to get the administration to step in with military aid. And you know their position on that!"

"Zach, are you volunteering to go in?"

Zachary thought of the quiet, peaceful life he'd built for himself. No demands, no pressures, no emergency missions in the middle of the night. He didn't even have a dog to feed.

He had things set up just the way he wanted them. He taught political science at Silver Shores Junior College, because it was easy and because it allowed him to live near the ocean, and he grew tomatoes in clay pots.

"Zachary?" his friend and former employer prompted.

"Yes, damn it," Zachary replied, thinking of defiant green eyes and long brown hair that caught the sunlight and turned it to fire. "I want to go in and get Kristin. And don't remind me that I resigned from the agency eighteen months ago. Nobody's better qualified, even now."

Perry sighed again. "That's true. But I can't just give you the go-ahead—I have to make a few calls before I can do that. So sit tight—you hear me?"

"I hear you," Zachary grumbled, then hung up with a crash. He was already planning to leave within the next twenty-four hours, whether the trip was sanctioned by Washington or not. He knew a thousand ways in and out of Cabriz.

An hour later, showered and clad in blue jeans, dry sneakers and a navy sweatshirt, Zachary stood at the stove, stirring a pan of canned spaghetti and watching another update on the cable news channel. The telephone jangled, and he had the receiver in his hand before the first ring faded.

"Harmon," he snapped.

The answering voice belonged to one of the president's favorite men—and Zachary's *least* favorite—

Kristin's father. "This is Kenyan Meyers. I've just spent some time on the telephone with Perry King, over at the State Department. He tells me you're willing to go into Cabriz and bring Kristin home."

"That's right," Zachary replied. He wasn't awed by Meyers; he'd dealt with more powerful men, but he was on guard because of all that had happened between him and Kristin. And because he knew the Secretary was about as benevolent as a cobra with PMS.

Meyers paused for a moment before replying. "You're aware, of course, that Kristin may well want to stay in Cabriz. Especially if the marriage has already taken place."

"I'll take that chance."

"Fine. One of our planes will pick you up in Seattle in exactly ten hours—you know the procedure, I'm sure. You'll be briefed on the current state of affairs during the flight."

"Thanks." Zachary was moving to hang up when Meyers spoke again. He put the receiver back to his ear.

"Bring my daughter home, Harmon, whether she's agreeable or not. She has no idea what kind of situation she's gotten herself into."

The only thing Zachary could have promised anyone at that point was that if Kristin was still alive when he arrived in Cabriz, he was going to strangle her personally. And he wasn't laboring under any flowery delusions that Meyers's true concerns were for Kristin. He definitely had some important political ax to grind. "I'll be in contact with you as soon as I can, Mr. Secretary," Zachary replied evenly, and the call was over.

KRISTIN'S BRAVADO WAS beginning to desert her as she stood beside a veiled servant woman at one of the windows, watching as Jascha's troops drilled in the dusty streets of the city of Kiri, Cabriz's capital. The place seemed so different now, so unfamiliar. It was hard to believe she'd grown up only a few blocks away, in the American embassy.

With a sigh, Kristin sank into a rattan chair, one blue-jeaned leg slung over the arm, and let her head fall back. She closed her eyes and thought of the day she'd left Cabriz, at seventeen. She'd finished her high school work, with the help of her tutor, and now it was time to return to America....

"I don't want to leave you," she sniffled, looking up at Jascha's face through a blur of tears. Overhead a lemon tree blossomed, dropping delicate white petals all around them, like snow.

Jascha was a prince, in every sense of the word. With his dark hair and eyes and exquisitely tailored clothes, he could have stepped out of the pages of a storybook. He kissed her lightly on the forehead, his strong hands holding her shoulders. "Do not cry, Kristin," he said, his voice a ragged whisper. "One day you will come back to Cabriz, and you and I will reign together."

Kristin swallowed, hardly daring to believe the fairy tale even though she and Jascha had discussed it many times. "But your father has seven wives," she said, echoing her mother's pet reason why nothing could ever come of Jascha and Kristin's bittersweet romance.

Jascha traced the line of her cheek with a smooth thumb. "You will be my only wife, little lemon flower. This I promise you."

Kristin believed him, perhaps because she was seventeen and he was the first man she'd ever loved, and threw herself into his arms even as her father called impatiently from the other side of the embassy courtyard. Jascha kissed her soundly before stepping aside, his hands caught together behind his back, to await the ambassador's appearance.

Almost regretfully, Kristin came back to the here and now. Her parents had looked upon her earlier relationship with Jascha as a teenage infatuation and therefore hadn't taken it too seriously, but they were strenuously opposed to the marriage that was about to take place.

Even if the political system hadn't been in chaos, they probably wouldn't have attended the wedding.

Kristin sighed, possessed by a strange loneliness. She loved Jascha, she insisted to herself. She had loved him since childhood, when the two of them had played on the palace lawn.

But it wasn't Jascha's handsome face that came into her thoughts as she rose from her chair and went to stand looking out on the courtyard. It was Zachary Harmon's.

Just the memory made her furious. She had no business thinking about Zachary—he was nothing but a self-centered adventurer, afraid of commitment and responsibility. She'd never really cared for him.

The swift, secret sensations in Kristin's body gave the lie to that idea. Maybe the emotional attachment had ended, but she still felt a physical response every time he invaded her mind.

Mercifully, she reflected with a lift of her chin, that didn't happen often.

She turned from the glass door and surveyed the sumptuous bedroom that would be hers until after the wedding ceremony. There was a lovely gauzy white spread on the enormous teakwood bed, and rattan chairs with bright floral cushions were everywhere. In less than twenty-four hours Kristin would leave this room for Jascha's.

She sank her teeth into her lower lip as she went to a nearby table and picked up her camera. She wondered what kind of lover Jascha would be, then put the thought out of her mind. She would find that out soon enough.

After attaching the telephoto lens, Kristin carried her camera back to the terrace door, focused and began taking pictures of Jascha's troops drilling in the courtyard. "The photo-diary of a future princess," she muttered to herself.

Kristin was so involved in picture taking that she didn't hear the door of her room open, didn't know Jascha was there until he turned her gently to face him.

As always, she was struck by his imperial good looks. His exiled father was Asian, but his mother had come from India, and he had her round, dark eyes. He wore slacks, a jacket and a tailored shirt, putting on his uniform only for state occasions. He took the camera from her hands—a little impatiently, it seemed to Kristin—and set it aside.

"Do you wish to go back to the United States?" he asked, glancing over her shoulder at the troops she'd been capturing on film. "There could be war at any moment."

Kristin had some feelings she didn't want to explore just then, but she'd been well trained in the art of loyalty. She smiled, laid her hands on Jascha's broad shoulders and shook her head. The two of them had played together as children, fallen in love as teenagers, and later Jascha had persuaded his father to allow him to go to college in Massachusetts—the same one Kristin had attended. They'd dated steadily then.

Later, when Kristin had moved to California to work on an advanced degree and Jascha had returned home, they had written each other long, soul-searching letters.

Until Zachary came along, that is. Kristin had truly thought she was in love with him—it must have been the secret-agent mystique—and even moved into his apartment.

Kristin had crawled away from that relationship, emotionally speaking, not caring whether she lived or died. It had been Jascha who had made the difference; somehow he'd learned what had happened and he'd come to her. Twenty-four hours a day he'd pursued her, sending flowers and jewelry, whisking her off to other parts of the world in his private jet, promising he would never, ever hurt her.

In her vulnerable position, it had been easy to buy into the fantasy. Now, far from her friends and family, Kristin was beginning to come out of the daze induced by her breakup with Zachary, and she could no longer ignore her doubts.

Jascha bent his head and kissed her, lightly at first and then with increasing passion. Kristin waited to feel some kind of physical response, as she had in the old days, before Zachary, but nothing happened.

Still unwilling to face the growing suspicion that she'd made a disastrous mistake, Kristin marked her coolness down to prewedding jitters.

There was a certain sadness in Jascha's dark eyes as he drew back to look at her. The edge of his thumb grazed her cheek lightly as he muttered, "Kristin. My lovely, lovely Kristin. I am afraid for you. I should not have brought you here."

In the distance Kristin heard the ominous popping sound of gunshots, and the drilling of the troops went on. She forced herself to smile. "Whatever happens, Jascha, I want to be with you."

He bent to nibble at the side of her neck, and one of his hands lightly cupped her breast.

To her own surprise, as much as Jascha's, Kristin bolted backward out of his embrace.

Jascha was not without temperament, and his well-sculpted lips formed a royal pout. "You still think of him," he accused. "The man you lived with in California."

Kristin shook her head, acutely aware that he was right. "No. it's just that—it's just that I think we should wait. Until after our wedding."

He folded his strong arms and cocked his head to one side, and for the first time, Kristin knew he was considering forcing her. Although he had always been kind, she was well aware of Jascha's legendary temper.

"You want to keep yourself chaste," he said evenly. "Yet for twelve months you slept in Zachary Harmon's bed. Surely you see that we have a contradiction in terms here."

Kristin retreated another step. Jascha had never used this tone with her before; it had to be the stresses of his precarious political situation. "The time I spent with Zachary was a mistake," she answered evenly. "If I could go back and change it, I would."

Jascha advanced toward her, trapping her between himself and the bed. "You will find me a more than satisfactory lover," he said in a low voice, pulling the tails of her cotton shirt from her jeans.

Panic wrapped itself around Kristin like a lash, sudden and strange. Where once she had burned to give herself to this man, now she was frightened, even repulsed, by his touch. "Jascha, no," she whispered, crossing her forearms in front of her chest and struggling to stay upright.

He flung her onto the bed and held her wrists together high above her head. With his free hand, he began unbuttoning her shirt.

Kristin twisted, trying vainly to break away, filled with fear and rage. The warnings she'd heard from her parents and friends screamed in her mind. *He'll have absolute control over you—in his culture, women are property—you've only seen the Jascha he wanted you to see....*

Just as Jascha bared one of Kristin's breasts and closed his hand over it, the door of the bedroom opened and Mai entered, carrying tea. Although her eyes were downcast, as became a lowly servant in the presence of her prince, she obviously knew what was going on. And she wasn't about to leave.

Jascha muttered a curse and released Kristin, storming out of the room and slamming the door behind him.

Too mortified to meet Mai's gaze, Kristin sat up, righted her bra and buttoned her shirt. Because she didn't know what to say, she was silent.

Mai busied herself laying out the tiny bowls in which tea was served, along with the small sweet cakes she knew Kristin loved. "Weather is hot. Perhaps Miss Kristin like to bathe in swimming pool," she said, pretending nothing out of the ordinary had happened.

Kristin felt sick. Something was wrong with Jascha—terribly wrong. In all the years she'd known him, he'd never mistreated her in any way, though she had to admit he'd been damnably arrogant on occasion. Yet only moments before, he'd been bent on raping her. Ignoring the tea, she made for the telephone at her bedside.

"I'm in no mood to swim," she muttered, while silently cursing herself for every kind of romantic fool. She should have seen this coming. She should have known she'd only been trying to revive her old feelings for Jascha because she couldn't bear the pain of grieving for Zachary. "I want to call my father."

"Line's cut," Mai said succinctly.

Kristin felt the color drain out of her face as she lifted the ornate receiver and put it to her ear. Sure enough, there was no dial tone, only an ominous silence.

But Jascha had offered to send her home to the United States before he'd gotten so angry and thrown her onto the bed. She had to find him, tell him she'd changed her mind.

She strode to the door and wrenched it open, her rising ire lending her courage as she marched along the elegantly carpeted hallway, down the curving stairs that led to the great entryway with its glittering crystal chandeliers.

A guard was posted by the front door. "Where is the prince?" she demanded, heedless of her untucked shirt and mussed hair.

The guard's expression didn't change. "There," he said in Cabrizian, pointing toward the towering double doors of Jascha's study with the barrel of his rifle.

Kristin knocked briskly, then marched inside without waiting for an invitation. Jascha was in hushed conference with one of his generals, and his glowering expression said he did not appreciate the interruption.

"I've changed my mind about everything," Kristin announced. "The wedding is off. I want to go home right now."

For a moment she saw the old tenderness in Jascha's eyes, but then they turned hard as ebony. "It is too late," he bit out, while the general looked on unabashedly. "Go to your room, Kristin, and do not come out again until you are told."

Kristin's mouth fell open, and she stood rooted to the center of the study floor. She was twenty-seven years old, and she hadn't been sent to her room in two decades. She wasn't about to set a new precedent.

"Go!" Jascha said with a dismissive wave of one hand.

Instead, Kristin stepped closer to him. "What's happened to you?" she whispered. "Why are you behaving like this?"

"This is Cabriz, not America," Jascha pointed out. "Things are different here. Now, do as I say before I decide you must be disciplined."

"Disciplined?" Kristin's fury was so great that it rose

into her throat and swelled, making it impossible for any more words to pass.

Jascha was livid. He called out a word Kristin couldn't translate, and the guard from the entryway appeared. A rapid conversation passed between them, of which Kristin caught only a few words. Then the guard took her arm and dragged her roughly toward the door.

Kristin struggled, but it was no use. "Jascha!" she cried, in an angry plea for reason, as she was propelled out of the study and up the stairs.

Minutes later, Kristin was flung unceremoniously into a large room and the door was locked behind her.

Wildly, she looked around. The place was huge, and sumptuously furnished. The chairs and sofas were all upholstered in colorful silk, and heavy damask curtains surrounded the enormous bed, which stood on a dais. There was an ivory fireplace, even though the temperature in that part of Cabriz never dipped low enough for a fire, and a beautiful Louis XIV desk stood in front of the windows.

Kristin's anger reached ferocious proportions when she realized that this was Jascha's room, and she'd been sent here, like a mischievous concubine, to await the prince's convenience. She hurled herself at the giant door, hammering at it with both fists and screaming, "Let me out! Damn you, Jascha, *let me out!*"

After a while Kristin sagged against the wood, exhausted. It was hopeless; no one in the palace, not even Mai, would dare to flout Jascha's authority by releasing her. She was going to have to find her own means of escape.

She went to the terrace doors. For a moment Kristin had hope, but then she looked over the stone railing. It was at least a thirty-foot drop to the courtyard below, and there were no trees or trellises to climb down.

Momentarily defeated, she went back inside, out of the blazing midafternoon sun.

She searched the desk drawers for a key, but found nothing other than a stack of letters scented with some spicy perfume and written in Cabrizian. Although Kristin could understand the language if it was spoken slowly and clearly, she had never learned to read it.

Still, it didn't take a genius to figure out that the letters had been written by a woman. Feeling more a fool than ever, Kristin put the envelopes back where she'd found them and continued her exploration.

After an hour, when she'd found nothing that would aid in her escape and had exhausted herself emotionally, she collapsed in the middle of Jascha's enormous bed. She awakened sometime later to find herself surrounded by women, all veiled, all clad in the colorful, gauzy robes worn by Cabrizian females.

Mai was not among them.

"What the hell?" Kristin gasped, bolting upright and trying to scramble off the bed, but the women wouldn't let her pass. They gripped her arms and legs, and one of them clasped the back of her neck in strong fingers. She struggled, but there were too many of them, and they subdued her. "Who are you?" she cried. "What do you want?"

"Open mouth," one of them ordered. Gone were the gentle, subservient tones that had always been used with her before.

"Let go of me!" Kristin ordered. "Right now!"

When the women ignored her, she threw her head back and screamed Jascha's name.

Her right arm was wrenched behind her back and pulled painfully upward. The command was repeated.

Kristin had no choice but to obey. She parted her lips, and a bitter-tasting wine was poured onto her tongue. Not daring to spit it out, she swallowed convulsively. "Stupid," she muttered, addressing herself, coming face-to-face with a reality she'd refused to consider before. *"Stupid!"*

The women were stripping her clothes away, but when Kristin moved to fight them again, she found that her muscles had turned to rice pudding. She was helpless.

Her eyes filled with tears of frustration and fear. Jascha had lied, both to her and her family. These women were his wives.

She was raised from the bed and propelled into the prince's private bath, where an enormous tub of inlaid tiles waited, filled with steaming, scented water.

The women—she tried counting them, but could not think clearly—lowered her into the tub and, remarkably, began to bathe her. They surrounded her and their swift, firm hands were everywhere, soaping her arms and legs, lathering her hair.

After a while Kristin was lulled into a state of half consciousness. They lifted her from the tub and dried her as carefully as they'd bathed her, and then she was ushered back to the bed again.

She felt silken sheets against her bare back as they laid her down. Now, she thought dreamily, they would let her rest.

But they didn't. They began rubbing scented oil into her skin, covering her breasts, her stomach, her thighs. Something stirred in Kristin; she felt herself drifting through space, back to another time and another place.

"Zachary," she whispered with a soft smile.

Her skin was powdered, her hair dried and brushed. Kristin lost track of time and reality.

A familiar masculine voice disturbed her erotic dreams. "Okay, princess, wake up. We're going home."

Slowly, Kristin opened her eyes. For a moment she thought she was still sleeping, because Zachary's shadowed face was looming in the darkness, only inches from hers. "Zachary?"

"That's me," he replied, reaching under her and lifting her off the mattress. "It's a good thing they used powder after they greased you," he said, holding her up with one arm and pulling rough cotton trousers onto her with the other. "Otherwise you'd be slippery as hell and I'd probably drop you right on your hard little head. Not that it would make any real difference in your thinking processes...."

The effects of the drug the wives had forced on Kristin were just beginning to wear off, but she still felt woozy and very unsteady on her feet. She shook her head. "Zachary, is that really you?"

"It's really me, princess. And keep your voice down. If His Highness finds me in the royal boudoir, I'll be in for a rough three or four days in the dungeon."

He pulled a shirt over her head and forced her arms into the sleeves. Then she rested her cheek against his chest, yawning. "How did you find me?"

"That's a long story. We'll talk about it when we're at least fifty miles from this place." He caught a curved finger under her chin. "Maybe it's a good thing you're stoned out of your mind," he confided. "We're about to climb down over the terrace, and there's always a possibility one of the guards might wake up. Whatever you do, princess, hold on tight and keep that legendary mouth shut."

Before Kristin could lodge any kind of protest, Zachary hoisted her over one shoulder and headed toward the terrace doors. It was dark and the ebony sky was littered with stars. When she saw the stone railing approaching, Kristin squeezed her eyes shut and sucked in a breath.

"Now remember," Zachary told her in a rough undertone, *"be quiet."*

There was an awful jostling sensation, and Kristin caught hold of the back of Zachary's belt and hung on with all her strength. The fact that she'd been drugged did nothing to ease her fear when she opened her eyes and saw that they were descending a thin rope into the dark courtyard.

If she hadn't still been holding her breath, she would have screamed her lungs out.

Presently they reached the ground and Zachary set Kristin on her feet, where she teetered for a moment, to flip the grappling hook loose from the terrace railing and wind the rope around one hand. Kristin lifted her hand to her mouth to stifle another yawn. "You'll never believe what just happened to me in there—"

Even in the thin light of an autumn moon, Kristin saw the muscle tighten in his jaw. "I've got a pretty good idea," he responded. "Now, let's get out of here."

Once they'd gained the palace wall, Zachary flung the grappling hook over the top, then wrenched on the rope to make sure it was secure.

"Not again," Kristin protested.

"Get on my back," Zachary ordered impatiently. "And for God's sake, stop bitching. In case you haven't noticed, your ladyship, I'm doing all the damn work!"

Kristin put her arms around his neck and climbed onto him piggyback style. "Think of it as just recompense for all the times I had to carry out the garbage and wash your socks," she replied sweetly, her head clearing by the moment.

He started up the wall. "You never had to wash my socks," he retorted, his voice sounding choked.

Kristin loosened her grip slightly. "It was a metaphor," she whispered back.

"You know," he grunted in response, straining to pull them both up the rope, "the prince probably deserves you. Maybe I should take you back there and let them finish the ritual."

They'd reached the top of the wall, and Kristin could just barely make out the outline of a Jeep below.

"Jump," Zachary instructed her. "We're like ducks in a shooting gallery up here."

Kristin's heart hammered in her chest. "I'm not jumping!" she protested. "It must be ten feet to the ground!"

"Aim for the bushes," Zachary answered, and then his hand pressed into the small of her back and she went sailing off the wall. He landed in the shrubbery only a moment after she did.

She flew at him, hands flying, bones aching from a jarring touchdown.

He caught her wrists and stayed the attack, and his perfect teeth flashed in an acid grin as he looked down at her. "No time for gratitude, princess. It won't be long before they miss you."

Kristin started to say that she didn't want to go anywhere with him, but the memory of Jascha hurling her onto the bed stopped her. If Mai hadn't come in when she had, Prince Charming would have slapped her senseless and then raped her. Anything was better than a lifetime of that. "If we hurry," she said with a meekness she didn't feel, "we can get to the Canadian embassy before Jascha's servants sound the alarm. It's just around the corner."

Zachary thrust her into the Jeep and got behind the wheel. "There isn't any Canadian embassy," he answered as they drove quickly away from the palace wall. "Not anymore. Hold on to your pedigree, princess—we're leaving Cabriz the hard way."

CHAPTER TWO

ZACHARY WHEELED THE JEEP through dark, narrow streets Kristin didn't recognize. The city seemed strangely quiet. Empty.

"Where is everybody?" Kristin asked, raising her voice to be heard.

"Hiding. This is a military Jeep."

Kristin swallowed and brushed her tangled hair back from her face with both hands. "You mean, people think we're soldiers?"

"Probably."

Uneasily, Kristin ran her hands down her thighs. She was wearing the pajamalike garb of Cabrizian peasantry, male or female. "Where did you get it?"

"I stole it," he answered with exaggerated politeness. "Given your station in life, I tried to get an embassy limo with little flags on the hood, but they were all booked up—it must be prom night."

Kristin's temper rose steadily as they left the ancient city behind and started up a nearby mountain. As far as she could tell, there wasn't any road. She folded her arms across her breasts. "Still jealous of the advantages I've had," she replied. "Honestly, Zachary, envy doesn't become you."

The Jeep stopped with a jolt. "Let's get one thing straight, princess. Anybody who wanted your life—" he jabbed at his temple with an angry forefinger

"—would have to be one can short of a six-pack. And if you wouldn't mind, how about a little gratitude? I didn't have to take this job, you know!"

Kristin subsided, stung. She hadn't had a chance to prepare for this encounter with Zachary, and the pain was intense. "You didn't even ask if I wanted to leave," she observed in a more moderate tone of voice.

Zachary guided the intrepid little vehicle into even more inhospitable terrain. There were towering pine trees all around, and enormous boulders. "Well, excuse me," he replied dramatically. "I'll drop you off at the next corner!"

"Stop yelling," Kristin said with a sigh. Zachary hadn't changed in the year and a half since she'd seen him. He was still bristly and uncommunicative—the dedicated agent through and through. "We're going to be together for a few hours, so we might as well try to get along."

The Jeep came to another lurching stop, and Zachary turned to her, smiling in amazed amusement. "A few hours?"

"Sure. There's a helicopter hidden around here somewhere, isn't there?"

He gave a hoot of derisive laughter.

"What's funny?" Kristin demanded.

"You are. There isn't any helicopter, your ladyship. We're going to travel through the mountains on horseback. If we're lucky—*damn* lucky—we'll be over the border into Rhaos in five days."

Kristin gulped. For a moment she actually considered turning back, going through with the marriage to Jascha. Held up alongside the prospect of five days with Zachary Harmon, under the harshest of conditions, life in the palace didn't look so bad. "Oh," she said.

Zachary jammed the Jeep into gear, and they were

moving up the mountain again. When they'd traveled for what seemed like hours to Kristin, in relative silence, he finally brought the vehicle to a stop. In the glare the headlights she could see two horses, saddled and tethered by long ropes to a tree. Nearby were canvas packs.

When Zachary shut off the lights, everything disappeared for a moment. Kristin waited for her eyes to adjust to the moonlight, but her recalcitrant rescuer immediately got out of the Jeep and started moving around in the darkness.

"I don't see why we have to take horses," Kristin reasoned as she lowered herself delicately to the running board and then the ground, "when we have a perfectly good Jeep."

"There are some places," Zachary told her, untying one of the nickering, restless animals, "where only a horse can go." He handed her the reins, and Kristin stood there looking at him, shivering. She hadn't been in the saddle since she was five years old and staying with her mother's parents while Alice and Kenyan put the embassy in order. Her grandfather had taken her for a pony ride at the beach.

Without her having to say she was cold, Zachary brought a fleecy jacket from one of the packs and handed it to her, along with a pair of sturdy boots and heavy socks. Only then did she realize she'd been barefoot through the escape from the palace.

With a little shake of her head, Kristin dropped the reins and sat down on a nearby stump to put on the socks and boots. Between those clodhoppers and her ill-fitting, scratchy cotton pajamas, she'd be a sight.

Zachary snatched back the reins and held them impatiently while she prepared to travel.

"I have to go to the bathroom," she told him sheepishly. She'd never even been to camp, let alone roughed it in a foreign wilderness, and all those trees were giving her the willies.

"Pick a bush," Zachary responded.

Kristin started to protest, then stopped herself. It was clear enough that Zachary still thought she was a spoiled, immature little rich girl, and she wasn't going to give him the satisfaction of showing weakness. "Thank you," she said with dignity, rising to her feet and walking regally across the small clearing.

When she returned, Zachary was waiting to strap a pack on her back.

"What's in this thing?" She frowned as she tried to hoist herself into the saddle, pack and all. The horse sidestepped nervously, and the saddle tipped. The next thing she knew, Kristin was between the animal's legs, and it was prancing in a frantic effort to keep itself upright.

"You been gaining weight lately?" Zachary asked as he caught the horse by the bridle and then soothed it with a pat on the neck.

After scrambling back to her feet, and out of the way of the horse's hooves, Kristin glared at him. "I beg your pardon?"

He shrugged and then made a beckoning gesture. "Come on, I'll help you into the saddle."

Kristin was still insulted. "If you're sure you won't get a hernia from the effort," she replied stiffly.

He laughed. "It may be too late. After all, I just carried you down a rope and up the palace wall." With a sound meant to indicate Herculean effort he lifted her into the saddle, and she clung to the pommel with both hands, hoping he wouldn't see how afraid she was.

It didn't help that he swung into his own saddle as easily as a TV cowboy. "Relax, princess," he said, and it was the first kindly tone he'd used since he'd awakened her in the palace. "These animals are hardly more than plow horses. They're not going to hurt you."

Kristin lifted her chin. "I'm aware of that," she lied in a lofty tone of voice.

Zachary chuckled and shook his head, then spurred his horse toward a break in the trees. "Follow me, your ladyship."

Her lips moving in silent mimicry of his remark, Kristin gave her mount a nudge with one heel. "How did you know which room I'd be in back there?" she asked when about fifteen minutes had passed. Even though she didn't like Zachary—indeed, he was the last man in the world she would have wanted to rescue her—she was curious. Besides, five days was too long to keep quiet.

His broad shoulders stiffened in the bright moonlight. "That didn't take a genius—you were about to marry the guy. I looked up an old friend who used to work in the palace, and he sketched the floor plan for me."

Kristin was silent for a few moments, absorbing the fact that Zachary thought she'd been sleeping with Jascha. She didn't know why, but it hurt.

"I did get there before the wedding, didn't I?" he asked, glancing back at her.

Kristin sighed. "Yes. But I wouldn't have gotten married anyway—I'd already told Jascha the ceremony was off."

"I don't think he was convinced," Zachary replied.

She ducked to avoid a low-hanging branch, and her nostrils were filled with the sudden and paradoxical scent of Christmas. "Why not?"

"When I got there you were naked as hell, and you'd been powdered and perfumed for a night of pleasure, that's why."

Kristin blushed, remembering the strange, decadent sensuality of the experience. She'd grown up in Cabriz, but there were a great many things about its culture she didn't understand. After all, she'd always been very sheltered, living within the embassy walls, taking her schooling from a governess. She didn't speak.

Zachary looked back at her again, but the expression on his face was unreadable in the thin moonlight. "They were the Cabrizian equivalent of a harem, princess. It's their job, among other things, to prepare a new bride for their husband's enjoyment."

Kristin had already come to that conclusion, and she was ashamed of her naïveté in believing Jascha when he'd promised she'd be his only wife. "I know that, Zachary," she said quietly. "You can spare me the Cabrizian culture lesson."

He reined in his horse to ride beside her, even though the path was really too narrow. "If you knew, why the hell did you agree to marry the bastard?"

She sighed and ran one hand through her hopelessly tousled hair. "I didn't figure it out until tonight," she confessed, unable to meet Zachary's eyes. "Jascha promised—"

"Jascha promised," Zachary interrupted, and his voice conveyed such contempt that Kristin began to feel defensive.

"He was there for me when I needed him, Zachary," she said evenly.

Zachary glared at her for a moment and she saw the muscles in his throat work, then he rode ahead of her again.

Typical, Kristin thought. Whenever the conversation took a direction Zachary didn't like, he simply clammed up. In all the time they'd been together he'd never told her anything about his childhood or his family, if he had one. All she knew for sure about his past was that he'd never been married and that he'd joined the agency right after he left the air force.

"What if I hadn't wanted to leave Jascha?" she asked.

The path was broader there, but Zachary didn't wait so she could ride beside him. "I wouldn't have forced you," he replied quietly.

"Even though your orders were to bring me back no matter what?"

She saw the broad shoulders tighten under his battered leather coat. "I'm not here under anybody's orders," he answered.

"Not even Dad's?"

Zachary permitted himself a raspy chuckle. "Well, he did offer an opinion."

"I can imagine," Kristin replied ruefully. She and her father were certainly not close—she'd never, to her knowledge, done a single thing that pleased him—but she liked to think the man cared about her, at least a little.

The glimmer of the moon showed a rocky plateau up ahead, followed by another steep incline. "Why did you do it?" Zachary asked hoarsely. "Why did you come over here, when you knew the country was in an uproar? Did you love him that much?"

Kristin bit her lower lip, searching her mind for satisfactory answers. God knew, those were questions she'd asked herself often enough during the past few weeks as the fighting had grown worse and Cabriz's relations with other governments had collapsed. "A year ago, when Jascha and I started seeing each other again, in New York, things weren't so volatile over here. And there was the fairy-tale aspect of it all—we were on the covers of magazines, and Jascha sent flowers every day...." She

stopped and glanced at Zachary, trying to read his reaction in the set of his frame, but he gave her no sign of
his feelings. "I got swept up into the storybook-princess
element of the thing, and it wasn't until I came over here
that I began to have doubts."

For a long time the only sounds were those of night
creatures prowling the nearby woods and of the horses'
hooves on the stony ground. Then the question came
again.

"Did you love him?"

Kristin had been stalling, but she still wasn't prepared.
"I don't know, Zach."

He didn't reply, and they began the ascent up the side
of the mountain. Kristin felt as though the weight of her
backpack alone would pull her over the horse's rump and
onto the ground.

Finally they reached fairly level ground again. "Where
are we going to sleep tonight?" she asked, breathless from
the effort of holding on to the pommel of her saddle.

Zachary gave her a sour look. "The Ramada Inn," he
answered.

Kristin felt anger swell inside her, but she was too
tired, cold, hungry and frightened to give free rein to
it, so she just rode quietly until her temper had deflated
a little. "There's no need to be snide," she pointed out.

Holding the reins in one gloved hand, he bent in a
mocking bow. "I beg your pardon, your ladyship. I'll try
to keep a civil tongue in my head from now on."

Tears pressed behind Kristin's eyes and clogged her
sinuses, but she held them back. "I haven't had my dinner, you know," she said, keeping her chin high.

Zachary produced something from the pocket of his
leather jacket and shoved it at her.

She took the item from him with trembling fingers.

It was a candy bar—her favorite combination of chocolate and coconut—and though it was a little squished,
it looked like a feast to Kristin. She thanked him, unwrapped it with awkward haste and indulged in a bite.

"Want some?" She felt duty bound to offer, though
she hoped Zachary would decline.

He shook his head. "No, thanks. I'll have something
when we stop for the night."

So they *were* stopping. Kristin was relieved to hear
that. "Umm," she said, enjoying her candy bar.

Zachary spared her a grin. "Did you think I'd forgotten what you like?"

Her throat constricted with unwanted emotion. It was
just like him to remind her of old times, when they'd
lived together. He'd left her favorite candy on her pillow in those days, or tucked it into her pocket, or hid it
in her camera case.

She blinked several times and swallowed hard. "I
doubt if you've given me a thought since the day I moved
out of your apartment," she said evenly.

They were moving into the trees again, and Zachary rode ahead, forcing Kristin and her horse to fall in
behind. He spoke in a terse voice. "Then you're wrong.
I've thought about wringing your neck a million times."

Kristin sighed. Despite the jacket Zachary had bundled her into, she was cold, and the candy bar had only
taken the edge off her appetite. Worse, she was beginning to consider the reprisals Jascha might use if they
were caught. "If you hate me so much, why did you come
into Cabriz to get me?"

He didn't look back. "Because I get a kick out of
sneaking into countries with names that sound like a
line of sportswear," he answered tartly.

"Jascha will kill you if he catches us."

"You'd better pray he doesn't, princess. He's probably not real fond of you right now, either."

Kristin remembered the look on Jascha's face when he'd been about to force himself on her, and she shuddered. "I don't know what's come over him lately. He was always so sweet, and so gentle."

Zachary's tone was wry. "Little things like the overthrow of a throne tend to upset a guy."

Kristin's weary mind had gone on to other possibilities. "What will they do to Jascha—the rebels—if they do overrun the palace?"

He waited a long time to answer, and when he spoke his voice was gruff with reluctance. "They'll kill him, princess."

The grief that surged through Kristin shouldn't have come as a surprise, but it did. Jascha had been her friend, if not her lover, for a very long time. After she'd lost Zachary, the prince had dried her tears and listened patiently while she tried to work out the things that had gone wrong.

Her shoulders hunched under the heavy load of the backpack and tears trickled down her cheeks.

Zachary must have known she was weeping—try as she might, she couldn't seem to cry quietly—but he didn't make any comments. He did take the reins from her and lead her horse behind his.

By the time he brought both horses to a halt in the shelter of a small circle of trees, Kristin had recovered some of her dignity.

She felt abject relief when Zachary reached out, still mounted on his horse, to unfasten and remove her backpack. "I can hardly wait till we get the fire built," she said with a sigh, summoning up a tremulous smile.

He swung down from the saddle, carrying her backpack, and tossed it into the leaves that covered the ground. "No fire tonight, your ladyship," he answered in clipped tones. "We're still too close to Kiri, and there are probably patrols out looking for us right now."

Kristin shivered and glanced around at the woods. They looked eerie in the silver glow of the stars and moon. "Do you really think so? It would make better sense if they started out in the morning."

He shrugged out of his backpack and set it down beside hers. "Right. And if we just follow the yellow brick road, we'll be home in Kansas by morning and Auntie Em will bake us an apple pie."

It was a struggle, but Kristin managed not to lose her composure. She watched as Zachary took the reins of both horses and started off toward the woods, and when it was clear he wasn't going to apologize for patronizing her, she stormed after him.

"Why do you always do that?" she demanded.

"Do what?" Zachary retorted, all innocence. A stream flowed a few yards ahead, shining like a silver ribbon in the night.

"Why do you always make me out to be so damn naive? I happen to have a degree in journalism, you know, and I've been all over the world on professional assignments!"

While the horses drank, Zachary turned to Kristin, his nose less than an inch from hers. "Some assignments— you took pictures of embassy parties and wrote cutesy articles to go along with them. And as for *this* little adventure, you came halfway around the globe to marry a prince who already has half a dozen wives, in a country that's been teetering on the edge of disaster for ten years, and then you have the gall to stand there and ask me why I think you're naive?"

Kristin stepped back, stung, and would have fallen if Zachary hadn't been so quick to reach out and steady her. She blinked, unable to refute the charge that her job with *Savoir Faire* had amounted to little more than writing the occasional society column. "I didn't know about the wives."

Zachary let her go. "In fifteen minutes," he said, "you'll have convinced yourself there were never any wives. Well, you have it your way, your ladyship. You've always arranged the world to suit your perceptions, anyhow. Why should this be any different?"

"You're being cruel, Zachary. I'm not trying to deny that I made a mistake."

"*A* mistake? Sweetheart, you've made a dozen. Why did you think all those women were hanging around? Did you have them pegged as members of the palace sewing circle?"

Kristin's eyes brimmed with tears and she whirled to walk away, but Zachary reached out and caught hold of her arm, turning her back to face him with surprising gentleness.

"Kristin, I'm sorry," he said softly. Unwillingly.

Kristin bit down hard on her lower lip.

Zachary touched her cheek, brushed away a tear with the edge of his thumb. "Don't cry, princess."

When Kristin didn't respond, he released her and turned back to the horses. She walked a little way upstream and knelt down to splash clear, icy water onto her face.

It restored her a little, and when she joined Zachary in the clearing she was almost her old self. He tied the horses where they could graze, then knelt beside her and took a bedroll from her backpack.

"It's going to get cold tonight," he said as he zipped his sleeping bag and Kristin's together.

Kristin's eyes widened. "You mean we're sleeping in the same bag?"

Zachary gave her one of his impatient looks. "It's not like we've never shared a bed," he pointed out.

Kristin's mind filled with sweet, fiery and completely unwanted memories at the prospect. "But we're not—we were involved then."

"Relax, your ladyship. I don't intend to touch you."

Chilled, not only by the night wind but by the timbre of Zachary's voice, Kristin shivered. "I'm hungry," she said.

He reached for one of the backpacks again. "I'll get you something. Take your clothes off and get into the sleeping bag."

Kristin had been unlacing one of her clunky hiking boots, but she stopped cold. "You expect me to strip? In your dreams, Zachary Harmon."

Holding a package of something in one hand, he turned his broad and singularly imperious back. "Get undressed," he reiterated. "If you don't, your clothes will draw moisture and you'll end up with pneumonia."

Kristin studied his back, trying to decide whether he was telling the truth or not. "If you're lying to me—"

He turned to face her, tossed the small package into her lap and took off his hat. The moonlight shimmered in his rumpled brown hair. "I've never lied to you in my life," he said. And he unzipped his jacket and laid it aside, then pulled his shirt out of his jeans and began to unbutton it.

Kristin's cheeks felt as though they'd caught fire, and she dropped her eyes. "All right," she said. "I'll take off my clothes. But you have to look the other way until I tell you it's okay."

He turned away in a leisurely fashion, and Kristin heard a slight clinking sound as he unfastened his belt buckle. "Were you this shy with the prince?"

Kristin wasn't about to dignify *that* question with an answer. She took off her hiking boots and socks, then the odd, rough-spun pajamas. Beneath them she was naked, and she practically dived into the double sleeping bag, pulling the top up to her chin and huddling as far as she could to one side.

She squeezed her eyes tightly shut when Zachary slid into the bag beside her, but she could feel the heat of his body, and she was awash in memories of other nights.

"I thought you were hungry," Zachary remarked.

She opened her eyes and felt around on top of the sleeping bag for the packet he'd given her earlier. "I am," she said. The stars seemed to crowd around the moon, determined to outshine it.

Instead of the packet she found rock-hard thigh, which she released instantly.

Zachary laughed. "Here," he said, dangling the packet in front of her face.

Kristin snatched it out of his hand and sat up so rapidly that the sleeping bag nearly slipped down to reveal her bare breasts. She held on to her virtue with one hand and used her teeth to tear open the little bag.

Inside were roasted peanuts, and Kristin gobbled them down, thinking sadly of the spicy, scrumptious meals that were served at the palace.

When she was finished she lay down again. "I wish I could floss."

"Thank you for sharing that," Zachary replied in a sleepy voice.

She resisted a fundamental urge to nestle close to him, not for love but for protection. Her voice was small. "Zachary?"

"Hmm?"

"Are there wild animals in the woods?"

"Umm-hmm."

"Suppose they come after us? I mean, since we don't have a fire or anything—"

Zachary yawned. "Between the two of us, princess, we ought to be able fend off a squirrel attack. Now quit talking and go to sleep—tomorrow's going to be a hard day."

Kristin wriggled farther inside the bag. It was made of some kind of space-age material; although it was thin and light, she was perfectly warm. The ground was a little hard, though. "What do you suppose Jascha's doing right now?"

"Planning our executions. *Go to sleep,* Kristin."

She closed her eyes, but sleep was elusive. Every sound in the woods seemed to be magnified. "I left my camera at the palace," she said with real despair.

Zachary rolled onto his side, turning his back to her. She saw the familiar mole between his shoulder blades and barely resisted the urge to touch it with the tip of one finger.

"Next time I carry you out of a prince's bedroom," he said between yawns, "I'll give you a chance to pack a few things first."

The urge to touch Zachary's mole was replaced by one to give him a kidney punch. "I had taken some very important pictures," she told him, struggling to keep her voice even.

His reply was a theatrical snore.

Kristin rolled onto her stomach in a vain effort to get comfortable, and burrowed down deep into the bag. She fully intended to cry, feeling she had every right after the day she'd put in, but she was too tired. In five seconds she was asleep.

She awakened hours later, in the depths of the night, to find herself cuddled close to Zachary, enfolded in his strong arms. For just a few moments she thought she was back in their apartment, that their breakup had never taken place.

She sighed softly and ran one hand along his muscular thigh; he stirred in his sleep and spread one hand over her bottom, fitting her against him. The size and power of him jolted her back to reality and she jerked away, reaching blindly for her clothes, ready to spend the night sitting bolt upright if it came to that.

But Zachary caught hold of her wrist and stayed her efforts. "You're not going anywhere," he said clearly.

Kristin knew she couldn't fight him; her strength didn't begin to compare with his. If he were to imprison her under his weight and take her, there wouldn't be a thing she could do to stop him.

She was horrified when a thrill of pure lust moved through her, leaving her to shudder in its wake. The words came out of her mouth before she could stop them. "Make love to me, Zachary."

His reply was like a slap in the face. "Not in a million years, princess. I don't travel in your social circles."

Kristin didn't know who she hated more—Zachary for cutting her to emotional ribbons or herself for inviting the intolerable, crushing pain of his rejection. To make her humiliation complete, she began to cry.

"Oh, damn," she sobbed miserably. *"Damn!"*

To her utter surprise, Zachary took her into his arms and held her close. "Go ahead and cry," he said raggedly, his lips moving against her temple. "If anybody's earned the right, it's you."

"I'm not crying because you wouldn't make love to me!" Kristin wailed, clinging to her pride even in the depths of indignity. "Don't you dare think that I am!"

He chuckled and laid a light kiss on her hair. "Whatever you say, princess."

She cried until her grief was spent, her head resting on Zachary's shoulder. Then she hiccuped. "Is there somebody—are you—?"

"No," Zachary answered. "I'm not involved with any particular woman." He patted her bare bottom lightly.

She swallowed. She didn't know why it was important to tell Zachary, but it was. "I never slept with Jascha," she said softly. "In fact, there was never anybody but you."

He didn't reply, and Kristin couldn't decide whether he didn't believe her or he'd fallen asleep again. And she was afraid to find out.

Pure exhaustion rendered her unconscious in the next few moments, and she awakened, hours later, to find herself alone in the sleeping bag. Zachary was up and dressed, and he tossed her another packet the moment she sat up.

"Here's your breakfast," he said cheerfully.

Kristin looked at the packaged food with a baleful expression. "What is it?"

"Dried fruit. Keep your chin up, princess. Tonight we sleep in a cabin, with a real fire on the hearth." He threw Kristin her clothes and calmly led the horses toward the stream.

CHAPTER THREE

KRISTIN HELD ON grimly as her horse plodded along behind Zachary's, scaling hillsides so steep that only scrub brush grew there. She would have given her passport for a cup of hot coffee and a powdered sugar doughnut. If she'd still *had* her passport—it was back at the palace, with her camera and journal and other personal possessions.

She tilted her head back, saw that the sky had turned the color of charcoal.

"Aren't we sort of out in the open?" she called after Zachary, mainly to make conversation. She was much too tired to be alarmed.

"Yes," he answered, "so hurry it up."

Resentment simmered in Kristin's cheeks as she spurred the panting horse. After all, *she* hadn't been the one to pick this route. If it had been up to her, they would have left the country in an airliner, or a helicopter at the very least. Before she could frame a retort, however, a blood-freezing *ping* rang in the air.

Zachary yelled something, and Kristin's horse took off at a breakneck pace with no urging from her. She very nearly fell off, and in her mind she saw herself rolling end over end down the slope, backpack and all.

They gained a grassy plateau, with trees, and once he was certain Kristin was safe Zachary leaped off his horse and crept back to the edge of the slope with a formidable pistol grasped in one hand.

"Who are they?" Kristin asked, crawling up beside him as she'd seen soldiers and cowboys do in movies.

Zachary's eyes were narrowed as he surveyed the apparently empty countryside. "Rebels," he speculated with a shrug of one shoulder, "or maybe bandits."

Kristin shivered. "You mean we have to worry about crooks, besides rebels and Jascha's soldiers?"

"Stay back," he growled, still scanning the wooded area at the base of the steep incline they'd just climbed.

"You didn't answer my question."

"Excuse me," was the brusque response as he checked the chamber of the pistol and then produced more bullets from his jacket pocket and thrust them into place with a practiced thumb, "but I'm a little busy at the moment. Maybe we could chat later."

Kristin was about to accuse him of being ridiculous when a second bullet struck the ground not half a dozen feet from where they lay. She scooted closer to Zachary. "I'm scared," she whispered.

"Smart girl," Zachary answered, drawing a bead on something at the edge of the woods. "The good news is, these guys are either lousy shots or they don't want to hit us. We were vulnerable as ducks in a rain barrel while we were climbing the hillside."

Just as Kristin was about to comment, he squeezed the trigger, and the explosion seemed deafening. She covered her ears with both hands and moved closer still to Zachary's side. "Did you hit anything?" she asked, peering toward the trees.

"Probably not. I just want them to know we're prepared to fight back—sometimes that's enough."

"Don't you have binoculars or something?" Kristin queried, watching Zachary squint. She wished she had her camera.

"That would be a great idea, princess," he answered with a long-suffering sigh. "Then they could pinpoint us by the reflection off the glass and blow us to little quivering pieces."

Kristin shuddered. "You don't need to be so graphic."

"Start moving backward, toward the horses," Zachary ordered. "And don't stick that sweet little rear end of yours up in the air. You're liable to get it shot off if you do."

She obeyed, but only because it was a matter of life and death. "I suppose this means we can't have a fire at lunchtime," she lamented as she wriggled along the ground like an earthworm in reverse.

"It means we may not *live* till lunchtime," Zachary replied.

When they were a good thirty feet away from the edge, he rose to a crouching position, one hand splayed on Kristin's back to keep her down. When no shots were fired, he released her.

"Stay as low as you can until you get to the trees," he said.

Kristin was trembling, but she did as she was told. Her clothes were covered with dirt now, and her hair was all atangle around her face. She thought with yearning of her makeup case, and her toothbrush, and a big bathtub filled with steaming, scented water.

Only moments had passed when they mounted their skittish horses, but they seemed like hours to Kristin.

"Ride ahead," Zachary told her.

She knew he was protecting her, but it was little comfort. Surely there were easier, safer ways out of the country. "Are they gone?" she asked. "The people who were shooting at us, I mean?"

"Probably," Zachary answered. But he was obviously on the alert.

At noon they stopped by a stream to water the horses and rest. Zachary produced two more packets of food, this time little pieces of dried meat.

Kristin sat on a log and gobbled down her share, too hungry to complain. "Do they have McDonald's in Rhaos?" she asked as Zachary, having finished his meal, rummaged through his backpack.

He chuckled. "Not yet," he answered. "But I'm sure they're working on it." To her wonder and delight he brought out a new toothbrush, still in its box, and a little travel-size tube of toothpaste.

Kristin accepted them eagerly. "I don't suppose you have soap?" she asked in a hopeful voice, kneeling by the clean stream, taking the brush from its package and dipping the bristles in the water.

He grinned. "It just so happens that I do. But you won't need it until later."

Kristin was too busy brushing her teeth to comment. It felt glorious to have her mouth clean and fresh again. When she was finished, she put the toothbrush carefully back into its box and tucked it, along with the tube of paste, into the pocket of her jacket.

"Do you think those guys are still following us?" she asked.

Zachary shrugged. "I don't know. They may have decided we weren't worth the trouble."

"So they probably weren't soldiers."

He shook his head. "No. Soldiers would have surrounded us—probably without firing a shot."

Kristin shook off the horrifying thought. "How do you know they're not going to do that, in an hour, or this afternoon, or tomorrow?"

"I don't," was the blunt reply.

When the horses had rested, eaten a little of the lush grass growing along the stream bank and had their fill of water, Zachary helped Kristin back into the saddle and they set out again. The two of them rode side by side, keeping to the edges of meadows and clearings. Thankfully, they didn't encounter another hillside, but Kristin knew it was only a matter of time.

"I think it's remarkable," she said once in an effort to start some kind of civil interchange with Zachary, "that this part of the country is forested, while the southern section is practically all jungle."

"It's a weird place," Zachary allowed, not so much as glancing in her direction. His eyes moved constantly in this direction and that, like those of a Secret Service agent protecting a high government official.

Not that Kristin thought he had any particular regard for her. He was just doing his job, that was all.

Near nightfall they came to a little hut nestled into the crook of a canyon. The place looked uninhabited, but there was wood piled along one tilting outside wall, and a crooked chimney jutted from the warped roof.

"How did you know about this place?" Kristin asked, getting down from the horse on her own even though she nearly stumbled under the weight of the backpack while doing it.

With a self-confident grin, Zachary unfastened her pack and lifted it away, setting her free. He was standing close, and Kristin felt as though her insides had suddenly been magnetized to his. Her mind gave the command to retreat, but her legs didn't move. She simply stood there, looking up at Zachary and remembering all the times he'd turned her inside out, whether in bed or elsewhere.

He removed his own pack and tossed it aside, his

wicked hazel eyes never leaving her face. There was an insolent confidence in his expression but, for the life of her, Kristin could neither move nor speak to thwart him. The old feelings had all come back in force, and it was as though no time at all had passed, as though no wounds had been dealt.

She knew that if he took her then and there, she wouldn't have the strength to object.

It seemed the entire world had shifted to slow motion, with only Kristin's rebellious heart beating a speedy rhythm. Zachary's hands cupped the sides of her face, his thumbs moving gently over her skin. Then he lifted her chin.

She saw his mouth descending toward hers and gave a little whimper, but that was all the protest she could manage. Perhaps, she thought wildly, it had not been a protest at all, but eager submission.

Every subtle injury he'd done her was healed in those moments, at least temporarily, and Kristin would have given her soul to be part of him again.

Everything within Kristin focused on the sensation of his lips touching hers. She felt as if she were standing in a mud puddle, gripping an electric fence with both hands.

His tongue caressed, then parted her lips and boldly explored. Heat surged through her, and her clothes might have been aflame, she was so warm. Her hands ached to tear them off.

He lifted her, without breaking the kiss, and her legs automatically wrapped around his hips, clutching him tightly. This, too, was a part of the familiar pattern between them, one that could have stretched back over other lifetimes besides this one. She could feel the hard promise of his masculinity at the crux of her thighs.

Kristin was trembling when, without warning, Zachary tore his mouth from hers and set her roughly on her feet.

For a moment she was too dazed to react. She just stood there, bewildered, using all her energy to keep from swaying to one side. And when she did manage to speak, all that came out was one word. "Why—?"

He turned away. "I'll take care of the horses," he said, and then he caught hold of both sets of reins and strode off through a copse of trees, leaving Kristin to stare after him in confusion and hurt.

Automatically, her hands rose to her tangled hair. She probably looked a fright, but that didn't explain why Zachary had rebuffed her. She'd felt his passion, burning hot enough to fuse with her own.

Not quite bold enough to brave the hut alone—it looked like the kind of place that would be filled with rats and spiders—Kristin busied herself with her pack instead. Searching through it she found, to her enormous relief, a sturdy comb, the promised soap and another set of clothes, besides packaged food, matches, her sleeping bag and a few first aid supplies.

By the time Zachary returned with the horses, she'd brought her wounded pride under control. She even managed to smile at him as though nothing had happened.

"I guess we're going inside now," she said cheerfully after he'd unsaddled the horses and tied them to separate stakes driven into the ground.

Zachary brushed off his hat and scratched his forehead. His rich brown hair was rumpled and damp with sweat; he needed a bath as badly as Kristin did. "You might have started the fire."

Kristin sighed. "The only fire I've ever started was with those little logs from the supermarket," she reminded him patiently.

There was a distinct chill in the air, since night was approaching, but Zachary's grin warmed her a little. "You're doing all right for a princess," he conceded, picking up her pack and striding toward the door of the hut.

The compliment was strangely sweet, and it found a hiding place in Kristin's heart. "Thanks," she answered, sounding as if she had a frog in her throat.

It was fairly dark inside the hut, since there were no windows to speak of, but Kristin could see cobwebs swaying in the shadows like ghosts, and she had to force herself not to turn and run outside. She wanted to be worthy of the sparse but sincere praise Zachary had given her.

She heard the strike of a match, and then a lone, flickering kerosene lamp lent the place a sickly glow. Suppressing a shudder, Kristin looked around until she spotted a crude homemade broom.

Grabbing it by the handle, she began sweeping down the cobwebs. Darkness still hovered around the ceiling and floor, and Kristin heard tiny clawed feet skittering everywhere. A scream of pure horror rose in her throat when something brushed against her ankle in passing, but she swallowed the cry.

Zachary went outside and returned moments later with an armload of wood, which he dropped in front of a small, strange-looking stove.

"There are probably things living in there," Kristin observed on her way to the door to shake out the make-shift broom.

The door of the stove creaked ominously as Zachary opened it. "They've moved to a better neighborhood," he responded. For a few moments his hands worked mysteriously with the wood, and then a cheerful fire leaped to life.

Kristin felt better immediately. In the temporary illumination, before Zachary closed the stove door, she spotted candles on a rude shelf and appropriated them. Soon after, the place was much more brightly lit.

Unfortunately, that only showed up its many shortcomings.

There was no bed, no sink, no toilet, and there were no tables or chairs. The kerosene lamp sat on an upturned crate marked with Chinese letters.

In one corner a pile of skins, probably crawling with lice and littered with rat leavings, provided the only place to lie down. The floor itself, Kristin could clearly see, was even dirtier, despite the sweeping she'd given it.

"Everything will be all right, princess," Zachary said gently, and she was embarrassed to realize he'd been watching her, reading her cowardice in her face. "I promise."

Kristin hugged herself and ran her tongue quickly over her lips. "I have to go to the bathroom," she said.

"It's out back," Zachary replied, taking cans and small cooking implements from his pack. His gaze was averted now. "Take the broom—you'll probably meet some wild-life."

After drawing a deep breath and ordering herself to have courage, Kristin snatched up the only weapon available to her and marched around back to find a crude privy. The structure was made of very old wood, and it leaned distinctly to the left.

Kristin opened the door and flailed around inside with the broom until she was satisfied that no spider-filled cobwebs would drop onto her head. Something small ran between her feet at the last second, and she screamed.

Zachary was there immediately, but the look in his eyes made her wish she'd encountered a bandit or one of Jascha's soldiers instead of a rat or squirrel. He handed her the flashlight and walked away, and she inspected the inside of the privy thoroughly before stepping in and closing the door.

When she returned to the hut, Zachary was heating water on the stove, along with two tin cans.

Kristin had been to the nearby stream, thanks to Zachary's flashlight, where she had washed her face and hands as best she could. "What's for supper?" she asked.

"Stew," he replied, gesturing toward the pile of skins, which he'd covered with a blanket. "Sit down."

Even before she obeyed, Kristin could feel things crawling on her. "I don't like this place," she said. "Couldn't we just sleep outside?"

"We could," Zachary replied, handing her one of the cans of stew and a spoon. "But it's going to rain like hell tonight, so it wouldn't be very comfortable."

Kristin tried not to think about the things that might be living in the skins beneath the blanket. The stew, at least, was surprisingly good. "Whose place is this?"

Zachary shrugged. "It's been empty as long as I can remember," he answered, taking a place beside her on the blanket and beginning to eat from his own can of stew.

"So you've been here before."

He nodded.

Because she was tired, and dirty, and her hair was a mess, because she'd wanted Zachary so desperately and he'd rebuffed her, Kristin felt a bit testy. "Did it ever occur to you that if you know the place is here, the bandits and rebels probably do, too?"

Zachary's spoon was poised between his mouth and the stew. "Yes," he answered patiently, "it did. But when the sky opens up and dumps the contents of your average reservoir on the countryside tonight, they're going to be holed up somewhere, not out looking for us."

With some difficulty, Kristin got to her feet. Still eating from the can of stew, she made her way to the door, opened it and looked out. Sure enough, there was no sign of the stars and the moon, and the sky was frighteningly dark. Even as she looked up at it, lightning snaked across it like a crack in black glass and the earth shook with the power of the thunder.

Kristin forced the door shut against a sudden and angry wind and turned, with what dignity she could manage, to face Zachary. "It's inhumane to leave those poor horses outside in the storm."

Zachary didn't even stop eating. In fact, he went so far as to talk with his mouth full. "They're in a lean-to."

Again, the very air vibrated with thunder, and particles of dirt sifted down from the roof of the hut. Zachary automatically shielded his can of stew with one hand, but Kristin set hers aside with a thump, all appetite gone.

"This is some rescue," she fretted.

Zachary glared at her. "Don't start," he warned. "Coming here and going through all this just to get your backside out of trouble wasn't high on my priority list, either."

"What was?"

He was chewing. "Wine, women and song."

Kristin was unaccountably stung, and she turned away to hide her feelings. "I need a bath," she announced, just to be saying something.

"Tough," Zachary replied.

She looked around until she found an old wooden bowl that might serve as a basin. Using a little of the water heating on the stove and the sleeve of her shirt, she wiped it out. Then she rummaged through her pack until she found the soap.

"If you wouldn't mind stepping outside—"

Another blast of thunder made the walls of the hut

shimmy, and torrential rain battered at the thin roof. "I'm not going anywhere," Zachary replied.

Having set her heart on a bath, Kristin couldn't bear not to have one. She might not get another chance for days.

"Zachary, please."

"I'll turn my back," he conceded, finishing the stew and tossing the can into a corner, where it rattled against other cans from other visits, now rusted.

"I don't trust you."

"You'd better start. Your life depends on it." He grinned and opened his pack, taking out soap and a real washcloth. "All right, you win. I'll just step outside and have a shower. Either you're finished by the time I'm through or you're not. It doesn't make any difference to me."

"Just don't come back in here before I'm dressed."

He arched both eyebrows, one hand on the wooden latch that served as a doorknob. "And if I do?"

"I'll report your behavior to your superiors," Kristin replied out of pure bravado.

Zachary laughed and began removing his clothes, tossing them past her onto the blanket-covered skins. Kristin watched him for a few moments as though mesmerized, then, realizing he'd soon be naked, whirled away.

He laughed again and went outside, into the pounding rain.

Kristin practically ripped off her clothes. Then she poured hot water from the kettle on the stove into the wooden basin and hastily bathed herself from head to foot. She washed her hair, too, and was purloining a T-shirt from Zachary's pack when she felt a rush of cold, moist air.

Her nipples puckered, not just because of the chill but

because she knew Zachary was looking at her. Goose pimples raced over her skin, fast as wildfire.

She wrenched the drab olive T-shirt on over her head and turned to look at him, only to find that he was magnificently naked. She swallowed and, with a great effort of will, turned her head.

"You might have knocked."

"And you might have asked if you could use that T-shirt," Zachary replied philosophically, "so we're even."

She saw the flash of his skin as he bent to take another T-shirt and a pair of shorts from his pack. Kristin noted with despair that they weren't boxer shorts, but the kind that fitted close to his form.

She squeezed her eyes shut.

The next thing she knew, Zachary was zipping the sleeping bags together again and laying them out on the skins. She was only too aware of his tanned, soap-scented skin. It would be cool from a shower in the rain....

"I don't suppose you brought along a deck of cards or anything," she said in a desperate effort to put off lying down beside Zachary, stretching out. Remembering the kiss he'd given her when they arrived, she felt her blood heat and knew she wouldn't be able to trust herself once he'd zipped that bag around them.

He grinned and brought a worn deck from his pack.

"What else do you have in there?" Kristin asked.

"I would have thought you'd know, since you felt free to help yourself to my T-shirt," Zachary responded. Deftly, he shuffled the cards. "I could insist that you give it back, you know."

The shirt carried his scent, even though it was freshly laundered, and Kristin wanted to keep it next to her skin. "I'm too much of a lady to give it to you," she answered evenly, "and you're too much of a gentleman to take it by force."

He sat cross-legged on top of the double sleeping bag, and his chuckle was an evil rasp. "Is that what you think? You *are* naive."

Biting her lower lip, Kristin joined him, carefully arranging the hem of the T-shirt when she crossed her legs. "What's your pleasure?" she asked, referring to the card game.

"Don't ask," Zachary responded, and his eyes moved lazily from her lips to the swell of her breasts to the part of her she most hoped was hidden by the T-shirt.

Kristin flushed. "Stop being such a bastard and tell me what we're playing."

"Strip rummy," Zachary answered, beginning to deal the cards.

Kristin's heart hammered with an emotion that was not entirely made up of dread. There were, if she was to be honest, threads of pleasure woven in, too. That spell that had possessed her earlier was still very much in evidence. "I've never heard of that," she said quietly.

"Every time you lose a hand," Zachary replied knowledgeably, "you have to take off an item of clothing. In your case, it means living on the edge."

Kristin picked up her cards, arranged them, and threw them down again. "I demand a redeal. You cheated."

Using just one hand, he ferreted a flask from a pocket in his canvas backpack. "Now, now, your highness," he scolded, unscrewing the lid of the flask with his teeth. "Don't be a stick-in-the-mud. Sometimes you just have to play the hand you're dealt."

"Okay," Kristin answered, laying out her cards on top of the sleeping bag. "Gin."

Zachary looked at the perfect hand of cards and pulled off his T-shirt, revealing his broad, hairy chest.

Kristin's eyes strayed to the odd little scar beneath his right nipple, the one he'd always refused to explain, then she lifted her gaze to his face. He looked insufferably pleased with himself. "This time I deal," she said, reaching for the cards. She was all too aware that Zachary was wearing nothing now but a pair of skimpy briefs. "Where do you buy your underwear?" she demanded, to let him know she wasn't moved. "In adult bookstores?"

Zachary ignored her sarcasm and offered the flask, which she refused with a shake of her head. He picked up the cards she'd dealt him and arranged them as though the fate of the free world depended on their order. Then, a slow, insufferable grin spread across his face.

"I don't want to play anymore," Kristin announced, flinging down her hand and scrambling into the sleeping bag. By controlling her thoughts, she reasoned, she would be able to forget the filthy skins beneath, and all the things that had probably nested on them.

"Chicken," Zachary responded, pulling his T-shirt back on. He went to the table and blew out the candles and the kerosene lamp, then returned to the makeshift bed by the beam of his flashlight. "You were afraid you'd lose, weren't you?"

"Or win," Kristin answered quite honestly.

He switched off the flashlight and climbed into bed beside her, and the storm outside seemed to shake the very core of the earth. With an exaggerated yawn, he settled in to sleep.

Kristin was afraid to think of what might be outside, sneaking toward them through the storm, and she'd already ruled out contemplation of the things that might be under them. Her mind drifted, as she tried to keep

her distance from Zachary, back to another night, when
she'd known terror of another kind.

Zachary had been away on one of his mysterious missions when sudden, violent pains had grasped Kristin's
insides and wrung a strangled shriek from her throat....

The baby, she'd thought in desperation. Something
was wrong with the baby she and Zachary had barely
conceived, hadn't even really talked about. Something
was terribly wrong.

Stumbling to the phone, doubled over in agony, Kristin had called the paramedics, and they'd arrived in re-
cord time—but not soon enough to save the child. She'd
lost it on the way to the hospital.

Her doctor had admitted her for a D and C and a night
of rest, and the next day Kristin had gone home in a daze
of disappointment and grief. Reassuring herself there
would be other babies didn't help.

She'd been lying in their bed, alone and sick, when
Zachary called. She couldn't tell him the child was gone;
that would mean letting go, and she wasn't ready.

But he'd heard the pain in her voice. "Kristin, what's
wrong?" he'd demanded. When she didn't answer, he
guessed. "Is it the baby?"

She'd remembered the conversations they'd had about
babies then, how she'd told him she wasn't ready to be
a mother and a wife. And a horrible premonition came
over her. "It's gone," she'd answered.

Zachary had been very quiet, and Kristin had known
by the questions he asked that he believed she might
have gotten rid of their child on purpose, even though
he hadn't come right out and accused her of that. And
she'd hated him for it.

That very night she'd packed her clothes and left, sending a moving company a few days later for the rest of her things.

Now, lying beside Zachary in the darkness, Kristin was crushed by that same sense of hopelessness. Softly, brokenly, she began to cry, not only for that lost baby but for the lost weeks, hours and minutes, as well. She and Zachary might have found their way through the grief and confusion together, if only they'd tried.

She'd been a fool to run away, and Zachary had been a fool to let her, and now things would never be the same between them again.

CHAPTER FOUR

KRISTIN FELT ZACHARY'S hand come to rest on her shoulder. Gently he turned her over onto her back and, with a thumb, he caressed her cheek.

He didn't ask why she was crying—he was just arrogant enough to assume he knew—and his lips brushed her forehead lightly.

A violent shudder ran through Kristin's exhausted body, and it was as though she'd been thrust back through time, into happier, less complicated days. The barbs they'd exchanged and Zachary's cold looks faded from her memory like golden leaves in autumn.

She wrapped her arms around his neck and snuggled closer to him, needing his warmth and strength.

With a groan, Zachary found her mouth with his own and possessed it fully. Again Kristin was electrified, with nothing to ground her. Her hands moved frantically up and down the muscular expanse of his back, seeking a place to hold on, a way to anchor herself.

He left her mouth to taste her neck, pushing aside her damp hair, and one of his hands closed lightly over her breast. Kristin arched her back and whimpered as he stroked the nipple with the pad of his thumb, causing it to harden in anticipation.

Zachary kissed her again, then went to her breast and boldly took the puckered morsel into his mouth.

Kristin groaned as she felt his tongue circle its prey,

cried out when he began to suckle. He brought his hand down over her belly to the fevered mound where her womanhood was hidden, one finger creeping through tangled silk for a preliminary conquering.

While Kristin's bottom rose and fell on the flannel lining of the sleeping bag, her knees falling wide, Zachary treated her other breast to the same thorough loving he'd given the first. Then he began kissing his way lower and lower, and her moist flesh quivered under the passing of his lips.

She pleaded with him, softly, senselessly, and gave a strangled shout of triumphant surrender when he parted the damp curls and took her. Her legs went over his shoulders, her hands flailed wide of her body then raced to his hair.

His strong hand cupped her bottom, holding her high, and she felt his hard back under her heels.

"Zachary," she wailed, and he lashed her lightly with his tongue, rendering her nearly mad with need. Her head flew from side to side, her flesh was wet with perspiration from her hairline to her toes, and outside nature built toward a crescendo to parallel the one Kristin's body strained for.

He gave her two kisses, soft as the touch of a butterfly's wing, and then nipped her gently with his teeth.

She cried out as the torrent broke within her, her body stiffening to align itself with the ferocious flow of pleasure that came from Zachary. She was gasping with exhaustion when he finally lowered her back to the sleeping bag and praying he would give her what she needed most of all, but he wasn't through pleasuring her.

He set her on her knees and brought her down onto the warm moistness of his mouth. His hands reached up to cup her passion-heavy breasts and, while he toyed with

her nipples, Kristin writhed on the tip of his tongue, her
breathing ragged and harsh.

"Please," she whimpered, "oh, Zachary, please..."

But still he teased her, mercilessly. She danced to the
tune measured out by his tongue and lips.

At last, even he could no longer hold back the tide of
Kristin's response. She bucked violently as satisfaction
overtook her, wringing hoarse, repeated cries from her
throat, causing her body to curve into a supple rigidity
as everything was demanded of it.

She fell down beside Zachary, convinced she had nothing more to give. But when, after several minutes of
slow, tender caresses, he entered her, Kristin's very soul
was aflame.

Perhaps because she'd been so thoroughly tamed, she
was the first to achieve the pinnacle. She knew immense
satisfaction as she used her voice and her hands to guide
Zachary through the treacherous territory of his own release, and his gruff cry made her heart catch.

They lay entangled afterward, the sleeping bag twisted
around them, their hair and flesh soaked. Outside the
little hut the storm continued to rage. Inside, the lovers
slept, leaving regrets for the morning.

AND KRISTIN HAD plenty of regrets when she awakened
in the drizzly dawn and remembered.

Zachary, fully dressed, brought her a mug of coffee,
made in a small enamel pot on the stove, and kept his
eyes averted.

His voice was rough, like the sound of two pieces of
rusty metal being rubbed together. "You and the prince
weren't planning to have a family right away, were you?"

She knew what he was asking—whether or not she
could have gotten pregnant the night before—and she

was annoyed by his assumption that birth control was her problem. "No," she said coldly, "I have an IUD."

He turned away, still without looking at her. "The rain's slacked off, and it's a nasty day out all the same."

Kristin squeezed her eyes shut, fighting for control. What was it about this man, that he could injure her so deeply just by what he said or didn't say? "We're moving on, aren't we?" she managed to ask.

"Yeah."

She pulled her pack close and went through it until she found the food packets Zachary—or someone—had put there for her. In one was a biscuit, hard as a hockey puck, in another, dried fruit. She choked the rations down, not because she had any discernible appetite but because she knew she would need all the strength she could garner for the day ahead.

"About last night..." she began. But her voice died away; there were no words.

Zachary tossed the grounds from the coffeepot out the door, rinsed it with water from the kettle he'd apparently refilled at the stream, and flung it into his pack. "Let's not talk about that, okay?"

Kristin felt a surge of anger. That had always been Zachary's stock statement whenever the conversation got too heavy for his liking. She heard echoes from the past.

It bothers you, doesn't it, Zachary, that my social background is so different from yours?

It's not important, Kristin. Let's discuss it some other time....

I think I'm going to have a baby, and I'm really, really scared.

We'll talk about it when I get back from this mission.

When will that be, Zachary?

Soon.

She reached for her pack and pulled out jeans and a T-shirt, the only outfit she had besides the pajamalike garb Zachary had put on her before they left the palace. After a few awkward moments had passed, she was dressed, and she climbed out of the sleeping bag to face him.

"It's interesting that you haven't changed in all this time," she observed, her voice betraying no emotion at all.

Zachary, wearing his jacket and hat, turned slightly to watch as she combed her hair. "What the hell do you mean by that?"

With deft fingers she wove her hair into a French braid and tied it with a tiny piece of string she'd found in the pocket of her jacket. "I mean you still deal with everything you find difficult or distasteful by refusing to talk about it. Don't look now, secret agent man, but that's the coward's way out."

She watched as a muscle tightened in his whisker-bristled cheek, then relaxed again.

"What did you expect, Kristin? A few stanzas of poetry? A declaration of my undying love?"

The words wounded Kristin far more cruelly than she would ever have guessed they could. "No, Zachary," she answered, with a calmness that surprised her. "Not from you."

Outside she tried to saddle her horse, but Zachary said she didn't do it right and elbowed her aside. Her ire simmered and bubbled, but she wouldn't let him see.

"I wouldn't have let you make love to me," she said stiffly once they were mounted, their backpacks in place again, "if I hadn't been so scared. It won't happen again."

He tossed her a cocky grin underlaid with cold steel. "We've got a long way to go before we're out of Cabriz, princess," he replied. "So don't be too sure of yourself."

Kristin wanted to run him down with her horse, but since he was mounted she had to settle for the fantasy. "You are so arrogant!"

He touched the brim of his hat. "Just self-confident," he countered with an obnoxious grin. "You didn't seem to mind my being sure of myself last night, princess."

Her face went crimson. "You go straight to hell, Zachary Harmon. I would have responded that way with *anybody.*"

Zachary laughed and reined his horse into the woods, and Kristin had no choice but to follow. Impossible as he was, Zachary was her ticket out of Cabriz, and she wanted desperately to go home.

"Did you ever finish college?" Zachary asked when the hut was well behind them.

The branches of trees hung low over the narrow path in a green arch, filling the crisp morning air with their scent and dripping moisture left from the rainstorm in the night. Kristin ducked. "Yes," she answered in a stony voice. When she and Zachary had lived together, she'd been attending UCLA—the third college in her academic career—finishing up her master's. On more than one occasion he'd accused her of being a professional student.

He glanced back at her with an expression of wry annoyance. "Now, there was an answer abounding with pertinent information. I was thinking about that paper you wrote for one of your journalism classes—'Chauvinists I Have Known,' or something like that."

Kristin couldn't help smiling. "'A Chauvinist's Profile.' It was about you, and I got an A."

"So," he went on, apparently content to ignore the gibe, "once you got your sheepskin, you thought you might as well marry a prince."

"I had a job at *Savoir Faire* magazine," she pointed out in self-defense.

"Did they fire you?"

"No. They sent me all over the world on photojournalism assignments."

"Tracking the diamond-breasted embassy bird, no doubt."

His good-natured contempt hurt, but she was determined not to let him know. "Somebody has to cover those parties," she said.

Before he could make a comment on that statement, which Kristin already regretted wholeheartedly, the sounds of laughter and gunshots rang through the air.

Zachary immediately put up a hand, signaling Kristin to halt and be silent. He took off his hat and put it on again, then spoke in a raspy whisper. "Stay here," he said.

Kristin opened her mouth to protest, then closed it again. Zachary was already moving into the woods on foot, disappearing. She was suddenly terrified that he would be killed or captured, and her heart began to beat so hard that she could practically hear it.

She got off her horse and left it untethered beside Zachary's. Then she made her way through the woods in the direction he'd gone.

She'd traveled only a few yards, catching not so much as a glimpse of him, when suddenly a strong hand reached out and closed over her mouth. An arm encircled her waist and hauled her backward, off her feet.

Thinking of bandits, and of Jascha's revenge, she struggled wildly. Relief and fury clashed inside her when she turned her head and saw that her captor was Zachary.

She glared at him.

"Their camp is about twenty-five yards ahead, through

those trees," he breathed into her ear. "Maybe you'd rather I'd just let you stumble right in?"

Kristin's eyes were wide as he set her on her feet and slowly lowered his hand from her mouth. "Bandits?" she whispered, curiously drawn to the noise even though she had the good sense to be properly terrified.

Zachary touched his finger to her lips and gave her a stern look, then started back through the trees, pulling her after him.

"I wanted to get a look at them," she complained once she figured they were a safe distance away.

"You almost got more than a look, princess," Zachary replied through his teeth, fairly hurling her up onto her horse. "You damn near struck up an intimate friendship. Now keep your mouth shut until I tell you it's safe to talk."

She bit down on her lower lip, chagrined but not cowed, and dutifully followed Zachary when he guided his horse in another direction. They'd probably traveled a full two miles before he turned to her and said, "There must have been fifty of them. We're going to have to be extra careful tonight."

Knowing that probably meant no campfire, and thus no coffee, Kristin was deflated. "What do we have that's worth stealing?"

"Although it's debatable," Zachary replied tautly, glowering at her, "some of them might consider taking *you*. Of course, once it was too late, they'd understand their error, but I'm afraid that wouldn't help you much. Or me."

Kristin sighed. "All right, I'm sorry. I was just trying to help, that's all. I got to thinking what would happen if you were captured—"

"And you were going to save me, right? Listen, princess, just do us both a favor in the future and follow your usual modus operandi—which, of course, is looking after your own skin and letting the devil take the hindmost."

Kristin bit back an angry response and fought to hold in the tears of frustration and pain that burned behind her eyes. She didn't expect Zachary to like her, much less love her, as he once had, but she wasn't prepared for hatred, either. And while she'd known the events of the night before would never lead to anything permanent, she'd hoped civility would be possible.

After all, once they were out of Cabriz, they could go their separate ways and forget they'd ever seen each other.

"I'm sorry, Zachary."

He reined in his horse to ride beside her. "I shouldn't have said what I did," he admitted. "It's just that when I saw you walking past me, headed straight for that nest of vipers, I lost it. I'm sorry, too."

She smiled at him. "Thanks for catching me before I made their acquaintance," she said, relieved to find that they could still talk without going for the psychological jugular.

After riding for several more hours they stopped again to eat more dried fruit and meat. Kristin would have given anything for a cheeseburger deluxe with fries.

In the distance they could see a small village huddled against the mountainside. Industrious Cabrizians in dark clothes milled around the huts, and smoke curled from the chimneys.

"Are they friendly, Kemo Sabe?" Kristin asked, crunching on a dehydrated apricot.

"They were the last time I came through, but things might have changed. I'm going to have a word with them, and I want you to stay here." He glared at her, shaking one finger in a mock threat. "And I mean it—cross me again and I'll take a bamboo switch to your backside!"

There weren't many things Kristin could be certain of where Zachary was concerned, but this was one—he would never lay a hand on her in anger, no matter what she did. "Bamboo grows only in the south," she reminded him, holding back a smile. "But I'll stay put."

His eyes widened and then narrowed, and Kristin knew he was trying to read her. "Really?"

"Yes," she said, clasping her hands together behind her back, now that she'd been relieved of her pack. "Really."

Zachary took his pistol from the holster under his jacket and extended it, butt first. "I'll be back as soon as I can. If anybody gives you any trouble, shoot them."

Kristin's inner smile faded, and she felt the color drain from her face. "I don't know if I could do that," she answered, trying to hand the gun back.

He wouldn't accept it. "Just don't go looking down the barrel," he grumbled, mounting his horse and setting off toward the village. Then he was gone.

With a sigh, Kristin plunked down on a large rock to wait, the pistol dangling between her knees, pointed at the ground. "I just hope I don't have to shoot anybody, that's all," she fretted.

Her horse nickered in response.

A full hour passed before Kristin saw Zachary riding back toward her, and she was embarrassed by the extent of her relief. She'd begun by imagining that the villagers had proved unfriendly, then pictured herself storming the place to save Zachary from a fate worse than death.

She held the hateful pistol wide of her body by two fingers, like something that smelled bad, as Zachary approached.

He dismounted and took it from her with a chuckle

and a shake of his head. "Here," he said, tossing a parcel wrapped in some kind of skin into her hands.

"What is it?" Kristin asked, turning the bundle over. There was a low-grade stench coming from the package. "Don't tell me what kind of skin it is," she added quickly. "I don't want to know."

Zachary laughed. "It's nothing worse than what you slept on last night."

Kristin made a face as she unwound the twine that bound the package, rolled it neatly and tucked it into the pocket of her jacket. She might need it later to tie back her hair.

Inside the package was a gossamer yellow robe, of the kind Mai and the other palace women had worn, complete with a veil. The gown was beautiful, but hardly suitable for riding, and Kristin looked at Zachary in confusion.

"In case we run into a situation where you have to pass as a Cabrizian," he said, averting his eyes.

Beneath the robe was a round, curious lump of something hard and white. Kristin's nose wrinkled as she assessed the stuff.

"Cheese," Zachary explained, flipping open his jack-knife and cutting off a wedge. He laid the morsel, still resting on the edge of the blade, to Kristin's lips.

"What kind?" Kristin asked, chewing. For all that it smelled like dirty socks, it wasn't bad.

"You're happier not knowing," he answered, giving her another piece.

After Kristin had packed away the robe and, with considerably less enthusiasm, the cheese, Zachary fastened on her pack again and helped her into the saddle. They headed around the village and up the mountain.

They didn't talk much, and Zachary was on the alert. Maybe it was just that they'd nearly stumbled onto those bandits that morning, but Kristin didn't think so. She figured it was more likely that the villagers had warned him about something.

And she was nervous.

Late that afternoon her horse picked up a stone and started to limp.

Zachary lifted the animal's foreleg and inspected the damage, talking with gruff gentleness to comfort the beast, and Kristin felt an unwanted tenderness rise within her.

She turned away resolutely, her arms folded. She couldn't afford to let herself fall in love with Zachary Harmon again, knowing that he could never feel the same way about her. Maybe, for that matter, he never had.

There were some berries growing at the side of the path and she began to pick them, mostly for something to do. In a glance back over one shoulder, she saw that Zachary was using his jackknife to pry the stone out of the horse's hoof.

She raised one of the purple berries to her lips and ate it, enjoying the tangy sweetness. She followed that with another, and another.

When Zachary had finished doctoring the horse, Kristin strolled back to him and held out her hand. "Berry?" she asked cordially.

He just glanced at the fruit at first, but then his eyes widened and he grabbed Kristin's hand, lifting it so he could get a closer look. He muttered a swearword, wrenched off his hat and hurled it onto the ground.

"What's the matter?" Kristin asked. But even as she uttered the words, a sudden spate of nausea overwhelmed her, sending her scurrying for the bushes. She retched violently, repeatedly, and Zachary stood at her side the whole time, one hand resting on her back.

"They were poison," she managed, once her stomach was empty, and Zachary nodded, handing her a mug filled with spring water.

She rinsed her mouth and spat, then drank. "Am I going to die?" she asked shakily. The joke was awkward. Flat.

"No," Zachary answered seriously, "but for the next few hours you're going to wish you had. Weren't you ever a Girl Scout, princess? You don't go around eating whatever you find growing on a bush, you know—"

Kristin was sick again, and Zachary stood by her until the spasms stopped. Then he helped her onto her horse.

"Just hold on," he told her gently, patting the elderly gray mare on the neck. "The Silver Bullet and I will do the rest."

"But I need to lie down," Kristin fussed. She was never at her best when she was sick. In fact, Zachary always used to say that a simple cold could regress her to the age of five.

Zachary had taken the reins from her. "We've got to keep moving until nightfall, princess," he said reasonably. "There are rebels and robbers all over this mountain."

Kristin's stomach clenched wildly, painfully, even though there was nothing inside it to expel. "Just shoot me, then," she pressed, only half in jest.

They rode until they came to another stream, toward dark, and Kristin was so miserable that she would have fallen out of the saddle if Zachary hadn't lifted her down.

"Can I sleep now?" she asked.

He chuckled and kissed her forehead. "No, princess. Not yet. But the horses need water." He unfastened her pack and then went through his own. Finding his washcloth, he carried it to the stream and dipped it.

He was wringing the cloth out as he walked toward

Kristin. "Here," he said quietly, laying it across the back of her neck, under her bedraggled braid. "This ought to help a little." He sat her down on a rock. "Wait here."

Kristin was too woozy to wander off. She couldn't keep her mind on anything except the unceasing pain in her stomach.

When Zachary returned, he was holding something in the palm of his hand. "Close your eyes and open your mouth," he said. "And then swallow."

She was trying to see what it was he was offering her, but he wouldn't permit that. And the awful stomach spasms were getting worse. "What—?"

"Just do as I ask for once, princess."

She drew a deep breath and squeezed her eyes shut. "It's not that cheese, is it? I don't feel like—"

Suddenly her head was pulled back and something cold and slimy slithered into her mouth. She tried to spit, but Zachary caught her lips between his fingers and held them closed.

"Swallow," he ordered.

Kristin did so, having no real choice. "What was that?" she sputtered when he let her go, bolting off the rock.

"It was a raw egg."

Kristin whirled away just in time to keep from throwing up on his boots. But this time was different. After the first spate of sickness, her stomach settled down and she almost felt normal.

"Do you need another egg?"

She gave him a look fit to kill and stomped over to the stream, where she knelt and splashed water over her face and into her mouth. Although she was still dizzy, the violent nausea was gone.

"I suppose I don't want to know what kind of egg that

was," she said as Zachary squired her back to her horse, strapped on her backpack and helped her mount.

"You're right," he answered, giving her bottom a little swat before she plopped into the saddle. "You don't want to know."

They rode on and on, it seemed to Kristin, up slopes as steep as the side of a refrigerator, through trees so dense that it was hard to pass between them. She thought with longing of her old chenille bathrobe and a cup of hot, strong tea, but she didn't ask Zachary to stop. Her pride had taken enough of a beating that day.

Finally, when it was not only dark but the moon was riding high in the sky, they reached another canyon, and Zachary instructed her to wait while he rode through the opening.

The minutes that passed before he returned seemed like generations to Kristin, but she waited as she'd been told, grateful that he hadn't left his pistol as well.

"It's clear," he said, returning to the gap in the rock to take off his hat and lean slightly forward in the saddle. "Come on in, princess. This is the closest thing you're going to get to luxury accommodations."

With a slight frown, Kristin rode through the breach and looked around.

The moon seemed to be pouring its light into the canyon, where it collected in a silver glow. A spring or stream rippled in the background, but there were only a few trees.

Kristin took off her pack on her own, once Zachary had lifted her to the ground, and headed straight for the water. There was something strange about it, though she couldn't quite decide what it was.

When she reached the pebble-strewn banks of the

spring, she knew. It was as hot as bathwater, and steam billowed off the surface.

She whirled, full of weary delight. "We can stay—can't we? We can spend the night here?"

He came to her, kissed her lightly on the forehead. "We can spend the night here," he confirmed. "Go ahead and get a bath. I'll build a fire and see what I can rustle up for supper."

Kristin's eyes went wide as she looked at the spring again. "There wouldn't be any leeches, or anything like that—"

Zachary shook his head, grinning.

With a little whoop of joy, Kristin shed her jacket and bent to untie her work shoes. Only then did she remember that she had an audience. "You'll turn your back, of course?"

Zachary was still grinning. "Of course," he answered.

She took from her pack the robe he'd gotten her that day, along with a bar of soap, and made her way to the edge of the spring. Once she'd taken off her jeans and T-shirt and climbed into the water, she looked back and found Zachary standing in exactly the same place she'd left him, staring at her.

"You lied," she called, but she couldn't work up any real anger. Not when he'd done his best to look after her and had brought her to a place like this.

She was mildly disappointed when he didn't offer a comeback but simply turned and started gathering twigs for a fire.

Kristin settled into the luscious water, soap in hand, and began to bathe.

CHAPTER FIVE

"I THOUGHT WE WEREN'T going to have a fire," Kristin said, combing the tangles from her clean, wet hair as she approached Zachary. "Because of bandits and rebels and bogeymen."

He was crouching beside the small blaze, and his eyes wandered over Kristin's gauzy yellow robe for several moments before rising to her face. "The campsite is sheltered by the canyon walls," he pointed out, his expression solemn.

Kristin glanced uneasily around her. The place was too perfect, too much like Eden or Shangri-la. There had to be a serpent somewhere, waiting to offer her an apple. "If you know about it, they probably do, too. And tonight there isn't any rain to keep them away."

Zachary bent to take his miniature coffeepot from the coals of the fire and pour the contents into their mugs. He held one out to Kristin as he sipped from the other, then lowered it slowly from his mouth. "We're as safe here as we would be anywhere else on the mountain," he responded.

"Which isn't saying much," Kristin speculated, hugging herself with one arm and tasting her coffee. "Maybe we should just have kept moving."

"You've been sick most of the day," Zachary reminded her. "And you're not used to this kind of life. You couldn't have gone much farther."

Kristin took another sip of the coffee. Even though there were grounds floating in it, since Zachary always made the brew without benefit of basket or filter, it was delicious. "I should have asked you about those berries before I ate them," she confessed with a sigh. "I'm sorry. This trip is difficult enough without my complicating it."

He approached her, kissed her lightly on the forehead. "It was an innocent mistake," he said. And then he set his coffee mug down and ambled toward the spring, where Kristin had taken such a luxurious bath.

She watched him toss his hat aside, shrug out of his jacket, kick off his boots. Then, realizing that she was staring, Kristin looked purposefully away.

"How many more days until we're out of Cabriz?" she called, her voice unnaturally loud even considering the distance between them.

"Three," he answered. "Two if we're lucky." She heard a splashing sound and envisioned him washing his hair.

She poured the dregs from the coffeepot into her cup. "And then?"

"And then we'll go our separate ways," he replied easily. "You'll probably want to spend a little time recuperating at the embassy in Rhaos. You can look now, Kristin—I'm not exposing any relevant parts of my anatomy."

She realized how tense she was—silly, really, after giving herself to this man so completely the night before—and made a diligent effort to relax. She even strolled toward the spring and sat down on a log. The truce between them was comforting, and she wanted to maintain it. "You haven't told me anything about your life. How's the spy business these days—rescuing former roommates aside?"

He had rinsed his hair and was soaping his armpits,

the water reaching to his rib cage. "I wouldn't know," he answered. "I've been teaching at a junior college on the Washington coast ever since...well, for the last year and a half."

He'd been about to say, "since we broke up," Kristin knew. The reminder hurt, and so did the knowledge that he'd resigned from the agency. Before their parting she'd begged him to do that so they could build some kind of sane life together, and he'd steadfastly refused.

"You're teaching," she said in a small voice. "What's your subject? Survival in the wild? Covert operations?"

In the thin light of the moon she saw his lips twist into an expression that might have been either a grimace or a smile. "Political science," he answered. "I also do the occasional seminar on Asian culture."

Kristin scraped her lower lip with her teeth. "I'm surprised," she said evenly, still grappling with the unexpected pain. "I wouldn't have thought you'd ever want to do anything as tame as teaching." She wouldn't have thought he'd reveal so much about himself so easily, either. She wondered if it was too much to hope that Zachary was loosening up a little.

He was splashing away the lather from his chest and underarms. "People change, princess," he said. And then she felt his eyes move over her, assessing, finding her wanting. "At least, some of us do."

And here she'd been thinking charitable thoughts about him. "What's that supposed to mean?"

"You're still impulsive," he said in a totally objective tone of voice. "And you still can't make up your mind what you want to do with your life. You go to this college, you go to that college. You take a job, then you give it up to marry a prince. After that, you decide maybe that isn't such a good idea...."

Kristin's cheeks were hot. She started to speak, then stopped herself. It galled her that she couldn't deny Zachary's charges.

"You seem to have a serious problem with commitment," he finished. "Maybe you ought to get some counseling or something."

Kristin gave an angry hoot. "That's a good one, coming from you! If I remember correctly, you were the one who didn't want to be 'tied down' to an everyday job—"

He stalked out of the hot spring before Kristin had a chance to prepare herself and stood there before her, gloriously naked, glistening with mineral water and moonlight. Reaching down, he caught hold of her robe and wrenched her to her feet. "My life is in order," he said in a ragged, angry whisper. "But you're still running, aren't you?"

Kristin tried to pull away, but his hold was too firm. "Running? I was practically abducted!"

"Abducted, hell. You could have stayed in the palace if you'd wanted to and you damn well know it."

She whirled, and this time he let her go. When she looked at him again he was dressed, except for his jacket, hat and boots. He used her comb, then tossed it back to her, and there was a dismissal in the gesture that stung Kristin to the quick.

She busied herself looking through her pack for something to eat that hadn't been dried, and came up with a small can of chicken and noodles with a pop-up lid.

"Do you regret leaving him?" Zachary asked, and her hand tightened around the can.

"Jascha?" Kristin paused, considering. "Yes, in a way. I miss the man I thought he was." She opened her supper and set the can carefully in the embers to heat.

There was an awkward silence, then Zachary said, "I saw your picture on the cover of that magazine."

The engagement photograph of her and Jascha. He'd worn his official uniform for the shoot, and someone had found a rhinestone tiara for her. Kristin smiled sadly, mourning the pretty dream.

"You looked like a real princess," Zachary added, and his voice was hoarse.

She raised her eyes to his face, wondering what he'd thought and felt, looking at that picture. Had there been any pain, any remorse for all the two of them had lost? "Thanks—I think."

He grinned, strapping on his shoulder holster, then busied himself for a few minutes wiping down the barrel, cleaning the chamber. Then he spun the chamber once with an expert thumb. "Your noodles are about to burn," he pointed out.

Disappointed, yet not knowing what she'd expected from him or even hoped for, Kristin carefully removed the can from the fire, using the T-shirt she'd worn that day as a pot holder. "Expecting trouble?" she asked, spooning a bite of food into her mouth and nodding toward the pistol. The noodles tasted smoky and good.

Zachary shrugged, pulling on his jacket. "It wouldn't hurt to have a look around," he answered, then he raised a finger. "And Kristin—"

"I know, I know," she interrupted. "Stay here."

She told herself it didn't make her nervous, having Zachary leave her alone in camp. She finished her supper, disposed of the can and washed her spoon in the spring.

Then, because Zachary still wasn't back and inactivity was unbearable, she took out her sleeping bag and unrolled it next to the blaze. Tonight, with the fire and the warm spring nearby, there wouldn't be any need for them to sleep together.

By the time she'd finished the task, Zachary still hadn't returned.

Kristin brought out her toothbrush and paste and attended to her teeth, using water from Zachary's canteen in lieu of going to the spring. After that there was nothing more to do.

Kristin looked at the high, invisible walls of the canyon, at the V of stars visible in the cleft overhead. Zachary was probably right, she concluded. They were as safe there as they would be anywhere on the mountain—which meant they were in mortal danger at every moment.

Telling herself to be brave, Kristin pulled back the top of her sleeping bag and climbed in, still wearing the yellow robe. It was soft and comfortable, and it made her feel a whole lot less vulnerable than she had in Zachary's T-shirt.

She had just snuggled down, her eyes on the hypnotic, dancing flames of the campfire, when Zachary returned. She was so glad to see him that she sat bolt upright and blurted out, "Did you see anybody?"

"No," he answered with a sigh, taking in the single sleeping bag without a noticeable reaction, "but that doesn't mean a damn thing."

"Maybe one of us had better sit up and keep watch," she ventured.

Zachary grinned and took off his hat and jacket. The firelight gleamed on the pearl handle of the pistol. "Good idea. If anybody comes into camp, princess, you just interview them. Promise them a spot in *People* magazine."

"Funny," Kristin replied, swallowing. Something had been troubling her all evening, just beneath the surface of consciousness, and now it bobbed to the top with brisk clarity. "If you're not with the agency anymore, what are you doing here in Cabriz?"

In the dim light of the fire and the moon, Kristin couldn't read Zachary's expression. He was a long time answering. "I have a specialized knowledge of the country," he finally said. "You know that."

A tiny flame of crazy optimism flared in Kristin's heart, and it made her bold. "And no one else does?"

He drew nearer, crouching beside her, taking her chin roughly in hand. All hope died when she saw the cold expression in his eyes. "The current administration probably would have left you here if it hadn't been for me," he said. "Their reasoning was, 'she made her bed, let her sleep in it.' And under any other circumstances, I would have agreed with them."

Kristin felt painful venom spread through her veins, made up of shame, frustration and pain. She looked away, and Zachary finally let go of her chin. She lay down and turned her face toward the darkness so he wouldn't know how much she was hurting.

It came as a total surprise when she felt her sleeping bag being unzipped. She sat up, her heart hammering. "What are you doing?"

He attached his bag to hers with such practiced deftness that Kristin was filled with searing jealousy, imagining him lying in such close quarters with another woman. "I think that's fairly obvious," he answered, kicking off his boots.

"You're not sleeping with me!"

"You're right. I don't plan on sleeping."

Kristin was furious, not because she thought Zachary would force her but because she knew he could change her mind in the space of one kiss. She started to scoot backward, out of the sleeping bag, but that only made the robe bunch up around her thighs.

He unbuckled the holster and set it carefully aside, and before she could pull down the hem of her robe he was lifting it over her head, tossing it aside in a billowing cloud of softness. She was naked, shivering in the heat of his gaze.

"Stand up," he said quietly. "I want to look at you."

Kristin shook her head, already falling under his spell, using all her strength to break the enchantment. "No."

He reached out, cupped her breast gently in one hand. The nipple went taut as he stroked it, and Kristin gave a little moan and let her head fall back.

Zachary chuckled and leaned forward to drink languidly from her breast, and in that moment she was lost. Try though she did, she couldn't summon the words to put him away from her.

Once he'd taken nectar from both her nipples, he again asked her to stand, and this time Kristin complied.

She trembled, knowing what was coming, and made a soft whimpering sound as he parted the silken veil to taste her. "Zachary—"

He teased her with nibbles, with darting flicks of his tongue. "What?"

Kristin moaned. She was exhausted from riding all day; every muscle in her body ached. And yet a treacherous energy was gaining strength within her, holding her up for Zachary's pleasure and her own. Her fingers were entangled in his hair. "I want it to happen when you're inside me. Please."

To her surprise, he lowered her to the sleeping bag, laid her gently on the flannel. The backs of her knees rested against his shoulders while he opened his pants.

He found the velvet passageway and entered with a

forceful thrust, his hands gripping Kristin's ankles as she arched her body to receive him.

"That's good," she whispered. "So good—"

Zachary took her fully, then retreated almost to the point of withdrawal. His chuckle was raw with any emotion but humor. "And tomorrow—you'll say you would have responded the same way—to anybody."

"No one," Kristin half sobbed, because the pleasure was already too much for her. She couldn't bear it. "No one else—oh, Zachary, fast—hard—"

He didn't change his pace at all. He held her legs where they were and moved in and out of her with excruciating slowness.

She tried to writhe but he wouldn't permit that, either. He glided in and withdrew and she felt the friction in every nerve, and gloried in it.

Kristin arched her neck and groaned through clenched teeth. "Please."

"No," he answered, pushing her legs forward slightly so that his penetration was deep.

The stars blurred against the dark sky as Kristin climbed toward them, hand over hand, her breathing fast and harsh. Her feet rested against the sides of Zachary's head now, and he held her tightly around the thighs, moving with more speed as his own body began to make demands that would not be ignored.

With a broken cry, he slammed deep and stiffened against her, and in that moment Kristin went wild. She was a woman untouched by civilization, and she was not simply making love—she was mating for life.

Later, when she lay still in Zachary's arms and the last aftershocks had finally subsided, she faced facts. Although what had just happened was of profound significance to her, there was no reason to think anything had changed for Zachary.

She turned her face into the bare flesh of his shoulder, holding back weary tears, and a tremor moved through her.

In response, Zachary held her closer, pulling the top of the sleeping bag up so that it covered them both comfortably. "Cold?"

Kristin shook her head. "Scared." She couldn't add that it wasn't Jascha, or the rebels, or even the bandits that frightened her. It was the thought of going back to a life that didn't include Zachary and trying to pretend seeing him again hadn't awakened all the old feelings.

He kissed her lightly on the temple, his breath ruffling her hair. "In a way," he said, "I'm going to be sorry when this is over."

Kristin closed her eyes tightly so she couldn't cry. She didn't answer, not daring to speak.

Somehow, Zachary seemed to know that she needed holding as much or more than she'd needed his lovemaking. He kept her tucked close to his side long after he'd drifted off to sleep. And even though she was wide awake, Kristin dreamed.

She dreamed of being married to Zachary, and of bearing his children, and of finally making a real place for herself in the scheme of things. She saw herself taking pictures for a newspaper and writing about things that really mattered.

Because she was so caught up in her thoughts, she was startled when Zachary suddenly stiffened beside her and then groped for the pistol.

A strange voice came out of the darkness, speaking in swift Cabrizian dialect, and Kristin caught enough of the general meaning to be terrified.

"Leave the gun where it is and you won't get hurt."

The horses nickered and fretted in the darkness, and Kristin finally picked out the figure of a small man standing on the other side of the dying campfire and pointing a rifle at them.

Zachary's body was perfectly still, his words evenly modulated. "Who are you?" he asked in the robber's own language.

"We need horses," the bandit replied, and it became obvious to Kristin that he was nervous. "We won't take the woman, we won't take the food. Just the horses."

"No," Zachary said as forcefully as if he had a choice in the matter. "The horses are ours. Leave them here."

The man was insane as far as Kristin was concerned. Why else would he talk that way to someone who was holding a gun on him? "Go ahead," she said in the halting dialect she remembered from embassy days. "Take the horses. Just so nobody gets hurt."

Zachary's elbow landed in the middle of her stomach, just hard enough to cut off her wind.

The bandit came close enough to kick Zachary's pistol out of reach, then backed out of the firelight. Moments later the clip-clop of hooves was heard as the horses were taken away.

Zachary spat a swearword and scrambled out of the sleeping bag, searching the ground for his pistol. By the time he found it, the horses and the bandit were long gone.

And Zachary took his frustration out on Kristin. "I ought to drag you out of that sleeping bag and blister your backside!" he yelled.

Kristin shimmied out on her own and quickly pulled on the yellow robe, as though that could offer some protection. "What did I do wrong?"

"What did I do wrong?" Zachary mimicked furiously. "You drew his attention, for one thing. You should have kept your mouth shut!"

"That wouldn't have stopped him from stealing the horses," Kristin replied reasonably, folding her arms. "Do you think he was alone?"

"Probably not," Zachary answered, picking up his shoulder holster and jamming the pistol inside.

"I told you one of us should have kept watch."

"Right." Zachary was putting on his clothes in jerky, outraged motions. "I can see it now. You probably would have invited them for coffee and asked them if they wouldn't like to steal our food and sleeping bags, as well as our horses. Then we could have been totally annihilated, instead of just in the biggest damn trouble of our lives!"

Kristin stirred the fire and added a few of the twigs and broken branches Zachary had gathered earlier. "Don't you dare try to foist the responsibility off on me—it isn't my fault we were bested by one skinny little bandit!"

Zachary glared at her for a long moment, then startled her completely by chuckling. "He was skinny, wasn't he? If this ever gets back to the guys in the agency, I'll never live it down."

Kristin's concerns were more immediate. "What are we going to do now, Zachary?"

"Sleep," he answered with a deep sigh. "Tomorrow we walk."

"Carrying our packs?"

"That's the idea."

She got back into the sleeping bag, still wearing the robe, and snuggled down. "Do we have enough food?"

Zachary didn't join her, but sat up beside the fire,

staring ponderously into the flames. "Probably not," he replied. "Get some rest, princess. Tomorrow is going to be a long day."

HE WAS RIGHT.

In the morning Kristin washed up in the spring and dressed in the blue jeans and T-shirt she'd worn the day before, then drank a cup of Zachary's campfire coffee. She had no appetite for breakfast, given the situation and yesterday's berry binge.

At first, hiking with a loaded pack on her back was a novelty, and Kristin enjoyed it. It just went to show that all those people who thought she was nothing more than a social butterfly—Zachary and her father, for instance— were dead wrong. Inside her slender form lurked the spirit of an intrepid adventurer.

Then they started traveling uphill.

After advancing only about a hundred yards up the incline, Kristin sank onto a fallen log and covered her eyes with both palms.

Zachary had gone some distance before he realized she wasn't behind him, and stopped. "What's the matter?" he called back, sounding for all the world like a big brother forced to let a small and helpless child tag along on an important mission.

Kristin struggled ingloriously to her feet, almost unbalanced by the pack. "Nothing," she returned with stubborn good cheer. "I just wanted to take a little breather, that's all."

"We've got to keep moving," Zachary replied. And then he turned and went on, and Kristin had no choice but to trudge after him.

The next challenge was a narrow path leading around the edge of a steep slope.

The last of Kristin's bravado teetered on the edge of extinction as she looked down the rocky grade to a pile of mean-looking boulders about a hundred feet below. The path seemed inadequate to say the least—it was hardly more than a line drawn in the dirt—and the weight of two people was sure to send it sliding downhill.

Zachary must have seen the fear in her face, because he laid one hand gently on her shoulder and said, "It's okay, princess. Just hold on to the back of my belt until I tell you to let go, and don't look down."

Kristin drew a deep breath and let it out again. She couldn't fold now, when the time element was even more important than before. With a trembling hand, she reached out and clasped Zachary's belt.

They began to edge slowly along the narrow path, and Kristin looked neither right nor left, up nor down. She just fixed her gaze on the back of Zachary's head, where the hair on his nape curled against the tanned flesh of his neck, and moved as he did.

For all her careful obedience, something went wrong. She set her right foot down and the path fell away beneath it.

With a shriek, Kristin went over the edge, still clinging to Zachary's belt, both feet flailing in an effort to find solid ground.

How he kept his balance Kristin would never know, but Zachary managed to turn and grasp her arm and somehow get her back onto the path.

"Are you all right?" he asked when she was beside him again, face pressed to the rock wall above the ledge, eyes squeezed shut as she battled down the lingering terror.

"My knee," she whispered. "I hurt my knee."

Zachary reached around her, unfastening the backpack. "Okay, Kristin," he said in a reasonable, steady tone of voice, "listen to me. I want you to stay right here while I take your pack to the other side. Once I've gotten rid of it, I'll come back and help you go the rest of the way. All right?"

Kristin swallowed, still afraid to open her eyes. If she so much as glanced down and saw those huge boulders below, waiting to smash her bones, she'd panic and then everything would be lost. "All right." She felt relief as the weight of the backpack was removed.

"Don't try to move," Zachary reminded her, and she could hear the distance growing between them, even though she dared not look. Pure fear rushed into her throat, scalding and vile. "I'll be back in a minute, Kristin. I promise."

Sweat trickled between Kristin's shoulder blades and breasts, and the pain in her right knee intensified. Somehow, when trying to break her fall, she'd twisted it. "Please hurry," she whispered, having no hope that he was close enough to hear.

But he was. "One minute, Kris."

Struggling not to lose her tenuous grip on composure, Kristin nodded and began to count slowly, silently, to sixty.

She felt Zachary's heat and strength just as she reached fifty-seven.

"How's the knee? Can you walk?"

Kristin tested the idea and felt stabbing pain, but she nodded. "I can make it if you'll help me."

His hand rested, firm and strong and very reassuring, on the small of her back. "Just one step at a time, babe—that's all you have to do. I'll be right here to keep you from falling."

Their progress seemed impossibly slow to Kristin, who finally dared to open her eyes but could look nowhere but at Zachary's face. Finally, though, after several minutes, they reached a grassy plateau on the other side.

There Kristin collapsed, engulfed in pain and relief, and sat clasping her knee.

Zachary knelt beside her and gently felt the injured limb, looking for obvious injury. "I don't think anything's broken," he said softly.

Kristin leaned forward and let her forehead rest against his shoulder. The pain was starting to subside, but she didn't have the breath to say so yet.

He put his arms around her, kissed the top of her head. "It's okay, princess. We'll rest until you're ready to move on."

Kristin nodded, and he released her to go and rummage through his backpack. When he returned, he thrust a little package of half-crumpled cookies into her hand.

"I was saving these for the last night, but I think you need them now," he said.

Kristin looked at the treat in disbelief for a few moments, then laughed and wiped her dirty, sweaty face with the back of one hand. "You've been holding out on me!"

He grinned and opened the package for her. "Didn't you tell me once that when you were hurt you used to go to the kitchen for a medicinal cookie?"

Kristin sank her teeth into her lower lip, touched, afraid she'd cry and spoil all her efforts at being brave. Since she didn't trust herself to speak, she just nodded.

Zachary took the only cookie that hadn't broken from the rigors of the trip and touched its edge lightly against Kristin's mouth.

CHAPTER SIX

"I'M ALL RIGHT," Kristin insisted, running one hand over her sore knee. At least it had stopped throbbing. "I just pulled a few muscles, that's all."

Zachary smiled, still kneeling beside her, brushed the cookie crumbs from her lips and rose to his feet. "Let's see if you can walk," he said, offering Kristin his hand.

She took it and allowed him to pull her up. A shaft of pain shot from her injured knee up her thigh, and she grimaced, turning her face so Zachary wouldn't see. Her first step was sheer agony, but then she took another and another.

A memory flashed into her mind: she was seven, and she'd fallen from the embassy banister and broken her arm. She heard her father's clipped, impatient voice. *Stop sniveling, Kristin. It's your own fault that you fell.*

She held her chin high. "I can make it," she told Zachary quietly.

Zachary caught her chin in his hand and made her look at him. "You can barely stand," he countered, reading the expression in her eyes. For good or ill, he'd always been a master at that.

Stubbornly, Kristin reached for her pack and moved to sling it into place, only to have Zachary take it away again.

"Sit down before you collapse," he ordered tersely, and his manner was nothing short of cantankerous.

"Thanks for the concern," Kristin retorted, "but we can't stay here. You know that as well as I do."

"So have it your way!" Zachary hissed through his teeth. Then he grumbled, "Come on," and set off across the plateau.

Kristin limped along behind him, her teeth sunk into her lower lip, but when Zachary glanced back at her she was ready with a smile and a firm gait.

Grudgingly he moved on, leading the way through thick pine and fir trees. The ground was uneven, but at least they weren't climbing. Kristin didn't know if she could maintain the charade on an incline, even without her pack.

By noon, when Zachary stopped, the pain in Kristin's knee was only a dull ache, but it had sapped her strength, and she knew she was pale.

While she sat on the ground eating cold corned beef from a can Zachary had given her, he paced, agitated and watchful.

"Are we being followed?" Kristin asked, chewing.

"No," Zachary answered, standing on a high ledge and looking down over the mountain they'd been climbing for almost three days. "But I think I see our horses."

Kristin bolted to her feet, wincing at the resultant pang in her knee. "What? Where?"

He pulled a small pair of field glasses from the pocket of his leather jacket and, after checking the position of the sun, peered into them, squinting. "At the edge of that village down there. Looks like our horse thief is a hometown boy."

"What are we going to do?" Kristin asked, following Zachary as he turned away from the ledge with a thoughtful frown on his face.

"*We're* not going to do anything," he said without looking at her.

"Zachary," Kristin warned, staying doggedly at his side as he shed his pack, took the pistol from its holster and checked the chamber. "I'm not staying here by myself."

"Yes, you are," he answered without missing a beat or even bothering to look at her. "You'll lie down, and you'll rest, and when I come back I'll bring the horses with me."

"I want to go."

"And I want the Nobel Peace Prize," Zachary informed her. "Guess we're both out of luck, princess." With that, he kissed her on the forehead and started to walk away.

"What if some bandits come and attack me?" Kristin called, hurrying after him, forgetting to hide her limp.

He turned briefly and glared at her with such ominous intensity that she stopped in her tracks. "Ask them what their sign is," he replied, spreading his hands. "Make small talk."

"Zachary!"

He was leaving her again. "If you keep yelling, princess," he warned good-naturedly, "they're bound to find us."

Kristin sank despondently onto the ground. There was no way she could keep up with Zachary's long strides; even without a sore knee it would have been difficult.

She watched him until he disappeared into the trees, then got up and went back to the vantage point at the ledge. All she could see of the village were specks that might have been the roofs of huts and a haze of smoke against the sky.

Kristin ran the tip of her tongue over dry lips and prayed that Zachary would return safely, with or without the horses.

Now that he wasn't there to see, there was no point in trying to pretend she wasn't a physical wreck. Kristin collapsed on the cushiony grass of the plateau, drinking in the thin warmth of the sunshine.

It was inevitable that she would remember the tender moments she and Zachary had shared, there in Cabriz and back in California, where they'd lived together.

The ache in Kristin's heart was worse than the one in her knee. To escape it she drifted backward in time, to a party her parents had given in their home in Williamsburg, Virginia....

The ballroom of the mansion glittered. The women wore dresses as jewel bright as the lights on the towering white Christmas tree in the entryway, and the men were elegant in tailored tuxedos. A string quartet played Mozart, a fire blazed on the hearth and snow drifted past the windows in huge, swirling flakes.

And all the atmosphere was lost on Kristin, who shared a dutiful dance with every man who asked and kept one eye on the big double doorway the whole time. Zachary had promised to spend Christmas with her, but so far there had been no sign of him—and no telephone calls, either.

Instead of visions of sugarplums, Kristin was seeing crashed helicopters and sprays of dust raised by machine-gun fire splattering some dusty Middle Eastern road. Normally she didn't allow herself to think about the things Zachary might be doing when he was away on a mission, but that night she couldn't seem to help it.

She managed a shaky smile when her father, a tall, fit man with a full head of gray hair and shrewd blue eyes, cut in on her bewildered dance partner and took her into his arms for a waltz.

"You look beautiful tonight," Kenyan Meyers told her

brusquely, and there was no love in his voice, despite the compliment. "But you're a bit on the pale side. What's the matter? Worried about your soldier of fortune?"

Kristin ached inside. Just once she'd like to feel that her father really cared about her, that she didn't have to put out an effort to win even the most cursory acceptance. She nodded. "Dad, what if Zachary's been shot—or captured?"

Kenyan was annoyed. "Do you see what this relationship is doing to you, Kristin? There are too many uncertainties, too many grim possibilities. Surely you realize that you're headed toward emotional disaster?"

Although she knew her father was probably right, that she should give Zachary up before the fear of what might happen to him made her crazy, Kristin hadn't been able to walk away.

It wasn't that she couldn't live without Zachary—she knew she could. But life would be a flat and endless round of classes and parties without him. "I love him," she answered simply.

Just then, as though the words had conjured him, Zachary appeared in the doorway. His glossy brown hair was dusted in snowflakes, and his eyes searched the long, crowded room for Kristin.

Her heart leaped and, as always, all thoughts of making her way through the world without him dissipated like vapor.

As the dance ended, she stood on tiptoe to kiss her father's cheek, then swept toward the doors, her white lace ball gown whispering as she walked.

Zachary's eyes lit up when he saw her, and one side of his mouth lifted in a smile. He looked uncomfortable in formal clothes, and yet he was the most attractive man in the room.

Catching Kristin's hands in his, he pulled her through the doorway and into the limited privacy of the entryway.

There Kristin flung her arms around his neck, and he picked her up and swung her around once. And then he kissed her.

It was the way it always was when they'd been apart. Kristin suffered a sweet form of cardiac arrest, and all her carefully cultivated gentility deserted her. She took Zachary's hand when the kiss ended and pulled him up the stairs and into the library, carefully locking the door behind them.

The room was lit only by outdoor lights shining through the ever-increasing flurries, but Kristin could see the admiration in Zachary's eyes as he held her at arm's length, taking in her extravagant white dress.

"You look," he said hoarsely, "like a snow fairy."

She smiled, and the music from the ballroom seeped through the venerable floors. "I'll have this dance, if you please."

He grinned, and her heart turned over, as it always did. "I love you, sweetheart," he said, and then he took her in his arms and they whirled through the darkened library, passing between the desk and the fireplace, the pool table and the leather sofa where at least one president had sat.

The dance ended when Zachary lifted Kristin off the floor, pressing her body to his even as their mouths met. Their tongues sparred, greedy for conquest, and Kristin gave a little whimper of welcome as she felt one of Zachary's hands curve around her breast.

He set her on the edge of the pool table and nuzzled her neck with warm, moist lips.

Kristin trembled when he gently lowered her bodice, baring both her breasts. They glowed like alabaster, tipped with rose, and stood out proudly for Zachary's caress.

"I missed you so much," she managed.

He kissed her again, thumbs moving over her nipples, fingers supporting the sweet, plump weight of her. Finally he broke away. "God kelp me, Kristin," he rasped, "I need you—I want you—"

Kristin laid her palms to either side of his face and pressed him to her breast, where he took suckle at a waiting nipple. With his hand he sought a pathway through the voluminous billows of Kristin's skirts.

He circled her nipple with the tip of his tongue before raising his head and chuckling. "Darlin', I need a little aiding and abetting here. I can't find you under all this lace and satin."

Kristin's laugh caught in her throat as she felt his lips close over the pulsing tip of her breast again. She moaned as he pressed her back onto the cool felt of the pool table, and the motions of her fingers were nothing short of frantic as she raised her skirts for him.

"Yes," he whispered, bending to nip her lightly through her panty hose.

Kristin's breath was quick and shallow. Delicious tension coiled within her as Zachary gently rolled down her hose and tossed them aside. She gasped when he brought her heels up to rest on the edge of the pool table.

"I'm going to enjoy this a great deal, princess," he told her, his lips moving against the satiny flesh of her inner thigh. "And so are you."

Kristin's first release came rapidly; it rumbled deep within her, like an earthquake, and left her shuddering in a series of mellow aftershocks.

"We're going to have to do better than that," Zach-

ary said, as he proceeded to bring her to the brink of an
emotional volcano. "Much better."

"Just take me," Kristin pleaded softly as he consumed
her. "Please, Zachary—"

He lifted his head. "I'm only giving in because I'm
so damn desperate," he replied. In the next moment he
was inside her, and Kristin was buoyed up on geysers of
hot lava. She was a sacrifice. Her flesh was molten, she
became a part of the liquid rock flowing from the center of the earth.

And Zachary swallowed her cries of passion even as
he sent his own hurtling into her throat....

Kristin came out of her reverie and was disgruntled
to find tears on her cheeks. She wiped them away with
dusty palms and looked around.

There was no sign of Zachary, and everything was
quiet. Too quiet.

She went to Zachary's pack and rifled through it, just
in case he might have another candy bar tucked away in
there somewhere. Sure enough, there was one, mashed
to bits but made of chocolate nevertheless. And he was
hiding a well-thumbed paperback mystery as well.

Since she hadn't read anything since she'd left the palace, Kristin was as hungry for the book as she was for
the candy bar. She opened them both, and gobbled them
simultaneously.

Of course, the chocolate was gone first. She was up
to page seventy-four in the book when she thought she
heard the nicker of a horse.

Jubilation surged within her, followed immediately
by fear. The rebels definitely had horses and Jascha's patrols would, too. Someone was approaching, but it wasn't
necessarily Zachary.

Wildly, Kristin looked around for shelter. There was

nothing except for a shallow recession in the hillside, where the shadows might hide her.

She dragged both backpacks over to it and hid them, along with herself. Her knee gave silent screams of pain at the sudden exertion, and her heart thumped against her breastbone in fright. She watched with wide eyes, her breath solid as a peach pit in her throat as the sounds grew nearer.

And then Zachary rode into sight, looking none the worse for wear and leading Kristin's horse behind his.

"You did it!" she cried, scrambling out of the indentation, ignoring the agony in her knee and brushing away the cobwebs that clung to her hair. "You got the horses back!"

Zachary grinned wearily as he dismounted.

"What did you do?" Kristin demanded eagerly. In spite of the fear she felt, she was caught up in the drama of imagining the scene. Zachary must have been magnificent.

"I gave them money."

Kristin was momentarily deflated, but she was too glad to see the horses—and Zachary—to dwell on the fact that things hadn't gone as they would have in an adventure movie. She went to the mare she'd come to think of as her own and patted its neck affectionately.

"We'd better get moving while there's still some daylight left," Zachary said, and Kristin realized that he was watching her with a peculiar expression in his eyes.

"Is something wrong?"

He shook his head. "Where are the packs?"

"In there," Kristin answered, pointing toward the cave that wasn't a cave. "I wasn't sure it was you when I heard the horses, so I hid."

Zachary nodded and went to retrieve the packs. He

found the mystery, too, with page seventy-four dog-eared. "You know I hate it when people do this to my books," he grumbled, holding the volume up as damning evidence. A moment later he carefully closed the book and tucked it into the pocket of his jacket.

Before Kristin could apologize and point out that she still had a hundred and fifty pages of the story to read, Zachary stormed over to her with his hands on his hips.

It was his standard intimidation pose, and Kristin didn't intend to be swayed by it.

"Come to think of it," he began, "what were you doing going through my pack?"

"I was looking for a candy bar," Kristin responded, folding her arms. "And I found one. You lied to me, Zachary—you said you didn't have any more!"

With a muttered curse he turned away from her, grasped her pack and practically flung it onto her back. "Since you won't be walking, you can carry this," he said as he fastened it.

Kristin glared at him, but it wasn't anger that soured her expression. It was pain. "You're doing it again," she accused.

He practically hurled her up onto her horse's back. "Doing what?" he snapped.

"Making a distance between us. Refusing to talk about what you're feeling. We're mad at each other! Why can't we just fight, like other people?"

The brim of Zachary's hat hid his face. "We have nothing to fight about," he muttered. And then he turned away.

"The hell we don't!" Kristin yelled, making her horse dance nervously beneath her. She watched with grim satisfaction as Zachary's shoulders stiffened under the worn, supple leather of his jacket. "I walked out on you. Didn't that make you angry?"

He turned and, for just a moment, Kristin was frightened by the raw emotion she saw in his face. Then, typically, he regained the formidable control that had probably served him well as an agent. "I wasn't surprised," he answered in an even voice. "I knew you'd feel the pea under our mattress, like a real princess, and go looking for a softer bed."

If Kristin had been close enough, she would have slapped him with all her might. "You bastard, are you insinuating that I left because I cared for someone else?"

His shoulders moved in an insolent shrug. "A princess needs a prince," he replied coldly, and then he turned and mounted his horse.

Kristin felt as though he'd backhanded her. She was torn between conflicting needs to cry and to rave like a wild woman, but she did neither. She just rode along behind Zachary, her teeth sunk into her lower lip, wishing she'd never come back to Cabriz at all.

They rode for hours before they stopped in a densely forested place that sheltered the mouth of a cave.

Kristin got down from the horse before Zachary could help her, biting back a cry at the response of the muscles in her knee, and began unbuckling her pack. She'd had to go to the bathroom for a long time, but she'd suffered in silence, too proud to ask Zachary for a break.

He was making up time, undoubtedly anxious to get her into Rhaos and off his hands.

Kristin went into the woods, attended to her business and returned. "There's a stream back there," she said in tones she might use to address a stranger. "I washed my hands in it."

Zachary had unsaddled the horses and tied them to separate stakes. "Fine," he said.

It was probably her exhaustion, Kristin told herself, and her injured knee, that brought tears so close to the surface. "Are we going to have a fire?" she asked, and her voice trembled. Zachary might be unpleasant, but having him ignore her was like being alone in that vast wilderness.

He nodded and disappeared into the timber without another word.

Kristin found a stump and sat down on it, despondent and bone tired. If she survived this ordeal and made it back to the United States, she vowed she would burrow in somewhere and write one hell of a book about the experience.

Of course, she'd leave out the times Zachary had made love to her. Those memories were naturally too private to share with the world. And too precious.

Zachary returned to camp with an armload of wood, which he tossed down in front of the cave. He glanced at Kristin once or twice as he laid the fire, but he was too damn stubborn to say anything. And that left Kristin with no choice.

"I'd like to finish that mystery novel, if you don't mind," she said.

He pulled it from his pocket and with a flick of his wrist sent it winging toward her.

It landed close enough that she could pick it up without leaving the stump. "Thank you."

Zachary crossed his stomach with one arm and bowed deeply, and there was no humor in the gesture, only mockery. "At your service, your ladyship."

Kristin bolted off the stump and limped over to him.

"Damn you, Zachary, stop patronizing me! All I want is a little honest conversation. Is that too much to ask?"

"Honest?" he rasped, towering over her, wrenching off his hat and flinging it aside. His hair, damp with sweat and crusted with dust, bore the impression of it. "You walked out without even giving me a chance to talk to you! Do you call that honest?"

"So you *are* angry."

"You're damn right I am! I loved you, lady! For six months after you left, I spent most of my time lying on the living-room floor, listening to somebody-done-me-wrong songs! I couldn't eat, I couldn't sleep, I couldn't think!" He leaned forward until his nose was a fraction of an inch from hers. "You, on the other hand, were probably running around with the prince!"

Kristin swallowed. She'd wanted Zachary to vent his anger, but she hadn't guessed how intense it would be. "I wasn't 'running around' with anybody," she said quietly. "Jascha and I were old friends. When he found out I was hurting, he wanted to help."

"You were hurting?" The question was harsh, like the rusty blade of a saw grating against metal. "Why, princess? Were your charge cards at their limits?"

Kristin stood her ground, refusing to be daunted. "I'm getting tired of your snide comments about my lifestyle and my background, Zachary Harmon! Maybe I've been a little indecisive in the past, but I'm a good person!"

She watched as the muscles in his jawline tensed, then relaxed again. After giving her a look of utter contempt, he turned and started to walk away.

Kristin caught hold of his arm and held on with all her strength. "I'm sorry I hurt you," she said when he glanced back at her.

He wrenched free of her grasp and straightened his

jacket with a shrugging motion. "Hurt me? Sweetheart, it would have been kinder if you'd taken a hammer to my kneecaps." With that, he returned to the fire and Kristin hobbled back to the stump, sat down and purposefully opened the mystery novel.

She gave up trying to read it after only one attempt; the print was blurred.

Once the fire was going, Zachary took something from his pack and disappeared into the woods. Kristin watched him vanish over the top of the paperback and dragged herself over to the blaze when he was gone. The heat felt good against her knee.

She was still sitting there, dazed with heartache and plain weariness, when Zachary returned, carrying two large fish on a stick.

Her stomach rumbled at the thought of something fresh to eat, but she was careful to hide her eagerness. "I didn't know you liked to read mysteries," she said, almost defiant in her insistence that they carry on some sort of conversation. Actually, there were a great many things she didn't know about Zachary.

Zachary didn't look at her as she brought a lightweight aluminum frying pan from his pack and set it over the coals. "That's one of my grandfather's," he said, his voice so low that it was barely audible.

Kristin remembered then that Zachary had been raised by his widowed grandfather. She turned the book in her hand and studied the battered cover. "A Dan Harmon mystery," the blurb read. "I guess when you read this you feel close to him," she ventured.

He looked at the book, then at her face. He didn't have to say his grandfather had been the only person in the world to give a damn about him, the belief was plain in his hazel eyes.

"When did he die?" Kristin asked. She couldn't remember Zachary sharing even that.

"The year I graduated from college," Zachary answered somewhat to Kristin's surprise, laying the fish he'd caught in the pan.

She put her hand on his arm; he brushed it off.

"Zachary—"

"Just leave me alone, Kristin," he bit out, rising to his feet again and walking away.

Kristin dropped her eyes to the novel, opened it to the dedication page. "For Zachary," it read. With a sniffle and a squaring of her shoulders, she flipped forward to page seventy-four and began reading.

The fish burned, but Kristin ate her share anyway, along with what was left of Zachary's.

"How's your knee?" he asked finally, as she lay propped on her elbows, reading by the light of the fire.

"It's okay," Kristin lied, turning a page.

"The cousin did it," Zachary announced.

It was a moment before Kristin realized he'd just given away the ending. And she was a mere fifteen pages from the finish.

"He did not!" she cried, slapping him on the shoulder with the book.

"With a monkey wrench," Zachary added.

Kristin looked at the last page. "That was mean-spirited," she protested when she saw that he was right.

He smiled at her, but there was no humor in his face or in his eyes. "Maybe I feel mean," he replied. And then he got up and laid out his sleeping bag beside the fire.

It shouldn't have bothered Kristin that he didn't join their two bags together, but it did. She felt a sting in her heart.

"You're not the first person who's ever had a hard

childhood, Zachary," she pointed out reasonably. "Or been hurt when a relationship went wrong."

"All right, Kristin," he invited, his tone cutting straight through her flesh to her soul. "Tell me how tough it was to be the only daughter of an ambassador."

"Will you stop playing Oliver Twist, please? Maybe you didn't have the privileges I did, but your grandfather was not a poor man. And my home life wasn't so great. My father never offered me one scrap of encouragement or respect in my life!"

Zachary said nothing for a long time, but when he did speak, his words left Kristin shaken. "I called you once. After you left."

The words stunned Kristin so much that for a long time she could only sit there, trying to absorb them. "You did?"

"Yes." Plainly, he wasn't going to give anything away. She would have to work for every word.

"Where was I?"

"Williamsburg. You were there with your parents and the prince—remember?"

Kristin was filled with an overwhelming sadness, and the beginnings of outrage. No one had told her about Zachary's call. "I didn't know," she said, thinking about her father. *If I survive this, Dad, you and I are going to war.*

"I talked to the ambassador." Zachary's voice was calm, matter-of-fact.

Kristin squeezed her eyes shut. "He didn't tell me."

Zachary gave a raw, mirthless chuckle. "The ambassador never saw me as an acceptable son-in-law," he replied, surprising Kristin. She'd expected him to accuse her of lying. "And I'll be damned if he wasn't right. You and I would never have made it, princess. We didn't have anything going for us except great sex."

Kristin was glad of the darkness; it hid the tears that had brimmed in her eyes at his words. "You're right," she said with all the dignity she could summon. "We should never have gotten together in the first place." She rolled out her sleeping bag, took off her shoes and crawled into bed. She'd wanted to fight it out with Zachary, and she'd gotten her way.

She hadn't counted on losing.

CHAPTER SEVEN

KRISTIN'S SLEEP WAS fitful that night; she missed the warmth and substance of Zachary's body lying next to hers. Several times she awakened and reached for him, only to remember that another rift had opened between them. And this time there would be no crossing the chasm.

Morning brought chilly fog and the welcome smell of something frying. Kristin sat up, drawn out of her sleeping bag by the almost-visible aroma. "Umm?" she muttered, hugging herself. "What is that?"

Zachary spared her a scant smile. "Corned beef mixed with freeze-dried potatoes and powdered eggs," he answered. "It tastes better than it sounds."

Kristin shook her head as he handed her a mug of his special campfire coffee. "You really are a marvel. Did they teach you this in secret agent school?"

Again he smiled, but there was something sad in the response that touched Kristin's heart like the back of a cold spoon. "I learned it from my grandfather. He had periodic yearnings to return to the land, like his hero."

"Who was?" Kristin prompted, taking a cautious sip of the hot, delicious coffee.

"Henry David Thoreau," Zachary replied. He wasn't looking at her then; he was busy dishing up his breakfast concoction. "Eat hearty, princess. I have a feeling today's going to be a challenge."

Kristin felt reasonably contented, except for a distinct case of heartbreak, as she accepted the plate he handed her. She thanked him automatically, but her brow was furrowed as she tried to catch his eye. "Why should this day be any worse than the rest?"

"Just a hunch," he answered, his voice low, his eyes scanning the trees that surrounded the cave.

Because she was hungry and the food smelled so good, Kristin began to eat. "You know," she said after swallowing, "if you ever get tired of teaching, you could always work as a short-order cook."

Zachary chuckled at that, albeit reluctantly. He was pulling his familiar trick of distancing himself from her, and he was all too adept at the technique. "Thanks, princess. I'll remember that."

Kristin was lonely for their old bristly camaraderie, and she tried to fan the flames of the conversation. "Do you like teaching?"

He shrugged, chewing. "It's all right," he said presently.

"But it isn't what you really want to do?"

His eyes linked with hers briefly, then turned away. "Sometimes," he said in quiet tones, "a man can get his life so screwed up that nothing pleases him, no matter how good it is." With that cryptic statement, he turned his concentration to his breakfast.

Kristin cleaned her plate, even though there was a lump in her throat, then got out of the sleeping bag to walk down to the stream and clean up. She yearned for a hot bath, clean clothes and a real bed, surrounded by solid walls, in a country with a stable government.

"How's your knee?" Zachary asked when she returned to camp. She'd groomed herself as best she could and washed her plate so it wouldn't appear that she had to be waited on all the time.

"It still hurts a little," Kristin replied honestly. "But I think it's getting better."

He was sipping coffee, and his gaze never quite met hers. "Maybe I'd better examine it."

Kristin's temper flared. "Heaven forbid," she said. "Then you'd actually have to look at me!"

His hazel eyes came swiftly to her face, fiery with some emotion Kristin didn't want to recognize. "Take your jeans off," he ordered brusquely.

In spite of all the times they'd made love, Kristin's cheeks went crimson at the suggestion. "No."

Zachary advanced toward her. "I'm going to look at your knee, Kristin, whether you take your jeans off or I do. The choice is yours."

Now it was Kristin whose gaze was averted. "I'm fine, really."

"Let me see." He was nearer now; she could feel him towering over her.

She knew she'd lost. With her teeth digging into her lip, she undid the snap and zipper of her jeans, pushed them toward her knees and sat down on the tree stump. "If anybody sees us," she said in a voice barely above a whisper, "I'll never forgive you!"

"If anybody sees us," Zachary countered, squatting down on his haunches to lay gentle fingers on her bruised, swollen knee, "we'll both be in big trouble. This is one time when we don't want the cavalry riding to the rescue."

Kristin winced involuntarily as he touched her knee, and he gave her an angry look.

"I'm glad it's better, princess," he said with cold sarcasm, "because if it were any worse, you'd need to be in a hospital."

"It isn't as bad as it looks," Kristin insisted, and when Zachary stood she followed suit, quickly pulling up and refastening her jeans.

He turned and walked away, only to return a few moments later with two pills in his hand. "Here," he said, holding out his palm. "They're just aspirin, but that might help."

"You've got practically everything in that pack of yours," Kristin said, trying to lighten the moment a little. "I don't suppose you have this week's issue of *People?*"

Zachary grinned in spite of himself. "Sorry, princess. The aspirin was it. Swallow them while I saddle the horses."

Kristin returned to the stream and knelt beside it, scooping up the cold, fresh water in her palms after tossing the aspirin into her mouth. An eerie feeling possessed her as she swallowed; it was as though she was being watched.

Shivering, she got awkwardly to her feet and looked around. Seeing nothing, she made her way back to camp.

Zachary helped her into her pack, making her feel a little like a child in a snowsuit with a balky zipper, then hoisted her onto her horse. The day ahead looked long and cold to Kristin, as well as painful, and she didn't have the heart to ask again how long it would be until they were over the border into Rhaos.

She knew she wouldn't like the answer.

They rode uphill throughout the morning, raising a lather on the patient horses, and the aspirin did little to quiet the persistent ache in Kristin's knee. It didn't help that she'd hurt that same joint during a game of tennis the year before, but nothing could have made her complain. She wasn't the spoiled princess Zachary thought she was, and she was going to prove that if she accomplished nothing else beyond survival.

During those first few hours Zachary spoke to her only once. He turned as they were about to pass through a narrow opening between two enormous rocks and said, "You'll be able to see the Rhaotian border in another few minutes."

Kristin was elated, though her joy was tinged with a shading of sadness because she knew she and Zachary would soon be parting forever. She wished, for one wild moment, that she could have conceived Zachary's baby; at least then she wouldn't have lost him entirely.

In the next few seconds it seemed that the world was shifting on it axis. One moment Kristin was lamenting the impossibility of pregnancy, the next she was frozen with horror.

Just as she followed Zachary through the cleft in the rocks, men in shabby trousers and shirts came from every direction, including overhead. They shouted and shrieked, and their faces were twisted with vicious concentration.

Zachary fought, but he was vastly outnumbered. They wrenched him from the saddle and swarmed over him.

Through it all she heard him shout, "Run, princess! Get the hell out of here!"

Kristin couldn't have left even if she'd wanted to. Her muscles were rigid with fear, her eyes wide. Bile rushed up into her throat as she watched the men beating Zachary.

Only when he fell unconscious to the ground did she scream.

She was dragged from her horse only moments later, and she had no reason to expect a fate different from

Zachary's. She braced herself, but the men only shuffled her along between them, their hands strong on her arms.

She looked back over one shoulder to see Zachary being half propelled and half dragged behind. *Don't hurt him any more,* she pleaded silently. Behind her the horses nickered and whinnied in confusion and panic. Kristin's hands were tied and she was flung unceremoniously into the back of a Jeep.

A bolt in the floor scraped her cheek, and her knee hurt so badly that she thought she might be sick. For all that, her mind and soul were full of Zachary. Where was he? What had they done to him?

Kristin squeezed her eyes shut and offered a silent prayer. *If one of us has to die, God, let it be me. Zachary was only trying to help.*

The Jeep's engine roared to life, and the dusty vehicle began to jolt and jostle its way down the mountainside. Kristin wondered whether their captors were rebels or guerrillas fighting on Jascha's side.

Either way, she and Zachary were in more trouble than the wildest imagination could have dreamed up.

Kristin consoled herself with the idea of writing a book about her experiences—should she be fortunate enough to survive. At the moment it looked as if she was bound to die young.

And probably in intense pain.

After what seemed like hours, the Jeep finally came to a lurching stop. Once again, strong brown hands lifted her, and she nearly fainted at the protest in her knee when the men set her on her feet.

"Who are you?" she asked angrily in her halting Cabrizian, and her captors laughed. There must have been a hundred of them, and there were at least twenty Jeeps.

A group of ramshackle huts stood nearby, their roofs covered with taut animal skins. Curious children and women, in the same trousers and pants as the men, gathered around, staring. Kristin turned her head, searching for Zachary, but there was no sign of him.

Dear God, Kristin thought, her numb hands still bound behind her, maybe they'd already killed him. Left him lying on the ground...

Hot tears filled her eyes. *Zachary,* she called silently.

She distinctly heard a response, though the sound seemed to come from inside her own head. *I told you this was going to be a bad day.*

The words were so distinctly Zachary's that Kristin actually smiled. He was alive, then. And he was nearby.

The relief nearly made her sag to the ground; the strangers pulled her roughly back into an upright position.

It was only later, when she'd been thrown onto a pile of skins in one of the huts, her hands still tied tightly behind her back, that she began to analyze the experience and thus to doubt it. She'd only thought she heard Zachary speak to her; she didn't have psychic episodes and neither did he.

Her heart was so heavy that she just lay still for a long time, held down by the weight of her sorrow. If Zachary died because of her silly fantasies about marrying a prince and ruling over a storybook land, she was never going to forgive herself.

Not that she was likely to live much longer than he did.

Finally Kristin struggled into a sitting position and looked around. There was no one else in the hut, although she could hear excited voices outside, arguing in rapid Cabrizian. Although she'd forgotten most of the language, she got the gist of the conversation—one faction was in favor of rape, the other wanted to sell her back to the prince.

She lowered her head. It probably hadn't been difficult to figure out that she was Jascha's runaway bride. She and Zachary were without a doubt the only Caucasians in the entire country. What had made them think they could get away?

Presently a woman came in. She brought a ladle of water and held it to Kristin's lips. Thinking of typhoid and hepatitis and all the other diseases that flourished in these remote villages, Kristin drank. She was simply too thirsty to refuse.

"My friend," she began, grappling with the language. "Is he well?"

The woman, who wore the prescribed trousers and shirt, did not look at Kristin. Nor did she answer. She just scurried out of the hut and let the crude wooden door fall shut behind her.

"Excuse me," Kristin called, lapsing into English in her frustration. "Excuse me, but I need to use the bathroom!"

There was no answer, and Kristin sat in utter misery, her wrists throbbing where the thongs chafed against her skin, her fingers so numb she couldn't feel them. Her heart and her knee, however, fairly pulsed with pain, one keeping time with the other.

After a long time the woman returned and untied Kristin's hands. She chattered incomprehensibly and shook one finger, then led her captive toward the door.

Kristin took the indecipherable discourse as a warning and tried to look submissive as she followed her keeper out into the afternoon sunlight. Another look around reinforced the dismal fact that there would be no escaping.

The woman led her to a pit some distance from the village. Even in the cool, crisp air there were flies, and the stench was enough to curdle Kristin's stomach.

Nonetheless, she did what she had to do and allowed herself to be ushered back to camp.

Again, she searched eagerly for Zachary as she passed among the people. Again, there was no trace of him.

Inside the hut, the woman tied Kristin's hands behind her back again, though this time the thongs were not pulled so tightly. She sank down onto the skins, which were considerably cleaner than the ones she and Zachary had slept on in that other hut just a few nights before, and closed her eyes.

There had to be a way out of this situation, she thought. Perhaps if she told the men her father would pay ransom...

But that would be difficult. Someone would have to bring the money into Cabriz, and a trade would need to be made. There would be nothing to stop her captors from taking the money and still killing her and Zachary, as well as the messenger. Provided a messenger could be found in the first place.

Cabriz wasn't exactly a hot tourist attraction at the moment.

Kristin's reflections were interrupted when the door of the hut opened again and one of the men came in, carrying a rifle across one arm. His eyes were quick, black and mean, and they skittered over Kristin's prone figure like a stone over smooth water.

Instantly she tensed. "Don't touch me," she breathed in English, too frightened to search her mind for the Cabrizian words.

The man laughed and spoke to her in her own language, though his words were so heavily accented that she could barely make them out. "You cannot afford to give orders, pretty one."

Kristin was silent, watching him, waiting.

He squatted beside her, reached out to sift her hair through grubby fingers. She tried to pull away; he tightened his grasp and gave the lock a painful wrench.

"The prince will pay much money for you," he said. "And for your friend."

Kristin tried to suppress the shudder that went through her. Jascha would not be forgiving of her actions or of Zachary's—it was the code of his culture to take vengeance when it was called for. To do anything less would be to lose face. "You are rebels," she said calmly. "Why would you want to please the prince?" She paused, swallowed. "My father is rich. He'll give you more money than Jascha would, if you'll just let us go."

The rebel laughed and thumped his chest with one fist. "You think we are fools? The prince will give us more than gold. He will pay in guns and prisoners, and medicine and food."

Kristin knew he was probably right. And that Jascha would make her and Zachary wish they'd never been born long before he finally relieved them of their lives. "So you're turning us over to the prince?"

Her visitor nodded, black eyes glittering. "Tonight you stay," he said, and once again his gaze ran the length of her.

"You'd better not lay a hand on me," Kristin said, operating on pure bravado as she struggled to sit up. It was an awkward pursuit, with her hands caught together behind her that way. "I was to be the prince's wife. He won't pay if you've used me."

He gestured toward the door with a slight motion of his dark head. "The other one, he use you. And Jascha will kill him for it." A slow, insolent grin spread across the man's face.

Kristin thought it was probably a good thing she was bound; otherwise, she would have slapped him. "Jascha's a jealous man. He'll kill you, too. And all your friends."

The rebel gave a shout of laughter at that. "He try. He fail. I do what I want."

Kristin's blood turned cold in her veins, but she kept her chin high and her gaze remained defiant. Not for one moment did she think her opponent was intimidated; his boast had not been an idle one. He could do what he wanted, and Kristin had no real way to protect herself.

But suddenly an argument erupted outside, just when she thought all was certainly lost, and the man disappeared.

Although she was nearly faint with relief, Kristin couldn't allow herself to fold. She scrambled to her feet and sneaked to the door, pressing her ear to the wood. The rebels were still engaged in their earlier debate, one side in favor of savagery and murder, the other leaning toward the money, food and guns Jascha could provide.

Kristin didn't find either prospect appealing, but of course she would have chosen being returned to Jascha if they'd offered her an option. That, at least, would give her and Zachary some time to escape.

When she heard someone approaching the hut, a man talking in a voice as loud and angry as the others, she drew back, eyes wide, wondering if the prisoners' fate had at last been decided. Whatever happened, Kristin hoped she wouldn't have to see Zachary suffer.

The door opened and a man came in. He was older than the first visitor, and he moved with authority. "Hakan," he said, tapping his chest with one finger. Then he pointed the same digit at Kristin.

"Kristin Meyers," she answered.

He took her arm in a firm but painless grasp and turned her, and Kristin's cheeks burned. He was assessing her value, just as he might that of a broodmare or a ewe in the marketplace.

With a cocked thumb, he gestured toward the door. "Harmon is your man?"

Kristin knew Zachary would love that question, their circumstances notwithstanding, and she vowed he'd never hear about it—or know what her answer had been. "Yes," she said with a lift of her chin. There was always the chance the men in the village wouldn't trouble her if they thought she belonged to someone else. Even among bandits there was a code where such things were concerned.

Hakan laid the palm and splayed fingers of one hand over Kristin's belly, and while she flinched, she forced herself not to try to wrench away. "Make child?"

She shook her head. "No. I—I can't make children." She wasn't about to explain why; it was none of Hakan's business.

The shrewd leader looked surprised, then downright contemptuous. "No make child, what use?" he asked.

Kristin's responses were necessarily limited. This guy wouldn't care that she could put on a party for two hundred people or write a sparkling article for the social pages of a magazine or newspaper. Nor would it matter that she played a mean game of tennis.

To his way of thinking, and that of the rest of his culture, women were good for two things—cooking and making babies.

"I can cook," she lied.

Hakan's expression revealed frank skepticism. Again, Kristin had the feeling that if Zachary had been there, he would have laughed. "You go Jascha," he decided. "We take money. Guns."

For all that she'd just been given a reprieve of sorts, Kristin was vaguely insulted. She held on to her temper, reminding herself that this was no time to indulge in tantrums. "What about my friend?"

Hakan smiled, revealing large yellow teeth. "Jascha pay much for him. More for him than for you."

"Could I see him, please? My friend?"

Hakan's lip came down like an automatic garage door, and the smile disappeared. "No!" he raged. And for a moment Kristin thought he was going to strike her.

Although her every instinct called for it, she refused to cower. "He won't be any use to Jascha if he's hurt," she reminded Hakan in a reasonable tone of voice as he turned away to open the door. "Please. I want to see him."

The man turned and studied her for a long moment, and she thought she saw something like respect flicker in his eyes. Whatever the emotion was, it was gone in the space of a heartbeat.

"Come," he said tersely. "You see Harmon."

Silently thanking a friendly fate, Kristin stepped toward the door. Hakan took her arm and thrust her outside, into the last blazing brightness of the sun. In just a few hours it would be dark.

While the other rebels looked on in silence, Hakan led Kristin across the village to another hut, opened the door and gestured.

Because she'd just come from darkness into blazing light and was now going into gloom again, Kristin had to pause a moment on the threshold to let her eyes adjust. When they had, she saw Zachary lying half-conscious on the floor.

Kristin turned her head and looked Hakan straight in the eye. "Untie my hands," she ordered.

The rebel leader paused a moment, probably stunned by her audacity. Then, remarkably, he reached down and loosened the thongs binding her wrists together. His face left no doubt in her mind that his leniency had distinct limits. "You try to run away, we kill," he said.

Kristin nodded and turned toward the only man she'd ever loved. "I need cold, clean water and some cloth," she said to Hakan. And then she went and knelt beside the prone form on the dirt floor of the hut. "Zachary?"

His hand locked around hers. "Princess." He breathed the word, rather than speaking it. His eyes didn't seem to focus, and his face was covered with dried blood. "Did they hurt you?"

Although Kristin wanted very much to cry, she knew it would be the worst thing she could do. She kissed his forehead. "Looks like you got the worst of it," she replied gently. "Are any of your bones broken?"

Zachary thought for a moment, then shook his head. "No. But they probably will be soon. When we get to the palace, princess, tell Jascha I kidnapped you—"

Kristin felt her throat tighten. "No. That would only make it worse for you."

"It's going to be bad for me any way you look at it, Kris." His fingers entangled themselves gently in her hair, his thumb soothed her pulsing temple. "There's no reason for you to suffer if you can avoid it. And if you can save Jascha's pride, you'll also save that shapely little rear end of yours."

She wrapped her arms around him, held him close. "Oh, Zachary, I'm so sorry for getting you into this. I was such an idiot, believing in fairy tales—"

The door creaked open, and a woman came in with a

basin of water and a piece of cloth. By the time she and Zachary were alone again, Kristin had gathered her frail composure.

Gently she began to wash the blood from his face, too stricken by the cost of her foolishness to talk.

Zachary laid a very dirty hand to her cheek. "Princess, I can handle anything but seeing you hurt. Now promise me you'll mollify Jascha in any way you can."

Kristin ran her tongue over dry lips and shook her head. "No. I couldn't live with myself—"

Zachary's voice was suddenly harsh. "Listen to me. You won't live at all if you don't tell Jascha that I forced you to leave the palace. You think you know the man, but *I* know the culture, and the prince's honor won't be worth spit if he doesn't avenge this."

She let her forehead rest against his. "Okay, Zachary," she said, wanting only to calm him. But even then she knew she couldn't betray him to protect herself. "Okay." She kissed his forehead. "Whatever you say."

He smiled and kissed her lightly on the lips. "Of course, if we get a chance to skip out, we'll take it," he whispered. "Be ready, princess."

Kristin nodded as Hakan came in and pulled her roughly back to her feet. He tied her hands behind her back again, as much for Zachary's benefit, she thought, as his own, and then pushed her toward the door.

There were so many things Kristin wanted to say that she didn't manage to voice one of them. She just looked at Zachary for a long moment, then allowed Hakan to drag her out into the hot sunshine again.

She was taken back to the other hut and, when the same woman returned to keep an eye on her, her wrists were unbound. She was allowed to wash her hands and face in cold water and given a small dish of rice and a bowl-like cup of tea.

Since there were no chopsticks, or utensils of any kind, Kristin ate with her fingers. She was hungry, despite everything, and if the chance to escape presented itself she didn't want to be in a weakened state.

Her knee was hurting again, now that Zachary's aspirin had worn off, but Kristin had other things to think about.

Perhaps, she reflected as she drank the strong, flavorful tea, she could reason with Jascha. Cultural dictates aside, he was a gentle, sensible man. He'd attended college in the United States and, of course, he'd dressed like an American then, though now he seemed to be embracing Cabrizian ways again. Surely Kristin could make him see that a marriage between the two of them would have been a mistake anyway, and that there was nothing all to be gained by punishing Zachary.

By the time Kristin huddled up on the skins to sleep that night, she'd convinced herself that Jascha would forgive her and Zachary both, and let them go back home in peace. Believing that was the only way she could have gotten any rest.

When she awakened to a chilly morning, however, all her doubts returned to haunt her.

Once, she'd truly believed that she knew Jascha. She would have put her very life in his hands. Now, however, logic told her that Zachary was right. The prince had been conditioned by centuries of tradition, and one socialite probably wasn't going to change his mind.

Kristin was given more rice and tea, but this time she couldn't eat or drink. She could think only about all the horrors that might well lie ahead.

It was about ten o'clock, she judged, when she saw

Zachary being led from his hut. Like her, he was bound, but his manner was inexplicably cocky. He caught her eye and grinned.

She glowered at him, silently reminding him that he might at least have the good sense to be scared, and his grin stretched from one side of his dirty, bruised face to the other, showing his strong white teeth.

I love you, Kristin thought desperately as she was lifted into the back of another Jeep. *And isn't this a hell of a time to think of it.*

CHAPTER EIGHT

ANOTHER RUSTY BOLT bruised Kristin's cheek as she bumped along in the back of the rebel Jeep toward almost certain doom. The bright sunlight was frying her, her head and injured knee were both throbbing and her stomach was threatening revolt, but her mind was on Zachary, not herself.

He wanted to take the blame for what had happened, to spare her from Jascha's rage. She wondered if Zachary knew he still loved her, or if it was a secret his subconscious mind was keeping from the rest of his brain.

Despite everything, Kristin smiled. Zachary loved her. Maybe, if by some miracle they got out of this fix, there was a chance of making their relationship work.

Because present reality was so painful, Kristin let her mind wander into a rosy future, where she and Zachary were married. In her fantasy they were furnishing a large split-level house with a view of the ocean. Zachary was teaching, and she was pregnant and hard at work on the book about Cabriz....

Cabriz. Kristin was jolted back to the floor of that filthy Jeep just as it came to a screeching halt.

What now, she wondered, biting her lower lip. They couldn't have reached Kiri so fast—that would take hours more. She waited, fighting down a wave of panic, until someone came and lifted her out of the vehicle.

She looked around, dazed. There were only two Jeeps

now, instead of twenty or more, and Zachary was handcuffed to the roll bar of the other one.

Only then did Kristin realize that the rebels couldn't just drive boldly up to the palace door with their prisoners, no matter how valuable. She and Zachary would be hidden until a deal had been struck, and that could take days.

She was both relieved and fearful. The more time that passed before the two of them were turned over to Jascha, the better the chances of their escaping. On the other hand, the rebels could get bored and decide to play a few games of their own.

The driver of the Jeep Kristin had been riding in jabbed her in the back with the tip of a rifle barrel and ordered her to move. She stumbled into the woods toward a hut and prayed that her captor loved his wife.

The doorway was covered only by the tanned hide of some animal, and this curtain was pushed aside as Kristin approached. A tiny Cabrizian man smiled at her, showing broad gaps between his teeth, and gestured for her to come in.

She risked a backward glance and saw that Zachary was behind her. He gave her an almost imperceptible nod, and she stepped into the darkened hut.

Something made with cabbage was cooking on a little oil-powered stove in the corner, but there was no other furniture except for the inevitable pile of skins where the residents probably slept.

To Kristin's surprise, her hands were untied, and she was given water in a cup made of some smoothly polished wood. With trembling fingers—only a little sensation had returned—Kristin held the cup to Zachary's lips.

He resisted for a moment, then sipped. His face and hair were filthy, and every visible inch of his skin seemed to be covered with abrasions, bruises and cuts. Kristin knew he was in pain, but he was too stubborn and too proud to complain.

Although the apparent owner of the house had slipped out, one of the two rebel soldiers who had escorted Kristin and Zachary into the hut was still in evidence. He lost patience and, with a muffled exclamation, slapped the cup from Kristin's hand.

Flames of fury licked to life inside her, and Zachary must have seen their reflections in her eyes.

"Hold your tongue, princess," he said evenly, just as she was about to tell her captor what she thought of his manners. "This guy's not an insolent waiter biding time until he gets his big break in the theater. He's a trained killer."

Kristin averted her eyes and hugged herself, fighting down a rage that was born more of fear and panic than anger.

Since his hands were bound and there was a gun trained on his head, Zachary could offer comfort only by words and the timbre of his voice. "We've got to stay calm, Kris. It's our only chance."

At this the guard grew angry and shouted at Zachary in such rapid dialect that Kristin failed to understand it.

"He wants me to go outside," Zachary explained with a philosophical sigh as he turned toward the door. "Remember, princess—don't needle these bozos. They're all about five seconds from liftoff as it is."

Kristin swallowed. "I'll be careful," she promised.

And Zachary was led out, but she was alone for only a moment. When her guard returned, he handcuffed her to a rusted metal ring lodged in the dirt floor of the hut, restricting her movements so that she could only lie on the smelly skins. She watched him with wide, fearful eyes—his thoughts were plainly visible in his face.

He was wondering if he could get away with raping her.

He must have decided not to risk angering his superiors, because he left the hut, shoving the hide curtain aside with a furious motion of one hand as he passed.

The small man returned almost immediately, but he didn't frighten Kristin so much as the guard had. He'd smiled at her earlier, and she'd seen no irony or hatred in his face.

He knelt beside the skins and spoke to Kristin with gentle patience. He wanted to know why she'd been limping.

Under the circumstances, kindness was an unexpected weapon, and Kristin had no defense against it. She wept softly and told him about the injury to her knee, knowing all the while that he understood nothing beyond the gesture of laying her hand to the offending joint.

He found a knife somewhere and cut a slit up the leg of Kristin's blue jeans, then laid the fabric aside to look at her knee. He prodded the swollen flesh with a careful finger, then crept away into the shadows.

By that time her knee was hurting so badly that Kristin was afraid she'd faint. When her host returned and held a cup containing some warm liquid to her lips, she raised her head and drank.

Sleep consumed her almost instantly, dragging her down into its black, healing folds and secreting her there.

When she awakened, the pain in her knee had subsided and the smell of boiled cabbage was dense enough to choke her. She sat up and squinted, trying to see through the smoky shadows.

Zachary was sitting with his back to the opposite wall,

his knees drawn up, holding a bowl to his mouth with cuffed hands. "Feeling better?"

Although her knee was definitely improved—when she touched it gingerly with her free hand she found that the swelling had gone down—Kristin was far from her best. "Just terrific," she answered. "My hair is matted and probably full of bugs, and my skin is so dirty it's a wonder someone hasn't written 'wash me' on my forehead. I'm hungry enough to eat anything that won't try to crawl away from me, and one of my wrists is chained to an iron ring. All in all, Zachary, I'd say 'better' isn't the way I feel."

The thin moonlight seeping into the hut through various cracks and crevices showed that he was grinning. "You're bitching. With you, that's a good sign."

Kristin sighed. "What's in that bowl?"

"Some kind of cabbage and fish concoction. Want some?"

"Every part of me except my stomach is voting no," Kristin answered, brushing tangled hair back from her face.

Zachary chuckled then called out in Cabrizian, and the little man came in. He beamed at Kristin, went to the small, smoky stove, and dished up some soup.

The stuff looked, smelled and tasted terrible, and yet Kristin could hardly keep herself from gobbling it down the way a hungry dog would.

"How do I tell him I have to go to the bathroom?" she asked, once the hunger pangs had stopped gnawing at her middle. Since her host was still smiling at her, she smiled back.

Zachary spoke the dialect deftly, but his request made Kristin lower her eyes and blush a little all the same.

Their gentle guard went out and returned moments later with a rusted tin can.

Kristin looked at it in horror. "He doesn't mean—?"

"He's got orders not to release us under any circumstances," Zachary put in helpfully.

Looking at him more closely, she saw that his feet were hobbled with rope, as well as tied to the same iron ring that held her virtually immobile. "But I need privacy," she sputtered.

"I need a steak dinner, a hot bath and a back rub," Zachary answered. "We're even, princess."

"Hardly," Kristin snapped back, her earlier charitable thoughts fleeing as she considered her predicament.

"This doesn't have to be a problem, your ladyship. I'll turn my head," Zachary offered reasonably, "and Ward Cleaver here will step outside."

Kristin looked in desperation from one male face to the other and finally nodded her capitulation. Her choices were, after all, limited.

"What about those goons with the guns?" she asked, once she'd taken care of the humiliating business and her birdlike host had carried away the can. "Are they around somewhere?"

Zachary shook his head. "They've been gone for hours. It isn't likely they'd want to be in this neck of the woods when Jascha's soldiers come to pick up the spoils of battle."

Kristin had to work up her courage to ask, since she was so afraid of the answer. "When do you think that will be?"

He shrugged. "My guess would be dawn, since both sides are probably anxious to make a deal. But it could be days, or even weeks, if negotiations hit any kind of snag."

Kristin nodded toward their happy jailer. "This guy

seems pretty friendly. Maybe if you talked to him he'd see reason and let us go."

The reply was another shake of the head. "I offered him everything from money to a boxcar load of Hershey bars. Not unlike the rest of us, he prefers to keep his hide."

There wasn't much to say after that. Kristin didn't have the courage to ask Zachary if he still loved her; she was too afraid he'd say no.

After an hour, Kristin was given another cupful of the mysterious herbal tea that had taken away the pain and swelling in her knee. She slept soundly, dreamlessly, until she was roughly awakened.

Someone shook her, spoke to her sharply and wrenched her to her feet before she'd even managed to open her eyes.

She recognized Jascha's favorite lieutenant, a solidly built man called Quang. His face was twisted with cruel satisfaction as he spat an insulting Cabrizian word.

"You'll forgive me, princess," Zachary stated as two of Jascha's soldiers hoisted him to his feet, "if I don't defend your honor."

"Kindly keep your smart remarks to yourself," Kristin told him, rubbing the wrist of the hand that had been cuffed to the ring throughout the night.

Quang interrupted the process to manacle her to his own wrist and stride out the door. Zachary, still hobbled and bound, was dragged behind.

The sun was rising, and birds chirped in the trees.

During the ride into Kiri—more Jeeps—Kristin was at least allowed to sit in the front seat with the driver, instead of lying in back on the floor. Her fear increased with every passing mile, and when the palace came into sight she thought her heart would stop beating.

Cruelly, on the way the little procession passed the compound that had once housed the American embassy. The unexpected reminder of long-ago, carefree times nearly brought tears to Kristin's eyes.

Just as they approached the palace, and the towering iron gates swept inward to admit them, a roar filled the sky and the treetops swayed as if caught in a gale. Kristin looked up to see a helicopter hovering over the courtyard.

Jascha.

Kristin suppressed a shudder and lifted her chin a little higher. No matter what happened, she would maintain her dignity.

The Jeep screeched to a stop on the cobblestones in front of a side door. Quang got out of the Jeep, forcing Kristin to climb between the steering wheel and the seat to follow, since she was handcuffed to him.

Inside the palace, in a cool, shadowy entryway, Quang unlocked the cuffs and released Kristin into the custody of Mai and a half-dozen women in robes and veils.

Color climbed her cheeks as they took her arms; these were Jascha's wives—the women who had drugged her the night of the escape with Zachary.

Kristin was filled with fear. She turned wildly in an effort to find Zachary.

His hazel eyes were calm, if weary, as he looked back at her. And his solemn expression reminded her to keep her composure at all costs.

Drawing in a deep breath, Kristin absorbed the courage he lent her and allowed herself to be taken away.

The wives led her upstairs, into Jascha's private living quarters, where they clucked and fussed over her as though she were a naughty child caught playing in a mud puddle in her Sunday dress.

Kristin tried to shift her mind to another place, a secret

hideaway in the center of her soul, and made no protest
as the women removed her clothes.

A bath filled with hot, scented water was waiting.
Under any other circumstances, it would have been pure
luxury. Knowing what could lie ahead, it was an ordeal
instead.

Kristin was bathed—the women allowed her to shave
her own legs and underarms, at least—and her hair was
shampooed. The tub was drained and then filled again,
and she lay in the fresh water still concentrating on nothing. She couldn't afford to think or feel.

There was a clapping sound, a muttered order, and the
wives disappeared like a flock of colorful birds.

Kristin held her breath as Jascha walked into the bathroom.

He wore a tailored navy blue suit with a striped shirt
and a smart tie, and his dark hair was expertly cut. He
might have been a successful businessman, rather than
the future head of the faltering Cabrizian government.
Certainly no one expected Jascha's father to return from
exile and rule again.

"Hello, Kristin," the prince said, coming to sit on the
wide edge of the enormous marble tub.

His brown eyes moved over her naked body, which
was only veiled by the water of her bath, not hidden.

She swallowed. Here was her chance. She could tell
Jascha that Zachary had taken her away by force and,
perhaps, save herself from the prince's vengeance....

"What happened?" Jascha asked reasonably, reaching
for one of the enormous white towels Kristin had found
so to her liking when she'd first arrived at the palace.

She took the towel and got shakily to her feet, hiding
behind the terry cloth as best she could. "I told you be-

fore," she said evenly. "I changed my mind. I don't want to be your wife."

Jascha's eyes were hot as he watched her cover herself, even though his manner was still strangely placid. "You love this Zachary Harmon, then—the American who took you away?"

Kristin hesitated. To say she loved Zachary, even though it was the truest thing about her, would only intensify Jascha's yen for revenge. "No," she said. "I only used him. There is a man at home."

"You lie," Jascha accused, and Kristin could see that he was seething. Any moment now he would erupt.

"What are you going to do?" she asked with a tranquillity that surprised even her.

A bitter smile curved Jascha's sculptured lips, and it occurred to Kristin that the situation in his country might have driven the prince a little mad. She had never seen that particular expression on his face before, in all the years she'd known him.

"Jascha?" she prompted, standing on the other side of the vast marble tub, one hand holding the towel tight.

"You will be punished," he said with a sort of pleasant resignation. "And then you will be my wife, as we planned."

Kristin trembled with the effort to raise her next question nonchalantly. "And Zachary?"

Jascha smiled again, as though he anticipated some festival or longed-for gift. "He will die. That, my pretty bride, will be the fate of all your lovers, so I would advise you not to take more."

For a moment, the air around Kristin seemed as heavy and dense as water. There was a queer buzzing in her ears, and she thought she would faint. She swayed, caught herself. "You mustn't do this, Jascha. It's murder. Give me whatever punishment you wish, but don't kill Zachary. *Please* don't kill him."

"So," Jascha said, and his smile turned sad, philosophical. "You would beg for him. And yet you say you do not love this man."

Kristin drew a deep breath, let it out slowly. "I would beg for anyone, Jascha. It isn't right, taking an innocent life—"

"Innocent?" Jascha gave a bitter chuckle after uttering the word. "Do not think me a fool, Kristin. I felt the fire burning between you and Harmon. I heard your cries in the night as he made love to you."

The color drained from Kristin's face, and Jascha laughed at her shock.

"So it's true," Jascha said with a sort of wounded mockery. He sighed and rubbed his eyes with a thumb and forefinger. "You grieve me, Kristin. I trusted you. I believed you when you said you loved me."

Kristin edged closer to the wall, more afraid and more vulnerable than she'd ever been in her life. "I believed it, too, Jascha—when I said it."

"And now?"

"Now I want to go home."

"This," Jascha said, with aggrieved patience, "is your home." He cocked his thumb toward the sumptuous quarters beyond the bathroom archway. "And that is your bed. You will lie in it whenever I summon you, and you will be a loving wife."

Kristin's hand tightened on the towel, and she tried to sink into the wall behind her.

"Remove that," Jascha ordered, gesturing toward the towel.

Kristin swallowed hard. "Jascha, please..."

"Remove the towel!" he shouted.

Closing her eyes tightly, Kristin forced her fingers to release the fold of terry cloth she held, and she felt cold air touch her flesh as she let it fall.

She sensed Jascha's approach, used all the strength at her command to keep from screaming. His gaze seemed to burn into her skin.

And then his finger curved under her chin. "Open your eyes, Kristin," he said with a deceptive softness.

She obeyed, having no other choice, and her soul went cold at the fury she saw in his face.

"You are very beautiful," he told her, "for a whore."

Kristin stood still, waiting, knowing she had no option but to endure.

Jascha reached down, picked up the towel and draped it almost gently around her. "You will be taken to the room you occupied before," he said. "Dress as you please, but wait there until I send someone for you."

Too grateful for a reprieve, however temporary, to argue, Kristin nodded and proceeded into the bedroom beyond. A blue silk robe had been laid out for her, and she put it on, letting the towel fall away beneath as she closed it, never once meeting Jascha's gaze.

When she bent to pick up the discarded towel, he stopped her. "Leave it," he said, and she did.

He escorted her down the hall to the guest room where she had stayed until the day of her escape with Zachary, and even opened the door for her.

Mai was waiting inside. She'd brought a tray containing hot tea in a delicate porcelain pot, the sugary little cakes Kristin loved and a bowl of fresh fruit.

Jascha went out without a word to either Kristin or Mai.

Kristin ate hungrily, then fondly touched her camera, her journal, the clothes that filled the drawers and the closet. As terrible as her situation was, there was some comfort in having her own things around her again.

When Mai had taken the tray away—and locked the door behind her—Kristin took off the robe and put on clean underwear, a pair of trim gray slacks and a silk shirt in dark blue. Then she sprayed herself with her favorite cologne, brushed her hair and wound it into a French braid, and put on makeup.

After that she paced, waiting, feeling as Anne Boleyn must have felt locked away in the Tower. One hour passed, and then another, and no one came for her.

She got out her journal and wrote, her pen flying rapidly over the pages as she put down memory after memory of her flight with Zachary. And only after the condensed account was completed did she realize that committing what had happened to black and white was probably not the smartest thing she'd ever done.

Anxiously, Kristin searched the room for a place to hide the leather-bound book, but there was none where it would really be safe. She glanced at the hearth and considered burning the volume, but everything within her resisted that. She was a writer, and those pages contained firsthand accounts of her experiences.

Finally, she tucked the journal into a flap in her camera case. That would have to do until she could think of something better.

Kristin began to pace again, but odd noises in the courtyard drew her to the window. She looked out to see a handful of Jascha's soldiers erecting a large wooden pole, and a chill went through her as she watched them hoist it into place.

The sound of a key turning in the lock drew her attention, however, and she turned her back on the strange pillar. The possibility that Jascha had sent for her, or come in person, took precedence over all other concerns.

But it was Mai who entered, moving silently in her gossamer blue gown, her face hidden behind the veil.

"Yes?" Kristin couldn't bear the quiet; if she was being summoned to Jascha, she wanted to know it. "Has the prince asked for me?"

Mai looked at Kristin with exotic, unreadable eyes. "No," she said. "He will not send for you tonight."

Kristin felt hope leap within her. "He won't? Why not?"

The woman glanced away. "He is going."

"Going? Where?"

Mai shook her head, and even as she made the motion, the great blades of the helicopter filled the air with noise. Kristin rushed to the window and saw Jascha getting into the cockpit, along with a woman dressed in a flowing green gown.

"That woman," Kristin said, staring out the window. "She's one of Jascha's wives?"

"Yes," Mai answered softly.

"And you?"

"I am also his wife."

Because Mai had attended her since her arrival in Cabriz, Kristin had assumed the woman was a servant. She watched thoughtfully as the helicopter rose into the air and then swung off sideways toward the horizon. Then she turned to look at Mai. "Surely you don't want your husband to have me for a bride, in addition to the others."

Mai simply looked at the floor. It would not be proper for her to express such an opinion.

Impulsively, Kristin grasped Mai's hands in hers and squeezed them. "Please—you must help me. I've got to find my friend, Mr. Harmon, and leave here before Jascha comes back."

Mai lifted her eyes to meet Kristin's, and they were filled with dread. "No! There is no escaping—not for you or for your Mr. Harmon. There is no way I can help you!"

"You must know where they're holding Zachary."

The woman shook her head. "You cannot help him. He will die when Jascha returns, and you will be punished for your treachery."

Kristin raised a hand to her temple, then lowered it again. There was no sense in arguing with Mai; she would never be able to change her mind. She went back to the window. "That big pole out there—what is it for?"

Mai was silent so long that Kristin finally turned to stare at her.

"Mai?"

"I do not know," said Jascha's wife, so quickly and so fiercely that Kristin knew she was lying.

"Tell me!"

But Mai was in retreat. She opened the door, hurried out and turned the key in the lock.

Kristin looked at the pillar again, shivered, and pulled the thin curtains closed over the window.

The room was full of books—Jascha had been so eager to please her when she first returned to Cabriz— and Kristin needed refuge desperately. She went to the shelves, found a volume of Walt Whitman's poetry and stretched out on her bed to read.

At first her worries made it difficult to concentrate, but she persisted, and finally the beautiful words reached out to enfold and shelter her. They carried her far away from Cabriz, and Jascha, and all the problems she couldn't solve.

Mai did not deliver Kristin's dinner that night. It was

brought instead by one of the other wives, a younger woman wearing a pink robe.

"What's your name?" Kristin asked quickly when the girl would have hurried out.

"Tala," a soft voice answered from behind the ever-present veil.

Kristin had no doubt that she too would be forced to cover her face and most of her body once she was officially Jascha's wife.

"What do you think of my marrying the prince?" Kristin asked casually, watching the lovely eyes closely as she spoke. She was, at the same time, pouring tea into a cup.

Tala's eyes flashed fire for a moment. "You will wear white," she said, and the statement sounded like an accusation. Kristin couldn't remember whether white symbolized virginity in Cabriz, the way it did in the Western world. In the East it was the color of mourning.

"I would leave—and not marry Jascha—if you would help me."

"Leave?" Tala failed to keep a note of hope from sounding in that one word.

"If you would just do two things—forget the key to this room when you go out, and tell me where to find Mr. Harmon—"

Tala's eyes grew wide and she retreated a step, shaking her head. "Jascha would be angry."

Kristin took her hand and dragged her forcibly to the window, where she pushed aside the curtain. "That pole out there—what is it for?"

Tala looked at her fearfully. "It is a whipping post," she answered. And then she pulled free of Kristin's grasp and rushed out of the room.

CHAPTER NINE

A WHIPPING POST.

Kristin's fingers turned white, so tight was her grasp on the window ledge. Horrible images, splashed with crimson, flipped through her mind.

After several minutes, using every ounce of resolution she possessed, Kristin came away from the window and went to the mirror over the vanity table. She was trembling visibly, her eyes were enormous and there was no color at all in her face.

She began to pace, unable to bear standing still, but the harrowing pictures would not leave her mind. Jascha had deliberately ordered the pillar set up in that part of the courtyard so that she would be aware of its presence at every moment. Which meant Zachary was probably being held somewhere on that same side of the palace, too.

Knowing the fate that awaited them was a form of torture in its own right, and Kristin felt sure Jascha would withhold their punishment until their nerves were shattered by waiting.

Helpless rage surged up into her throat like hot acid. "You bastard," she gasped. Turning back to the vanity table, she picked up the photograph Jascha had given her along with a bevy of other engagement presents, and flung it across the room.

It struck the mantel, and the glass in the frame shattered violently, giving Kristin keen, if temporary, satisfaction.

ZACHARY HADN'T BEEN surprised to find out the palace had a dungeon; he would have bet on it. The bars on his small, dank cell were ancient, like the ones on the single window that looked out onto the courtyard, but they were sturdy.

God knew, he'd tried them often enough.

He looked around at his quarters with a sigh. The furniture consisted of a toilet stained with rust and a metal cot with a thin, filthy mattress.

Because he needed the fresh air, he went to the narrow window and looked out. He could plainly see the pillar—knowing it was there, awaiting him, was part of Jascha's vengeance, of course. What really angered Zachary was the awareness that Kristin could see it, too. And she was probably climbing the walls.

Zachary wasn't a religious man, yet in that moment he prayed devoutly that Hakan, the rebel leader, would go along with the plan he'd suggested. After all, Hakan had people on the inside of the palace, and the chance to double-cross Jascha had to appeal to him in a big way.

With a sigh, Zachary shoved splayed fingers through his dust-encrusted hair and turned his thoughts to his beach house in faraway Silver Shores, his quiet job at the college, his tomato plants. "I'm getting too old for this stuff," he muttered just as a distant clanking sound came to his ears.

Two of Jascha's men appeared in front of the cell, their faces grim. One carried a tray of food, the other pointed a rifle at Zachary, to make sure he didn't try to escape when the door was opened.

"Do I get a last wish?" he asked in leisurely Cabrizian.

The guard set his tray on the bed and backed out of the cell again, never once taking his eyes off Zachary. He didn't answer until the door was safely shut and locked.

"What do you want?"

"A bath," Zachary replied idly, sitting down on the bed and resting the tray across his knees. The conditions in the dungeon were horrific, but the food looked good. "And clean clothes. Jascha's stuff would probably fit."

The guards looked at him in amazement. "You ask to wear the prince's clothes?" one of them marveled.

Zachary shrugged, chewing on a piece of fresh, doughy bread. "Just an idea," he said.

The sentinels went away, muttering between themselves, and Zachary grinned. It never hurt to ask.

He finished the food and shoved the tray through a three-inch gap under the cell door. A rat the size of a full-grown Pekingese immediately appeared to nibble at the leftovers. Zachary wondered if anyone had ever taught a rodent to fetch sticks or roll over and play dead.

He stretched out on the skimpy mattress, his hands cupped behind his head, and watched as the rat finished his meal, gave Zachary a curious inspection and disappeared into the darkness that loomed around the cell like fog.

"So long, Rover," Zachary said with a sigh, closing his eyes.

Immediately he saw a collage of bittersweet portraits—Kristin standing by their bed long ago, wearing one of his shirts and nothing else, holding out her arms to him. Serving him a dinner she'd botched with a sort of forlorn hope in her eyes. Bucking beneath him as they lay in the double sleeping bag on the mountain, their bodies fused.

Pure anguish twisted in his gut. She was going to suffer, unless Hakan came through, and there was nothing he could do to help her. That knowledge was the worst torture of all.

He got up, tried the bars in the window again, found them as immovable as ever. Even if he could have pulled them out, however, he wouldn't have been able to squeeze through the opening.

Hours had passed, the sun had gone down and come up again, before Jascha appeared outside his cell.

"Did you have her?" the prince asked bluntly.

A new energy surged inside Zachary. Even sparring with this bastard was better than pacing or lying on the cot staring up at the ceiling. At least it was something to do. "Yes," he replied.

Although Jascha tried to hide the fact, that single word quivered in its mark like an arrow still vibrating in a bull's-eye. "And she responded to you?"

Zachary shrugged and shoved his hands palms out into the hip pockets of his jeans. "I didn't give her a choice."

Again, Jascha's confidence seemed to waver. "You mean you forced her?"

"Yes." Zachary prayed the prince would believe the lie and grant Kristin some kind of clemency.

Jascha's expression was skeptical, but he gave away nothing more of his private emotions. "I understand that you have had the audacity to ask for a bath and a set of clean clothes."

Zachary's gaze was steady, even though inside he was fighting an urge to beg Jascha not to hurt Kristin. The cool, rational side of his mind knew that would be a mistake. He managed to grin. "You know what they say about Yankees. No manners."

A raw chuckle burst from Jascha's throat, and he shook his head in amused incredulity. "You shall have your bath, Mr. Harmon, and the clothes, too. Never let it be said that I forced you to die in a state of such disarray."

Zachary inclined his head slightly but said nothing.

Jascha walked away after giving him a look of undisguised hatred, and two sentries came to fetch him before he had time to lapse into boredom again.

He was manacled between them and led out of the cell and up slippery stone steps into a dusty storage area. From there they entered the kitchen—no one so much as glanced in their direction—and stepped into a service elevator that took them to the upper floor.

Zachary was sure Kristin was behind one of the doors they passed, and he ached to find out which one, but he didn't bother to ask. His escorts probably didn't know, anyway.

They took him into a sumptuous guest suite graced with an enormous marble tub. Three soldiers stood at various points around the room, armed with automatic machine guns.

Zachary grinned to think they considered him so dangerous. In a way it was a compliment.

The guards unmanacled themselves from him and left the room, and Zachary started the taps running to fill the tub, then began taking off his clothes.

"Excuse my impatience, fellas," he said to the soldiers, who looked at him with suspicion. It was obvious they didn't understand English.

He climbed naked into the tub and reached for the fresh bar of soap that had been set out, he suspected, for more esteemed guests. "How about this weather, huh?" he went on, lathering one armpit as he spoke. His prattle unnerved the men, and there was no telling what unexpected advantage that might present.

Zachary scrubbed himself clean, taking his sweet time and talking constantly. He covered politics, professional football, and carried on a one-man debate as to whether the queen liked Diana or Fergie better.

He emptied the tub, rinsed it out and refilled it. Then, lounging, with a mirror in one hand and an old-fashioned razor in the other, he shaved away the stubble of a week's beard.

Not once during any of these processes did he allow himself to reflect on the fact that this might well be the last bath he ever took, but the pillar out in the courtyard was lodged in a dark corner of his awareness like a sliver.

He was given clothes to wear—underwear and socks, comfortably worn jeans and a beige Irish cable-knit sweater. He whistled softly as he dressed, put on his own scuffed, dusty boots and carefully combed his hair. There was even a toothbrush and paste, which he used with aplomb, humming through the foam.

At last the ritual could be extended no longer. One of the guards barked an order and gestured with his gun, and Zachary sighed. He waited for the manacles to be put back on, but no one made a move to confine him.

He left the guest chamber with one soldier walking ahead and two behind, but his hands and feet were free, and that filled him with a singular, tremulous sort of hope. He and Kristin might just get their chance after all.

KRISTIN WAS TOO distracted to think about clothes that morning when Jascha sent word that he wished to see her in his study. She put on tan corduroy pants, sneakers and a blue sweatshirt with large, white letters on the front that said God Bless the U.S.A. Her hair was brushed back into the customary French braid and she hadn't bothered with makeup, except for a little mascara and some blusher to give her ashen cheeks color.

Her palms were sweating when she was brought before Jascha's desk, and she rubbed them against her thighs.

She tried to smile, out of old habit, but her lips wouldn't make the gesture.

Jascha sat back—at one time he would have risen to greet her—and once again Kristin was struck by the fact that he was a stranger. "I can see that you are thoroughly frightened," he remarked cordially, his hands resting on the tufted arms of his chair. If he had any compunction at all about what he was about to do, she could see no sign of it.

Kristin folded her arms, squared her shoulders and lifted her chin. "Isn't that what you wanted? Does it make you feel better to know I'm afraid?"

At that, Jascha shot out of his chair. "Silence!" he shouted, bending toward her and resting the palms of his hands flat on the surface of the desk.

Terrified, but still too proud to fold, Kristin retreated a step.

Jascha drew a deep breath and let it out slowly. "Harmon tells me that he forced you to submit to him. Is that true?"

Kristin's cheeks ached with color. "No," she whispered hoarsely after a long pause.

"You willingly submitted to his—attentions?"

She nodded. "Yes."

"Why did he lie to me?" Jascha asked, and his tone was a mockery of bewilderment. "What did he hope to accomplish?"

Kristin swallowed. "He wanted to spare me punishment," she said quietly. "But I won't allow him to take the whole brunt of your anger."

The prince laid a hand to his heart. "This is all so touchingly romantic. Tell me, would you also suffer in his place, as he apparently would in yours?"

"Yes," Kristin answered without a moment's hesitation.

"And he did not kidnap you?"

"I left willingly."

The muscles in Jascha's handsome face contorted briefly, twisting it into a frightening mask. He cried out the Cabrizian word for guard, and Kristin's jailers reappeared.

She was taken from the room with one gripping each arm, and her heart rose into her throat and hammered there. The inevitable, she knew, could be avoided no longer.

The sunshine was hot and dazzlingly bright, glaring on the brick surface of the courtyard. Jascha's helicopter sat nearby, unmanned, and the wives, dressed in their colorful gowns, stood like a human rainbow behind a first-floor window, looking on.

Kristin assumed they were present in order to learn firsthand the fate of a disobedient bride. Doubtless, the morning's spectacle would nip any thoughts of unwifely rebellion in the proverbial bud.

She stood between her guards, watching in silence as Zachary was brought from the palace. He was clean, and dressed in jeans and a sweater, and he favored her with a brazen grin. For just a merest moment, Kristin's spirits rose.

Then she remembered that she and Zachary were about to become examples.

She looked around again. Besides Jascha, there were just three soldiers present. No doubt many others were watching from the palace windows.

Jascha gave an order Kristin was too dazed to decipher, and Zachary was thrust forward, toward the ominous pillar. He went right on grinning and tossed the prince a cocky salute.

Fool, Kristin thought miserably. *Don't you know he's*

about to kill you? Only then did she notice that Jascha was holding a cruel-looking black whip coiled in one hand.

"You will see now," he said close to Kristin's ear, "what becomes of those who tamper with what belongs to me."

Zachary's arms were taken, and he was hurled against the pillar. Kristin's heartbeat pounded in her ears, and everything seemed to be happening in slow motion, as in a bad dream. Just as the guards were about to bind Zachary's hands together so that he could not step away from the pole, the sky seemed to explode with noise.

A huge, battered helicopter loomed overhead, shadowing the sun. There were shrieks of angry terror as a barrage of machine-gun fire peppered the ground.

Kristin saw Jascha dive for shelter while the guards scrambled for their rifles, neatly stacked against the courtyard wall. Zachary made a sound that was half laughter and half a whoop of triumph and ran toward her.

"Come on, princess!" he shouted, grabbing her hand. "Hakan came through—let's get out of here!"

He grabbed a pistol from a wounded guard and held it on the others as he dragged Kristin toward Jascha's grounded helicopter on a dead run. Kristin looked back, saw troops pouring from the palace doors, but their attention was on the air attack, not the escaping prisoners.

The courtyard was alive with gunfire, but all of it seemed to be coming from the sky.

Swallowing a throatful of bile, Kristin followed Zachary's shouted order and jumped into Jascha's aircraft. The very air seemed to vibrate with the exchange going on outside.

Zachary's hands worked the controls with hasty deftness, and Kristin closed her eyes for a moment and held on.

Overhead, the blades caught, then whirled, deafening Kristin. She put her hands over her ears and looked back once more, just in time to see Jascha pointing at them and yelling orders to the soldiers.

"I hope you know how to fly this thing!" she cried, just as the 'copter lifted off the ground and lurched dizzily away. Bullets pinged against the runners and the aircraft shuddered wildly, but it didn't go down.

Zachary grinned, cocky as hell. "Don't worry, princess," he called back. "I'm a quick study when it comes to things like this!"

Realizing that they were clear of the palace and out of range of the guns, Kristin sagged back against the seat and fought down an urge to be violently sick. "Stop showing off, Zachary," she retorted. "I know you flew a helicopter in the air force."

The city of Kiri fell away rapidly beneath them as they streaked north, toward the border. Below was the timbered mountainside where they had lived out an adventure Kristin would never forget.

"Would you mind explaining how that helicopter happened to show up just when we needed it most?"

Zachary's teeth flashed in an obnoxiously confident grin. "While we were being held at the rebel camp, I made a little suggestion to Hakan."

Kristin remembered the guerrilla leader; he hadn't seemed to her like the sort to take unsolicited advice. "Such as what?"

He shrugged. "I just told him how bent out of shape Jascha would be if the rebels not only collected guns and money for us humble prisoners, but stole us back at the last minute, before the prince could save face."

Kristin was nodding, her brow crumpled in a frown. "But how did Hakan know when to strike?"

Zachary was concentrating on the helicopter controls. "He had people on the inside of the palace, Kristin," he said impatiently. "Haven't you ever seen a James Bond movie?"

Rolling her eyes, Kristin pulled her journal out from under her T-shirt, retrieved a pen from the top of the instrument panel and flipped to a fresh page.

"What the hell are you doing?" Zachary yelled conversationally.

"Writing down how we got away, that we're safe, all that."

Zachary looked regretful. "There is one problem we still have to deal with, princess."

Kristin smiled. Their relationship, of course. Well, with love and work, they could make that fly just like a helicopter. "What?" she asked, only because she wanted Zachary to be the one to say they belonged together.

"We don't have enough fuel to make the border."

Kristin's disappointment was profound. "What?"

Zachary was surveying the rugged country below. "The best we can hope for is a chance to steal a Jeep or a couple of horses. We're running on fumes as it is."

Horror welled up in Kristin at the reality of the situation. "Fumes? Oh, great! Now we're probably going to crash fifty yards from the rebel camp or something! Imagine what Jascha would pay for us now!"

"Well, excuse me!" Zachary bellowed, glaring at her. "Next time we're about to be whipped to death in a palace courtyard, I'll be sure to steal a 'copter with a full tank!"

Kristin's arms were folded tightly across her chest; her journal had slipped, forgotten, to the floor. "Just keep your snide comments to yourself," she snapped.

The aircraft's engine began making an alarming sound midway between a sputter and a pop. Kristin sat bolt upright and screamed as the machine zigzagged drunkenly toward the ground, while Zachary concentrated on grappling with the controls.

They came down in a meadow, and the blades hadn't even stopped whirling when Zachary shoved Kristin out the door and scrambled after her. She went back long enough to grab her journal and the pen, and then Zachary caught hold of her hand and dragged her into the woods at a full run.

"What's the big hurry?" she demanded breathlessly when they were well into the timber.

"Don't be an idiot," Zachary retorted. "By now the attack is over and Jascha's called for another 'copter. He'll be on our trail like a hound dog chasing a fat rabbit!"

Kristin wrenched her hand from Zachary's and walked at a slower pace, struggling to keep her respiratory system from overloading. "If Jascha catches us, we'll wish we'd never been born."

"You always were insightful," Zachary breathed.

"Zachary, this is serious!"

"You're right," Zachary answered, still moving so rapidly that Kristin could barely keep up. "But we're overdue for some good luck."

Kristin hadn't caught her breath. "Where are we going?" she asked impatiently.

Zachary looked back at her, and she saw his jaw tighten. "I spotted a village just before we went down. We're going to try talking them out of a couple of horses."

"Suppose they're bandits—or rebels?" Kristin cried, panicking. "Suppose they sell us to Jascha again?"

He stopped and grasped her by the shoulders, breathing hard himself. "Get a grip on yourself," he ordered, and while his voice and his grasp were hard, Kristin saw concern in his eyes. "We've got to keep moving. Jascha's goons are going to spot that 'copter sooner or later, and we'd better not be in the area when they do. Now, have you got anything we can swap with the villagers, like jewelry or something?"

Kristin attributed her involuntary smile to hysteria and reached under the neck of her sweatshirt to pull out a gold chain with two rings dangling from it. One was a four-carat diamond Jascha had given her when they became engaged, and the other sported a gold lion's head with perfect rubies for eyes. "How about these?"

Zachary cupped the rings in his hand and whistled as he inspected their design, but when his eyes lifted to meet Kristin's she was unsettled by the shadow of pain she saw move briefly in their depths. "Where did you get these? I mean, I know the prince gave them to you, but you didn't have them when we were trying to get out of the country before."

Kristin dropped the chain and rings back down inside her shirt, and she shrugged one shoulder. "I grabbed them before I left my room this morning. I don't really know why."

He took her arm, just above the elbow, in a grip just short of bruising. "Let's keep moving."

"What's the matter with you?" Kristin wanted to know as she scrambled along beside him, trying to keep up with his long strides. "And don't say 'nothing,' Zachary Harmon, because I saw that look in your eyes."

He stopped and wrenched her against his chest, but it was a gesture of anger, not passion. "It just reminded me of how little we really have in common, that's all," he ground out. "You're a rich princess, and I'm just an ordinary guy. It's been great, Kristin, and I'll get you out of Cabriz, but after that it's over. I'm never going to look back."

For several moments Kristin reeled inwardly, just as stunned as if he'd slapped her. "What?" she managed to squeak. "But I thought—"

It was as though a veil had dropped down behind his eyes, hiding the soul Kristin had seen on more than one occasion. A bitter smile twisted his lips. "This isn't a movie, princess. Just because we had great sex and got shot at together doesn't mean we can make a life. It would never work."

Kristin started to protest that she loved him and furthermore that she damn well knew he loved her, but her pride stopped her. She just nodded and pulled free of him.

In another half hour they reached the edge of the village Zachary had seen from the sky. The villagers proved to be curious but friendly, and they gladly accepted Kristin's rings and chain in return for two worn-out plow horses, some blankets and a little food.

"We're spending the night here," Zachary told Kristin when the animated negotiations had been completed and the transaction was made.

"Isn't that a risk?" Kristin asked, and she made her voice sound casual even though just looking at Zachary made her want to cry. She'd had such hopes, such dreams—and he wanted to walk away from her the moment they were safe in Rhaos and never think about her again. "You said it yourself. Jascha's probably right behind us."

"There was a lot of damage to the 'copter when we landed," Zachary answered without looking at her. "I'm hoping they'll think it was a crash and we're already dead."

Kristin felt as though that were the case. She was like

a ghost, numb and cold, condemned to wander, never caring where.

She sat with Zachary that evening, staring into the fire while he talked with the villagers in their language, and when he led her to the hut they were to share, she didn't resist. She didn't even argue when he enfolded her in his arms, kissed her forehead and fell asleep, still cuddling her close.

Kristin was exhausted, emotionally and physically, and though she slept, her slumber was not restful. She awakened in the depths of the night, aching with a loneliness so profound, so hopeless, that she was sure nothing could assuage it.

It drove her through the barrier of her pride, that need, and she raised herself to her knees and bent to kiss Zachary's mouth softly.

He stirred, searched her body with his hands, found her breasts. Her name came ragged from his lips, and he moved to pull her down beside him on the skins.

"No," she whispered. "This time is mine." She pushed his sweater up, letting the moonlight seeping in through the roof of the hut dapple his chest. She stroked him, running her fingers through the tangled swirls of golden-brown hair, then bent to taste his nipple with the tip of her tongue.

He moaned. "Kris—"

She rose up again, and calmly unfastened his jeans. "Maybe this will be goodbye," she said. "And maybe you'll walk away without looking back, just like you said. But you'll *never* forget me, Zachary—I mean to see to that."

Kristin bent then to nip at his belly, and she smiled when his manhood was there to meet her.

Zachary groaned and arched his back when she

touched him with her tongue. His hands entangled themselves frantically in her hair. Soon he was delirious, beg-
ging senselessly in a gravel-rough voice, and Kristin
showed him no more mercy than he'd ever shown her.

But at what must have been practically the last second,
he gripped her shoulders and in one swift move wrestled
her beneath him. His mouth covered hers in a consuming, fiery kiss while his hands moved under her sweatshirt to release her breasts from the restraint of her bra.

"You're right," he rasped as he shoved her sweatshirt
up and found one of her nipples with his warm, wet
mouth. "I'm never going to forget this night. But damn
you, you won't either!"

A whimper escaped Kristin as he took her breast,
teased her with his lips and tongue. His hands gripped
her wrists, pressing her hands wide of her shoulders into
the depths of the skins they lay upon. She writhed under
his hips, aware of his length and power in every part of
her being.

She grew wilder, more desperate as he made his way
to her other breast and sampled that. He held her wrists
together above her head now, in one hand, while the other
unsnapped her jeans and smoothed them away. He was
less patient with her panties, however.

"So beautiful…" he told her hoarsely, nibbling his way
down over her belly. His tongue moved swiftly through
the silken jungle to administer sweet menace.

"Take me," she pleaded. "M-make love to me—
please—"

She felt the tip of his shaft at her entrance, teasing,
gently prodding.

"Zachary," she sobbed, and he cupped his hands under
her bottom and drove into her hard.

The friction set them both afire, and Kristin grasped at

Zachary's head and dragged him into a kiss as their bodies rose and fell together in an ancient dance of wonder and need. Her moans collided with his, and their tongues mated frantically.

Kristin felt the sky rushing toward her as despair and joy clashed inside her like great, silent cymbals. Her body convulsed wildly, once, twice, three times, and then she was in the eye of the storm.

Zachary stiffened, gave a low warrior's cry and spilled himself into her, and the two of them lay gasping on the skins for a long time. Kristin cuddled close to Zachary, her arms around his waist, her heart already grieving because there would not be a lifetime of nights just like that one.

When he abruptly thrust her onto her back and loomed over her, Kristin was startled. Her eyes widened when she saw the unrestrained fury in his face, the tears shimmering along his lashes.

"Damn you," he grated out, his thumbs digging into her shoulders. "Why did you do it? Why did you abort my baby?"

CHAPTER TEN

WHY DID YOU do it? Why did you abort my baby?

The questions demolished Kristin's spirit like a steel wrecker's ball, and with every strike a little more of her crumbled away.

She opened her mouth to answer, but no sound came out. And Zachary's thumbs were like rivets, bolting her shoulders to the floor.

"Why?" Zachary demanded.

Finally Kristin found her voice. "It was a miscarriage," she croaked, her words barely audible. "I—I wanted our baby, Zachary. I wouldn't have gotten rid of it."

He just stared at her for a long time, his lashes glistening, and she watched as hope and suspicion warred in his face. He thrust free of her and turned away. "You're a liar!" he rasped, and even in the thin moonlight Kristin could see his shoulders shuddering as he struggled to regain control of his emotions. "You were scared—you didn't think our relationship was going anywhere...."

Kristin sat up, wrapping her arms around her knees. She was facing the most crucial conflict of her life—the battle for Zachary's trust—and she was too exhausted to fight it. "You're partly right—I was scared. And I didn't want to go on just living together forever. But I wanted our baby. I meant to raise it myself, if you refused to marry me."

He shoved spread fingers through his hair. "Save it, Kristin. Your father told me the truth."

"My father?" Kristin was confused. Kenyan Meyers hadn't even known about the miscarriage until afterward; he'd been on the other side of the country when it happened.

"He called me about twenty minutes after I came in from that last mission and found you gone." Zachary didn't turn to look at her, and his voice sounded haunted, bewildered; he seemed to be reliving the pain. "He said you had finally come to your senses, that there had been a 'little problem,' but you'd gone to the hospital and had it taken care of."

Kristin was reeling. She'd known all along that her father didn't like Zachary, didn't think he'd make a suitable husband for his only daughter, but she would never have dreamed he was capable of such cruel treachery.

"Damn it," Zachary breathed, whirling around to glare at her in the cold, sparse light, "he called our child a 'little problem'!"

"Zachary—"

He held up one hand to silence her. "No more lies, Kristin. It's better if we just don't talk about this anymore."

Kristin had had enough. She bolted to her feet, using energy from some reserve she hadn't known she possessed, and stormed over to Zachary. "If you think you can drop an emotional bomb like that and then pull your old trick of refusing to talk about it, Zachary Harmon, you're full of sheep dip!"

"Keep your voice down—you'll wake up the whole village!"

"I don't give a damn if I wake up the whole *country!*" Kristin yelled, hands on her hips, jaw set at an obstinate angle. "We're going to talk this out! I don't know what he thought gave him the right—and I swear I'm going to strangle him when I get back to Virginia—but my father lied to you. Do you hear me, Zachary? *He lied.* I wanted that baby more than anything else in the world!"

She saw the torment in his eyes, the struggle to believe, and at the same time she knew she'd lost.

It was the final blow; Kristin could bear no more. She turned slowly away from Zachary, lay down on the skins, wrapped herself in one of the blankets and willed herself to die.

"Kristin," Zachary said raggedly. And she could feel him reaching for her, with his heart if not his hands. But what did that matter, when he'd take another person's word over hers?

"Leave me alone," she whispered, too broken even to cry. She lay curled up throughout the night, caught in that hazy state between waking and sleeping.

In the morning she ate the rice Zachary brought her, but she didn't speak to him. She wasn't punishing him, she wasn't even angry anymore. She simply had nothing to say.

They prepared the bartered plow horses for travel and set out toward the border.

Zachary tried to talk to her again when they stopped for a midday meal of some dried meat Kristin didn't care to categorize. "We'll be out of Cabriz sometime tomorrow," he said.

Kristin just looked at him. She supposed she probably had dark circles under her eyes; she always got them when she was overtired.

"Damn it, will you say something?" Zachary rasped.

She shrugged. "Thank you for saving me from the bad guys," she said. "But then, that's what a macho-man like you is supposed to do, isn't it? Rescue damsels in distress?"

He was plainly annoyed—and he was going to persist in pursuing his point. "Why would your father lie to me?"

"He didn't like you very much," Kristin replied with bald honesty. "I don't suppose it was anything personal—he just thought you had a lousy job. So did I, for that matter. And if I know Dad, he probably ran a background check on you and found something he didn't care for."

Zachary's face tightened, then relaxed again. He threw down the last of his dried meat and hoisted himself upright from a crouching position. "Let's get moving, princess," he said, revealing no emotion at all in his tone. "The evil prince could still catch up with us."

There was no more mention of the lost baby, or of Kristin's father. They traveled in silence, communicating only when necessary. Even when they stopped to make camp they avoided each other as much as possible. At five o'clock the next afternoon they reached the border station Zachary had been aiming for all along.

The Rhaotian guards greeted them with broad grins—the Cabrizians just scowled at Zachary's drawn pistol—and one of the friendly soldiers rushed to telephone the news to their superiors. Soon a representative of the Rhaotian government arrived in a dusty little sedan and, after giving the horses to a surprised farmer as a gift, Zachary and Kristin sped toward Isi, Rhaos's capital city.

Kristin sat numbly in the back seat, her shoulder touching Zachary's, her heart lost in the farthest, loneliest reaches of the universe.

The embassy was in an uproar when they arrived, and reporters waited at the gate, snapping pictures and shouting questions.

Neither Kristin nor Zachary so much as looked in their direction, let alone spoke.

Inside the embassy compound they were immediately separated and subjected to an extensive "debriefing." Kristin told the ambassador and the man from the CIA everything that had happened—except, of course, for the lovemaking. That was private, and she wasn't going to share it with anybody.

"You'd better talk with the reporters, however briefly," the ambassador's assistant advised, after the CIA had subjected Kristin to exhaustive questioning. The aide was a woman in her middle thirties, with sleek dark hair and an air of authority about her. "The whole world has been waiting for a development of some kind."

Kristin's shoulders sagged at the prospect, but before she could frame a reply, the ambassador, an old friend of her father, interceded.

"Great Scott, Caroline, the poor girl is on the verge of collapse. She needs food, rest and perhaps even medical care. Issue some kind of statement to keep them at bay and send for a doctor."

Caroline looked at Kristin reproachfully, but she left the ambassador's study and closed the door behind her.

Mr. Binchly, an old-timer in the diplomatic corps, laid a gentle, beefy hand on Kristin's shoulder. He was a tall man, with a shiny pate and kindly blue eyes. "Were you hurt, Kristin?" he asked, and he looked as though the answer to that question really mattered to him.

A lump formed in Kristin's throat. *Yes,* answered an inner voice, silent but nonetheless eloquent for that. *Yes, I was hurt. I found the man I was meant to love, and he doesn't want me.* "I'll be all right in a few days," she said, and then tears welled up in her eyes.

Mr. Binchly laid his hand lightly on the back of her

head and pressed her face to his shoulder. "There, there, you're safe now, dear. We'll see that you get back home to your family as soon as you're ready to travel."

Kristin felt a flicker of rage as she thought of her father, but she suppressed it. She would deal with Kenyan Meyers when she'd recovered her strength. "My friend, Mr. Harmon—is he all right? He was beaten once…." Her voice fell away.

The diplomat seated Kristin in the chair she'd bolted out of after her grueling interview with the CIA and went to pour brandy into a snifter. "Here," he said, handing her the glass. "This will brace you up a little. Harmon is fine, as far as I know. He'll be checked over by a doctor, just as you will."

Kristin nodded distractedly and took a sip of the brandy. The liquor rolled like a fireball down her throat and into her stomach, and her eyes were watering when she looked up. "If I could just lie down—"

"Surely," Mr. Binchly said quickly, and he immediately went to his desk and used his intercom to summon another aide.

Kristin set her brandy aside and followed the young Rhaotian man out of the room with as much dignity as she could manage. He led her up the main staircase and deposited her in a large guest room.

After a brief exploration, Kristin started water running in the bath and asked the aide to send up tea and a platter of fresh fruit. He nodded politely and left.

The bath Kristin took was a leisurely one. She soaked, she washed her hair, she shaved her legs and armpits. And then she let the water out and ran a fresh supply.

When she reentered the bedroom sometime later, wrapped in a towel, she found a white silk robe draped over the back of a chair and a tea tray on the nightstand.

She put on the robe and combed her hair, then sat cross-legged in the middle of the bed with a cup of tea and her journal. Although she'd never been more tired, she felt a need to set down what had happened to her in black and white. Maybe then she'd be able to grapple with the experience and make some sense of it.

Unfortunately, all she could think about was Zachary. Kristin realized now that she'd loved him all along—the episode with Jascha had been a grand-scale attempt to forget her broken heart.

She sighed, cupping her chin in one hand and setting her teacup aside. Zachary was not the kind of man a woman loves once; with him, it was for always. And he couldn't have made it clearer that he wanted nothing whatever to do with her now that they were safe.

Kristin abandoned all attempts to write about her escape from Cabriz and crawled into bed, pulling the covers over her head. She fell into an almost immediate sleep, and didn't awaken until she felt someone pulling back the covers to prod and push at her.

"Zachary," she scolded with a half smile on her face. But when she opened her eyes, she was looking up at a stranger—a doctor, judging by the stethoscope hanging around his neck. He was an Asian of indeterminate age, and his expression was a kindly one.

"I'm sorry not to be Zachary," he said with pleasant formality. "My name is Chong. Paul Chong."

Kristin smiled, despite the sting of disappointment, and sat up, pulling the covers up to her waist. "I really don't need an examination—"

"All the same," interrupted Dr. Chong with a shake of his finger.

"There was a slight injury to my knee," Kristin recalled, frowning. "But a man gave me some sort of tea, and it improved right away."

"Let me see, please," the doctor urged.

Kristin obediently laid the robe aside to reveal her knee. It was still bruised, but there was no swelling and certainly no pain. The doctor examined it with gentle fingers, then covered her.

He nodded thoughtfully. "I wish I had the knowledge of herbs some of the villagers have. They can sometimes accomplish remarkable things."

"Where did you go to school?" Kristin asked cordially as he listened to her chest through his stethoscope.

His smile broadened into a grin. "Harvard," he replied. "If we covered ancient herbal remedies, I must not have been paying attention."

Kristin might have chuckled another time; as it was, she couldn't manage. "Have you seen my friend—Mr. Harmon?"

The doctor took a tongue depressor from his bag, unwrapped it and gestured for Kristin to open her mouth. "He's next on my list."

"Where is he?" Kristin asked, speaking around the wooden stick.

"A few doors down, I think." Dr. Chong tossed the depressor into the wastebasket and took out a little vial of pills. "You are suffering from severe exhaustion, Ms. Meyers. I would like you to take one of these tablets and get some sleep."

"I just want to see Zachary for a minute—"

He handed her one of the pills, along with a glass of water from the carafe on the nightstand. "I will tell him," he said. "In the meantime, please take this."

Kristin threw the pill to the back of her throat and swallowed a gulp of water. "He can be sort of stubborn."

The doctor nodded. "It would require a certain intractability of spirit to effect such a daring escape."

Kristin yawned and sank back against her pillows. "It's not as though he did it all by himself, you know," she pointed out. "He had me to help him."

Chong smiled again. "He is a very fortunate man." With that, he took his bag and left the room.

Eyelids growing heavier with every passing moment, Kristin gazed fixedly at the door. When Zachary came in, she would tell him—well, she didn't know what. There had to be some way to persuade him not to give up on their alliance so easily.

Presently Kristin glanced at the clock on the bedside stand. The doctor had had plenty of time to check Zachary over. So where was that boneheaded ex-spy, anyway?

She tossed back her covers and started to sit up, only to find that the pill and her own fatigue had left her too weak. She sagged back against the pillows and closed her eyes.

ZACHARY DREW UP a chair beside the bed and sat down. Taking the note from his shirt pocket, he tucked it into Kristin's journal, which had been lying on the nightstand, and then turned his attention back to her.

Even with her long eyelashes resting on her cheeks, the shadows under Kristin's eyes were evident. Her soft brown hair framed her face, and Zachary could catch the scent of it even from a distance.

He pulled the chair closer, reached out to awaken her, drew back his hand.

God knew, he should have trusted Kristin; he should have been there for her when she was hurting so badly. Instead, just when she'd needed him most, he'd flown into a rage and accused her of something she would never have done.

"Kristin." Her name came out as a raw whisper; she stirred slightly, but didn't open her eyes.

Zachary leaned over and kissed her ever so lightly on the forehead. Her father was a bastard, but he'd probably been right, too. Kristin needed glamour and excitement; she wouldn't be happy in Silver Shores, with a teacher for a husband. She belonged with the jet set.

He couldn't resist touching her mouth with his, and she gave a soft whimper that made his heart turn over.

In the doorway he paused, memorizing her face, her shape, her hair. As if he could ever have forgotten.

"I'm sorry I'm not your prince," he said gruffly. And then he went out.

KRISTIN AWAKENED FEELING physically restored, ate a huge meal, took a shower and dressed in her jeans and T-shirt, which had been laundered for her. "I want to see Mr. Harmon immediately," she told the maid when the woman came in to pick up her tray.

The response was a blank stare and a spate of chatter Kristin didn't understand. All the same, she grasped the fact that the maid didn't speak English and would send someone who did.

The ambassador's wife, Kitty, came in shortly.

"I'm sorry to have bothered you," Kristin told the pretty, middle-aged woman, who had been a college classmate of her mother. "All I really wanted was the precise location of Zachary's room."

Kitty clasped beautifully manicured hands in front of her blue silk sheath, and her brown eyes showed bewilderment. Once, nervously, she touched her fluffy gray hairdo. "You mean Mr. Harmon, of course. Well, Kristin, he's—gone."

Kristin's heart came to a screeching stop, then limped back into its regular beat. "Gone?"

"Oh, I don't mean dead," Kitty said with an endearing smile. "He left yesterday. He said he'd been away from his classes too long."

A hard knot was forming in Kristin's throat. She didn't know Kitty well enough to cry in front of her, so she held on to her dignity with all her strength. "I don't suppose he left a note or anything?"

"Mr. Harmon did ask me to have you look in your journal," she said. "Oh. And you do have a press conference scheduled for this afternoon, if you feel up to it."

Kristin practically dove for the nightstand where she'd left her diary, and flipped it open. Sure enough, there was a folded note tucked between the pages.

"Kris," Zachary had written in his bold, clear hand, "You were right, princess. It will never work. Thanks for all the things we shared. Love, Z."

"Coward," Kristin whispered. And because there were tears in her eyes, she didn't turn to face Kitty. She drew a deep breath and spoke bravely. "I'll take care of the press conference, and then I'd like to leave for the United States as soon after that as possible."

"Caroline will make the arrangements," Kitty promised, and the door closed gently behind her when she went out.

Kristin dried her face with the backs of her hands. Zachary didn't want her and, since that was something she couldn't change, she would have to accept it.

She used the makeup either Kitty or Caroline had so kindly lent her, and then she took her journal, went out into the courtyard and wrote until her fingers were too numb to hold the pen. After that she marched stoically into the embassy, met with eager representatives of the press from all over the world and told them her story.

Except for the parts she regarded as personal, Kristin told the complete, unvarnished truth. And she didn't cry once, the whole time.

"Your rescuer was Zachary Harmon," called out one American reporter, an attractive woman smiling thoughtfully. "Weren't you and he romantically involved at one time?"

Kristin swallowed, but her gaze snapped with anger. "I hardly see what that has to do with anything," she said curtly.

The reporter was undaunted. In fact, her smile widened. "Well, it might make this into quite a different story. Didn't you and Mr. Harmon live together once?"

There was a general buzz among the others while Kristin frantically formulated an answer.

"Zachary—Mr. Harmon and I were involved some time ago," she said, keeping her tones even. "But that's all over now. There's nothing between us."

With that, Kristin pushed back her chair and stood. Flashbulbs went off all over the room, blinding her, and she went out gripping Ambassador Binchly's arm.

Early the next morning she boarded an airplane. It touched down in Singapore, then Honolulu. Kristin would have a four-hour layover there before flying on to the mainland.

Since her passport was still in Cabriz, Kristin had special papers from the ambassador to show at customs.

Her mother was there when she finished, however, and the surprise was a welcome one. Kristin flung herself into Alice Meyers's arms with abandon.

Alice embraced her daughter, one gracious hand press-

ing the back of Kristin's head. "Dear heaven," she said
with tears in her voice. "We thought we'd lost you."

Kristin stiffened. "You haven't," she said, putting only
the slightest emphasis on the word *you*. She would discuss her father's part in her initial breakup with Zachary
when they reached Virginia.

Crystal-blue eyes swept over Kristin's clothes. "Just
as I thought. You need to do some shopping before we
go home." Alice linked her arm with Kristin's, and they
started toward the door. There was no point in going to
baggage claim, since Kristin had nothing but the clothes
she was wearing and her journal. "I have a lovely room
at the Hilton. We could swim and sunbathe and shop
and talk—"

"Not all at once, I hope," Kristin said with a faltering
smile. It was the closest thing to a joke she'd be able to
manage for a long time, she suspected.

"It was Zachary who came and got you, wasn't it?"
Alice pressed when they were settled in the back of a cab
and heading toward the hotel.

Kristin nodded, biting her lower lip.

Alice reached out, took her daughter's hand and
squeezed it. "I don't imagine Jascha was happy to see
you leave," she said, probably sensing that the subject of
Zachary was painful for Kristin.

She shook her head and said nothing, hoping her
mother would guess that she didn't want to talk about
Jascha, either. Not just yet.

"Well, you'll be almost as good as new by the time
you've had a few days in the sunshine and restocked
your wardrobe," Alice stated, still valiantly searching
for a safe topic. "I think we ought to spend a great deal
of your father's money."

Kristin nodded, watching the familiar beach and dazzling blue ocean slip past the cab window. "How's the weather back in Virginia?" she asked, mostly to rescue Alice.

The older woman shivered. "Chilly. After all, dear, it's nearly Thanksgiving. It won't be long until we have snow. Perhaps if your father can get away we'll all fly down to Bermuda and have our turkey dinner there."

"No," Kristin said. "I mean, I just want to have a few words with Dad, then I'll be going back to L.A. Or maybe to New York."

Wisely, Alice didn't push. She was no slouch when it came to diplomacy herself, having spent all those years in Cabriz.

When they reached the hotel, Kristin bought a swimsuit in one of the shops. After putting the garment on in the suite Alice had rented, she went out to the pool and swam rapid laps, moving with such determination that the other tourists got out of her way.

Only when her arms refused to make another stroke did she grasp the tiled side of the pool and whisk the hair back from her face.

Alice was sitting comfortably in a lounge chair, sipping a colorful tropical drink. Her stylish dark hair was neatly covered by a white bathing cap. "I'm exhausted just from watching you, dear," she said, taking a maraschino cherry from her cocktail and popping it into her mouth.

Kristin was studying her mother, seeing signs of strain around her eyes and mouth. Although no one else was nearby, she lowered her voice. "You were frightened for me, weren't you, Mother?" she asked gently.

"Yes," Alice answered. "Fortunately, we didn't know what had really gone on until after you reached the embassy in Rhaos. Mr. Binchly called your father right away, of course, and told him the whole story."

Not the whole story, Kristin thought sadly, remembering how Zachary had held her, caressed her, made her cry out in the night because the pleasure was too keen to be endured in silence. "I'm sorry you were worried. I should have known better than to think a marriage between Jascha and I could work, especially when the Cabrizian government was toppling."

Alice set her drink on a table, approached the pool and lowered herself into the water beside Kristin. "Jascha seemed like such a charming young man when you used to bring him home from school," she said fretfully. "What happened?"

Kristin shrugged. "He was putting on a facade for all of us back in the States, I think," she speculated. "But in Cabriz, he was surrounded by his own culture. And that required that he have more than one wife, among other things."

A sigh escaped Alice. "Don't think your father and I don't blame ourselves for what's happened. We lived in Cabriz for years. We *knew* the culture permitted a man of Jascha's status to marry more than once. It's just that he seemed so westernized, and he promised us he loved only you."

Gently, Kristin laid a hand on her mother's shoulder. "It wasn't your fault. I was chasing fairy tales long after I should have grown up."

Alice reached out, smoothed a tendril of wet hair away from Kristin's cheek. "That hollow look I see in your eyes—it's there because of Zachary, isn't it? Kristin, what really happened in Cabriz?"

Kristin swallowed and averted her eyes for a moment. She wasn't sure she could keep the truth from her mother, wasn't sure she even wanted to. "I think I was on the verge of getting Zachary back. But I lost him, Mother. I lost him all over again, and it's tearing me apart."

"This calls for a drink," Alice replied, and held up one hand to call over a waiter.

Kristin asked for white wine and stood at the side of the pool sipping it as she told her mother how deeply she'd cared for Zachary.

"What are you going to do now?" Alice asked when her daughter had finished.

Kristin sighed, studying the blue Hawaiian sky. "I want to have a few words with Dad—in person—and then I'm going to hole up in an apartment somewhere— pick a city, any city—and write. Zachary aside, I have one hell of a story to tell."

She and Alice left the pool behind after that, along with the subject of Kristin's adventure. They spent the coming days just as they'd planned to—shopping, sunning, relaxing.

When Kristin flew on to the mainland, she was tanned, rested and ready to do battle, first with her father, then with the world.

On her first night back, network newscasters announced to the world that the Cabrizian government had fallen. Jascha had escaped with his life and was living in exile in Singapore.

CHAPTER ELEVEN

KRISTIN'S FATHER ROSE from behind his desk and came toward her, arms extended for a hug. She drew back against the towering study doors, her manner wary, and his delighted expression faded.

"What is it?" he asked.

"Sit down—please," she said woodenly.

When Kenyan had returned, albeit reluctantly, to his leather swivel chair, his daughter took a seat facing his desk.

"A year and a half ago, when I miscarried, you called Zachary and told him I'd had an abortion instead. I'd like to know why."

Kenyan's gray hair glinted in the light of his desk lamp, and his face was in shadows. "I think you know, Kristin," he said reasonably. "Harmon was a government agent. The things he's done, independently and by order of his superiors, would horrify you. And his background couldn't have been more dissimilar to yours—"

Kristin's hands tightened on the arms of her chair and, for virtually the first time in her life, she interrupted her father. "My God, Dad, I *loved* the man—I was living with him, expecting his baby. How could you interfere like that? What gave you the right?"

His voice rose slightly as he replied, "You had already left Harmon, remember? I merely wanted your decision to stand. And the fact that you're my daughter gave me the right, damn it!"

The reminder that she had been the one to instigate the whole problem in the first place brought pulsing color to Kristin's cheeks. "I was wrong, Dad," she said brokenly. "I should have stayed and tried to work things out with Zachary. But that doesn't change the fact that you had no business messing with my life."

Kenyan sighed heavily. "Harmon would never make a good husband or father," he said. "The man has no conception of what family life means."

"And you do, I suppose?" Kristin demanded, leaning forward in her chair. "Are lying and meddling things a father should do?"

The ambassador-turned-cabinet-member held up one hand in a bid for silence. "I'm willing to concede that what I did was wrong, Kristin. But I still maintain that Harmon wouldn't be able to give you what you need."

Kristin's tone was cordially acidic. "Which is?"

"A regular home."

"Come on, Dad. What did you find out about Zachary that worried you so much? That he cheated on a third-grade history test? That he was raised by his grandfather?"

"Damn it," Kenyan blurted, slamming one fist down on the desktop, "both his parents were alcoholics. There was an automobile accident and not only were the Harmons killed outright, so were a young mother and her two children, on their way home from the supermarket!"

Sickness rushed into Kristin's throat as she thought of what Zachary and his grandfather must have suffered, along with the family of the mother and children. "That wasn't Zachary's fault," she said softly.

"I'm not saying it was," Kenyan insisted, his face flushed with conviction and, probably, the desire to redeem himself. "But things like that tend to run in families. Forgive me, Kristin, but I didn't want it running in ours!"

At last she stood. "That wasn't your decision to make," she said calmly. "Now, if you'll excuse me, I've got some packing to do."

Outside, a light snow was drifting down from gray afternoon skies. The view framed Kenyan's impressive physique as he stood to protest. "You're leaving? But it's almost Thanksgiving. Your mother—"

Kristin paused at the doors and turned to face him again. "I suppose I'll forgive you, in time. After all, I love you very much, God help me. But right now I don't want to be in the same state with you, Dad, let alone the same house. Goodbye."

"Kristin, I've apologized!"

She hesitated, her hand on the doorknob. "To me, yes," she conceded. "But not to Zachary." With that, she walked out of the study and climbed the stairs. In her room, she cried as she packed.

Five hours later she landed in New York, a destination chosen for its proximity to the publishing world, checked into a hotel room and set up her computer. Writing about her experiences in Cabriz would be her salvation; it would give her life focus and meaning.

She hoped.

Kristin worked straight through Thanksgiving, making no telephone calls and marking the occasion only with a turkey sandwich from the coffee shop down the street. Although she didn't allow herself to think about him consciously, Zachary hovered at the edges of her life like a phantom.

The week before Christmas, Kristin was finally ready to show her work to someone. She'd drafted an extensive outline of her prospective book, and had written the first chapter.

She called John Claridge, a family friend in the publishing business, and he eagerly agreed to look at her proposal. Of course, that left her with a holiday to face and nothing to keep her occupied until it had passed. Since she was in New York, Christmas was everywhere; the only way to avoid it would be to hide out in her hotel room. And Kristin couldn't do that, not without the book to absorb her attention.

She finally telephoned her mother.

Alice wept with relief. "Kristin! Are you all right? In the name of heaven, where are you?"

"New York," Kristin answered, and gave her mother the name of the hotel. "Listen, I was just thinking, well, maybe I could come home for Christmas?"

"Of course you can," Alice was quick to sniffle. "What time will your plane be in?"

"I'll take a train tomorrow, Mother," Kristin answered a moment after the idea came to her. "I want some time to think about a few things."

"You've had phone calls," Alice told her in the same tone of voice she'd used years before, when Kristin had been full of Christmas curiosity and there were presents hidden all over the house.

Kristin's heart leaped out of its normal beat and hammered at the base of her throat. "From whom?"

Alice hesitated. "Zachary Harmon, for one. He left several numbers. Would you like them?"

"No," Kristin said impulsively. "Who else called?"

As if you cared, her mother's tone of voice replied. "Just some of your college friends, dear. I'll tell you all about it when you get home."

Zachary's name buzzed in Kristin's heart like a pesky bee hovering around a picnic while she packed her clothes and arranged for her computer to be shipped back to Virginia. She had no idea where she'd be going after that.

All during the train ride the following day she thought about the man who had rescued her from Cabriz. The fact that his parents had been alcoholics explained Zachary's difficulty with trust and his fear of commitment. It must have been hell, growing up knowing the two people who had given him life were responsible for taking that same gift from others.

"Oh, Zachary," she whispered, staring out the window at the wintry countryside. "If I had it all to do over again, I'd change so many things."

When the train pulled into the station at Williamsburg, Alice Meyers was there to meet Kristin, looking splendid in a full-length mink coat and matching hat. She embraced her daughter and took her arm, leading her straightaway to the waiting car. The baggage would be sent out later.

"I haven't done any shopping," Kristin mused, seeing that lights and decorations were everywhere. It was a giant commercial conspiracy, and yet she loved Christmas.

Alice squeezed her arm. "We still have tomorrow," she said. "Tell me, what have you been doing?"

"Working on a book," Kristin confessed. "I gave the outline and the first chapter to John Claridge to read. Now there's nothing to do but wait."

Alice had a mysterious look on her face. "I think there's much more to do than that, dear," she answered sweetly. Then she opened the car door and got behind the wheel.

"What are you trying to tell me?" Kristin asked, a smile tugging at the corners of her mouth.

Her mother simply shrugged. "Nothing at all."

Kristin fastened her seat belt as Alice started the car. "You said Zachary called," she ventured. "What did he say?"

The engine roared, and the large car rolled into traffic. Alice shrugged one mink-swathed shoulder. "He asked for your number. Of course, I couldn't give it to him since I didn't know what it was myself."

Kristin sighed. "It's just as well," she said, putting down the springing hope she'd felt at the news.

Alice said nothing more about Zachary. She simply drove through the familiar streets of Williamsburg and came to a stop in front of the Meyers's house. There was a funny-looking compact car blocking the driveway, and the lights were burning in Kenyan's study.

Kristin glanced in her mother's direction, but Alice was studiously avoiding her gaze. The two women entered the house by way of a door with an enormous holly wreath hung upon it.

"We're here!" Alice cried gleefully, shrugging out of her coat and shaking off the snowflakes. That done, she hung the garment and hat neatly in the closet, and not once did she glance in her daughter's direction.

The study doors opened, and Kristin froze where she was. Standing there in the chasm, looking as uncomfortable as she felt, stood Zachary Harmon. He loosened his tie and swallowed visibly as he ran his eyes over her.

"Hello, Kristin," he finally said, and his voice was hoarse.

Kristin's muscles became mobile again, and she unbuttoned her coat and hung it in the closet with her mother's. "What are you doing here?"

He rested his hands on his hips. "Well, that's one hell of a greeting," he grumbled as Alice crept past him into the study and closed the doors. "I came to get you—that's what I'm doing here."

A tangle of sensations gushed up inside Kristin like a geyser. "You thought I'd just let you take me by the hair and drag me back to your cave, huh?"

Zachary loomed above her now, and his hazel eyes snapped with annoyance. "Why don't you just keep quiet and listen for once?" he barked. "I'm here because I love you, damn it. Because my life isn't worth a pile of wet seaweed without you. And the least you could do is listen while I tell you I'm sorry I didn't trust you before!"

Kristin stared at him, wide-eyed. "Dad admitted he lied?"

"He didn't have to. I knew." Zachary came to her, bundled her into her coat and put on his own. "Come on. We're going somewhere where we can talk." With that, he shuffled her out of the house, down the driveway and into the ugly little car.

"I hope you rented this," Kristin said. She was in such a state of shock that inanities were all she could manage.

Zachary tossed her a wan grin. "That's your first wish, princess. You have two more coming." He pulled into the sluggish, early-evening traffic typical of the neighborhood.

Barely able to believe he was really there, Kristin reached out and touched his upper arm. It felt sturdy and solid beneath her fingers and the cloth of his coat. "I love you, Zachary," she said.

He laughed, and there was something merry in the sound, a release of old ideas and fears. "Hey," he protested, "that's *my* wish."

"Well, I'm granting it," Kristin replied softly, letting her head rest against his shoulder. "I don't know if we can make a go of it now any more than we did then, but there's no question that I'm in love with you. Hopelessly."

Zachary's lips touched the top of her head. "We'll start with that, then, and work out the rest as we go along. Tell me what you've been doing."

Kristin looked up into his face. "I've been missing you, mostly. Though I did manage to work up a proposal for a book about Cabriz."

He grinned. "I suppose you left out the fact that I can drive you crazy in bed," he said.

She laughed and jabbed him lightly in the ribs. "I did leave that out, in fact," she replied. "But since you also drive me crazy everywhere else, there was no lack of material."

Zachary guided the car through the snowy streets, coming to a stop in front of a coffee shop across the street from an historic inn with a boastful sign on the lawn. "That George Washington sure got around," he muttered as he helped Kristin from the car.

They entered the coffee shop, which was almost deserted, and took a table at the rear. Once the waitress had brought them both steaming cups of espresso and left them alone again, Zachary reached across the table and took both Kristin's hands in his.

"That's terrific—that you started a book, I mean," he said gravely.

Kristin shrugged. "I haven't sold it, Zachary. And there's a big difference between starting and selling."

"It'll be a hit," he said with quiet certainty. "You're a good writer, Kris."

She felt defensive. After all, Zachary had never said a positive word about her efforts, either before their breakup or after they'd gotten together in Cabriz. "How do you know?"

"I've been following your career for the last year and a half, that's how. Maybe the subject matter left something wanting but—"

Kristin's cheeks reddened. "Okay, so I wrote about parties," she snapped. "The editors wouldn't trust me with anything but fluff!"

"Calm down," Zachary said. "I'm not criticizing you. I really believe this book is your chance to make a name for yourself."

She found herself itching to show him a copy of the work she'd done so far. "What were you and Dad talking about when I came in?"

He sighed and sat back in the booth. "You, of course. He apologized—albeit grudgingly—for lying to me, and I asked him for your hand in marriage."

Kristin's cup stopped midway between the saucer and her lips. "You did what?"

"You're an old-fashioned girl, Kris, or you wouldn't have been sucked into that whole fairy-tale setup over in Cabriz. So I flew out here—after your mother called and told me you were coming—and asked your father if I could marry you. Of course, if he'd said no, I still would have proposed to you."

"He said yes?"

Zachary nodded, a grin lifting one corner of his

mouth. "What about you, Kris? Are you going to say yes, too?"

She hesitated, but not because there was any question in her mind. She was just wondering if this was really happening. "If I do, where will we live?"

"I like Silver Shores," Zachary replied. "I have a cozy little beach house there. But if that doesn't work for you, then we'll find something else. Now, would you mind putting me out of my misery and answering my question?"

"Yes."

"Yes, you'll answer my question, or yes, you'll marry me?"

"Yes, I'll marry you. Gladly. But we've got to promise each other one thing—there'll be no refusing to talk about things—"

"And no running away from a problem," Zachary interceded, leaning forward and raising his eyebrows.

Kristin nodded. "I regret leaving you, Zachary," she said. "With all my heart."

He got out his wallet and laid a bill on the table to pay the check and cover the tip. "Let's get out of here."

"Where are we going?" Kristin asked. He hadn't even kissed her, and her heart was fluttering like a trapped bird. Her body seemed to be opening up to Zachary, preparing for him, and the heat that surged through her was surely glowing in her face.

"We're going to buy a ring," he answered. "And a license."

"No storybook wedding?"

He faced her, his fingers locking gently over her shoulders. "Is that what you want, princess? A white dress and all the trimmings? If it is, we'll wait."

Kristin swallowed. "The last thing I want to do is

wait, Zachary. If you don't make love to me, I'm going to burst."

He caught his forefinger under her chin, lifted, and gave her a teasing kiss on the mouth. "Don't worry, babe. I'm going to love you all night long. But first I want an engagement ring on your finger, at the very least. And some promises have to be made."

Kristin looked up at him. "What are we going to tell my parents if we stay out all night?"

Zachary was helping her into her coat again. "I don't suppose we'll have to tell them anything. They're intelligent people—" he paused to nibble at the side of her neck "—they'll figure out what's going on."

An hour later the two of them selected a beautiful diamond ring in a nearby jewelry store, and Zachary slipped it on her finger right there in front of the clerk. Then he pulled Kristin close and kissed her thoroughly, while the onlookers applauded.

By the time they were back in Zachary's car, Kristin was in a heightened state of anticipation. She looked hopefully at every decent hotel and inn they passed, but Zachary didn't stop. He drove straight to her parents' house.

"I want to tell them we're getting married," he explained.

"But just a little while ago, you said they'd figure it out for themselves—"

"They would. After going through hell picturing you dead beside the highway because of some accident."

Kristin nodded and got out of the car, and she and Zachary linked arms as they walked toward the house. Kenyan and Alice were waiting for them in the entryway.

"Zachary and I are getting married as soon as possible," Kristin said.

Alice looked disappointed. "But I've always dreamed of giving you a beautiful wedding—"

"Great Scott, Alice," Kenyan interrupted, "can't you see they're hardly able to wait as it is? The kind of shindig you're thinking of takes months to prepare."

Kristin went to her mother, took both her hands. "We could still have a formal wedding, if it means so much to you. But there has to be a ceremony *soon*."

Kenyan's eyes widened, and he looked at Zachary with renewed rage. "By God, Harmon—"

"I'm not pregnant, Dad," Kristin said. Then she glanced back at Zachary. "Not yet, anyway."

"Just how soon would you two like to be married?" Kenyan asked.

"Tonight," Zachary answered without a moment's hesitation.

"I suppose that could be arranged," Kenyan said, his expression thoughtful. He had lots of friends in high places, naturally, and a simple marriage license would not be hard to expedite. His gaze turned to Kristin. "You're sure?"

She nodded.

"Very well, then," Kenyan responded, extending a hand to Zachary. "I hope you and I can let bygones be bygones, Harmon. I love Kristin, and I want her to be happy."

Zachary shook his future father-in-law's hand. "There's something we agree on," he said quietly.

The ceremony was performed an hour later, in Kenyan's study, by a very distinguished judge who had also arranged for a special license. There were flowers from the greenhouse, and Kristin wore the same lacy, romantic dress she'd worn when she'd danced with Zachary at that long-ago Christmas party.

The slight flush on his face and the sparkle in his eyes told Kristin he remembered not only the dress but the episode on the pool table as well.

Kenyan took pictures with his personal camera, and Alice served fruitcake in lieu of wedding cake. When the Meyerses were satisfied that the occasion had been duly celebrated, Alice said with a sniffle, "I've had the guest house prepared as a honeymoon cottage. If you need anything, just use the intercom and someone will see that you get it."

Zachary loosened his tie again, and Kristin felt his fingers tighten around hers. "Great," he said.

A few minutes later he carried her, laughing, down the snowy, slippery walk to the guest house and over the threshold. Inside the one-bedroom cottage, there was a fire blazing on the fieldstone hearth, and a bottle of Kenyan's best champagne was cooling on ice.

Zachary gave a teasing growl, then covered Kristin's mouth with his own, still holding her in his arms. She whimpered as a fire kindled deep within her and then grew hotter with every passing moment. Her arms tightened around Zachary's neck, and her tongue sparred with his.

Finally, with a gasp, he tore his lips from hers, carried Kristin into the bedroom and dropped her unceremoniously on the bed.

Kristin's heart beat faster as she watched her husband undo his tie and toss it aside, then shrug out of his suit coat. A tremor went through her. "Is this the part where you love me all night long?"

"This is the part," he replied, beginning to unbutton his shirt. "I hope you're in top shape, princess, because you're about to get a workout."

Kristin kicked off her shoes, but that was all the undressing Zachary would allow her to do. He took off her stockings personally, kissing each of her knees as he bared them, then tossed aside her voluminous petticoats. After that, he lifted her to her feet long enough to divest her of the dress, and she was naked before him.

She reached for the fastener on his slacks, but he caught hold of her hand and lifted it to his mouth, kissing the palm lightly, then flicking it with his tongue.

Kristin drew in a harsh breath, and her eyes drifted closed. "Zachary..."

He lifted her, just as he'd had to carry her to the guest house, and raised her high enough that he could take one of her nipples into his mouth.

Kristin cried out and arched her back, making herself more available. Zachary took her to the rug in front of the fireplace, enjoying her all the while, and laid her gently on the floor.

She stretched as she watched him open his trousers and remove them, held out her arms when he lowered himself to her side. The light of the fire danced over their bodies like some sort of pagan blessing.

"I love you," Zachary whispered, his lips tasting the length of Kristin's neck even as his hand deftly separated her legs.

She gasped with pleasure when she felt one of his fingers burrow in to prepare her. "And I love you—oh—so much—oh, Zachary..."

He chuckled, nuzzled her breasts, boldly captured a nipple. "Umm?" he asked, suckling at the same time.

Kristin writhed as he clasped her moist mound in his hand and slipped deft fingers inside her. The heel of his palm moved against the sweetest secret of her womanhood. "Love me—oh, please—love me *now!* You have all night to tease!"

Zachary nudged her legs apart with one knee and cradled himself between them, his fingers still working their singular magic. He bent his head and touched one of her nipples with his tongue, training it to pebble hardness. "You shock me, Mrs. Harmon. Are you asking me to consummate this marriage?"

"Yes, damn you!" Kristin cried, her eyes closed, her head back, her hips rising and falling under Zachary's hand. "Yes!"

He withdrew his fingers and clasped his hands under Kristin's bottom. She felt his shaft pressing against her, gave a long, crooning moan as it slid inside her.

She tried to raise herself, to start the friction she needed so badly, but Zachary stilled her by grasping her hips. "Easy," he breathed, giving her another slow, delicious stroke.

Kristin cried out, her fingers flying over Zachary's back, searching for a handhold, a way to push him into her. He teased until she flung her legs around him and imprisoned him in her depths, then his control snapped.

He grated out her name and bent to suckle briefly, desperately, at each of her breasts. Then, raising himself onto his hands, he drove into her powerfully, withdrew, and drove again.

Kristin lowered her legs, heels digging into the rug as she hurled herself at Zachary, receiving every lunge, welcoming it. Her head tossed from side to side and her hair was a wild tangle around her face, but she didn't care.

She matched Zachary stroke for stroke, and when her body began to convulse, gripping his, drawing at it, she pulled his head down and took his mouth with her own. He stayed with the kiss as long as he could, but then his powerful body buckled and he flung back his head. A low, muffled shout came from his throat as he gave himself up in final surrender.

When it was over, Kristin held him close, running her hands over his back to soothe him. She was too exhausted to talk, and there were tears glimmering in her eyes—tears she didn't want him to see.

He rolled onto his back, pulling Kristin with him, holding her close. A long time passed before either of them spoke.

"I want you to quit the birth control as soon as possible," Zachary said.

Kristin laughed. "Mother's doctor already took care of that, handsome. You and I had broken up, and I didn't plan on sleeping with anybody else."

"Good. Then let's get down to some serious baby making." He rolled onto his side, smiling, and traced the circumference of her nipples with his fingertip. Kristin felt sweet tension coiling inside her, knowing it would only be a matter of minutes before he suckled her. "I'd like to be a father by this time next year."

Kristin pulled a face. "Oh, yeah? How do you plan to manage that?"

"By taking you to bed on a very regular basis." The words rumbled from his throat; he was already kissing the plump breast he'd selected. "I'll come home for—" he paused to draw her into his mouth and enjoy her for a few moments "—lunch. And, of course, when I get back from school in the afternoon, you'll be through writing and ready to welcome me properly."

Kristin could no longer bear to lie still; she began to stroke him gently in retaliation. "Of course," she purred.

"Oh, Kris—"

"And there will be times, naturally, when I'll visit you during the day. Your office door does have a lock, doesn't it?" She nipped at his earlobe with her teeth, was delighted by Zachary's lively response. "Doesn't it?" she repeated.

"Yes," Zachary groaned, completely in her power.

Kristin felt both triumph and passion as she maneuvered her husband into position for another session of loving. This time, she wouldn't have to plead.

He would.

And she was prepared to be generous.

* * * * *

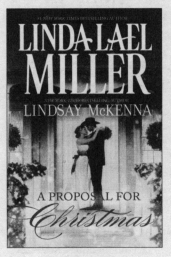

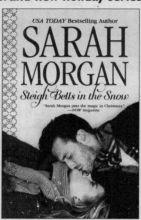

There's nowhere better to spend the holidays than with *New York Times* bestselling author

SUSAN MALLERY

in the town of Fool's Gold, where love is always waiting to be unwrapped...

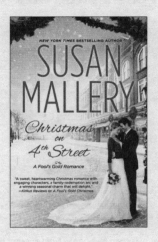

Available now wherever books are sold!

"Susan Mallery is one of my favorites."
—#1 *New York Times* bestselling author Debbie Macomber

www.SusanMallery.com

REQUEST YOUR FREE BOOKS!

2 FREE NOVELS
FROM THE ROMANCE COLLECTION
PLUS 2 FREE GIFTS!

YES! Please send me 2 FREE novels from the Romance Collection and my 2 FREE gifts (gifts are worth about $10). After receiving them, if I don't wish to receive any more books, I can return the shipping statement marked "cancel." If I don't cancel, I will receive 4 brand-new novels every month and be billed just $6.24 per book in the U.S. or $6.74 per book in Canada. That's a savings of at least 22% off the cover price. It's quite a bargain! Shipping and handling is just 50¢ per book in the U.S. and 75¢ per book in Canada.* I understand that accepting the 2 free books and gifts places me under no obligation to buy anything. I can always return a shipment and cancel at any time. Even if I never buy another book, the two free books and gifts are mine to keep forever.

194/394 MDN F4XY

Name	(PLEASE PRINT)	
Address		Apt. #
City	State/Prov.	Zip/Postal Code

Signature (if under 18, a parent or guardian must sign)

Mail to the **Harlequin® Reader Service**:
IN U.S.A.: P.O. Box 1867, Buffalo, NY 14240-1867
IN CANADA: P.O. Box 609, Fort Erie, Ontario L2A 5X3

Want to try two free books from another line?
Call 1-800-873-8635 or visit www.ReaderService.com.

* Terms and prices subject to change without notice. Prices do not include applicable taxes. Sales tax applicable in N.Y. Canadian residents will be charged applicable taxes. Offer not valid in Quebec. This offer is limited to one order per household. Not valid for current subscribers to the Romance Collection or the Romance/Suspense Collection. All orders subject to credit approval. Credit or debit balances in a customer's account(s) may be offset by any other outstanding balance owed by or to the customer. Please allow 4 to 6 weeks for delivery. Offer available while quantities last.

Your Privacy—The Harlequin® Reader Service is committed to protecting your privacy. Our Privacy Policy is available online at www.ReaderService.com or upon request from the Harlequin Reader Service.

We make a portion of our mailing list available to reputable third parties that offer products we believe may interest you. If you prefer that we not exchange your name with third parties, or if you wish to clarify or modify your communication preferences, please visit us at www.ReaderService.com/consumerschoice or write to us at Harlequin Reader Service Preference Service, P.O. Box 9062, Buffalo, NY 14269. Include your complete name and address.

ROM13R

LINDA LAEL MILLER

77623	THE McKETTRICK LEGEND	___ $7.99 U.S.	___ $9.99 CAN.
77606	HOLIDAY IN STONE CREEK	___ $7.99 U.S.	___ $9.99 CAN.
77600	THE CREED LEGACY	___ $7.99 U.S.	___ $9.99 CAN.
77580	CREED'S HONOR	___ $7.99 U.S.	___ $9.99 CAN.
77561	MONTANA CREEDS: LOGAN	___ $7.99 U.S.	___ $9.99 CAN.
77555	A CREED IN STONE CREEK	___ $7.99 U.S.	___ $9.99 CAN.
77502	THE CHRISTMAS BRIDES	___ $7.99 U.S.	___ $9.99 CAN.
77492	McKETTRICK'S CHOICE	___ $7.99 U.S.	___ $9.99 CAN.
77446	McKETTRICKS OF TEXAS: AUSTIN	___ $7.99 U.S.	___ $9.99 CAN.
77441	McKETTRICKS OF TEXAS: GARRETT	___ $7.99 U.S.	___ $9.99 CAN.
77436	McKETTRICKS OF TEXAS: TATE	___ $7.99 U.S.	___ $9.99 CAN.
77388	THE BRIDEGROOM	___ $7.99 U.S.	___ $8.99 CAN.
77364	MONTANA CREEDS: TYLER	___ $7.99 U.S.	___ $7.99 CAN.
77358	MONTANA CREEDS: DYLAN	___ $7.99 U.S.	___ $7.99 CAN.
77330	THE RUSTLER	___ $7.99 U.S.	___ $7.99 CAN.
77296	A WANTED MAN	___ $7.99 U.S.	___ $7.99 CAN.
77200	DEADLY GAMBLE	___ $7.99 U.S.	___ $9.50 CAN.
77198	THE MAN FROM STONE CREEK	___ $7.99 U.S.	___ $9.50 CAN.

(limited quantities available)

TOTAL AMOUNT	$ _____
POSTAGE & HANDLING	$ _____
($1.00 FOR 1 BOOK, 50¢ for each additional)	
APPLICABLE TAXES*	$ _____
TOTAL PAYABLE	$ _____

(check or money order—please do not send cash)

To order, complete this form and send it, along with a check or money order for the total above, payable to HQN Books, to: **In the U.S.:** 3010 Walden Avenue, P.O. Box 9077, Buffalo, NY 14269-9077; **In Canada:** P.O. Box 636, Fort Erie, Ontario, L2A 5X3.

Name: _____
Address: _____ City: _____
State/Prov.: _____ Zip/Postal Code: _____
Account Number (if applicable): _____
075 CSAS

*New York residents remit applicable sales taxes.
*Canadian residents remit applicable GST and provincial taxes.

HARLEQUIN® HQN™
www.Harlequin.com

PHLLM0113BL